**He pulled her onto his lap an** ... **with a wild, passionate a** ...

Somewhere in the back of his head, ... iful part of him was telling him this was ... But it felt so right.

Ilysa felt right. She was perfect. E: ...

She splayed her fingers into the ha ... his neck and pressed herself against him. ... and moans as she returned his fevered kis; ... im, too. Though she looked young, she ha ... She must know what she was doing to ... this was leading.

Still, a twinge of guilt made him hesitate and start to pull back. Ilysa sensed it and wrapped her arms more tightly around his neck.

"Please, Connor." Her voice was breathless. "Just this once."

When she pressed her lips against his neck, he shivered with the force of his desire.

*Aye. Just this once.*

# Praise for the novels of
# Margaret Mallory

## *The Warrior*

"4 ½ stars! Top Pick! Mallory's Return of the Highlanders series continues in this riveting story with great depth and sensuality. Her vibrant characters are so real readers will feel they are experiencing everything with them . . . Readers will be completely caught up in the beautifully crafted and compassionate love story."
**—RT Book Reviews**

"Margaret Mallory creates magic with her words, and draws the reader into her story from page one."
**—TheReadingReviewer.com**

"Margaret Mallory's Return of the Highlanders series is pure satisfaction guaranteed for Highlander lovers . . . *The Warrior* is dark and dangerous with its impassioned couple and remarkable story . . . [It] is as mighty as it is fierce. This romance is a stand-out, and I'm Joyfully Recommending it!"
**—JoyfullyReviewed.com**

"An entertaining second chance at love tale . . . Fans will appreciate this engaging sixteenth century Scottish romance as love heals the mind and soul."
**—GenreGoRoundReviews.blogspot.com**

# The Sinner

"Sizzling and captivating . . . Mallory weaves a fine yarn with plenty of spice and thrills."

**—Publishers Weekly**

"4 ½ stars! Mallory's portrait of 16th-century Scotland and the lively adventures she creates for her characters certainly engage readers' emotions. The sizzling sexual tension between the hero and heroine will leave readers breathless."

**—RT Book Reviews**

"*The Sinner* is perfect! Alex and Glynis are sexy, stubborn and simply divine together. *The Sinner* should not be missed!"

**—JoyfullyReviewed.com**

"A wonderful novel led by two powerful personalities . . . *The Sinner* is an exciting, turbulent read from beginning to end. I will be waiting impatiently for the next installment of this story."

**—FreshFiction.com**

"Captivating . . . Alex is a delicious male lead that would send any woman's heart aflutter . . . The chemistry and the fire that this couple had was explosive and just seemed to leap off the page . . . This book needs to be savored with a nice glass of wine . . . I am anxiously awaiting Duncan's story."

**—NightOwlReviews.com**

# The Guardian

"4 ½ stars! Top Pick! Mallory imbues history with a life of its own, creating a deeply moving story. Her characters are vibrantly alive and full of emotional depth, each with their own realistic flaws. Her sensuous and highly passionate tale grabs the reader and doesn't let go."

**—RT Book Reviews**

"Masterfully written . . . Mallory has created a series that every romance reader must read. *The Guardian* is truly a sizzling romance with high-impact adventure that captures the Scotland readers long for. The characters created by Mallory have found places in my heart, and I am impatiently awaiting the next of this spectacular series!"

**—FreshFiction.com**

"An amazing introduction to what is fated to become a dangerously addictive series. With characters capable of breaching the most impenetrable of readers' defenses, riveting story lines (and even more intriguing subplots), quick, witty dialogue, as well as wild sexual tension—the only thing readers will crave, is more."

**—RomanceJunkiesReviews.com**

## Knight of Passion

"Top Pick! As in the previous book in her All the King's Men series, Mallory brings history to life, creating dramatic and gut-wrenching stories. Her characters are incredibly alive and readers will feel and believe their sensual and passionate adventures. Mallory raises the genre to new levels."

**—RT Book Reviews**

"I really enjoyed this story . . . Very intense . . . Fans of medieval historicals will especially love this one."

**—CoffeeTimeRomance.com**

"An amazing story . . . a series that readers won't want to miss . . . Filled with hot romance as well as adventure with a fascinating historical background."
**—RomRevToday.com**

## *Knight of Pleasure*

"4 Stars! A riveting story . . . Such depth and sensuality are a rare treat."
**—*RT Book Reviews***

"Fascinating . . . An excellent historical romance. Ms. Mallory gives us amazingly vivid details of the characters, romance, and intrigue of England. You're not just reading a novel, you are stepping into the story and feeling all the emotions of each character . . . *Knight of Pleasure* is amazing and I highly recommend it."
**—TheRomanceReadersConnection.com**

"An absolute delight . . . captivating."
**—FreshFiction.com**

"Thrilling, romantic, and just plain good reading . . . An enjoyable, historically accurate, and very well written novel."
**—RomRevToday.com**

## *Knight of Desire*

"An impressive debut . . . Margaret Mallory is a star in the making."
**—Mary Balogh, *New York Times* bestselling author of *At Last Comes Love***

# THE
# CHIEFTAIN

Also by Margaret Mallory

**All the King's Men**

*Knight of Desire*
*Knight of Pleasure*
*Knight of Passion*

**The Return of the Highlanders**

*The Guardian*
*The Sinner*
*The Warrior*

# THE
# CHIEFTAIN

The Return of the Highlanders

## MARGARET MALLORY

FOREVER

NEW YORK   BOSTON

Forever
Hachette Book Group
237 Park Avenue
New York, NY 10017

www.HachetteBookGroup.com

Printed in the United States of America

First Edition: February 2012

10 9 8 7 6 5 4 3 2 1

OPM

Forever is an imprint of Grand Central Publishing.
The Forever name and logo are trademarks of Hachette Book Group, Inc.

The Hachette Speakers Bureau provides a wide range of authors for speaking events. To find out more, go to www.hachettespeakersbureau.com or call (866) 376-6591.

The publisher is not responsible for websites (or their content) that are not owned by the publisher.

*For my husband, Bob,*
*with love and gratitude for our Happily Ever After.*
*Some things are forever.*

# ACKNOWLEDGMENTS

I want to give a special thank-you to my editor Alex Logan and my agent Kevan Lyon, who have supported me in countless ways from the beginning. (Hard to believe it's been seven books!) Thanks also to the entire team at Grand Central Publishing for skillfully guiding my books through every stage of the publishing process. I am grateful to Anthea Lawson and Ginny Heim for their enthusiasm, moral support, and friendship, as well as their helpful feedback on drafts. Dr. James R. MacDonald and Sharron Gunn have been kind to help me with Gaelic phrases and Scottish history, though any mistakes are mine.

Writing can be a lonely task. Especially during those long stretches before deadlines when I don't get out of the house—or my sweatpants—for days, I am grateful to my online community of writers, readers, friends, and acquaintances on Facebook, Twitter, and RWA loops for much-needed laughter, support, and diversion. As always, my love and thanks to my wonderful family. And finally, a huge thank-you to my readers. You make it all worthwhile.

*Is sleamhainn leac doras an taigh mhòir.*

The chieftain's house has a slippery doorstep.

# THE
# CHIEFTAIN

# PROLOGUE

Fornicator, philanderer, liar," Connor's mother called out as she circled the crackling fire dragging a stick behind her through the sand. "*Mo mhallachd ort!*" My curse on you!

Connor hugged his knees to his chest as he watched her long, unbound hair swirl about her in the night wind like black snakes.

"May your seed dry up, Donald Gallach, chieftain of the MacDonalds of Sleat," she said in a high, quavering voice as she circled the fire a second time, "so that no woman shall bear you another child."

Connor wished his friend Duncan or his cousins were here, instead of asleep in the castle hall with his father's warriors, as he should be. His father said a seven-year-old who slept on a pallet next to his mother's bed would never be a great warrior and had forbidden it. But his father was away, and Connor had been afraid something bad would happen to his mother if he did not stay close to her.

"May your sons already born by other women die young," his mother said as she raked her stick around the fire again.

She had been weeping and tearing at her hair for days. She was like that sometimes. Other times, she was like sunshine that was so bright it hurt your eyes.

But she had never done this before.

"Three times 'round, and the spell is bound." His mother straightened and raised her stick in the air. "And may ye know it was I, your wife, who cursed you!"

Connor heard running feet coming through the darkness just before a familiar voice called, "No, Catriona!"

Connor's heart lifted when Duncan's mother, Anna, appeared. Her soft voice and kind words could sometimes soothe his mother. But if Anna saw him, she would send him back to the castle. Before she noticed him, Connor crawled through the beach grass until he was safely out of the firelight.

"Please, ye mustn't do this," Anna said. "An evil spell that's unwarranted can come back on ye."

"Donald Gallach deserves every evil wish," his mother spat out. "With passion and sweet promises of eternal love, he persuaded me to leave a man who adored me. And now, I discover he's been keeping a woman up at Trotternish Castle—and she's borne him a son!"

"Men have done far worse." Anna put her arm around his mother's shoulders. "I beg ye, take back this curse before it's too late."

"It was too late the moment he took another woman to his bed," his mother said and pushed Anna away. "I swear

I will make that man regret what he's done to me for the rest of his days."

"I'm certain you're the only one the chieftain loves," Anna said, brushing his mother's wild tangles back from her face. "Please, return to the castle and rest."

"If he believes I will accept this and remain here, a dutiful wife, he has forgotten who I am." His mother stared into the fire and smiled in a way that frightened Connor. "How he will rage when I leave him for another man."

"Ye can't mean to do that," Anna said. "What about your children?"

Connor held his breath, trying not to cry, as he waited for her answer.

"Ye know very well that Highland children—especially a chieftain's children—belong to their father," she said.

"But they need their mother," Anna said, gripping her arm again. "And young Connor adores ye."

"You're better at mothering them than I am, and I know you'd never let Donald Gallach touch you," his mother said. "Promise you'll take care of Connor and Moira after I leave."

"I will, but—"

"Don't go!" Connor ran to his mother and buried his face in her skirts. As always, she smelled of rose petals.

"My sweet, serious lad." His mother dropped to her knee and embraced him, then she leaned back and asked, "Ye want your mother to be happy, don't ye?"

Connor nodded. If she were happy, she would stay.

"You were begat of fiery passion, when I owned your father's heart," she said, holding his face between her hands. "Every time your father looks at you, he will remember how it was between us and regret what he's lost."

*  *  *

One night, Connor slept too soundly, and his mother disappeared.

When he awoke, a storm raged outside, and the castle was in an uproar. His father had returned after weeks away and was bellowing at everyone.

"Ye follow your mother about like a dog." His father lifted Connor off his feet, shook him, and shouted in his face. "Ye must have seen her with someone. Who did she leave with? Tell me!"

His father's fingers dug into his arms, but Connor did not say a word. Even if he had known where his mother was, he would never betray her. And if he was very good, she might come back for him.

His father sent his galleys in every direction, despite the storm. By the next day, an eerie calm had settled over the sea. Connor was outside with Ragnall, his father's son by his first wife, when one of the galleys returned. As soon as he saw a warrior carrying his mother from the boat, her limbs and long black hair swaying with his long strides, Connor started running.

"No, Connor!" Ragnall shouted.

He darted out of his brother's reach and scrambled down to the beach. But Ragnall was ten years older, a grown man, and he caught Connor before he reached her.

Ragnall neither chastised nor tried to soothe him, but simply held Connor against his solid frame, heavily muscled from constant training. Connor strained to see his mother through the warriors who had crowded around her.

"Even in death, she commands the attention of every man," Ragnall said under his breath. "By the saints, your mother was beautiful."

*Was?* Connor did not understand, but fear knotted his belly.

The men suddenly parted to let the chieftain through. As their father brushed past Connor and Ragnall, his gaze was fixed on the limp body that was draped over the warrior's arms like an offering.

"Their galley capsized in the storm, and all were lost," the warrior said when his father came to a halt before him. "A farmer found her body washed up on shore."

The muscles of his father's jaw clenched and unclenched as his gaze traveled over her.

"Let me see her!" Connor wailed, reaching his arms out to her.

His father pivoted and fixed his fierce golden eyes on him. Ragnall tightened his grip and turned sideways to protect him from their father's wrath, but Connor was too distraught to fear him.

"What's wrong with her?" Connor usually kept silent in his father's presence, but he had to know.

"She was unfaithful, and now she's dead," his father said, anger vibrating off him. "There will be no weeping for her."

Grief sucked the air from Connor's lungs, and it was a long moment before any sound came out. Then he howled, "No!" and clawed at his brother's arms. "Let me see her! Let me see her!"

"Praise God I have one son who is a fit heir to lead this great clan," his father said.

"Connor's only a bairn, Fa—" Ragnall started to say.

The chieftain cut him off with an abrupt wave of his hand. "Keep her son out of my sight."

# CHAPTER 1

## 1516

Ye can't go with Connor," Duncan told her.

"Who else will set up his household at Trotternish Castle?" Ilysa continued sorting and packing her clothes while her brother, who was twice her size and all brawny muscle, glowered down at her. "Ach, there will be so much to do."

"I won't allow it," Duncan said, crossing his arms.

Ilysa paused to give her brother a smile because he meant well, though she was not going to let him stop her. "For heaven's sake, Duncan, why shouldn't I go?"

"If you're keeping his household, everyone will believe that you're also warming his bed," Duncan said in a low hiss.

"I've been managing his household here at Dunscaith Castle since he became chieftain, and no one thinks that." It would not occur to any of them, least of all Connor. Ilysa stifled a sigh and returned to her packing.

"That's because I live here," Duncan said. "Ye grew up here. This is your home. Following the chieftain to Trotternish Castle is a different matter altogether."

What would she do if she remained here? Now that Duncan had married Connor's sister and been made keeper of Dunscaith, Ilysa had lost her place. Though she and Duncan's new bride were friends, there could be only one mistress of a castle.

"If you're troubled about this, why don't ye speak to Connor?" Ilysa asked. "He's been your best friend since the cradle."

"I won't insult my friend and chieftain by suggesting he'd take advantage of my sister!"

"But you'll insult me?" Ilysa asked, arching an eyebrow—though if Connor MacDonald wanted to take advantage of her, she would faint from pure happiness.

"I'm no saying anything would actually happen between the two of ye," Duncan said, raising his hands in exasperation. "But if the men think ye belong to the chieftain, you'll never get another husband."

"I don't recall saying I wanted one." Ilysa held up an old cloak to examine it for moth holes. "Should I take an extra cloak? They say the wind is strong on the north end of the island."

"Ilysa—" Duncan stopped abruptly.

Years of fighting had made her brother's instincts sharp and his reflexes quick. Before Ilysa could draw a breath to ask what was wrong, Duncan had run out into the castle courtyard and pulled his claymore from the scabbard on his back.

Through the open door, Ilysa heard shouting and raced out after him.

"What is it?" Duncan called up to one of the guards on the wall.

"Three riders are galloping hard for the gate," the man shouted. "One looks injured."

*Please, God, don't let it be Connor.* He had gone for a last hunt with his cousins before his departure for Trotternish. Usually, Duncan would be with them, but he had stayed behind to be with his bride. And to lecture Ilysa.

Ilysa followed in Duncan's wake as he ran through the warriors who were flooding into the courtyard. Through the open gate, she saw the three horsemen riding hell-bent for the castle. Her stomach dropped when she recognized Connor as the injured rider, flanked by his two cousins. He was slumped forward, looking as if he was barely holding on. The rest of his guard was several yards behind them.

As the three riders drew up to the narrow bridge that connected the castle to the main island, Duncan ran across it and blocked her view. Ilysa wanted to scream in frustration as she alternately rose on her toes and leaned to the side, trying to see.

"Clear the way!" Duncan shouted as he came back across the bridge.

The world fell away as Ilysa saw Connor enter the castle between his cousins, Ian and Alex, who were half carrying him. His black hair hung over his face, and the front of his tunic was drenched in blood.

"Run and fetch my medicines," Ilysa told the serving woman next to her before she ran after the others into the keep. As she entered the hall, she called out to another woman, "Bring blankets from my brother's bedchamber."

With one sweep of his arm, Duncan sent cups and platters clattering to the floor, clearing the high table just before Ian and Alex lifted Connor onto it and laid him down.

"*O shluagh!*" Ilysa said, calling on the faeries for help, when she saw the arrows sticking out of Connor's chest and thigh. *How many times will our enemies try to kill him?*

When Connor tried to sit up, Duncan held him down with a firm hand.

"I'm no badly hurt," Connor objected, but his face was gray.

"We rode hard for fear that he'd bleed to death before we reached the castle," Alex said as he sliced Connor's tunic open with his dirk to expose the wound.

"The arrows came from rocks above us," Ian said. "We were in the middle of an open field where we were easy targets, so we couldn't stop to take care of his wounds."

"We'll take the arrow out of his chest first, then the one in his leg," Ilysa said after she examined both wounds. She held her breath as she rested her fingertips on Connor's wrist. "'Tis fortunate that ye have the heart of a lion, Connor MacDonald."

Connor started to laugh, then winced. "Just get the damned things out of me. They hurt like hell."

"Someone bring us whiskey," Duncan shouted. "The rest of ye, out!"

When the whiskey arrived, Duncan cradled Connor's head and poured it down his throat.

Ilysa noticed the blood running down Ian's arm, but his injury could wait. Connor's could not. Still, this was not as serious as that other time, shortly after the four of them had returned from France. She shuddered as she re-called Ian carrying Connor's broken body into the seer's tiny cottage. Connor had been more dead than alive. With God's help, she and Teàrlag had snatched him back from death's door.

"Cutting the arrow out will be a wee bit messy," Alex said as he wiped his long dirk on his tunic. "I'll do that, Ilysa, and ye can do the sewing."

"I think we'll need all of ye to hold him down," Ilysa said, knowing the men would take that better than telling them a delicate hand was needed with the blade. "If Connor moves, it will make things worse."

While the men poured more whiskey into Connor, she made a poultice.

"Ready?" Duncan asked Connor. When he nodded, Duncan took the tooth-marked strip of leather from Ilysa's basket of medicines and put it between Connor's teeth.

Ilysa exchanged glances with the others, then took a deep breath and willed her hands not to shake. The arrow was deep, and it was barbed, so she had to work carefully. Thankfully, Connor passed out long before she finished.

After she cut out the arrow, Ilysa cleaned the wound thoroughly with whiskey and covered it with the poultice. Then she did the same with the arrow in his thigh. The three men were skilled at dressing battle wounds, so she sat down on the bench next to the table while they wound strips of linen around Connor's chest, looping the cloth under his left arm and over his right shoulder.

Now that it was over, a wave of nausea hit her, and she leaned forward to rest her forehead on the table. She slipped her hand into Connor's. When he was so badly injured the last time, she had washed his naked body with cool cloths to break his fever. Somehow, holding his hand now felt more intimate.

Ach, she was pathetic. She sat up and gazed at his face, which was eased of worry for once. Though his looks were the least of what drew her to him, a lass would have to be dead not to notice how handsome he was. He had scars all over his body, attesting to battles and attempts on his life, but his face was unmarked. He was perfect, an Adonis with black hair and silvery blue eyes.

Since Connor returned from France to find his father and brother dead and their clan near ruin, he had devoted himself with single-minded determination to restoring the clan's lands and making their people safe. If he lived long enough, he would be one of the great chieftains, the kind the bards told stories about. Whatever Ilysa could do to help him, she would.

"Connor will be fine," Ian said, squeezing her shoulder. "Ye did well."

"Let me see to that cut on your arm." Ilysa chastised herself for daydreaming while Ian needed tending and pushed up his bloody sleeve. "Looks like an arrow grazed ye."

"'Tis nothing," Ian said.

Ilysa rolled her eyes and set to work on it. "Connor's wounds are deep and will bear watching," she said for her brother's benefit. "He'll need a healer to travel with him to Trotternish."

"There must be healers in Trotternish," Duncan said.

"None that we can trust," she said as she tied the bandage around Ian's arm. "A healer wouldn't even have to poison him, though she could. 'Tis easy to let a wound go bad."

* * *

It should have been a clean kill.

Lachlan mulled over what went wrong as he waited at the meeting point for Hugh's galley, which would take him back to Trotternish. He had wasted his first arrow on the wrong man. When the rider entered the clearing, he fit the description Lachlan had been given: a tall warrior near Lachlan's age with a rangy build and hair as black as a crow. Fortunately, the man's horse had jerked to the side and saved his life. Lachlan was relieved he had only winged him. He did not make a practice of killing men who did not deserve it.

As soon as the next man charged his horse into the clearing, Lachlan realized his mistake. He could not have said why, for the two looked much alike, but he had known immediately that the second man was the chieftain. There was something about him that bespoke his position as leader of the clan.

Odd, how the chieftain had ridden directly into Lachlan's range when he saw the arrow strike his companion. Connor MacDonald had not hesitated, not spared a glance behind him to look for someone else to do it.

It was the chieftain's unexpected willingness to put the life of one of his men before his own that had caused Lachlan to falter, just for an instant, and send his next arrow into the chieftain's thigh instead of his heart. Lachlan recovered quickly, and his third arrow struck the chieftain in the chest, though it may have been too high to kill him.

Next time, he would not falter.

\* \* \*

The four men were in deep discussion when Ilysa slipped into the chamber with a tray. She glanced at Connor, who had no business being out of bed a day after he was wounded. Though he hid his pain well, she saw it in the strain around his eyes.

"We haven't found the man who shot those arrows," Ian said. "His tracks were washed out in the rain."

As Ilysa started around the table refilling their cups, Duncan gave her his icy warrior's stare to let her know that their earlier argument was not finished. Ilysa responded with a serene smile to let him know that it was.

"We all know Hugh is responsible for this attack," Alex said, referring to Connor's half uncle who was set on taking the chieftainship from him. "He's tried to have Connor murdered more than once."

"The MacLeods wouldn't attack us here on the Sleat Peninsula where we are strong," Ian agreed. "This was a single archer, and my guess is he was one of our own."

"We have vipers among us!" Duncan slammed his fist on the table, causing their cups to rattle.

As Ilysa refilled their cups, Ian shot her a quick, dazzling smile, and Alex winked at her. She had always been fond of Connor's cousins, though the pair had been philandering devils before they settled down to become devoted husbands. Ian and Connor had gotten their black hair from their mothers, who were sisters, while Alex had the fair hair of the Vikings who had once terrorized the isles.

"Will ye reconsider your decision to live at Trotternish Castle?" Ian asked Connor. "Up there, ye won't have us to guard your back as we did yesterday."

"Hell," Alex said. "if someone kills ye, we're likely to end up with Hugh as chieftain."

"By making Trotternish Castle my home," Connor said, "I'm sending a message to the MacLeods—and to the Crown—that I am not giving up our claim to the Trotternish Peninsula."

Connor's deep voice reverberated somewhere low in Ilysa's belly, making her hand quiver as she poured whiskey into his cup. For a moment she feared he would notice, but she needn't have worried.

"I want them to know," Connor continued, "that we will fight for the lands the MacLeods stole from us."

"*A' phlàigh oirbh, a Chlanna MhicLeòid!*"—a plague on the MacLeods!—the four chanted in unison and raised their cups.

Ilysa could see that she had arrived just in time with more whiskey.

"If you're intent on this," Duncan said, "I should remain as captain of your guard and go with ye."

"I need ye to protect our people here, just as I need Ian and Alex to hold our other castles," Connor said. "I'm sailing for Trotternish in the morning, so I suggest we discuss how to remove the MacLeods from our lands."

Ach, the man should let his wounds heal before leaving. Ilysa would have to watch him closely on the two-day journey.

She took her tray to the side table and stood with

her back to them, pretending to be busy. Because they suspected Connor's uncle had spies in the castle, Ilysa had always served them herself when Connor's inner circle met in private. The four men were so accustomed to her coming and going that they never noticed when she stayed to listen.

"The MacLeods are a powerful clan," Ian said. "We won't defeat them without a strong ally fighting at our side."

"If ye want us to take Trotternish," Alex said, "ye should make a marriage alliance with another clan."

Ilysa tensed, though she was certain Connor would say it was not yet time, as he always did.

"Several clans have already left the rebellion, and it will end soon," Ian said. "'Tis possible now to judge which clans will have power—and which won't—when it's over."

"Ye always said that's what ye were waiting for," Alex said. "Of course, we think ye were just stalling."

"You're right," Connor said. "'Tis time for me to take a wife."

Ilysa's vision went dark, and she gripped the edge of the table to keep from falling. Concentrating to keep her feet under her, she sidestepped along the table. When she reached the end of it, she turned around and half fell onto the bench that was beside it against the wall.

From the long silence that followed Connor's announcement, the men were as surprised as she was.

"We prodded the bull by taking Trotternish Castle. Alastair MacLeod could strike back at us at any time," Connor said. "The sooner I make a marriage alliance, the better."

*Soon?* Ilysa took deep breaths trying to calm herself. What was wrong with her? She had known Connor would wed eventually.

"God knows, ye need a woman," Alex said. "How long has it been?"

When the others began making ribald remarks, Ilysa knew they had forgotten her completely and was grateful for it. Connor's apparent celibacy since becoming chieftain had been the subject of a good deal of speculation and gossip. The men of the castle seemed almost as amazed by the chieftain's failure to take any lass to his bed as the women were disappointed.

The distance to the door suddenly seemed too far. As soon as Ilysa could trust herself to walk, she forced herself to get to her feet. She crossed the floor with her head down and bit her lip hard to keep from weeping.

\* \* \*

Connor let them have their laugh though he had little humor for this particular subject. He took a long drink of his whiskey. By the saints, he needed a woman.

His father and grandfather were great warriors, but the strife they caused with all their women had weakened the clan. His grandfather's six sons by six different women had all hated each other. After the murder and mayhem among them, only two remained alive. Connor's own father's philandering had caused another round of turmoil.

Connor was determined not to follow in their footsteps in that respect. During his years in France and before, he had taken pleasure in the company of women, as young warriors will. But when he returned to find his father and brother dead, everything changed. He could never again do as he pleased. As chieftain, his every decision had consequences for the clan.

He could afford no missteps. Connor's half uncle, who was called Hugh Dubh, Black Hugh, for his black heart, had nearly destroyed the clan before Connor took the chieftainship from him. Thanks to the help of the three men sitting with Connor now, the clan had recovered much of its strength. Relying on their swords and their wits, they had taken control of the clan's castles and secured most of their lands. All that remained was to reclaim the Trotternish Peninsula.

Connor would not destroy all he had built by leaving a legacy of strife and sorrow as his father and grandfather had done. He was determined to wed only once, provided he was not widowed, and to have no children except with his wife.

"This decision of who I marry is vital to the clan's future," Connor said when he grew tired of his friends' jests about his celibacy. "We must weigh the benefits and drawbacks of each possible alliance."

"The best match would be a daughter of the MacLeod chieftain," Ian said. "Remember, the oldest method of subduing an enemy is through the marriage bond."

"And it has the distinct advantage of requiring the sacrifice of only one man," Alex said with a twinkle in his eye.

"Alastair MacLeod will never agree to settle matters between our clans without blood," Connor said. "Besides, his daughters are too young."

"The MacLeod waited even longer than you to wed," Ian said. "Ach, he must have been well over forty."

That was unusual, indeed. The attempt on Connor's

life had been a harsh reminder of his duty to produce heirs and made him decide he could wait no longer to wed. In the violent world they lived in, it was important for a chieftain to have many children, both to be assured of an heir and to have children to make marriage alliances for the clan. In fact, it was common for chieftains to "put aside" wives who could not bear children—or who could no longer do so. Connor's father and grandfather had not bothered using that excuse.

"There are plenty of other chieftains with marriageable daughters," Ian said. "The upcoming gathering is the perfect opportunity."

So many chieftains and their sons had died in the Battle of Flodden that there was an abundance of chieftains' daughters in need of highborn husbands. Connor had avoided gatherings up until now for that very reason. But the time was ripe, and the chieftains would all be at this gathering, except for the few who were still in the rebellion. The Campbell chieftain, as the king's Lieutenant of the Isles, had summoned them to re-pledge their loyalty.

"No matter which chieftain's daughter I wed, I risk offending half a dozen other chieftains." Connor rubbed his forehead. If he had five or six siblings, he could spread alliances out like the Campbells did, marrying into clans all across the Western Isles.

"Shaggy Maclean said he'd make a gift of that sweet galley we stole from him if ye wed one of his daughters," Ian said, stifling a smile.

"I don't know that I'd want a father-in-law who is half mad and threw us in his dungeon," Alex said. "Besides, we already have his boat."

"Shaggy is mad and dangerous, which is precisely the reason I'd prefer to have him fighting on our side," Connor said, taking the suggestion seriously. It made him uneasy that the Maclean chieftain had joined forces with Alastair MacLeod as of late. "If Shaggy had not gotten himself on the wrong side of the Campbells, his clan would be a good choice for the alliance."

"Ye ought to consider the qualities of the lass as well as her clan," Duncan said. "She'll be the mother of your children."

"We're proof that ye can both please yourself and serve the clan with your marriage," Ian said.

Connor had seen these three, his closest companions, find happiness beyond all reason in their marriages. Despite their jesting, he knew they wanted him to have a love match as well.

But Connor neither hoped for nor wanted that for himself. He had seen the consequences of an unruly, all-consuming passion and would never trust it. Instead, he intended to have a smooth, cordial partnership with a lass whose father had enough warriors to defeat the MacLeods.

"Pick a pretty lass who's no afraid to argue with ye," Alex said and winked. "A man needs a wife who stirs his blood."

Any lass who was breathing could stir Connor's blood. After so long without, there was not a single one he did not find overwhelmingly appealing. He was like a man dying of thirst at sea, surrounded by water he could not drink.

"Frankly, lads, ye haven't been much help," Connor said, getting to his feet.

"Ask Teàrlag," Alex said, referring to the old seer as he and Ian drifted toward the door. "She'll give ye good advice, even if it makes no sense at the time."

Connor needed to get out of this room, but he stayed behind because he sensed that Duncan wished to speak with him. His head had begun pounding the moment he entered it. Like his father and grandfather before him, Connor had used this room as his private chamber. Even after he had stripped it of its ornate furnishings, he had felt his father's presence too keenly—stifling and choking him.

At his sister's insistence, the ornate furniture was back. The chamber was hers and Duncan's now that the two were wed and Connor had made Duncan keeper of this castle.

Connor hobbled over to look out the arrow-slit window. As his gaze traveled along the shore, he paused at the place where the warrior had carried his mother's body ashore all those years ago. Whenever he remembered that bleak day of his childhood, he thought of his brother Ragnall, who would have made a better chieftain.

But Ragnall, like his father, was dead, so the task fell to him.

"I'm honored that you've entrusted Dunscaith Castle to me," Duncan said.

"There are too many ghosts for me here," Connor said, though his personal reasons played no part in his decision. "I know ye will keep this castle and the surrounding lands safe for our clan."

"Have ye decided who will replace me as captain of your guard?" Duncan asked.

"I'll never find a captain who is as loyal or as fierce a

warrior as you," Connor said, turning to grip his friend's shoulder. "But I'll pick a man from among our warriors once I reach Trotternish Castle."

"Choosing the wrong wife could make things unpleasant for ye." Duncan paused. "But choosing the wrong captain could get ye killed."

# CHAPTER 2

A sense of freedom washed over Connor as he sailed away from Dunscaith Castle. He would have lived the rest of his life there if that met the needs of the clan, but praise God it did not. Every day at Dunscaith he lived in the shadow of two men—his father, whom he had never been able to please, and his older brother, whose place he had taken.

Before heading north to the far end of the island, he directed his men to pull onto the beach below Teàrlag's cottage, which was perched high on a cliff overlooking the sea. The questions he meant to put to the clan's ancient seer were private, so he left his guard in the galley. The steps cut into the stone cliff were black and slippery with rain, and his injured leg gave him some trouble.

He forgot Ilysa was behind him until he heard her cough.

"Careful," he said, turning to offer his hand to her.

"Does your leg pain ye badly?" she asked.

"No," he lied.

Teàrlag was not waiting for them at the top of the cliff, as she usually did. Perhaps the old seer was losing her gift. When he reached her cottage, he knocked on the weathered door, then pushed it open.

"I'm no losing The Sight," Teàrlag greeted him, glaring at him with her one good eye. "Has becoming chieftain gone to your head, lad? Ye can't expect an old woman to stand out in the rain waiting for ye."

While she spoke, her cow mooed in complaint from behind the half wall that divided the cottage.

"I see you and your cow are as cheerful as ever," Connor said, holding back a smile.

Teàrlag had two plaids wrapped around her and was so short and hunched over that he could not tell if she was standing or sitting until she shuffled over to the table where Ilysa was unpacking the basket of food she had brought. Connor was relieved that she looked no worse than the last time he saw her. When he handed her the jug of whiskey he'd brought, the old woman's wrinkled face brightened.

"There's a good lad," she said as she retrieved her cup from the shelf above the table.

"I'm making Trotternish Castle my home," Connor said. "I wished to pay my respects before I go."

"Hmmph, that's no why ye came." Teàrlag poured a large measure of whiskey into her cup. After she drank it down, she fixed her good eye on him. "Ye came because ye fear I'll be dead before ye come back."

Connor did not bother denying it, though that was not his only reason. He sat at the table and nodded his thanks to Ilysa, who had eased the jug out of Teàrlag's hand and poured him a cup.

"I wish to know what ye foresee for the clan," he said. "Do ye have any warnings I should heed to protect our people?"

"I told ye before," she said, looking sour again. "The clan's future depends upon ye wedding the right lass."

Connor had only been eleven or twelve at the time, though he remembered it well enough. He and the other lads had asked her about their future because they longed to hear about their great feats as warriors. Instead, she had disappointed them with predictions about women.

"I did harbor some hope," he said, "that in fifteen years ye might have gained a clearer picture regarding what lass I ought to choose."

"Ach, ye don't listen," she said. "I told ye that the lass will choose you."

Connor's chest was throbbing from the arrow wound, and the old seer was trying his patience. His bride would be a chieftain's daughter and would have no choice over the matter. Their marriage would be an alliance between two clans, agreed upon between Connor and the lass's father.

"I feel a vision coming," Teàrlag called out in a strange voice.

Connor suspected Teàrlag was warming up to re-enact a vision she'd had earlier, if she was not making it up altogether. The old woman did like to make a show of her gift.

Ilysa helped the old seer turn on her stool to face the hearth, then tossed a handful of the herbs Teàrlag used to enhance her visions onto the fire, causing it to spit and crackle. After drawing in several deep breaths of the pungent smoke, Teàrlag fell into an alarming fit of hacking. Connor started to get up, but Ilysa shook her head and helped the old seer turn around to face him again.

Teàrlag laid her palms flat on the table and closed her eyes. Then she swayed from side to side on her stool while making an unnerving humming sound. Finally, she opened her eyes and drank the draught of whiskey Ilysa had poured for her.

By the saints, how could such a wee old woman drink so much whiskey?

"'Tis just a wee nip," Teàrlag objected.

Connor kept forgetting that the seer could read minds.

"Take care who ye trust, Connor MacDonald," Teàrlag said, wagging a gnarled finger at him. "There are many who mean ye harm."

He did not need a seer to tell him that. If he forgot, he had the wounds in his chest and leg to remind him.

"Ye believe ye can decide everything here," she said, tapping the wispy gray hair at her temple. Her breathing was labored as she came around the tiny table to stand in front of him and lay a hand on his chest. "When the time comes for ye to choose who to put your faith in, forget what your head is telling ye and listen to your heart."

The old seer freely mixed advice with foretelling, and Connor suspected this was the former.

"Can ye advise me which clan chieftain I should seek to make an alliance with?" Before she could chastise him again, he added, "Then he can advise his daughter to choose me."

"Don't forget, 'tis no the lass's clan—nor her father— that you'll be sharing a bed with." The old seer cackled and slapped her hand on the table.

Ach, she was as bad as Alex. Connor would wed a lass who looked like a mule if it would save his clan. Still, he hoped his bride would be fair. Surely that would make it easier to be content with only her. He was so desperate to have a woman in his bed that he'd be happy at first with any lass who was warm and willing. But a lifetime? He did not like to think about it.

"Look for your bride among the faeries," Teàrlag said.

"The faeries?" What in the hell was she talking about?

Connor feared the old woman had lost her gift for foretelling, for which she was famed throughout the isles. That was a shame, for she had helped guide MacDonald chieftains through troubled times for many, many years, and there was no one to replace her.

"I need a word with Ilysa," Teàrlag said.

"Ilysa?" The lass was so quiet that Connor had forgotten her again.

"Now be a good lad and wait outside," Teàrlag said, as if he were still a boy of ten instead of her chieftain.

If anyone else called him a good lad and ordered him out, he'd have their heads. But it was hard to take offense at the old seer's lack of respect when she had treated his father the same. Besides, Connor was inordinately fond of her, and she had saved his life when he'd been badly injured soon after his return to Skye. He had been so close to death that he had seen an angel hovering over him.

"It wasn't me who saved ye," Teàrlag said as he leaned down to kiss her weathered cheek. "I gave ye up for dead."

Alas, the old woman's mind had grown confused as well. He hoped he would see her again in this life.

While he stood outside with rain dripping down the

back of his neck and his chest aching, Connor wondered what the old seer could have to say to Ilysa that he could not hear. A secret remedy for a headache or warts? No doubt, the old woman would miss Ilysa. She took good care of Teàrlag, visiting her often and bringing her baskets of food.

For the first time, it crossed his mind to wonder why Ilysa had chosen to go to Trotternish Castle. He had given each member of his household the choice of remaining at Dunscaith Castle, and all the others had chosen to stay. He'd probably never know her reasons. Ilysa was a lass who kept her thoughts to herself.

* * *

"While I'm away," Ilysa said, "Connor's sister Moira will make certain someone brings ye provisions regularly."

"You're a kind lass," Teàrlag said. "Tell me what is troubling ye?"

"Duncan doesn't want me to go with Connor," Ilysa said and made herself stop twisting the skirt of her gown in her hands.

"Ye never do what your brother tells ye, except when it suits ye," the old seer said. "That's no what's making ye uneasy."

"I could live here with you instead." Ilysa glanced around the small cottage and wondered whether it would be worse to share a bed with Teàrlag or the cow.

"Duncan is right to worry, child," Teàrlag said. "The path before ye is full of danger, but ye must go all the same."

"Why must I?" Ilysa asked, though she'd had the same feeling.

"It would serve no purpose to tell Connor, who's decided I'm an old fool," Teàrlag said, waving her hand dismissively. "But his future is hazy in my visions. I fear he may not live to see the summer."

Her words sent a jolt of fear through Ilysa.

"Connor must live! Our clan depends upon his survival." *I depend upon it.*

"Our young chieftain will need you to see dangers that he cannot," the seer said. "Trust yourself, and ye may save his life."

"Me?" Ilysa asked. "How am I to do that?"

"Ach, ye think far too little of yourself. Remember, ye carry the blood of the Sea Witch of legend, who built Dunscaith Castle in a single night," Teàrlag said, leaning forward and blinking her good eye. "And ye were born at midnight."

"That doesn't mean I have The Sight like you do," Ilysa said.

"Hmmph, no one has the gift like I do," Teàrlag said. "But The Sight comes to ye sometimes, doesn't it? Ye sense things coming."

"Perhaps," Ilysa whispered and dropped her gaze to her hands, which were folded in her lap. "But not often, and 'tis never clear."

"With you, lass, The Sight is strongest where your heart is," Teàrlag said. "That is why ye will see the danger to Connor when no one else does."

Ilysa turned her face away, embarrassed that Teàrlag knew how she felt about Connor.

"I've taught ye the spells of protection," Teàrlag said. "But most of all, ye must trust your instincts, for that is The Sight speaking to ye."

"I'll do what I can," Ilysa said.

Was she fooling herself into believing that Connor needed her, or should she admit, at least to herself, that she was going simply because she needed to be near him? Regardless, she listened carefully while Teàrlag told her of the places on Trotternish where the old magic was strongest.

"There will come a time when ye must part from Connor," Teàrlag said, patting Ilysa's arm with her gnarly hand. "It can't be helped. Ye will know when."

Ilysa already knew. When Connor took a wife, she would be gone.

"Tell me"—Ilysa paused to lick her dry lips—"will the lass Connor weds make him happy?" If so, she could bear leaving him.

"Our chieftain can only find happiness if he weds the lass who chooses him on Beltane night," Teàrlag said.

*Then two months is all I have left with him.*

"But for that to happen," the old seer said, "Connor must live to see Beltane."

# CHAPTER 3

## TROTTERNISH CASTLE

Connor stood in his new bedchamber watching the men practicing with their claymores in the courtyard below. The room extended the full width of the two-story building that adjoined the old keep and skirted the edge of the sea cliff. He chose this chamber for its windows, which afforded him views in both directions from which an attack might come.

He raised his gaze beyond the castle walls to the green fields an enemy must cross to reach the castle by land. When he dropped his gaze to the men again, he sighed. They were sadly in need of training. Unfortunately, he did not see one good candidate to serve as captain of his guard. The best of them was Sorely, who had been one of his father's guards and was getting old for the task. What Connor would not give to find one man here who was the match of his cousins and Duncan. But then, they were matchless.

Despite the daunting challenges he faced, Connor

could breathe here. His father had rarely brought him to this castle and never permitted him in this chamber, so Connor had no lingering memories.

He heard voices and turned toward the open door as two women entered with a wooden tub and buckets of steaming water.

"I can manage by myself," he said before one of them offered to wash him.

Being naked with any woman was far too dangerous in the state he was in, but the buxom lass with the chestnut hair had a gleam in her eyes that spelled temptation. As she poured a bucket of hot water into the tub, the rising steam enveloped her, sending dark, lusty thoughts swirling through Connor's head.

"Mind ye keep that door to the tower closed, Chieftain," the older woman said with a nervous glance at the small door at the far end of the chamber.

Connor had been warned not to take this chamber because the ghost of a nursemaid was rumored to haunt the tower. The nursemaid would not trouble him; he had left his own ghosts behind.

"So long as she stays in her tower," he said, with a wink at the old woman, "we'll get along fine."

The buxom lass laughed and gave him another look that led his imagination further astray. He was grateful— or at least he told himself he was—when the older woman pushed the tempting lass out the door before he changed his mind about needing help with his bath.

"Tell Sorely I want to see him when the men take a rest," Connor told the guard outside his door before he closed it.

After pulling his tunic over his head and tossing it

on the bench, he unwound the strips of linen around his chest. He winced as he pulled off the last layers, which had become stuck to his wound. That was the price he paid for ignoring Ilysa's pleas to let her change the bandages during the journey from Dunscaith. Until he was certain he had rooted out Hugh's spies, he could not afford to appear weakened by injury in front of his men.

While the heat from the bathwater soaked into his muscles, Connor leaned his head back and rested his eyes. The wounds had taken more out of him than he had admitted to himself. When he awoke, the water had gone stone-cold.

He was drying himself when there was a knock at the door. Thinking it must be Sorely, he called out, "Come in!"

"I've come to see to your woun—"

Connor turned around. *Jesu, 'tis Ilysa.*

She made a high-pitched squeak, and the tray she was carrying fell from her hands with a crash. Her face went scarlet, and she dropped to the floor and scrambled to gather her things.

Though Ilysa probably got a good look at his bare backside, Connor had covered his essential parts with the drying cloth when he turned around. Her reaction seemed extreme for a lass who was both a skilled healer and a widow. He still found it difficult to believe Ilysa was old enough to have been wed. She was a tiny thing, and in the loose gowns she wore, he could not tell if she even had breasts.

"I'll come back later," Ilysa said as she frantically reached for rolling jars.

She squeaked again when he knelt to help her pick up the pieces of a broken clay pot.

"No need to go," he said. "Just let me pull on my trews, and ye can see to my wounds."

He stifled a laugh when she sprang to her feet and turned her back to him.

"'Tis safe," he told her once he had his trews on and had settled himself on a stool.

As soon as Ilysa leaned over to examine the arrow hole in his chest, her manner changed completely.

"Ach, ye should have let me do this sooner," she scolded. "The bandages were stuck fast to the wound, weren't they?"

He did not bother answering. Despite her annoyance, Ilysa's touch was gentle. In fact, her fingers felt like feathers over his skin.

Oh, God help him, even Ilysa aroused him. Ach, he felt like the worst sort of scoundrel.

"How old are ye?" he asked her.

"Nineteen," Ilysa said as she briskly mixed herbs into a paste.

Though she looked like she was twelve, Connor did not feel quite so disgusting for getting a throbbing erection from her touch.

"I'm nine years younger than you and my brother, same as I've always been," she added with her dry humor.

Of course, he knew that. He could still remember when Duncan's mother had returned pregnant after disappearing mysteriously for weeks. It had been the talk of the castle, but Anna had never enlightened any of them regarding where she had been or who fathered her babe.

The ability to keep her own counsel was a trait Anna and her daughter had in common.

Ilysa's hands were on him again, spreading the poultice over his wound, and he could think of nothing else. Ach, he was a sorry man. When she leaned close, he felt her breath on his skin. He resisted the temptation to close his eyes and pretend a lass who was not his best friend's younger sister was touching him with a different purpose.

"Ye married young," he said. "Ye couldn't have been more than eleven when we left for France."

"Ye were gone a long time. Sixteen is not young to wed." She lifted his hand and placed it on the square of cloth that covered the poultice. "Hold that."

She commenced to wind a clean linen strip around his chest. She cupped his elbow and lifted it as she brought the strip under his arm, taking charge of his body with an assurance that both surprised and further aroused him. When she leaned forward, reaching around him to bring it behind his back and over his shoulder, her chest touched his. A jolt went through him as he discovered that Ilysa definitely did have breasts. Even through the thick layers of fabric, there was no mistaking the feel of the soft, rounded flesh.

He hoped to God Ilysa did not look down and see his shaft pressing against his trews. Considering how she had reacted to seeing his bare arse, he feared she would faint dead away.

"What made ye decide to wed Mìchael?" he asked to distract himself. Her husband had been a few years younger than Connor. He had known him, but not well.

"My mother was dying, and she wished to see me settled," Ilysa said.

Ilysa was a practical, sensible lass. No need to worry about her losing her head and running off with the wrong sort of man.

When she circled her arms around him again, Connor sucked in his breath. A lass who looked like a boy and dressed like a grandmother should not smell so good.

"Water lilies?" he asked without thinking.

"Aye," she said and gave a light laugh. "I used the dried flowers in the poultice so it wouldn't smell so dreadful this time."

Christ, he was going to smell like lilies?

When he felt her breast against his arm, he made himself focus on the hideously ugly brown cloth that was wrapped tightly around her head and covered every bit of her hair. That helped, but not much.

"Now I'll bandage the wound on your thigh," she said. "I'm afraid you'll have to get on the bed and take those trews off for me."

*Get on the bed and take my trews off?* Sweet Ilysa had no idea what a provocative suggestion that was to make to a man in his condition.

"Leave your things. I can bandage my leg myself," he said.

She started to argue, but he ignored her. Something out the windows on the sea side caught his attention. When he crossed the room for a better look, he saw three galleys sailing straight for the bay next to the castle.

* * *

Ilysa could not tear her gaze away from Connor's tall, powerfully built frame outlined against the windows. Her cheeks grew hot as she watched the muscles of his back ripple beneath the neatly wrapped strips of linen. The white lines of his many battle scars only made him look more dangerous and fierce. Helpless to stop herself, she followed the long sinews down his back to the muscles of his buttocks, which were tantalizingly visible beneath his trews.

"Damn it, why has no one alerted me?"

Connor's angry words jolted her attention. She tried to collect her thoughts while he jerked on his boots.

"I wish to God your brother was here," he said and snapped up his shirt from the bench. "You can be sure the men would be keeping watch."

"Let me help with that," she said, fearing he'd dislodge the bandages.

While he pulled the shirt down over his chest, she held her hands inside it to keep it from rubbing against his wound. Ach, a lass could swoon standing this close to Connor with her hands under his shirt.

"What did ye see?" she asked, when she remembered there was cause for alarm.

"Three war galleys are about to land." Connor grabbed his claymore and started for the door.

"Whose are they?" she asked as she followed behind him.

"They belong to Alexander of Dunivaig and the Glens."

"Is he attacking us?"

"I don't believe so," Connor said as he pounded down the stairs in front of her. "I invited him."

* * *

Men! Why did Connor not think to warn her that he had invited an important chieftain to the castle? Good heavens, what would she feed their guests? They had only just arrived themselves. At least she had set some of the servants to cleaning the hall and the bedchambers first thing.

She had not even had time to visit the kitchens yet. As the MacLeods controlled most of the countryside surrounding the castle, she suspected they barely had enough food to feed themselves. Three galleys full of warriors could clean out their stores in no time.

"When did ye invite him?" Ilysa asked as she ran to keep up with him.

"I told his son James when he visited Dunscaith a few weeks ago."

"But this castle was still in the hands of the MacLeods then," she said.

"I had confidence we would take it."

*Clearly.* "But why did ye invite him?" she asked as she followed him through the door that connected the newer building to the keep.

Connor turned and raised an eyebrow at her before pushing through the door that led out into the courtyard. Apparently, the chieftain viewed that as one question too many.

Ilysa crossed the hall to another set of steps that led down to the undercroft. This was not how she wanted to do this. Her plan had been to tread softly and take her time winning over the servants of the castle, particularly the fearsome cook in charge of the kitchens.

She'd heard murmurs since her arrival that he was the devil himself.

Though Ilysa had been only seventeen when she began managing the castle household at Dunscaith, everyone there knew her and had known her mother before her. For the most part, they had accepted her authority easily enough. Her Trotternish clansmen may know her brother and may have seen her at gatherings when she was a child, but that would not gain her much.

The cook, a sour-looking man in his fifties, glared at her the moment she came through the doorway to the kitchens.

"What is your name?" she asked.

"I'm called Cook," he said as if he expected an argument.

"Cook, I fear we find ourselves in a desperate situation," she said, standing before him with her hands folded. "The reputation of the clan depends upon you."

That brought a snide laugh from him. "The reputation of the clan depends on my oatcakes?"

"Alexander of Dunivaig and a hundred of his warriors are about to land," she said. "Ye know very well that a chieftain is judged by how lavish a host he is, so we require a grand feast."

The cook let out a long string of oaths, which Ilysa let pass without comment.

"'Tis important we not embarrass our chieftain," she said.

"'Tis no my fault," he said, raising his hands into the air, "that I don't have the supplies I need to create dishes to impress an important guest."

"As I'm sure you're aware, the MacLeods are waiting

to pounce on us and take back this castle," she said, keeping her tone calm. "The safety of the clan is at stake. We must do our part to make our clan appear stronger than we are."

"I'd need the help of the faeries to make that kind of feast," he sputtered.

"Tell me what ye need, and I'll see what I can do," she said.

His face grew redder still as he attempted to stare her down. After a long moment, he appeared to accept that she was not giving up or leaving.

"I have venison, oysters, and fish," he said, giving a calculating glance around the kitchen, "but I have no spices to make fancy sauces."

"I brought spices with me from Dunscaith."

The cook broke into a smile that seemed to surprise him even more than it did her.

"What else do ye need?" she asked.

"I can't cook a special feast without more help." He glared at two young girls stirring pots that hung over the huge kitchen hearth. "I only have these two, and they're useless."

"They're MacDonald lasses, so I'm sure they're hard workers," she said, casting an encouraging smile at them.

The castle had just been taken from the MacLeods three weeks ago. Former servants were drifting back day by day, but with no one in charge of the household, they were left to make their own choices. Ilysa suspected Cook had no other help because he was unpleasant to work with.

"I'll find ye some help, but ye must promise ye won't scare them off."

She did not wait to hear his response. A quarter of an hour later, she returned with four helpers and her precious store of spices. The cook, who was slicing venison with such speed that his knife was a blur, looked up and gave her a curt nod.

Her first victory, and an important one.

# CHAPTER 4

Ilysa's face was burning from the heat in the kitchen. She wiped her forehead with her sleeve and then brushed her gown.

"I must go upstairs now," she told Cook and peered over her shoulder at the back of her skirts. "Have I spilled anything on me?"

The cook gave her a look that said no one would notice. Ilysa sighed.

When she entered the hall, Ilysa paused to give instructions and encouraging words to the servants before slipping into a seat at the end of the high table next to Niall, Ian's younger brother. Bowls and trays of food crowded the table, and the savory smells of the venison and stews filled her nose. She was relieved everything appeared to be in order.

When she glanced toward the center of the table, her breath caught at the sight of Connor. He looked so handsome and at ease in the ornately carved chieftain's chair.

She recognized James, the eldest son of Alexander of Dunivaig, in the seat of honor to Connor's right. James must have come in his father's stead.

To Connor's left was a lass with golden hair woven into a thick braid that hung over her shoulder. Ilysa could not see her face, which was turned toward Connor, yet she could tell that the lass was beautiful. Her neck was long and graceful, her rich wine gown was perfection, and she had that aura of confidence that the most beautiful women had.

Ilysa's heart felt heavy as she heard the young woman's laugh above the noise in the hall and saw the light in Connor's eyes. When he shifted his gaze and met Ilysa's, she was embarrassed to be caught staring.

"'Tis not like you to be late for dinner," Connor called down the table to her. He made it sound as if she were a child who had been off playing instead of moving heaven and earth to put on a feast the day after her arrival. "This is Ilysa, my best friend's sister and the daughter of the good woman who had the misfortune to be my nursemaid."

Ilysa lowered her gaze and willed herself not to blush as all eyes were suddenly on her. Connor did not mean to embarrass her, but by introducing her without giving her father's name, he may as well stand on the table and shout that her father was unknown. Of course, no one knew her father's name, but why did Connor have to introduce her at all?

"You met James at Dunscaith," Connor said to her, "and this is his sister, Deirdre..."

Ilysa's heart dropped a little lower as Connor introduced the two tall, golden-haired guests. Deirdre looked

like a Nordic princess with her full, red lips, high cheek-
bones, and wide blue eyes. At the moment, she was
squinting those lovely eyes ever so slightly, as if she was
curious why she was being introduced to the mouse at the
end of table.

After Connor finished reciting Deirdre's lineage all the
way back to the first Lord of the Isles, he and his guests
fell into conversation again.

"Delicious dinner," Niall said as he speared another
hunk of venison. "This smells like heaven and tastes even
better."

Ilysa was proud of the meal and the honor it brought
to the clan. Cook was a master. But her pleasure waned
when she noticed how Connor's gaze kept returning to
Deirdre. No wonder. While nothing could have hidden
Deirdre's beauty, the wine-colored gown showed off her
fair hair and voluptuous curves to great advantage.

Ilysa looked down at her own plain brown gown, not
looking for spots this time, but truly seeing it. Normally,
she gave her clothes little thought. Her mother had drilled
into her from an early age to be inconspicuous, and it had
always served her well. But just this once, she wished she
had something pretty to wear.

Ach, as if a pretty gown could make Connor look at
her with lust in his eyes as he was looking at Deirdre now.

* * *

"Has your father accepted the Crown's offer?" Connor
asked James after they had withdrawn to his chamber for
a private discussion.

"Not yet, but I'm certain he will," James said.

He would be a fool not to. The Crown had been remarkably generous, considering the prominent role James's father had taken in the rebellion. Like prodigal sons, the clans that had joined the rebellion were being treated better than some of the clans—such as Connor's—that had not fought against the Crown.

"With the rebellion behind us, or nearly so," James continued, "there is no reason our clans cannot renew the close friendship we had before."

Connor was pleased that James was the first to raise the subject. He paused to take a sip of his whiskey. He did not wish to appear to be as anxious as he was for the alliance.

"The Crown gave Alastair MacLeod a royal charter to my lands here on Trotternish for turning against his former allies," Connor said. "I take a commitment to an ally more seriously."

"As does my father." James drummed his fingers on the table, then stopped and raised an eyebrow. "I'd say your worst problem is not the charter, but that the MacLeods control your lands."

That was the God's truth. Connor shrugged noncommittally, though they both knew he needed a strong ally like James's father to push the MacLeods out of Trotternish.

"'Tis a shame ye have this new trouble as well," James said.

Connor kept his face blank, though he had no notion what new trouble James was referring to. Whatever it was, it had made James confident.

"Your uncle Hugh has done the same as Alastair MacLeod," James said. "He captured two other pirate leaders and turned them over to the Crown."

Connor resisted the urge to throw his cup against the wall and took a slow sip of his whiskey instead. "Did he now?"

"Hugh pledged to quit pirating—or at least to stop plundering lands belonging to the Crown's allies."

"And who would be foolish enough to trust Hugh's pledge?" Connor asked.

"The regent and the council," James said. "From what I hear, the Campbell chieftain, as the Crown's deputy here in the west, is less inclined to bring Hugh into the fold. Still, this can't be good news for you."

Connor had intended to seek a marriage alliance at the gathering, which was only a few weeks away. In light of this news, he might do better to take advantage of the opportunity before him.

"My father has been approached by several chieftains seeking a marriage to my sister." James paused and smiled. "I suspect her beauty rivals my father's fleet of war galleys in fueling their desire for an alliance with us."

Deirdre had lush curves and the kind of overt sensuality that caught a man's attention like a ten-foot wave. In the days before Connor had become chieftain, when women came easy, he had preferred lasses with more delicate looks and subtle attraction. A sprinkling of freckles or an escaped curl played on a man's imagination. But in his current state of unrelenting need, Connor fully appreciated Deirdre's blatant appeal.

"I am considering marriage," Connor said, carefully approaching the subject as he would a pit of writhing snakes, "though I am in no hurry."

That was a lie, of course. The sooner he obtained a

strong ally, the sooner he could take back Trotternish. And if Deirdre's father was leaving the rebellion, this would be an excellent match.

"My father thinks well of ye and gave me permission to negotiate a marriage contract on his behalf," James said. "As long as I'm here, why wait?"

*Why, indeed?* In addition to his legitimate reasons for rushing the marriage, the plain truth was that Connor was tired of sleeping alone and *damned* tired of his own hand on his shaft. For the sake of the clan, he would have settled for a wife far less attractive than Deirdre.

She was not the sort of woman he dreamed of in those weak moments when he was weary enough to let himself daydream. In his secret heart, Connor had hoped for a lass who could be a friend as well as a lover, someone who would ease the sense of aloneness he felt as chieftain. Deirdre would never be that. She was vain and self-centered and had little to say.

But in this harsh life, he longed for a woman's softness at the end of the day.

\* \* \*

The kitchen was noisy with the sound of pots and pans being washed as Ilysa came through the door.

"What do ye want now?" Cook demanded and pointed a large wooden spoon at her. "If they have complaints, I don't want to hear them."

"I'm so proud of all of ye." Ilysa's voice hitched as tears suddenly stung the back of her eyes. "Everything was perfect. Ye did our clan and our chieftain proud." Whether Connor realized it or not.

Cook's sour expression gave way to a crooked smile.

"Thank ye, lass. Now shouldn't ye be upstairs conversing with our important guests?"

"Connor and James have gone to talk in private, and the lady wished to retire early." The saints be praised for that. "I think we each deserve a wee cup of the good wine, don't you?"

In a twinkling Cook and his helpers cleared the worktable and pulled up stools. Ilysa poured the wine, and they toasted themselves and had a fine chat. Eventually, the others left to find their beds, but Ilysa and Cook stayed.

"I worked in this kitchen for twenty years before the damned MacLeods threw us out," he said. "You're not like any of the other mistresses of the castle. They'd never lend a hand nor share a cup with me."

"I enjoy being useful," Ilysa said, then added, "and I was dead set on winning ye over."

Cook laughed. "You're a determined lass."

"Will we be friends then?" she asked.

"Aye." He lifted his cup to hers. "Ye remind me of a ripe plum, soft and sweet, but with a pit at the center hard enough to break a tooth."

It was Ilysa's turn to laugh.

"I hear the chieftain was displeased with our warriors today," the cook said. "Can't say I blame him. 'Tis nothing like it was in the days of his father, when our warriors on Trotternish struck fear in the hearts of the MacLeods."

"I'm sure they're good men who only lack for training," Ilysa said. "Connor will remedy that, though he can't do it all himself. He needs a new captain of his guard."

"Everyone here knows that the man the chieftain needs is Lachlan of Lealt."

"Who's he?"

"Lachlan is a hero in these parts for fighting the MacLeods when others fled," Cook said. "He's led raid after raid, and the MacLeods can't catch him. After he attacks, he slips away like an eel."

"This Lachlan sounds impressive," Ilysa said.

"Ach, women love a mysterious man," Cook said, waggling his bushy, gray eyebrows at her. "Lachlan is tall and fair-haired besides."

"Surely, he has no time for women between all that raiding and slipping away?" Ilysa asked with a smile. "If this Lachlan is loyal, he ought to come to the castle now that our chieftain is here."

"I expect he'll arrive soon," Cook said. "I heard he was visiting his father, who is in poor health."

"Truly," Ilysa said, leaning forward, "ye believe this Lachlan would make the best captain?"

"Aye, he has the respect of all the men here," Cook said. "They owe their allegiance to the chieftain, of course, but they don't know him. Most haven't laid eyes on him since he was a young lad. They'll be more willing to risk their lives to fight at his side if they see Lachlan there."

"I appreciate your telling me," Ilysa said.

"Ye should go to bed, lass," Cook said, stifling a yawn. "Ye worked harder than any of us, and ye look tired."

"You go on," she said. "I'd like to sit here in the quiet and finish my cup of wine."

Despite running all day, or perhaps because of it, Ilysa felt too edgy to sleep. Besides, she would be sharing a bed with Deirdre, and she was not in a hurry.

Tomorrow would be another long day, but it would

be easier because she had won a key ally. Cook was obstreperous, but he could work miracles in the kitchen with a little help and encouragement.

When she could not keep her eyes open anymore, Ilysa got up and lit a candle in the hearth fire to light her way to her chamber. As she left the kitchen, she heard something and paused before starting up the stairs.

Was that a light under the door to one of the storage rooms? She went to investigate. The last door did have a sliver of light under it. Leaving a candle or torch unattended overnight was dangerous. Tomorrow, she would find out who was responsible and speak to them. In the meantime, she would put it out.

She pushed the door open with her hip and then sucked in her breath. She was too stunned to move. In the warm glow of the torch in the wall bracket, she saw a pair coupling on the narrow wooden table.

"Aye! Aye!" the woman moaned as the table rocked with the rhythmic thrusts of the man standing between her legs.

The woman's bodice was pushed down to reveal ample, rosy-tipped breasts, and her golden hair spilled over the sides of the table. Rich, wine-colored skirts fell from the long, slender legs she had wrapped around her partner's waist.

*O shluagh!* The woman on the table was Deirdre.

The couple's obvious enjoyment brought a flood of unwelcome memories of Ilysa's brief marriage—the humiliation of her husband's awkward attempts, his limp member pressing against her.

So this was what it was supposed to be like. Ilysa's breathing went shallow as she watched how the man gripped Deirdre's hips while he thrust deep inside her. Slowly, she moved her gaze up the man's bare chest. When she reached his face, she started. His gaze was on her, and he had a wicked grin on his face.

He was laughing at her. Heat drenched her as she backed out and quietly closed the door.

When Ilysa reached her bedchamber, she undressed in the dark. Her care was unnecessary. There was no one else in the bed, confirming that the lass she had seen in the storeroom was, indeed, Deirdre.

Ilysa would be relieved when their guests departed. It was not that she begrudged Deirdre her lover or the attention of all the men in the hall. No, there was only one man whose regard she envied. When she recalled how Connor had looked at Deirdre, she wanted to weep.

Exhausted as she was, Ilysa stared up into the darkness. She had been so busy in the hours since she had gone to Connor's chamber to dress his wounds that she had succeeded in pushing the image of him naked from her mind. But now, as she lay alone in the dark, it would not leave her. It merged in her mind with the couple in the storeroom.

What would it be like to have Connor touch her like that? To have him look at her with smoldering passion in his eyes as he ran his hands over her skin?

# CHAPTER 5

Are ye any closer to choosing a new captain?" Ilysa ventured to ask.

Even after a week of dressing Connor's wound, Ilysa could not claim she was unaffected by being so close to him when he was bare-chested. But she was able to maintain at least an outward calm, and they usually fell into easy conversation. Today, however, Connor seemed distracted.

"Tait is a good fighter and loyal," he said. "But I fear he's no leader."

"That's for certain," Ilysa said, which earned her a smile.

"Ian's brother Niall will make an outstanding captain in a few years, but I need one now," Connor said. "The others are fine warriors, or will be with some training, but none is as good as a captain ought to be."

"Hmm," she murmured as she unwound the linen strips from around his chest.

"I've been watching the men every day, and I haven't seen one who has what it takes."

"What qualities are ye looking for?" she asked.

"He should be the strongest warrior, the most loyal man, and a leader the others respect enough to follow without question," Connor said.

"Ye can't expect to find someone who can replace my brother or your cousins," she said in a soft voice. "The four of ye trained and fought together all your lives."

"Aye." Connor's chest rose and fell under her fingers as he took a deep breath and blew it out. "I'd settle for one man who stands above the others."

Ilysa had raised the subject purposefully. Still, she hesitated, unsure of how Connor would take a suggestion from her on a subject so far from her knowledge.

"I may have to choose Sorely, for lack of someone better," Connor said, his gaze fixed on the sea out the window. "He's a strong warrior, and I know he's loyal."

"I've heard of someone who may be worthy of your consideration."

"Who?" Connor said, turning to fix steely-blue eyes on her.

Sometimes the shift in his manner from disarming friendliness to chieftain was startling. Ilysa forced her breathing to remain steady as she told him what she knew about the man Cook had described.

"I hope this Lachlan is all that you've heard," Connor said. "I'll send for him. Someone in the castle will know where to find him."

Ilysa smiled to herself, having accomplished one of the two tasks she had set for herself before coming into the room. Now for the second one.

"The wound on your chest is healing well, but I haven't seen the one on your leg since I removed the arrow," she said, praying her cheeks were not turning pink. "Ye should let me look at it."

Despite her embarrassment, she was faintly disappointed when he pulled his tunic on. She helped him, as usual, so that he would not ruin the bandaging she had just done. When he started unfastening his trews, she spun around. She could almost hear him chuckle.

"Wish me well," he said while her back was to him.

"Why?" she asked.

"I'm negotiating a marriage contract tonight."

Ilysa slowly turned around. "A marriage contract? For who?"

"For me," Connor said with a sudden, blinding smile.

"Who are ye marrying?" Her mind was moving slowly, as if she had thick mud in her head. "Is it . . . Deirdre?"

"Aye," he said. "She's a fair lass, isn't she?"

"She is that." Ilysa's heart pounded in her ears. She had to tell him about Deirdre and her lover, but how?

"Is something wrong, Ilysa? Ye look pale."

He startled her by grasping her around her waist and lifting her onto the stool he had been sitting on earlier. *Oh my.* That had not helped calm her at all. He leaned down until his face was inches from hers and scrutinized her with narrowed eyes, which set her heart beating harder still.

"I know it's not my place to say this"—she paused to lick her lips—"but I like to think we're friends."

"Of course we are." He straightened and looked impossibly tall standing above her. "I've known ye since ye were a babe in your mother's arms."

"Ye mustn't marry Deirdre," she said. "She isn't the right wife for ye."

"Her clan can help us defeat the MacLeods," he said, the concern in his eyes evaporating, "and that makes her right for me."

Ach, Ilysa did not want to tell him what she had seen in the storeroom. And that was not all. When she saw the man Deirdre had been with again, she realized he was one of James's warriors. All week, Ilysa had watched him leave the hall, time and again, shortly after Deirdre.

"If ye intend to bandage my leg, you'd best be about it," Connor said.

"I fear Deirdre will make ye unhappy," Ilysa said, dropping her gaze to her hands, which were folded in her lap, "and embarrass ye."

When he did not speak for a long moment, she glanced up at him. His eyes were so cold that she swallowed. What had she done?

"Like my mother embarrassed my father? Is that what you're saying?" Connor said. "You assume that being beautiful makes her untrustworthy?"

Ilysa had not given his mother a thought.

"You're quick to judge the poor lass," he said. "That is unkind of ye."

"I did not mean—"

"I have much to do," he said. "Ye may go."

"But your leg?" she asked.

"I said, ye may go."

It was a clear dismissal, but she must tell him. Deirdre could already be carrying another man's child. A chieftain, even more than most men, had to know that his heir was of his own blood.

"Connor, I must tell—"

"My close bond with your brother has made ye forget that I am your chieftain," he said, his voice like the deadly calm before a storm. "A marriage alliance is a complex matter. I asked for your good wishes, not your advice."

"But—"

"Go!" he thundered and pointed to the door.

\* \* \*

"Connor is still alive," Hugh said. "Ye failed to kill him."

Lachlan had suspected as much. He shrugged and glanced around the abandoned house Hugh was using as his base. It stank of dogs, unwashed men, and moldy rushes.

"And they say you're the best," Hugh said, his voice dripping sarcasm.

Lachlan met Hugh's glare without showing any reaction. He had not done it for Hugh, and he did not give a damn what Hugh thought of him. A common enemy made them allies, but that did not mean he liked the man.

"Ye said ye got two arrows in him, yet I'm told he's walking around as if nothing happened," Hugh said.

"You're perilously close to calling me a liar," Lachlan said, moving a step closer. "Unless you're certain that you're better with a blade than I am, I suggest ye don't."

Hugh's men, a motley bunch of clanless scum, began reaching for their weapons but stopped when Hugh threw his head back and laughed. What in the hell was amusing? Hugh's unpredictability was one of the traits that made Lachlan mistrust him.

"You're a tough son of a bitch." Hugh tucked his

thumbs in his belt and rocked back on his heels. "That's what I like about ye."

Hugh's woman, Rhona, a curvy lass with dark hair, sauntered over and put her arm around Hugh's neck. That lass was trouble, and no better than Hugh deserved. Whenever she thought Hugh was not looking, she gave Lachlan the eye. Rhona underestimated Hugh, a mistake Lachlan did not make. Hugh had a sly cleverness, and he did not miss much.

"Don't worry, you'll have another chance at Connor," Hugh said. "Go to Trotternish Castle and offer him your sword."

Lachlan nodded because he had already decided to do exactly that.

What troubled him was that the chieftain would require Lachlan to give his oath of loyalty, and it went against who he was to give a false oath. But sacrifices must be made. Killing the chieftain was a debt of honor, and this time he would complete the task.

"We'll get rid of him together," Hugh said, his eyes gleaming cold like a snake's.

"I'll tell ye again so that you're sure to understand me." Lachlan grabbed Hugh by the front of his tunic and pulled him up until they were nose-to-nose. "My dispute is with Connor, and Connor alone. I will do nothing that harms the clan."

Lachlan felt the prick of Hugh's dirk against his stomach.

"Keep your goddamned hands off me if ye want to leave here alive," Hugh said.

Lachlan had made his point and released him.

"Give me warning when Connor is outside the safety

of the castle walls," Hugh said, "and my men will see to it that he never returns."

"It had better be your men, such as they are," Lachlan said, throwing a scathing glance at them before returning his gaze to Hugh. "If I find you're dealing with the MacLeods, you and I will be enemies. I am not a good enemy to have."

"Connor's your enemy, not me," Hugh said. "Deliver him, and we'll both have justice."

# CHAPTER 6

Ilysa went up to her chamber to be alone to think. She groaned when she opened the door to find Deirdre there, being dressed by her maid.

"Have this laundered." Deirdre stepped out of her gown and tossed it to Ilysa, without actually looking at her, as if she were a common servant. "It has a tear that needs mending."

Ilysa could guess how it had torn. Her stomach hurt.

"Your mistress and I must speak in private," she told the maid.

Deirdre's fine eyebrows went up an inch, but Ilysa waited to explain until the door closed behind the maid.

"Are ye aware that your brother is negotiating a marriage contract between you and my chieftain?"

"I am." Deirdre shrugged. Then, watching herself in the mirror, she tugged a strand of hair loose from her braid to make a fetching curl at the side of her face.

"Is this what ye want?" Ilysa asked.

"Your clan is not as powerful as my father's, so Connor is a bit beneath me," Deirdre said, wrinkling her nose. "But he is undeniably handsome."

"He is more than that," Ilysa said. "He is an honorable man, and he'll be a devoted husband. Can ye promise him the same?"

"My, you are surprising, but 'tis not your place to question me." Deirdre waved her hand as if she were batting away a fly. "Do see about having that gown mended."

"Is there something ye ought to tell Connor before entering into this marriage?" Ilysa persisted.

Deirdre turned and leveled a hard look at Ilysa. Suddenly Ilysa understood. Deirdre was with child.

"Ye must tell your brother that ye cannot wed Connor," Ilysa said.

"It was my brother who suggested the marriage." Deirdre placed her hand on one shapely hip and smiled. "Connor wants the alliance. And he wants *me*."

"But ye love someone else," Ilysa said.

"Love?" Deirdre gave an amused laugh. "I'd hardly call it that."

Clearly, Deirdre was not going to put a stop to this. As for Connor, he could not see beyond the alliance and Deirdre's overflowing attributes. Yet when Deirdre had a child in six months—and later took a lover, as Ilysa suspected she would—it would tear Connor's pride to shreds.

Teàrlag had told Ilysa she must trust her instincts and protect Connor. She made up her mind what to do.

"As ye say, 'tis not my place." Ilysa heaved what she hoped sounded like a resigned sigh and began gathering her medicines. She picked up a few at random and put them into her basket. "I have other duties. A woman in a nearby cottage is having a babe and sent for me."

"Isn't it dangerous to leave the castle?" Deirdre asked, narrowing her lovely blue eyes at Ilysa. "And why would you be the one to go?"

"As anyone will tell ye, I'm a healer," Ilysa said and lifted her cloak from the peg by the door. "There's no telling when I'll be back. A first babe can take hours and *hours*."

Outside the door, Ilysa leaned against the cold stone wall. Before she did this, she must set aside her feelings for Connor and be sure she was doing this because it was best for him and for the clan. Even without Teàrlag's warning that Connor would not be happy if he wed before Beltane, Ilysa knew in her heart that Connor would suffer if Deirdre were his wife. As for the clan, any weakening of Connor's authority would make his tasks even more difficult.

This marriage must be thwarted.

It was nearly time for supper. Instead of leaving the castle as she had told Deirdre, she headed for the kitchens.

"I can't be seen in the hall," Ilysa said in a low voice to Cook as she joined him at the worktable, "but I must know the moment Deirdre leaves the table."

Cook raised an eyebrow, but she shook her head to let him know she could not tell him why.

"I'll tell one of the serving maids to keep an eye on her," he said, pitching his voice below the noise of the kitchen. "I'll invent a reason."

Ilysa was relieved that he understood she did not want anyone else to know the request came from her.

"You're a good friend," she whispered and squeezed his arm. Then realization dawned, and she turned to face him. "What do ye know?"

"I have a suspicion about the lass's *interest* in a certain warrior," Cook whispered, "and I'm no the only one."

That meant half the castle was abuzz about Deirdre's clandestine meetings with her lover. If Ilysa had any doubts before about the need to take action, they were gone.

"I'll wait in the wine cellar," Ilysa said.

Supper seemed to take an eternity, but at last Cook stuck his head through the door. "The lady's excused herself to retire early *again*."

Ilysa picked up her skirts and raced out. She stopped on the dim-lit stairs where she could see into the hall without being seen, her heart pounding. She did not have to wait long before Connor and James left the hall for the adjoining building.

*Hurry, hurry*, she chanted in her head as she fixed her eyes on Deirdre's lover. When he finally left the hall and disappeared into the stairwell that led to the upper floors of the keep, Ilysa realized that her plan might actually work.

She did not know how long to wait. Would Deirdre and her lover talk first? Ilysa recalled how the pair behaved in the storeroom and decided that, if they did talk, it probably would not be for long.

Once they actually started, how long did it take to fornicate? From all the remarks Ilysa had heard from other women, the time varied considerably. She did not want to act too soon, before it all began. On the other hand, if she waited too long, it could all be over and the man gone.

Ach, this would drive her mad. Ilysa took a deep breath and decided it was time.

* * *

"My sister has a sweet, biddable nature that would please any man," James said as the two of them sat at the small table in Connor's private chamber.

"Aye, she has," Connor said because it was expected, though Deirdre did not strike him as either sweet or biddable.

"I can tell that her beauty has charmed ye as well," James said, smiling.

Deirdre was undeniably attractive.

Over the last week, Connor had thought on it long and hard and concluded that he could do no better for his clan than make this alliance. Alexander of Dunivaig had the warriors and galleys Connor needed to fight the MacLeods, and he was offering an extremely generous *tochar*, or dowry, which Connor's beleaguered clan could sorely use.

And yet, Ilysa's caution about Deirdre not being the right wife nagged at him. He was still annoyed with her for suggesting Deirdre would embarrass him.

"There are two things that are essential to me when I take a wife," Connor said.

"Beauty and what else?" James said with a laugh.

"My first requirement is that her clan commit to fight the MacLeods with mine," Connor said. "Your father cannot fight for Trotternish while battling the Crown's forces elsewhere, and I cannot risk an alliance that could draw me into the rebellion."

"As I said before, I believe my father is very close to

accepting the Crown's terms," James said. "Very close, indeed."

Close was not good enough, but Connor needed this alliance, and he needed it as quickly as possible.

"My other requirement," Connor said, "is that I have my wife's absolute loyalty."

James bristled, but it had to be said.

"I've heard about your mother, of course, so I won't take that remark as an insult," James said in a stiff voice. "You've nothing to fear in that quarter. My sister comes to her wedding as an untouched virgin, and she will be a virtuous wife."

"In exchange for her loyalty, I will give her mine," Connor said. "We will have the usual trial marriage for a year to assure that she can bear children. But so long as she is my wife, I will take no other woman to my bed."

"I won't hold ye to that," James said with a wink.

Connor would hold himself to it, however. Thanks be to heaven that Deirdre was beautiful, for she was dull as dirt. He quickly chided himself for disparaging the woman who would be his wife. She deserved his respect, and he was determined to be content with her.

Bedding her would certainly be no chore. Ach, he had been celibate for far, far too long. He thought of her long legs wrapped around his waist, and his hands...

"I'm glad we have matters settled," James said. "If ye don't have your own clerk, I brought one with me who can prepare the marriage contract."

Before Connor could reply, the door burst open.

# CHAPTER 7

*God preserve me.* Connor clenched his fists as Niall, who was one of the guards at his door this evening, escorted Ilysa into the center of the room.

"Niall, I told ye I was not to be interrupted for anything short of an attack," Connor said between his teeth.

Although Niall had just turned eighteen, no man could have gotten past him. He was, however, pliable as warm wax when it came to females. He trusted every last one of them, and he thought Ilysa, in particular, flew with the angels. If Ilysa said one word about Deirdre being the wrong wife, Connor was going to strangle her.

"Ilysa has something urgent to tell ye," Niall said with a painfully earnest expression.

"Ilysa, do not—" Connor started to order her.

"I apologize for interrupting, but I fear for your sister's safety," Ilysa said, looking at James. "I'm sure ye won't want the whole castle to know, but I saw a man sneak into the bedchamber I share with her."

Connor leaped to his feet, ready to charge out to protect his guest. When he noticed that James was considerably slower to get out of his seat, a bad feeling settled in the pit of his stomach.

"I heard her cry out, but the door is barred," Ilysa said, clenching her hands in front of her. "Ye must hurry. Please. Who knows what he's doing to her?"

"You two wait here," Connor ordered Ilysa and Niall as he pushed past them. "James and I will deal with this."

When he and James reached the hall, Connor slowed his pace so as not to draw attention.

"Ilysa must have been mistaken," James said in a low voice. "Surely, none of your men would harm a guest."

Connor ignored him and went up the stairs to the keep's bedchambers. Without pausing to knock, he rammed Ilysa's door with his shoulder. It was barred, so he stepped back and kicked it, tearing it off its hinges with a *crack.*

When he stepped inside, Deirdre stared at him from the bed with her mouth open. She did not have a stitch on, and she was sitting astride a man, who was struggling to sit up. As soon as Connor saw that it was not one of his own men, he turned around.

"She's your problem, not mine," Connor said to James, who had come in behind him.

James was glaring at his sister with murder in his eyes, clearly furious with her.

But he did not look shocked.

\* \* \*

Connor never let his emotions rule his behavior, but he was so angry his vision blurred. He wanted to pound his fists into the stone wall and shake the building.

"Not a word of this to anyone," he hissed in Niall's ear as he held him by the back of his shirt and ushered him out of his chamber. "We shall speak of your role later."

He slammed the door shut and turned to Ilysa, who was perched on a stool. For once, she did not look serene in the face of danger.

"Ye knew Deirdre was in that bedchamber with a man," he shouted at her. "Ye embarrassed both me and my guests by what ye did."

"I tried to warn ye about her," Ilysa said in a soft voice.

"Ye led me to believe ye disliked the lass because ye were jealous of her," he said. "Ye did not tell me she was bedding one of her clansmen in my keep while her brother was negotiating a marriage contract with me!"

"I didn't know how else to stop ye."

"Ye came in here playing the innocent with that story about poor Deirdre being attacked," he said. "Ye deliberately deceived me and made fools of us all!"

Ilysa looked so small and pathetic sitting in her oversize gown that he felt like a monster for yelling at her. With an enormous effort, he forced himself to stop.

"A chieftain is judged by how he treats his guests," he said, though it was a ridiculous point and not the reason he was upset.

"They were not being very good guests," she murmured.

"I do not gauge my behavior by others," Connor said.

"I'm sorry for how I did it," Ilysa said, worrying her skirts in her hands. "But I had to do something before ye committed yourself."

Connor rubbed his neck and took a deep breath. "Ye should have simply told me what ye knew, instead of making vague remarks about her not being *the right wife.*"

"All right," she said. "Next time I will."

Next time? God help him, there had better never be a next time.

"There is something more ye ought to know," she said in her quiet voice. "I think Deirdre is already with child."

Connor sank into his chair and rested his head in his hands. Of course Deirdre was pregnant. And of course her brother knew it. Connor felt like a failure to have been duped like that. By tradition, the clan chose a chieftain from among the men who carried chieftain's blood. To avoid strife, it was essential there be no question that Connor's sons were truly his.

Ilysa was right to stop him, though he wished to God she had chosen a less dramatic method. If he had signed a marriage contract, it would have been a disaster.

Deirdre's child would have been born too early and then Connor would have two choices, both of them bad. If he returned her in disgrace, he would risk war with her powerful father. If he kept her, he would lose the respect of his clan and the other clans. A chieftain who was not respected weakened his clan.

He should have been suspicious when James was so intent on rushing the marriage contract. Connor was in need of a quick alliance, but their clan was not. Why had he failed to be more cautious?

Connor could tell himself it was because he was desperate to gather forces to attack the MacLeods before they attacked him. But that was not the whole of it. He had wanted to bed that lass so badly it hampered his judgment.

Lust had made him hasty and careless. It was unforgivable. He would not allow himself to be so weak again.

# CHAPTER 8

It was kind of ye to come with me," Ilysa said to Niall as they walked the final yards through the field to the castle.

"'Tis dangerous outside the castle," Niall said in an uncharacteristically gruff tone. "Connor said ye needed a man to protect ye."

Ilysa was surprised Connor was even aware that she had been called to a nearby cottage to assist a woman who was having a difficult birth. But then, he had promised Duncan he would protect her, and Connor was vigilant about his responsibilities.

"Ye won't tell anyone that I keeled over, will ye?" Niall asked, sounding young again.

Niall was over six feet and was a courageous warrior, but he had fainted dead away when the babe was born.

"Of course not," she said. "You're not the first man to do that, I promise ye. Now you'll know what to expect when ye have your own."

"What I'll expect," Niall said making a face, "is to be where I don't have to see any of it."

"I suspect you'll feel differently when the time comes."

Niall had a soft heart. He would be the sort of husband who refused to leave his wife's side and got in the way.

"I can smell spring in the air," he said, drawing in a deep breath as they neared the gate.

Beltane would be upon her in no time. In the week since James and Deirdre's hurried departure, Connor had been courteous but distant. She missed the talks they'd had when she re-bandaged his wounds each day, but he had informed her that his wounds were healed.

Niall grabbed her arm when she stumbled as they entered the castle.

"You've been up all night," he said. "Go up to bed, and I'll tell one of the serving women to bring ye something to eat."

"I am tired," she admitted. And she had not eaten since supper last night.

Ilysa intended to take Niall's advice, but she scanned the hall from habit to be sure all was well before going upstairs. Connor was not there. Most of his guard was gone as well, so she assumed he was away from the castle.

When she glanced once more around the hall on her way to the stairs, her gaze fell on a man she had never seen before. Her vision swam, and she halted in her tracks.

The Sight came to Ilysa so rarely that she was slow to recognize it. At first, she dismissed her reaction as due to an empty stomach and being overly tired. Then she realized that her weariness had made her mind open to The

Sight. Teàrlag always said that she resisted her gift.

The vision grew stronger, and vivid colors vibrated around the stranger. Alas, Ilysa had no idea what it meant.

The stranger sat alone on a bench against the wall with his arms crossed, as if waiting. From his dress, his muscular frame, and the claymore strapped to his back, he was a warrior. He had fair hair, and his skin was tanned from being outdoors, though it was early spring yet.

Ilysa was examining the strong, hawkish nose and broad cheekbone of his profile when he suddenly turned and met her eyes. Men usually looked past her or through her, but this stranger fixed his gaze on her with unwavering intensity. Ilysa wondered if he sensed that she saw something in him others did not. As they locked gazes, the feeling grew inside her that this warrior had a secret he did not want known.

Ilysa went to investigate.

"Good day to ye," she greeted him when she stood before him.

"I have business with the chieftain," the stranger said as he rose to his feet. He was a tall man, and he held himself taller.

"Our chieftain is away, but he would want me to bid ye welcome."

"Who are you?" he asked. "His wife?"

The man was rude.

"No," she said. "My name is Ilysa."

His sharp green gaze swept over her, making her recall her brother's warning that her role in the castle would lead men to assume she was the chieftain's mistress. She could almost hear this stranger wonder why the chieftain had chosen such a plain lass.

"My mother was our chieftain's nursemaid, and my brother is his best friend." She had never felt the need to explain herself before, but the stranger's scrutiny made her self-conscious. "The chieftain and I are nearly sister and brother."

"Nearly?" He raised one eyebrow.

"*Very* nearly," she said in a firm voice and held his gaze. "If you'll come sit at the table, I'll have refreshment brought for ye."

She was a trifle annoyed that no one had brought him anything already. It was midway between breakfast and the noon meal, but a traveler usually arrived hungry—and even a rude guest merited hospitality.

When she sent a meaningful look at one of the serving maids, the lass went scampering to the kitchens. The trestle tables were taken down between meals, so she directed him to sit at the end of the high table. By the time he settled himself, the maid was returning with a cup of ale and a bowl of steaming stew. Ilysa gave her a grateful smile.

"Sit and keep me company," the stranger said.

Ilysa was dead on her feet, but she could not rest until she learned more about him.

"I've told ye my name," she said sliding onto the bench beside him. "Will ye do me the same favor?"

"I am Lachlan."

"Are you the Lachlan who has been leading raids against the MacLeods?"

"Mmmph," he grunted in what she took as an assent and leaned down to scoop a spoonful of stew into his mouth.

So this was the warrior everyone thought Connor should make captain of his guard.

"This is tasty. Things have improved since I was last here." When he was halfway through his stew, he paused and said, "Since ye know our new chieftain so well, being *nearly* a sister to him, tell me about him."

Ilysa did not like his sarcasm. "Is there something in particular ye wish to know?" she asked.

"Is he a man worth serving?"

This Lachlan was direct, even for a Highlander.

"He's your chieftain and that should be sufficient," Ilysa said, sounding prim to her own ears.

Lachlan gave her a bored, sideways glance and resumed eating his stew.

"Ye shouldn't need a better reason," she said, letting her disapproval show in her tone, "but I'll tell ye that Connor MacDonald is as fine a man as any to walk this earth."

Lachlan set down his spoon and turned to look at her. "So that's the way of it."

"Ye misunderstand," Ilysa said and felt her face grow hot.

He gave a noncommittal shrug and commenced eating again. What an annoying man. Ilysa wanted to set him straight that she was not Connor's mistress, but continuing to protest was likely to have the opposite effect.

"How good a warrior is our new chieftain?" Lachlan asked.

"There's none better, save for my brother Duncan."

"Duncan, the former captain of the chieftain's guard?" he asked. "I've heard of him."

"Perhaps that will make ye think twice," she said, "before making judgments about me that ye have no business making."

"I apologize," he said, his expression softening a fraction.

At the sound of men's voices, they both turned toward the door just as Connor came through it with several of his guards. As always, Ilysa's heart made an odd little lift in her chest at the sight of him.

The next moment, she was disoriented by a burst of red colors emanating from Lachlan that felt like hostility washing over her. Then she was rocked by anguish as a vibrant blue color glowed behind the orange-red flames engulfing him.

She gripped Lachlan's arm to draw his attention. When he dragged his gaze away from Connor, his eyes held a fierceness that frightened her. But the anguish she had seen in his heart tempered her fear.

"Whatever ye think ye know about our chieftain is wrong," she said. "Connor is a good man."

"I've never met him before," Lachlan said, fixing his gaze on Connor again. "I don't think anything about him."

He lied.

Ilysa felt the tension in Lachlan's body as Connor turned his silvery blue gaze their way, then crossed the room to them. When the two men faced each other across the table, danger pulsed around them and echoed in Ilysa's head like a drumbeat.

* * *

"I am Lachlan of Lealt," the newcomer told Connor, identifying himself as being born near the Lealt River, which ran on the east side of the peninsula. "I hear ye have need of strong warriors and have come to offer my sword."

Lachlan was about Connor's age, well built and nearly as tall. His honed muscles bespoke long hours of practice, and he had the hardness in his eyes of a determined warrior. Connor liked what he saw.

"I've heard a good deal about ye," Connor said. "They say ye have been protecting the homes of our people here."

"Not all of us fled in the face of the MacLeods."

No false modesty from this one. "If ye want to fight MacLeods," Connor said, "I have need of you and your sword."

"I'm happy to demonstrate my skills," Lachlan said.

"I'd practice with ye, but I'm healing from a wound." Connor flicked his gaze to Ilysa. "I fear this wee lass will take a whip to me if I re-open it."

Lachlan's eyes widened a fraction, but he gave no hint of a smile. Connor supposed it had been too much to hope that the new man had a sense of humor as well as fighting skills.

"I'll fight him," Sorely said, stepping forward.

Connor was about to tell them it could wait until after Lachlan finished his meal, but Lachlan swung off the bench, nearly dislodging Ilysa, and strode toward the door. The other warriors stampeded out with shouts. Men did love to watch a fight. Amid the chaos, Connor noticed Ilysa was looking at him with an expression of alarm.

"I won't let them kill each other," he said, giving her a wink to reassure her. "I need them both alive to fight the MacLeods."

Ilysa did not respond with the amused glimmer in her eye that he expected. Connor regretted the discomfort that had been between them since the debacle with

Deirdre. But after letting lust interfere with his judgment, he was keeping his distance from all women, especially Ilysa.

The two combatants waited to begin until Connor joined them in the middle of the courtyard. As soon as he gave the signal, Lachlan attacked with force and no hesitation. Connor folded his arms and smiled as he watched. Sorely was good enough to make Lachlan work for it, but it was clear to Connor from the start who the victor would be.

The fight went on for some time, but Sorely remained on the defensive. When Lachlan knocked him on his back and took his sword, the men erupted into cheers. Lachlan's face showed no emotion as he let his opponent's sword clatter to the ground and returned his own to its scabbard.

"I'm glad ye decided to join us," Connor said after the shouting died down. "You'll want to finish your meal now."

Lachlan gave him a sharp nod and turned on his heel to return to the hall.

"But first," Connor said, bringing him to a halt, "I'll have your pledge of loyalty."

When Lachlan turned around, Connor caught a flash of resistance in his eyes. It was gone quickly, but Connor did not think he was mistaken.

"Of course." Lachlan dropped to one knee and laid his sword at Connor's feet. "I pledge my sword and my life to defend the MacDonalds of Sleat against all others."

Connor was not entirely satisfied, but he nodded and dismissed Lachlan to his dinner. A chieftain had the right to expect absolute loyalty from his clansmen. Thanks to his uncle Hugh's efforts to take his place and tear the clan apart, however, Connor understood that he had to earn his men's loyalty.

Sorely brushed off his clothes and came to stand beside Connor.

"He's an arrogant son of a bitch," Sorely said as they watched Lachlan go up the steps to the keep.

"Aye, but he is an impressive warrior," Connor said, "and I'm badly in need of those."

\* \* \*

While everyone else in the household was in the courtyard watching the fight, Ilysa frantically looked through her trunk for the bag of herbs Teàrlag had given her. When she found the bag, she hid it in her medicine basket and raced to Connor's bedchamber. As she hoped, the door was unguarded and the room empty.

She was relieved that the peat in the brazier still glowed hot and dropped to her knees before it. Here in Connor's chamber, she hoped she could bring on The Sight and discover if Lachlan of Lealt was a danger to him. To calm herself and clear her mind, she closed her eyes and slowed her breathing. Then she scattered the herbs that were supposed to enhance visions over the brazier.

A spray of sparks shot up from the fire followed by a pungent puff of smoke. As Ilysa leaned forward and breathed deeply, she felt as if the room were tilting. She tried to focus her thoughts on Connor and Lachlan. Instead she saw two women cooing over a babe. It should have been a comforting scene, but she felt a heavy sadness surround the women.

Then she sensed danger and a man's presence lurking just outside her vision.

When it was gone, Ilysa sat back on her heels. What on earth did it mean? And who was the man, Lachlan or Connor?

# CHAPTER 9

Connor would not permit himself to limp in front of the men. He gritted his teeth and concentrated on keeping his stride even as another shooting pain ripped down his leg. Once he passed through the doorway into the adjoining building, he paused to take a deep breath before climbing the stairs.

Damn the arrow that struck his leg, and damn the man who shot it.

He was sweating by the time he reached the top and pushed the door open.

"Ilysa?" What in the hell was she doing kneeling on his floor? Why was she in his bedchamber at all?

Her brown eyes were huge as she looked up at him from the floor. Surprise gave way to what looked suspiciously like guilt, though Connor could not imagine what sweet Ilysa had to feel guilty about.

"I was just...," she murmured as she started to rise.

Connor lunged to help her and winced as hot needles of pain jabbed into his thigh.

"I warned ye that ye should let me take care of that wound in your leg," Ilysa scolded him. "Now you're going to set aside your pride, Connor MacDonald, and let me."

It was not pride that had kept Connor from sending for her, but the memory of her hands on his bare skin. As it was, he thought of that every time he saw her. He'd even had dreams of sweet, innocent Ilysa's featherlike fingers running over every inch of his body until he was groaning with need and—*good God*—begging her to take him in her mouth. It made him damned uncomfortable to be around her.

Because of his lascivious imagination, he had let the wound fester too long. Now he let her take his arm and pull him toward the bed.

"What's that smell?" he asked, sniffing. It was vaguely familiar, but he could not place it.

"I thought you'd like it."

"Good God, is that what ye were doing in my chamber?" he said as he hobbled over to the bed. "Making it smell sweet?" First lilies, now this.

"I was waiting here for ye so I could tend to your leg." She held up her basket. "See, I brought my medicines."

Ilysa was not a practiced liar. It struck him as odd that she would make up a story, but perhaps she was embarrassed about smelling up his chamber with that odd scent.

"I'll heat some water and mix up the poultice while ye make yourself ready," she said, by which she meant that he should take off his trews.

The blood had soaked through them and onto his shirt, so he took that off as well. He stretched out on the bed and pulled the bedclothes across his hips to cover his manly parts.

Ilysa kept her gaze on the basin of steaming water she carried as she walked toward him with a cloth over her shoulder. After setting her things on the stool next to the bed, she turned toward him and sucked in her breath.

"I am so angry with ye! It's full of pus," she said, glaring at the wound in his leg. "That was careless and irresponsible of ye, Connor MacDonald."

He snorted on a laugh, making the bed shake. No one ever called him careless and irresponsible. Ah, but he wished he could be sometimes. At the very top of his list would be making love to a woman until neither of them could walk. That was the second and the third thing on his list as well. In fact, there was nothing else on his list but rolling in the bedclothes, making love to a lass, over and over. Ach, he was as hard as a battering ram thinking about it.

"Ouch!" He was jolted from his thoughts by the hot, wet compress Ilysa laid on the wound. Jesu, it hurt.

"Ye deserve it," she snapped.

Her sharpness was out of character, and Connor realized she was worried about him.

"Don't fret. This is nothing," he said and covered her hand where it rested on the bed beside him.

The air vibrated between them, and his mouth went dry at the feel of her soft skin. Connor jerked his hand away. He should not be touching Ilysa—not even her hand—when he was lying naked in his bed thinking of endless rounds of hot, sweaty sex.

"Sorry," he said. "I'm a bit jumpy."

"I know it's painful," she said, drawing her brows together.

She had no idea how painful, and he did not mean the wound. He clenched his teeth and tried not to groan aloud as she rested her free hand lightly on his thigh and then—*God, help me*—on his stomach, while she wiped the wound clean and covered it with her poultice.

*A little lower, please.* He wanted to beg her to touch him, to wrap her hand around his cock and give him the relief he needed. Better yet, crawl into bed with him and let him...

If Ilysa knew what he was thinking, the poor lass's heart would give out. He looked at the delicate features of her kind face and then at her hideous gown and ugly head covering and wondered how he could be so depraved as to actually be thinking of seducing her.

Connor covered his face with his arm and commanded himself not to imagine what Ilysa looked like under that dreadful gown.

\* \* \*

Connor MacDonald was not at all what Lachlan expected.

In the days since his arrival at the castle, Lachlan had watched the chieftain closely. Unlike Hugh, Connor met Lachlan's gaze directly and spoke to him with respect. Not once had he heard Connor make jokes at the expense of the lesser men or servants. In fact, his humor was self-deprecating, which Lachlan found disconcerting.

From everything his father had told him, he expected a man who carried the blood of the last chieftain to be a careless womanizer who was indifferent to the welfare of the lesser members of the clan. A chieftain had his choice of women, and Connor was undoubtedly handsome, judging by the way the women of the castle tripped over their feet watching him. The chieftain, however, did not appear to give any of them special attention.

Except for Ilysa.

Now, that was surprising. Ilysa was a funny, wee thing. Despite being highborn, she wore dull gowns that looked like hand-me-downs from an elderly relative twice her size. No, Ilysa did not look like a lass who would be sharing the chieftain's bed. If she were, Lachlan would have heard whispers about it by now.

And yet, there was something between them.

Lachlan watched Ilysa cross the hall, stopping on her way to say a kind word here and there and checking to see that all was well. Despite her youth and diminutive size, Ilysa controlled the household with a velvet glove. The servants would kill for her.

As she passed by, Lachlan put a hand on her arm. "You're always moving. Sit and rest a bit."

"I have a hundred things to do." She smiled as she made her excuse and started to move on, but then she halted and her smile faded.

There was always something in her eyes when she looked at him, as if she saw the blackness in his heart. Yet Lachlan never felt as if she condemned him for it.

After a moment, she perched herself on the bench beside him.

"Tell me why ye cover your prettiness," Lachlan said. "Is it the chieftain ye don't want to notice?"

Ilysa straightened her spine and blinked at him. "Mind your tongue, Lachlan. What a thing to say. And I'm not pretty."

Ilysa was a puzzle. When you really looked at her, you could see that her features were fair, but she tied that kerchief around her head so tightly it pulled her skin.

"What color is your hair under there?" he asked.

When he reached for her head covering, Ilysa slapped his hand away. "Stop it!"

He heard her gasp as a long blade flashed between them. Its point stopped an inch from Lachlan's throat. When he looked up the length of the blade, he saw Connor MacDonald at the other end of it.

"Is Lachlan bothering ye, Ilysa?" Connor's voice was as calm as the sea on a windless day, but his eyes were blue ice.

Lachlan did not move.

"No, he's not troubling me at all," Ilysa said.

"Ilysa is like a sister to me," Connor said. "If ye distress her, cause her even the tiniest bit of unease, you'll answer to me."

*Like his sister, my arse.*

"I don't want to leave any room for misunderstanding," Connor said, with the point of his blade pricking Lachlan's throat. "Have I been clear enough?"

"Aye, ye have," Lachlan said.

"I'm not certain I did right in defending ye to the chieftain," Ilysa said in a low voice after Connor walked away. "I want to trust ye, but you're hiding something."

"I spent the last two and a half years fighting the MacLeods," Lachlan said. "You've no right to question my loyalty."

"What have ye got against our chieftain?" she asked, undeterred.

"Nothing." Ach, she was as persistent as those wee dogs that bite at your heels.

"If ye endanger him, I'll kill ye myself." Ilysa got to her feet and looked down at him. "That's a promise, Lachlan."

Out of respect for her, he did not laugh. He had to admit that Connor MacDonald engendered loyalty from those who knew him well. That did not mean he deserved Lachlan's.

As his father so often told him, blood must be paid with blood.

# CHAPTER 10

Luck was against them.

Connor cursed under his breath. This time of year, he should have been able to count on a heavy mist to hide the boat. Instead a full moon shone bright on the sea. Their galley would be visible to any MacLeod who might be watching from the opposite side of the sea inlet that separated the Trotternish Peninsula from the traditional lands of the MacLeods.

"Hug the shore as close as ye can," Connor whispered in the ear of the man at the rudder. The other MacDonald warriors in the galley were silent, keenly aware of how well sound traveled over water on a clear, cold night.

"That's the place," the man next to Connor said in a hushed voice as he pointed toward a dark cottage with a gray plume of smoke rising from its chimney into the star-filled sky.

Each night, Connor took a handful of his warriors out under cover of darkness to visit homes of MacDonalds who had not yet left or been forced out in the face of the threat from the MacLeods. This was the farthest they had ventured from the castle, and it was also the closest to the MacLeods' home territory, where they were strongest.

Connor felt his men's tension as their small galley glided to shore. He flicked his gaze up and down the shoreline, ready to give the signal to reverse oars should enemy warriors spring from the bushes shouting their battle cry. All he heard in the still night was the rustle of reeds brushing against the side of the boat and the flap of wings when a startled waterbird took flight.

The steel blade of his claymore made the familiar *whoosh* as he pulled it from its scabbard. He dropped over the side into icy water up to his thighs. With barely a ripple, his men followed him into the water. Together, they hauled the galley onto the shore and hid it under low-hanging trees.

All Connor's senses were alert to danger as he and his five men climbed single-file up the small bluff to the cottage. He neither saw nor heard anything suspicious. And yet, he felt as if someone was watching them from the darkness.

Once again, he wished Ian, Duncan, or Alex were with him. They had saved each other's lives countless times, and he could trust them absolutely. Though he had hand-selected the warriors who accompanied him tonight, he did not know them well, except for Sorely. He would have added Lachlan to the group, but he could not find him.

When they reached the cottage, Connor held his sword at the ready while Sorely rapped on the door, his fist making a hollow sound on the weathered wood.

"'Tis me, Sorely." His soft voice sounded unnaturally loud after their long silence.

The door opened a crack, and a beak-nosed face peered out.

"Open up," Sorely said. "I've brought our new chieftain."

Connor wondered how long he would be known as the "new" chieftain.

The beak-nosed man stepped back inside, and the door creaked open wide. If Duncan or his cousins were here, one of them would have gone in first to make certain it was not a trap. Connor was not afraid of death for himself, but his death would very likely lead to Hugh being made chieftain—and that would destroy the clan.

To succeed in his mission to assure the clan's future, however, he needed more than the fealty of his clansmen. He needed warriors who were fierce in their loyalty and willing to die at his side. Highlanders respected fearlessness, whether it was foolish or no.

Connor stepped over the cottage's threshold, praying it was not an ambush.

Inside, a dozen men, mostly farmers, crowded the cottage. Connor swept his gaze over the men, the lone woman standing by the hearth, and the children peeking out from the loft overhead.

He signaled for three of the warriors who accompanied him to stand guard outside. With three, they could keep an eye on each other, as well as watch for MacLeods.

"I am Connor, great-grandson of the Lord of the Isles, grandson of Hugh, the first MacDonald of Sleat, and son of Donald Gallach, our last chieftain." Though it would be safer for all of them if this meeting was over quickly, the men would expect a certain amount of formality from their chieftain. "*Beannachd air an taigh.*" A blessing on this house.

"*Mìle fàilte oirbh,*" a thousand welcomes, his beak-nosed host greeted him. "I am Malcom."

As each man introduced himself, Connor fixed the name and face in his mind. Then he said, "Tell me how you and your families on this side of Trotternish fare."

"Our children are hungry," one man spoke up, "and our women fear we cannot protect them."

Connor listened patiently while several of the men took turns speaking.

"We hold Trotternish Castle again, but taking back all of the peninsula will be a more difficult task," he told them. "Every man must be a warrior and join in the fight if we are to remove the MacLeods and make your families safe from attack."

There was a general rumble of agreement from the men.

"When the time comes to fight, I will send the *crann tara,*" Connor said. The *crann tara* was a wooden cross that had been set on fire and then dipped in blood to extinguish the flame. It was the traditional method for raising the clan. "Every man who sees it will be expected to pass the word."

There was another rumble of agreement, then one man asked, "Where shall the clan gather?"

"It must be near here." That was the reason Connor had come to this particular place tonight. "The MacLeod warriors are spread thin among our own people here on Trotternish. Their strength lies on the other side of the Snizort River, so we must stop them there."

The room was quiet as the men took this in.

"Where is a good place for us to rally?" Connor asked. "It should be a place all our people know and can find in the night, without alerting the MacLeods."

As Connor shifted his gaze from man to man, each shook his head.

"What about a place men fear to go?" The voice belonged to the lone woman by the hearth. She was an attractive, plump woman in her midthirties, whom Connor assumed was Malcom's wife and the mother of the children in the loft.

"Hush," Malcom said, but Connor signaled for her to go on.

He had an inkling of what the woman meant and thought it a clever idea, though it did not appear to sit well with the men.

"There are three such places nearby," she said. "First is the graveyard on the island in the Snizort River, where the old church dedicated to Saint Columba is."

Connor felt the room grow tense. No man wanted to mingle with the dead after dark.

"We'd risk bringing ill luck upon us by disrespecting the dead chieftains and warriors who rest there," Connor said. "Where else?"

"The faery glen," the woman said. "'Tis hidden away, and the MacLeods won't go near it, day or night."

"That's because they're no fools," one of the men said.

"Riling the faeries is even more dangerous than disturbing dead chieftains," another said.

"And the third place?" Connor asked, though he was beginning to think he should have let her husband hush her.

"The standing stone," she said. "It doesn't hold much

magic except at the solstice, and it can be good magic. All the same, most folk avoid it at night."

"It's on a hill that overlooks the sea inlet, not far from the river," Sorely said. "'Tis a good choice."

"Then it's settled. When I raise the clan with the *crann tara*, we'll meet at the standing stone." Connor let his gaze move from man to man until each of them nodded. Then he signaled for the men to keep their voices down and raised his fist. "We will take the MacLeods by land and by sea!"

All the men in the room raised their fists and repeated the MacDonald motto. "By land and by sea!"

The moment Connor stepped out of the cottage door, he knew something was wrong. The men he had left standing guard appeared unaware of the threat. Connor stood still, listening and staring out into the night. He sensed no movement to his left or to his right.

As he peered out at the dark water, two war galleys made a silent appearance around the jut of land to the south. In the moonlight, he could see the row of shields along the length of the boats, each of which would carry thirty to fifty warriors.

Connor had six men, counting himself.

There were far too many enemy warriors to fight, and Connor could not afford to lose any of his. As he watched, the war galleys turned into the cove, which made it impossible for Connor and his men to reach their own galley and escape by sea.

By now his men had gathered around him.

"Our best chance is to split up and run like hell," Connor said in a hushed voice. "We'll meet back at the castle. Now go!"

As the men ran off, Connor went back inside to warn the others.

"Ye must be silent! MacLeod warriors are landing," he told them. "Everyone, run!"

Connor held the door, urging them to hurry, as he watched the MacLeod galleys glide into shore. The men left quickly, but it seemed to take a lifetime for the woman and her husband to gather their children. Tension thrummed through Connor as he watched the line of children climbing down the ladder from the loft. *Jesu*, how many did the couple have?

"Get your wife and children out quickly," he called to Malcom. "Hurry! Hurry!"

"Leave him to take care of his own children," Sorely said, pulling at Connor's arm. "Ye must escape. I'll stay at your side."

It seemed unlikely that two galleys full of MacLeod warriors happened upon them. Until Connor knew which man had betrayed him, he was not traveling alone with any of them, not even Sorely.

"Go," Connor said. "I'll find my own way back."

"But—"

"I said go," Connor commanded.

By the time Malcom and his wife had herded the last of the children out the door, Connor heard the thuds of feet running up the hill from the beach.

As he swung the door closed behind them, Connor caught sight of a curly-headed bairn coming down the ladder from the loft. He reached her in three long strides, plucked her off the ladder with one arm, and ran out.

As he rounded the corner of the cottage, he saw the

mother running toward him holding a child with each hand. She must have realized she had missed one.

"I have her," Connor told her. "We must get your family hidden *now*!"

"This way," she said.

They were in plain view, and the MacLeod warriors would reach the top of the hill at any moment. Connor scooped up the child who was lagging behind and holding his mother back, and together they ran for the copse of trees behind the cottage.

Shouts and the sounds of the enemy warriors smashing the family's pots and meager furniture reached Connor's ears as they entered the trees and continued running. On the other side of the small wood, they caught up with Malcom and the other children, who were waiting for them on a well-trod path.

"I'm grateful to ye for helping with my family," the woman said, her voice breathless. "But you're in danger here, Chieftain. Ye must go while ye can."

"I'll wait until you and your bairns are safely hidden," he said. "We're too close to the cottage. They'll find ye here."

"We can hide down the hill," she said.

They had evidently hidden there before because the older children were already disappearing down the side of the hill. As Connor left the path to follow them, he glanced over his shoulder. He saw no one yet, but they would be coming.

The family hid in an eight-foot-wide depression in the side of the hill created when a large tree had been uprooted.

"Ye must keep the children quiet," Connor whispered

to Malcom and his wife while he passed the two bairns he had carried down to them.

Connor lay flat in the grass next to their hiding place where he would be able to see anyone on the path above them. Sounds were still coming from the cottage, but he suspected the MacLeods would split into groups to search. At least, that is what he would order if he were in charge.

One of the children cried out and was quickly silenced.

"This way!" a voice called out. "I heard something!"

\* \* \*

"Put that knife down before ye slice your thumb off," Cook said and took it from her. "Ye shouldn't be doing kitchen work at all, but you're a danger to yourself today."

"I'm sorry to get in your way," Ilysa said. "I'm just worried."

After pacing her room until she could stand it no more, she had come down to the kitchen hoping to distract herself.

"The chieftain has gone out with some of the men several nights now," Cook said as he chopped onions with blinding speed, "and nothing's gone wrong."

Ilysa had told herself that over and over. Yet she could not shake this feeling of impending disaster.

"The men will return soon," Cook said. "You'll see."

"Of course they will," Ilysa said and kissed his cheek. "I'll leave ye to your work."

As she was going up the circular stairs to her chamber, Ilysa suddenly felt cold pass through her as if someone were walking on her grave. She held her hand against the stone wall to steady herself while her sight grew blurry.

Though she was aware of where she was, the stairwell disappeared, and she saw Connor bathed in moonlight. He was reaching his arm out to her, and his tunic was dripping with blood.

As soon as the vision passed, Ilysa raced up the stairs, knowing what she must do. She hurriedly collected the things she would need and put on her cloak.

# CHAPTER 11

On the ridge above them, Connor saw the outline of five warriors, clearly visible in the moonlight. Barely breathing, he glanced at the row of children flattened against the side of the hill and prayed they would keep silent.

Through the tall grass, Connor watched the five warriors, willing them to leave. They were close enough that he could make out their voices in the quiet night.

"The MacDonald chieftain was supposed to be here," one of them said. "Our reward will be great if we're the ones who find him."

The MacLeods knew he would be here. As Connor had suspected, one of his own had given him up. But which one?

Connor held his breath as the men turned north and followed the path in the direction of Trotternish Castle. He waited several long minutes after they disappeared before rising to his hands and knees for a better look.

"Are they gone?" Malcom asked.

"Hush!" Connor ordered when he heard the low rumble of the warriors' voices above him. "They're returning."

A short time later, the MacLeod warriors were once again standing above them.

"We should look down this hill," one of them said.

Connor tensed. Malcom was not a trained warrior, which meant Connor would have to take all five Mac-Leods himself.

"Ach, no, let's go back to the boat," another of the men said. "I have a jug of whiskey and a warm lass waiting for me at home."

Connor prayed the others would listen to him.

"We'll leave after we look down here," the first man said.

Connor heard the familiar swish of their claymores swinging through the tall grass as the five men walked down the hill. After signaling to the family to stay low, he ran across the side of the hill in a low crouch. He had to move fast to circle behind the men before they stumbled upon the family's hiding spot.

When he reached the path, he scooped up a handful of stones and climbed a large tree. As soon as he was out of sight in the branches, he hurled the stones, sending them bouncing up the path. Then he climbed out onto a thick limb that hung over the path and waited. If he did not hear the men coming toward him soon, he would have to shout to draw their attention. He smiled when he heard running feet.

He let the first three warriors pass and dropped on the last two, driving his dirk into one and then the other in quick succession. Before the others turned around to see what happened, Connor had his claymore in his hands. Three at once could be difficult. He was pleased when one charged him. With a swift stroke, he blocked the attacker's sword, then swung in a circle and drove his blade deep into the man's side.

The remaining two used their advantage and acted in concert, one coming at him from his left and the other from his right. Connor picked up the sword of one of the fallen men and fought them back using both swords. More MacLeod warriors could come looking for these at any moment. Damn, he needed to end this quickly.

He dove to the side as one of the men swung at him, and the blade glanced off his arm instead of piercing his chest. As he came up, Connor pulled the dirk from his boot. His opponent's arm was still extended with the force of his swing when Connor sank his dirk between the man's exposed ribs.

The last warrior charged at him with a roar before Connor could recover and block the attack with his claymore. He felt the wind of the man's sword on his back as he dropped to the ground. Before he could get up, his opponent raised his blade over his head and brought it down with all his force. Connor managed to roll to the side in time to avoid being split in two, but the blade caught his thigh.

Connor was on his feet again, and he had only one opponent left. When he could, Connor showed mercy. But this was not one of those times. He swung his great two-handed sword in deadly, rhythmic arcs, forcing his opponent back and back again.

Finally, the MacLeod warrior swung with all his might into Connor's injured leg. Connor had anticipated the move and jumped over the blade. When his opponent's sword met with no resistance, the force of his swing threw him off balance long enough for Connor to deal him a deathblow and end it.

As he leaned on his sword to get his breath back, Connor noticed that the family had crept out of their hiding place and were watching from the tall grass. He signaled for them to stay where they were and started dragging the dead bodies off the path. If the other MacLeod warriors came this way and found their comrades, they would be far more vigilant in their search.

"Just keep your children quiet and off the path," Connor told Malcom when he offered to help.

By the time he had dragged the five dead MacLeods into the bushes, his head was spinning.

"I must return to the castle, but ye should be safe if ye stay hidden," he told the family. "Don't go back to the cottage until it's daylight and ye can be sure that they've sailed away."

"Let me take care of your wounds before ye go," the woman said.

Connor only now realized that his sleeve was soaked with blood. He remembered being struck in the leg as well. That would explain why he was light-headed.

"Help me bind them, and I'll be on my way," he said.

Using Connor's dirk, she cut two strips from the bottom of her skirts. She tied the first around his arm while he tied the second strip around the gash on his thigh.

"'Tis a long way to the castle, and the path is overgrown and difficult to follow in the dark," Malcom said. "I'd better take ye."

"I'll manage," Connor said. "Stay with your wife and children."

"Mind ye don't enter the faery glen," Malcom said. "The path circles around it. Don't be tempted to cut through it to make your journey shorter."

Faeries were the least of his worries.

"If ye do find yourself in the glen, ye must have a token to leave for the faeries," the wife said. She reached into her pocket and brought out a stone that glittered in the moonlight. "Sometimes a gift will appease them, though ye can never tell with faeries."

Connor did not want to insult her, so he thanked her and put the stone in the leather bag tied to his belt. He had miles to travel, and he was anxious to be on his way.

"I see now why they say ye are the hope of our clan," the woman said. "May God watch over ye. We need hope."

# CHAPTER 12

Connor walked for what seemed like hours. He was grateful for the quiet of the night, even if the sense of peacefulness was false. He needed the time to think, and for once he was not accompanied by his guard. As chieftain, he was always surrounded, and yet always alone.

Which of his men had betrayed him? He considered each man who had come with him and dismissed each in turn. And yet, the traitor had to be someone who knew their destination.

After a couple of hours, Connor grew too light-headed to think anymore. He kept walking. Twice he lost the path and had to retrace his steps. Ahead of him, he saw the outline of odd, conical-shaped hills.

He stumbled ahead. As he drew closer, the night fog that lay between the strange hills transformed the moonlight into a soft glow. Above the mist, the tops of the hills had rows of ridges along their sides like ripples on the surface of water.

His mind was working slowly, but he had the uneasy feeling that he was forgetting something important. Something the woman with all the children had told him. The bindings on his arm and leg had loosened as he walked, and he was aware, in a distant way as if it were happening to someone else, that he was losing too much blood.

He sat down to tighten the bindings and dropped his head between his knees while he gathered his strength to do it. Then, forcing himself to stay alert, he retied the strip on his arm, using his teeth and one hand. Next, he unfastened the blood-soaked strip on his thigh and pulled that binding into a tight knot. With that done, he decided he could let himself rest for a moment before he got to his feet again.

Connor awoke shivering and realized he must have dozed off. With an effort, he lifted his head. The moon had not traveled far across the sky, so he could not have been asleep for long. He told himself he must get up and return to the castle before daylight. If the MacLeods—perhaps assisted by one of his own men—were searching for him, it would be safer to travel under cover of darkness.

His mind was thick and slow, but eventually it came to him that he was sitting in the midst of the faery glen. Though he had never been here before, the conical hills were just as they had been described to him. Strangely, the realization did not alarm him in the least.

Connor turned his head and saw the flickering light of a small fire through the mist. Friend or foe? A distinctly feminine form crossed in front of the fire. Whether she was a faery or a human, he did not know.

Was he imagining her? Connor blinked several times,

but she was still there. Her slender, alluring shape was draped in a translucent, gossamer cloth, just like an angel. Or a faery.

As he watched, she began to dance around the fire, swaying with the grace of a bird dipping and soaring through the sky. Each time she passed on his side of the fire, he could see her lithe, supple shape through the thin cloth of her robe. She appeared to wear nothing at all underneath it.

There was something so beguiling about the faery lass's movements that Connor did not consider leaving. Since childhood he had heard tales of enchantments wrought by faeries, but if this was one, he did not care.

She sang in a high, sweet voice. Though Connor was too far away to make out the words, the sound filled his heart with longing. Everything about her entranced him: the tips of her small breasts beneath the thin fabric, the graceful swing of her robe, and the long, fair hair that tumbled down her back like a shimmering waterfall.

Desire swept through him. Whether she was a faery or an apparition, he wished with all his heart he could have one magical night with her. He longed to sweep his hand along the graceful lines of her body, to cup her breasts, to feel her hair slide over his skin. One enchanted night with this faery lass that he could hold on to and remember after she returned to her world and left him in his, where he was the hope of his clan and must always, always put duty first.

Connor sucked in his breath as sparks flew from her fingers. What would it be like to touch this ethereal, magical lass? To run kisses along her swanlike neck? To bury his face in her hair...to feel her breasts pressed against his bare chest…to feel the sparks from her fingertips on his skin…

His eyelids grew heavy as he watched the slow sway of her body and listened to the sweet melody of her voice. He was not sure if he was awake or dreaming as he lay her down on his plaid and she wrapped her slender legs around him while he kissed her deeply. If he was dreaming, he did not want to wake.

* * *

The feather-light fabric slid sensuously over Ilysa's skin as she dipped and whirled in slow, arcing movements around the fire. At first, she felt self-conscious dancing with her hair loose and nothing on beneath the thin gown, but no one else would venture into the faery glen and see her. Ilysa had braved coming to this special place to enhance the potency of her spell. After seeing the black danger around Connor in her vision, she understood that no simple charm could guard against it. Teàrlag, who knew such things, said that the faery glen retained the power of the old magic.

Ilysa had never before attempted the fire dance, which called upon the power of the faeries, but Teàrlag had told her what to do. She concentrated on her movements, which, like her dress, were meant to flatter the faeries by emulating them.

The old seer claimed to have received the gown, which was made from cloth that had lain outside on three successive full moons, as a gift from the faeries when she was a young lass. Ilysa found it easier to imagine that the gown had been made by faeries than to imagine Teàrlag had ever been young.

As she swayed and twirled, Ilysa forgot herself and became lost in the freedom of the dance. Instead of the quiet, constrained lass no one noticed, she was a beautiful and beguiling faery princess. The power of the spell coursed through her as she sang the words.

> Blades may cut you,
>     Yet none shall kill you.
> False friends may deceive you,
>     Yet none shall kill you.
> Allies may desert you,
>     Yet none shall kill you.
> Enemies may trap you,
>     Yet none shall kill you.

> *Seun Dhè umad!*
> *Làmh Dhè airson do dhìona!*
> Spell of God about you!
> The hand of God protect you!

As she dipped and whirled, she sprinkled the special herb mixture into the fire with both hands, causing it to snap and shoot sparks into the darkness. This, too, was to please the faeries, who were known to like anything that sparkled or shone.

When she finished the dance, Ilysa collapsed onto the ground and stared into the fire. Doing the fire dance once would afford Connor a strong measure of protection. But to gain the full power of the spell, she must do it a second time, also on a full moon.

She had done everything just as Teàrlag had instructed. Still, she decided to add one more measure of protection and got to her feet. She had seen her mother do this many times in the years her brother, Connor, Ian, and Alex were in France—and the four of them had come home safely. It was a simple spell, just a charm really. The only important part was to make the circle in the right direction.

Ilysa moved around the fire left to right, *deiseal*, the direction that brought good fortune, dragging a stick along the ground.

"Protect him, heal him, bring him home."

She kept the image of Connor in her mind while she chanted the words over and over and made the circle, once, twice, thrice.

Weary and chilled to the bone, she put out the fire and wrapped her heavy cloak about her. She would have to hurry to make it back to the castle before the household woke.

With an expertise born of years of practice, she coiled her hair and tied a kerchief over it. Though it was the same one she always wore, the cloth felt rough beneath her fingers. The feather-light robe against her skin was the only reminder that, for a little while, she had been a beautiful faery princess.

* * *

Connor awoke to the gray light of predawn feeling stiff and wet from the rain that had fallen in the night while he slept. He glanced about him at the odd, conical hills, trying to recall where he was and how he got here.

Ahh, the faery glen. He had stumbled upon it last night on his way back to the castle after the attack...Connor sat bolt-upright as he remembered the faery lass.

She was gone. As he stared at the empty place between the hills where he had seen her dance, a sense of loss weighed down on his chest. Had he truly seen her? He shook his head. His dreams of making love to her had been so vivid that he could almost taste her on his lips.

For long minutes, he sat unmoving, hoping she would reappear. But no, she had disappeared with the night mist, like a dream or a faery in an old tale.

Connor was not a man given to fancy, but she had seemed so real that he was having a hard time convincing himself he had imagined her. Though it made no sense, he had felt drawn to her with all his being. He had felt lust for many women, of course. But this was a deeper kind of desire, the kind he feared was unquenchable. He felt as if he had glimpsed the only lass who could complete him. Was this faery magic she had worked on him?

Connor cursed himself. He had not been prone to such foolishness since he was a wee lad—not since the day his mother left. Catriona had captured all their hearts and made every day magical, but the magic died with her.

If his mother taught him anything, it was to be cautious when it came to women—especially the ones who could weave magic around men's hearts. Connor wanted a wife who, unlike his mother, was dependable and trustworthy—the kind of woman who did not leave.

Still, he was a man. Lust and yearning filled him as the image of the faery lass danced through his memory again. Though he had not been able to make out the features of her face in the night, he knew they would be as delicate and lovely as her graceful form.

Wanting was a useless waste of time. Though he was chieftain—or rather, because he was chieftain—Connor was not a man who could have what he wanted. Every choice he made, everything he did, must be in pursuit of restoring his clan and protecting his people.

And right now, that meant walking the remaining miles back to the castle on a wounded leg. When he got up, he was surprised to find he felt better for his night in the cold and rain. His head was clear again.

The coming dawn tinted the clouds pink as he walked through the wet grass between the odd hills. He remembered the glittering stone in his pouch and limped over to where he had seen—or imagined he had seen—the lass dancing.

When he saw the remains of a fire, he crouched down to touch the circle of rocks around it. The rain made it impossible to tell if the fire was from last night, but it was strange that someone had built a fire in the faery glen at all. As the sun broke over the hill, the slanting rays caused the wet grass to sparkle. Connor smiled, thinking of sparks flying from the faery lass's fingertips.

Was any of it real?

He took the glittering stone from his pouch and set it on a log near the fire, his thanks for the graceful beauty, whether real or imagined.

# CHAPTER 13

"Are ye well?" Lachlan asked Ilysa when he met her on the steps of the keep. He had not seen her at breakfast, and she was pale and drawn.

She ignored his question and asked, "Has the chieftain returned?"

"The men who went with him came back in ones and twos during the night," Lachlan said.

"But not Connor?" she asked, her face going still paler.

"Not yet."

"Do ye know what happened?" she asked.

"I'm told they were surprised by two galleys full of MacLeod warriors," Lachlan said since there was no point in attempting to keep the truth from her. "When they couldn't reach their boat to escape, they split up to make it harder for the MacLeods to track them."

Perhaps he should be glad if they had killed Connor and saved him the trouble of settling his blood feud, but

Lachlan could not be happy about any attack on his clan. When he turned his attention back to Ilysa, the lass was weaving on her feet.

"Sit down before ye faint on me," Lachlan said and sat with her on the steps.

"I don't faint," she said, and he didn't bother arguing with her.

Sorely came out of the keep then. When he saw them, he put his hands on his hips and looked them up and down. Lachlan had made an enemy when he knocked Sorely on his arse and took his sword in front of all the men. He suspected Sorely's sour attitude toward him was the reason Connor had not trusted him enough to take him on his night forays.

"You'd better have a damned good explanation for why we couldn't find ye last night," Sorely said in a tone that made Lachlan want to plant his fist in his face.

"Go to hell," Lachlan said. "You're not my keeper."

"We'll see about that," Sorely said.

Sorely was expecting to be named captain of Connor's guard, but it hadn't happened yet. Still, Lachlan should try harder to tolerate the man. He did not need to give anyone a reason to watch his movements too closely.

"Where were ye last night?" Ilysa asked after Sorely had huffed off.

Lachlan ignored her, hoping she would let it go, though he already knew her well enough to recognize that as a useless hope.

"Tell me ye had nothing to do with what happened," she said.

"I would never bring the MacLeods down on us," he said. "Never."

"I know you're a good man," Ilysa said, touching his arm, "and that you're contemplating doing something that troubles ye gravely."

Lachlan was not accustomed to having anyone read him so well. When he glanced sideways and met her honest brown eyes, he reminded himself that Ilysa was a bigger threat to him than Sorely. Ilysa had the chieftain's trust, and somehow she could see into the blackness of Lachlan's soul.

"Listen to your conscience," she said, "and don't do this."

Lasses liked to take him to bed, but having one fret over his conscience was new to him.

"Whatever it is, you must give it up and help Connor," she said. "He is the hope of our clan, the only man who stands between us and having Hugh as our chieftain."

"I'm here, aren't I?" he said. "Though I can't see where it makes much difference which of them is chieftain."

It was a mistake to admit that—Ilysa gripped his arm with surprising strength for such a tiny thing. By the saints, the lass was persistent.

"It makes *all* the difference," she said. "I was at Dunscaith when Hugh took it and proclaimed himself chieftain. Hugh did nothing while the MacKinnons attacked Knock Castle and the MacLeods took Trotternish from us."

"It wasn't Hugh's fault our former chieftain took our warriors off to fight the English and left us vulnerable to our enemies."

"I was there," she said in an insistent tone, enunciating each word. "Knock Castle is only five miles from

Dunscaith. Yet, when our men came from there begging for help, Hugh sat with two lasses on his lap laughing and drinking. We could see the flames and still he did nothing."

*The bastard.* Lachlan was shaken by her words. And yet, from what he had seen of Hugh, they rang true. "I doubt our former chieftain would have done any better," he said.

"Connor's father had his faults, but he would never have sat behind his castle walls feasting while our enemies took our lands," Ilysa said. "And neither would Connor."

Lachlan had been raised on his father's hatred of their former chieftain. Revenge was the reason for the constant training from the time he could walk. Lachlan tried to dismiss Ilysa's words, but he had never once heard a story of the former chieftain's cowardice, and no lands had been taken from them while he lived. The same could not be said of Hugh.

As for Connor, he risked his life every night he left the castle.

"Hugh brought his foul, clanless pirates into Dunscaith Castle," Ilysa said, "and no woman or child was safe."

"Did they hurt ye?" The thought of someone harming her made Lachlan feel ill. For some damned reason, he'd grown fond of Ilysa. Probably because her stubbornness reminded him of his sister.

"I made certain they heard I was learning the Old Ways," she said with a small smile. "They feared I would curse them."

"If Hugh and his men were so foul, why were you there at all?"

"To spy on Hugh, of course," she said. "I knew that the four of them—my brother, Connor, and Connor's cousins—would return as soon as they learned the clan was in danger, and they would need someone inside the castle."

Ilysa would make a better spy than he did, for certain. With her innocent face and quiet demeanor, no one would suspect her.

"Connor needs ye," Ilysa said. "For the sake of the clan, ye *must* help him."

Lachlan did not remind her that Connor could already be dead. Nor did he tell her that he wished he could change his course. The demands of honor were inflexible and unforgiving, and so must he be.

"There's a man crossing the field to the castle," one of the guards shouted from the wall.

Ilysa bolted from the steps, and Lachlan ran with her to the gate.

An unexpected rush of relief coursed through Lachlan when the guards flung the gate open and he saw the tall, black-haired figure in the midst of the broad, empty field.

"Praise God!" Ilysa said, pressing her hand to her chest.

Connor was using a thick stick as a crutch, and his sleeve was bloody, but he shouted a greeting and waved. The chieftain had survived another brush with death.

He was a hard man to kill, in more ways than one.

\* \* \*

"Can I speak with ye?" Sorely asked from the doorway of Connor's chamber.

Sorely shifted his weight from foot to foot and flicked

his gaze around the room. Connor was surprised to see him here at all. It had taken him a while to figure out why Sorely was always slow to answer a summons to come to Connor's chamber, never took guard duty at his door, and generally waited to speak with him until he was in the hall or the courtyard.

The tough old warrior was shaking in his boots for fear he would see the nursemaid's ghost.

"There is no ghost," Connor said. "I've been here a fortnight, and I haven't seen her once."

"There! She's there!" Sorely said, pointing toward the tower door. "Don't ye see her?"

Connor sighed. God help him, this was one of his best warriors. Once a story like the one about the nursemaid got started, people were likely to imagine they saw her ghost for centuries. Connor only hoped Alastair MacLeod had a few ghosts of his own to deal with.

"I'm telling ye, there is no ghost, but let's go down to the hall," Connor said, deciding there was no sense in torturing the man.

He used the stick for a crutch going down the stairs, though he was healing so quickly he hardly needed it.

"We must be cautious that no one overhears," Sorely said in his usual gruff voice as they entered the hall. Apparently, he did not fear that the ghost had chased them down the stairs.

"What is it?" Connor asked once they stood in a quiet corner.

"Someone alerted the MacLeods that we were going to that cottage," Sorely said.

Connor thought it far more likely that whoever betrayed them had told Hugh, expecting him to do the dirty task of eliminating Connor himself, rather than use the MacLeods. It was one thing for a MacDonald man to favor Hugh over Connor as chieftain and quite another to betray the clan to the MacLeods.

"Who do ye think told?" Connor asked.

"I can't say for certain," Sorely said, "but there's something ye ought to know about Lachlan of Lealt—something no one's had the ballocks to tell ye."

"I told no one where we were going but the men we took with us."

"One of them could have told Lachlan," Sorely said with a shrug. "Or he could have overheard them talking."

"I suppose." Connor hoped to hell it was not his best warrior in the castle who betrayed them.

"Lachlan wouldn't need to know our destination," Sorely added. "If he alerted the MacLeods in which direction we went, they could easily have watched for our boat."

Anyone could have done that. "What is it I should know about Lachlan that makes ye suspect him?"

"Lachlan's mother was one of your father's women," Sorely said. "She was married to Lachlan's father at the time, but ye know how the chieftain was about the lasses. When he wanted one, he had to have her."

Connor did know about his father and women. "I can't mistrust all the relatives of every lass my father bedded," Connor said. "That would be half the clan."

"There's more," Sorely said, glancing back at the doorway to the adjoining building. "It was her son that the nursemaid dropped out the tower window."

Connor had assumed the ghost story was as old as the

castle. It took him a moment to realize what this meant.

"That was my father's child who died?" Christ, he never knew he had a brother besides Ragnall. And that babe was Lachlan's brother as well.

"The chieftain put Lachlan's mother aside after the accident," Sorely said. "She killed herself by jumping off those two-hundred-foot bluffs between Lealt and Staffin Bay."

Was there no end to the grief his father had caused with his careless philandering?

"Some say she did it out of grief over losing the babe. Others say it was because your father lost interest in her." Sorely paused. "But Lachlan's father believed the chieftain forced his wife into his bed and that she killed herself for shame."

"I'm glad ye told me," Connor said, rubbing his forehead against the headache that had started pounding, "though it doesn't mean Lachlan is the one who betrayed me."

In the Highlands, grudges were passed from father to son for generations. Yet he and Lachlan shared the loss of a brother whom neither had a chance to know. Perhaps it was foolish, but Connor felt that loss created some kind of bond between them. While he would watch Lachlan closely, he prayed that Lachlan would not turn out to be his enemy.

* * *

That night, for the first time since he left Dunscaith, Connor dreamed of his mother. In his dream, he was on the beach as a child, hugging his knees against the cold and his fear.

."My curse on you!" his mother cried out as her hair blew around her like writhing snakes. "May your seed dry up, Donald Gallach…May your sons already born by other women die young…"

Connor felt as if he were looking down upon his child self while his nursemaid, Anna, tried to comfort his mother.

He sat up straight in bed, suddenly awake. He remembered what his mother had said to Anna that night. *He's been keeping a woman up at Trotternish Castle—and she's borne him a son!*

The woman she spoke of must have been Lachlan's mother and the son the babe who died. Pain seared through Connor as words he had forgotten for years and years rang in his ears.

*May your sons already born by other women die young.*

He had heard her chant as she circled the fire without comprehending it. His mother had cursed Ragnall, his older brother who had loved and protected him, and that innocent babe. Connor was the only son of his father's to survive. For such an evil, perhaps he did deserve to be punished.

Eventually, Connor recalled that he did still have one brother living, though he had never met him. Torquil MacLeod of Lewis was the son his mother had abandoned, along with her first husband, to marry Connor's father.

Connor lay awake until dawn, contemplating the hatreds that plagued his family. Between the rebellions and the rivalries among the clans, violent death was commonplace in the Highlands. But among Connor's closest kin, death usually came by the hand of one of their own.

Though this should serve as a warning, Connor decided he wanted to extend the hand of friendship to his last remaining brother.

# CHAPTER 14

Connor tensed when one of the guards burst into the hall and made a straight line for him. It was usually bad news that couldn't wait.

"There's a man at the gate claiming to be a relative of yours—and he looks as if he could be," the guard said. "He came in a fine galley with a dozen warriors."

This was good news after all. A week ago, Connor had sent Sorely with a message to Torquil MacLeod of Lewis. He had not expected his half brother to accept his invitation and offer of friendship, but he was very pleased that he had.

"Bring him in at once." Connor stood, too anxious to remain in his seat.

When the doors swung open and the guest led his warriors in, Connor covered his disappointment. This was not the relative he was hoping to see. Though Connor could not recall meeting this middle-aged man dressed in fine clothes, his guest looked unnervingly familiar.

"I am Connor, son of Donald Gallach, and chieftain of the MacDonalds of Sleat," Connor said when his guest stood before him in the center of the hall. "Welcome to Trotternish Castle."

"I hope I am welcome," the man said. "I haven't seen ye since ye were a young lad. I am your father's brother, Archibald Lerrich."

Connor had guessed as much. He had the same square face, fading golden hair, and barrel-chested frame as Connor's father and his hated uncle Hugh. Of the six sons his grandfather had by six different highborn women, Archibald and Hugh were the only survivors. Archibald was one of the middle brothers, in his midforties, with a reputation for staying out of trouble's way. The last Connor heard, Archibald had left Skye to live with his wife's clan in Lachalsh.

"I've come to swear my allegiance," Archibald said and sank to one knee. When Connor nodded, his uncle held his claymore out in both hands and gave his oath.

"Ye took your time," Connor said, not bothering to hide the coldness from his voice as his uncle rose to his feet again.

"I didn't join Hugh against ye," Archibald said, spreading his arms, "but neither did I wish to get between the two of ye."

Connor let that pass for the moment. He wanted to find out the true reason for Archibald's visit.

"Let us go where we can speak in private, *Uncle*," Connor said. Without waiting for Archibald's reply, he led the way into the adjacent building.

"You've grown into a fine man," Archibald said, when

they had settled at the table in Connor's chamber. "I can see your mother in ye."

Connor saw far too much of his father and his other uncles in Archibald.

"I've been chieftain for some time," Connor said. "Why have ye come now?"

"Ye may look like your mother, but you're direct like your father."

Archibald attempted a smile, but Connor did not respond in kind. He waited for his uncle to stop fidgeting and say what he had come to say.

"I am here in the hope," Archibald finally said, "of bringing peace between you and Hugh."

"Hmmph, 'tis late for that," Connor said. "I hold him responsible for the deaths of my father, my brother, and a great many other clansmen."

"Well," Archibald said, tilting his head, "Hugh blames you for the deaths of two of our brothers."

"There's a difference between justice and murder." Connor leaned across the table and grabbed Archibald by the front of his tunic. "Those two were marauding pirates guilty of taking food from the mouths of children and then raping their mothers, so do not speak to me as if their deaths are the same."

Connor released him and sat back, annoyed with himself for losing control.

"I understand your feelings about it," Archibald said after clearing his throat, "but there's been enough bloodshed among our family."

"I doubt Hugh would agree, judging by how many times he's tried to have me murdered," Connor said. "He won't be satisfied until one of us is dead."

"Hugh is mean as a cornered rat, but he's no fool—he can see that he's losing this fight with ye," Archibald said. "He sent a message through a lass named Rhona, asking me to serve as an intermediary."

So Duncan's former lover was still with Hugh. The mention of her name soured Connor's mood further.

"Now that Hugh has earned the Crown's favor by capturing a couple of other pirate leaders, he'd like to give up the game himself," Archibald said.

"As they say, there's no honor among thieves."

"Hugh wants—"

Archibald stopped speaking when the door opened and Ilysa came in with a tray. Connor was grateful she had brought it herself since her loyalty was beyond question. By the saints, he was tired of looking over his shoulder, wondering which member of his household was involved in treachery with Hugh.

As Ilysa poured the whiskey into two cups, Connor motioned to Archibald to continue talking.

"Hugh wants to settle his differences with ye." Archibald leaned forward. "I suspect ye could buy him off with a wee bit of land."

Connor kept his expression blank while rage rolled through him. Give that murdering bastard some of the clan's land?

"Surely it's worth at least meeting with Hugh and hearing what he has to say?" Archibald said.

The only way Connor wanted to meet Hugh Dubh again was with the point of his sword sunk in Hugh's belly. He forced himself to tamp down his temper and think it through coldly. This violent contest with Hugh was a distraction from the most important challenge, the battle with the MacLeods for Trotternish. The clan did not have the strength to fight both at the same time.

He did not believe for a moment that Hugh was ready to give up his quest for the chieftainship. Eventually, Connor would have to settle the problem of Hugh once and for all. Yet, if he could delay that final reckoning with his uncle until after the fight with the MacLeods, he would stand a far better chance of succeeding at both.

"Hugh asked me to host the meeting at my home," Archibald said. "You'll both be my guests, and as such, you'll be protected by the ancient code of hospitality."

"I'll consider it," Connor said, though he had already decided to go.

"If ye wish to meet Hugh," Archibald said, "be at my home in exactly five days."

\* \* \*

Ilysa's heart raced when she heard Archibald suggest Connor meet with Hugh. Unfortunately, she could not tell if it was fear or a true premonition. She needed to attempt to bring on The Sight. This time, she could not use Connor's chamber to help connect the vision to him, so she stole a loose hair from each of the men's tunics to mix with her herbs.

After ramming the bar across her door, she put an extra peat log on her brazier, then cut the hair into the herbs with her dirk. Her hand shook as she spread the mixture over the brazier.

Only rarely had she been able to see the future. On those times she did, what she saw was more a riddle than a clear vision. But now, when she breathed in the pungent fumes, a vision came to her so quickly and with such clarity that she gasped.

She saw Connor sitting at a table laden with food. On either side of him were two fair-haired, square-faced men—his uncles, Archibald and Hugh Dubh. As she watched, Hugh got up from the table and waved his arm, urging the other two to follow. Archibald went at once to join him at the window, but Connor held back.

*Don't go.* Ilysa did not understand why, but she knew Connor must not go to the window. *Leave the room. Leave the house. Now!* She tried to tell him, but he could not hear her.

"Come take a look at my new galley," Hugh said, his voice coming to Ilysa as if through a tunnel. "Isn't she a beauty?"

Tears stung Ilysa's eyes as Connor joined his uncles. She felt Connor's aversion when Hugh put a heavy arm around his shoulders and pointed out the window.

In a move so swift Ilysa barely saw it, Hugh drove a blade into Connor's back. Ilysa screamed soundlessly as Connor fell to the floor. Grief engulfed her. Connor lay unnaturally still, his blood seeping out of him. Archibald's face was horror-struck as he looked down at Connor. Clearly, he had not been party to this travesty, and he failed to grasp the danger to himself in time. In the next moment Hugh plunged his blade into his brother.

Ilysa had no idea how much time had passed when she found herself lying on her floor, covered in a cold sweat. After pulling herself up, she stumbled to the narrow table against the wall and poured water from the pitcher into the bowl. Her hands shook so badly that most of the water ran through her fingers as she splashed it on her face and neck. Holding the drying cloth to her face, she rocked back and forth.

She had to prevent this from happening. At all costs, she must stop Connor from going to the meeting with his uncles—or Hugh would murder him.

*  *  *

Connor stood by the window re-reading the royal summons commanding him to attend the upcoming gathering. He had avoided answering similar summons in the past. When the Crown was nervous, it had a nasty habit of imprisoning Highland chieftains on suspicion of treason or holding them hostage as a preventive measure. Now that the current rebellion was dying down, the Crown was calmer, and failing to obey the summons presented the greater risk.

The gathering was at Mingary Castle, the stronghold of the MacIains, who were steadfast supporters of the Crown in a region where few could make that claim. The gathering and the MacIains naturally led Connor to thoughts about treachery and marriage.

Not long after the Lord of the Isles was forced to submit to the Scottish Crown, the MacIain chieftain turned on his former allies, the MacDonalds of Dunivaig and the Glens. Through treachery, he captured the chieftain, his son, and his two oldest grandsons, who were all executed.

A younger grandson survived because he was in Ireland at the time. That was Alexander, Deirdre and James's father. After the executions, the Crown forced a peace through Alexander's marriage to MacIain's daughter.

At the gathering, Connor must choose which treacherous clan to ally himself with through marriage. But first, he had to spar with his vile uncle Hugh. *Please God, just put a sword in my hand.* Fighting was so much easier.

"May I speak?"

Connor started at the soft voice behind him and turned from the window to find Ilysa.

"I didn't see ye come in," he said. "What is it? Are our stores low, and I need to send the men out hunting? Or is it something far worse? Please tell me the whiskey isn't gone."

He was teasing her, glad for the diversion from his troubles. Ilysa, however, did not favor him with a smile. He narrowed his eyes and took a closer look at her. The usually unshakable Ilysa was twisting her hands in the skirt of her gown.

"What's wrong?"

"Ye mustn't go to your uncle's," she said.

"What did ye say?" Connor thought he must have misheard her.

"Don't go," she said, blinking her big brown eyes at him. "You'll be in grave danger if ye do."

Connor was aware that Ilysa had stayed in the room to listen when he met with his uncle, as she often did. He had never minded before because he trusted her loyalty absolutely and she never gave away secrets. But, by the saints, now she was trying to tell him what to do.

"I appreciate your concern," Connor said. "Now I have important matters to attend to."

He turned back to the window. After a moment, he realized she was still standing there. Did the lass not understand he had dismissed her?

"Leave me now," he said over his shoulder.

"Ye were angry with me for how ye learned about Deirdre," she said.

Connor's temper flared at the memory. When he turned and fixed his gaze on Ilysa, he did not attempt to hide it.

"Ye said I should have simply told ye what I knew," Ilysa said, her face pinched in an earnest expression.

"I did," Connor said, though he did not see why she was bringing this up.

"So that's what I'm doing now." Ilysa paused to lick her lips. "I'm telling ye that ye must not go to your uncle's."

Connor closed his eyes and rubbed the space between his brows where a raging headache was starting. He reminded himself that Ilysa was Duncan's sister, and therefore he should not yell at her. All the same, she needed to understand her place. He took a deep breath.

"I give ye a free hand with the kitchens and the servants," he said, biting out the words. "But I am your chieftain, and ye will not attempt to tell me what to do."

"Ye don't understand," she said, her voice rising. "I had a vision."

God help him, Teàrlag taught her how to mix a few salves and now Ilysa believed she had The Sight.

"I don't have time for such foolishness." Connor set the summons on his table and took her arm.

"Hugh wants to murder ye," Ilysa said as he led her to the door.

"There's nothing new about that. He's wanted to kill me for years." Connor opened the door and put a hand at her back. "Don't ever question my judgment again. Now go."

\* \* \*

Connor felt guilty when he saw Ilysa across the court-yard. Ever since he had spoken harshly to her after his uncle's visit two days ago, she dropped her gaze when-ever she passed him. She was a sweet, delicate lass. While he could not tolerate her interference, he had not meant to hurt her feelings.

She had barely spoken a word to him since. Odd, how much that unsettled him. He liked and respected Ilysa, and it did not feel right having this discord between them. When their paths crossed in the middle of the courtyard and she stopped to speak with him, he was relieved.

"Your favorite dog has had pups," she said, her face bright. "I can show them to ye when ye have a moment."

Connor had a great many things to do before he left, but this should not take long. Besides, he wanted to make things right between them.

"I can see them now," he said. "Where is Maggie?"

"She's hidden her pups well," Ilysa said, with a small smile. "Come inside, and I'll show ye."

Connor followed her down into the undercroft and past the kitchens, which were oddly quiet. When she opened the door to a storeroom, he followed her inside. He tamped down the impatience tugging at him when he looked about and did not see his dog amid the sacks of oats and barley.

Ilysa surprised him by dropping to her knees and lift-ing a board from the floor. Beneath it was a dark hole. Puzzled, Connor stooped beside her. On closer inspec-tion, he saw that there was a ladder in the hole.

"What is this?" he asked.

"Cook told me it leads down into a secret part of the dungeon, built for special prisoners."

"Special?" Connor grunted. "Why has no one told me about it?"

"Cook's grandfather showed it to him when he was a young lad. I don't think anyone else knows about it except perhaps a couple of the old folk." Ilysa smiled and added, "And your dog."

"How did Maggie get down there?" he asked, trying to see down into the hole.

"I couldn't find it, but there must be another entrance." Ilysa turned around to back down the ladder and put her foot on the first rung.

"No need for you to go," Connor said.

"I must show ye where she's hiding," Ilysa said. "You can carry the torch."

"All right, but I'll go first."

The smell of damp earth filled Connor's nose as he climbed down through the narrow tunnel. When he reached the bottom rung of the ladder, he dropped to the floor, then lifted Ilysa down. Such a slender waist she had. He looked around and saw that they were in a stone-walled passageway. Many castles had secret tunnels like this.

"Maggie and her pups are in there," Ilysa said, pointing into the darkness.

Connor followed the tunnel around a corner and through an open iron grate door into what was surely a cell. He lifted the torch to see into the corners, looking for his damned dog. Something was odd, but he could not quite put his finger on it. Ach, there were no rats scurrying before him, and no spiderwebs. That was it.

When the door slammed behind him, he thought it had been blown shut. *But there is no wind.* He turned around, wondering what happened.

"Ilysa?" He raised his torch higher. Where had she gone?

He pulled on the door, but it was stuck. He jerked at it. Then he glanced about the cell. There were no pups here.

"Ilysa!" he shouted and pounded his fist on the door.

Relief flooded through him when he saw Ilysa's head poke out from around the corner. She must have been waiting for him back by the ladder.

"The door's stuck," he said. "Ye may have to fetch some of the men to get me out."

"I'm sorry," she said, stepping out from behind the wall. "If you'd listened to me, I wouldn't have to do this."

"What in the hell are ye talking about?" he shouted. "Open this damned door at once!"

"I can't do that."

Connor's stomach dropped. She could not be betraying him. Not Ilysa.

"I told ye I had a vision," she said. "You were with your two uncles, and Hugh stabbed ye in the back. He murdered ye."

Instead of betraying him, had she gone mad? She stood outside of the circle of light from his torch so he could not see her face clearly, but she sounded as though she was weeping.

"Open the door," he said, trying to keep his voice calm. "Ye do have the key?"

"Can't ye see that I couldn't let ye meet your uncles?" she said. "I must protect ye."

"You, protect *me*?" he said, anger surging through his veins. "I am your chieftain, and I command ye to release me."

"Hugh was going to murder ye if ye went," she said. "I saw it."

"Ilysa!" he shouted.

"It won't be for that long," she said, brushing her skirts as if she were discussing a problem with the laundry. "Three days should be long enough for ye to miss the meeting, aye?"

She could not mean it.

"Ye have everything ye need down here. Plenty of candles and parchment," she said. "I'll bring ye food and fresh water every day."

By the saints, she had planned this all out. "You even cleaned it, didn't ye?"

He wanted to strangle her.

"If ye look under that cloth on the table, you'll find one of those apple tarts you're so fond of."

"An apple tart?" he said, clenching his fists. "Christ, Ilysa, ye think an apple tart will appease me!"

"No need for blasphemy and shouting," she said.

"I'm going to commit a far worse sin than blasphemy when I get out of here," he shouted. "I'm going to murder ye! Now release me at once!"

# CHAPTER 15

Ilysa listened to the men's snores as she crept through the darkened hall on silent feet. Guiding herself with one hand on the wall, she descended the stairs into the undercroft. After she was in the storage room and closed the door, she lit the lamp she had left there.

*I locked my chieftain in a cell.* The magnitude of the act struck her as she lifted the board from the floor.

She took a deep breath and steeled herself for another round of angry shouting. Once Connor realized she was not going to relent and let him out no matter what he threatened, they were usually able to have a reasonable conversation. Ilysa meticulously reported all the goings-on in the castle so he would not be caught unaware of anything important when he returned.

But this time, there would be no conversation after the shouting. She was releasing him.

After three days of hearing him make violent threats against her person, Ilysa was a trifle uneasy. She did not believe Connor would actually murder her with his bare hands, as he had said so many times. Yet she did anticipate she would receive some sort of punishment.

Was Connor angry enough to have her whipped in the courtyard in front of everyone? No, she felt certain it would be a private punishment.

Anxiety balled in her stomach as she climbed down the ladder. Connor was silent as she approached the door, which made her more nervous.

"I told everyone that ye left the castle after dark that first night for a secret meeting," she said as she drew the iron key from the pouch tied to her belt. "'Tis the middle of the night now. No one will ever know ye were here the whole time."

Her hand shook too badly for her to fit the key into the keyhole.

"*Aaah!*" she yelped when a hand reached through the grate and grabbed hold of hers. Connor did not say a word, and his hand was rock-steady as he twisted hers to turn the key in the lock. Ilysa jumped back as he shoved the door open with such force that it banged against the wall.

"I am sorely tempted to toss ye in that cell in my place and throw away the key," Connor said with such venom that a shiver went up her back.

Instead, he lifted her off her feet, carried her to the ladder, and flung her onto it. It did not matter that her legs were too wobbly to go up by themselves, because Connor was pushing her up from behind with a hand on her bottom. He was, understandably, anxious to be out of his prison.

A moment later, they were facing each other in the

storage room, which seemed far too tiny to contain Connor and his fury. In the light of the lamp she had left burning, she could see him clearly. His fists were clenched, and his chest heaving. With three days of beard and that black rage in his eyes, he looked so dark and dangerous that she could barely breathe. Yet he had never looked more handsome.

"I want ye to leave," Connor said. "Now."

"Leave?" Ilysa had not expected this. "Can't ye just order me whipped instead?"

"I don't have women whipped, for God's sake!" Connor said, his eyes narrow angry slits. "Besides, such a punishment would require an explanation, and no one is ever going to learn about this."

Ilysa could see that her worst offense had been hurting his pride.

"But ye need me here to take care of your household," she said, desperation taking hold. "I promise no one will know that I locked ye up."

"I will know," Connor said between his teeth. "You're leaving, and I don't want to see you in this castle ever again."

He turned on his heel and left, his anger like shimmering heat in his wake.

* * *

Connor sat in his chieftain's chair at the high table waiting for his breakfast. He ignored the questioning glances from his men. He owed them no explanation for where he had been for the last three days, and he was giving none.

Three days in his own dungeon, held prisoner by a wee lass. Even Shaggy Maclean had only succeeded in holding him prisoner a single day. Connor's fury was boundless.

Ilysa had the effrontery to tell him she was protecting him. Protecting *him*. And worse, she believed it! That was as offensive as deciding she had the right to dispute his judgment and ignore his commands. After pacing the floor the remainder of the night—he was too furious to sleep—he had decided to relent and not ship her home to Dunscaith. He was too kindhearted. Still, she did need to be punished.

Where in the hell was his breakfast? He was starving, which worsened his already black mood. The servants were scurrying about like confused chickens, but no one was bringing him food.

Was this Ilysa's way of punishing him for shouting at her last night? Three days ago, he would have dismissed the notion, believing her incapable of spite. But after living in the same household for much of their lives, he'd discovered that he did not know her at all.

Anger pulsed through him, making his pounding headache worse.

He slammed his cup on the table. "Where is my breakfast?"

Everyone in the hall was giving him nervous, sideways looks. He never abused his authority by shouting over small matters like a spoiled prince. This too, he blamed on Ilysa. By God, she deserved a dire punishment. If only he could think of one. He could not give her additional work, for no one worked harder.

Finally, the serving women scurried in with what looked like last night's supper. Cold.

"Where's my porridge?" he asked one of them.

"I'm sorry, Chieftain," the lass said, her eyes wide as if

she expected him to take a bite out of her. "We forgot to make it."

*Forgot?* He had porridge with his breakfast every single morning. Even in his goddamned dungeon, Ilysa had brought it to him.

"Just see that it doesn't happen again," he said, softening his voice with an effort because he did not want to send the lass into a dead faint.

Ilysa had let everything fall apart in the kitchen. Clearly, it did not pay to upset her.

After his miserable, cold breakfast, Connor went outside for some blessed fresh air. Nothing like spending time in a dank dungeon to make a man appreciate daylight. He walked along the side of the keep, drawing in deep breaths. As he was about to round the corner, he heard someone speak his name and paused.

"Where do ye suppose the chieftain was?" a woman asked.

He should have known the entire castle would be speculating about his absence.

"Ilysa's face went all pink when she told us he'd gone to 'a secret meeting,' and he didn't take his guard with him," a male voice responded. "I'd say that means he was visiting a lass."

"About time!" another man said, and this was followed by a round of bawdy laughter. "We'll have to stop calling him Saint Connor."

"Who's the lucky lass?" the woman asked.

The names of several women were raised and dismissed in turn.

"He wouldn't have to ask me twice," the woman said, which caused loud guffaws.

Connor rubbed his temples as he recognized the woman's voice as belonging to Flòraidh, a grandmother as round as a turnip.

"He's keeping it quiet," the second man said, "so I'd wager our *Saint* Connor is fooking another man's wife!"

It was time to put a stop to this. When Connor stepped around the corner, the three stared at him openmouthed.

"Since ye have time on your hands, you two will take night guard duty for a week," he said, pointing at the two warriors. Then he turned his glare on Flòraidh. "I'd better have hot porridge on my table tomorrow."

Connor spent the rest of the morning supervising the men's practice. Knocking his opponents to the ground for a few hours improved his mood considerably. He felt almost himself again by the time they went in for the midday meal.

The disaster of breakfast was repeated. Cold, tasteless food from the day before was served, and that was soon gone. He had enough troubles without facing them hungry.

Connor was tempted to give Ilysa the punishment she deserved after all: three days and nights in the hole of a dungeon. And no hot food, either. He took a long swallow of his drink and slammed his cup on the table. Even the ale had gone sour.

"Send Ilysa to my chamber," he ordered Lachlan, who happened to be standing by the door as he left the hall.

Connor paced his chamber, waiting. What in the hell was taking so long? Finally, there was a rap at his door. He turned, prepared to give Ilysa the berating of her life, but it was Lachlan.

"I couldn't find her," Lachlan said.

"Then look harder."

"Ilysa is not here."

"I suppose someone in one of the nearby cottages needed a healer." Connor hoped she had the sense not to go alone. "The moment she returns, I want to see her."

"Ilysa has gone from Trotternish," Lachlan said. "She sailed before dawn for Dunscaith Castle."

"No, that can't be." Connor stopped his pacing. "Ilysa couldn't sail a boat to Dunscaith by herself."

"Niall took her in that small galley," Lachlan said.

Two could sail the galley they had stolen from Shaggy Maclean. "How do ye know this?" Connor demanded.

"Cook was the only one Ilysa told, and it wasn't easy getting it from him," Lachlan said, looking uncomfortable.

"What do ye mean, it wasn't easy?" Connor said, narrowing his eyes at Lachlan. He did not approve of his warriors being rough with the servants.

"Ach, the man is a blubbering mess, weeping like a babe," Lachlan said, making a face. "I told him that's no way for a MacDonald to behave, but it did no good. I expect supper will be no better than breakfast and dinner were."

Connor went to the window to look out at the sea. Niall was a fine sailor, but they would be passing lands held by the MacLeods, which was dangerous with just the two of them.

*Why did they go?* Connor did not realize he had spoken the question aloud until Lachlan answered it.

"Ilysa told Cook that ye ordered her to leave."

# CHAPTER 16

Ilysa rested her head on her chin and stared at a crack in the wall. Since returning to Dunscaith, she had barely left her mother's cottage, which was really just two rooms built against the castle wall.

She was aware that she needed to make a plan, but she felt too weighed down to even lift her head. Ever since she was a young girl, she had been accustomed to being busy from morning until night. Yet, for a week now, she had done nothing at all. Not that it mattered. She had no responsibilities.

When she heard a knock on the door, she ignored it. The knocking turned into a loud banging, and then two faces appeared in her window. Moira and Sìleas, the wives of her brother and Ian, were both persistent women who would continue banging until she let them in, so she made herself get up and unbar the door.

Moira and Sìleas dragged her from her cottage and into the keep. The next thing Ilysa knew, she was standing in the middle of Duncan and Moira's bedchamber while the two women looked her up and down with narrowed eyes.

"Ach, that gown must go," Moira said, shaking her head.

"I suppose we can cut it up for rags," Sìleas said.

"What's wrong with my gown?" Ilysa asked. "'Tis a bit worn, but I've kept it mended."

Neither woman bothered answering, but their expressions were grim.

"The kerchief as well," Sìleas said, lifting her gorgeous emerald eyes to the top of Ilysa's head.

"For certain," Moira agreed.

The two women converged on Ilysa. Before she could say a word to stop them, Sìleas was pulling out the pins that held her kerchief, and Moira was unfastening the hooks at the back of her gown.

"Wait!"

When Ilysa ducked to the side to get out of their reach, her kerchief came off in Sìleas's hands. All three of them gasped as her hair came tumbling down and cascaded over her shoulders. Ilysa felt naked without her head covering. At least Sìleas and Moira had stopped grabbing at her clothes, but now they stood stock-still staring at her, which was even more disconcerting.

"What is it?" Ilysa asked, stepping back. Her face was scalding hot.

"Your hair is... lovely," Sìleas said in a soft voice that sounded like a sigh.

"You're being kind," Ilysa said, fixing her gaze on the floor. Her strawberry-blond hair was a poor, washed-out version of Sìleas's vibrant color.

Sìleas was a rare beauty, with red hair and emerald eyes, while Moira had black hair like Connor's, striking violet eyes, and the kind of voluptuous curves that left men with their tongues hanging out—unless Duncan was nearby.

"Why did ye cover this?" Moira said, running a long strand of Ilysa's hair through her fingers. "'Tis gorgeous!"

"I was married," Ilysa murmured, feeling uncomfortable with the attention.

"Ach, ye were barely married long enough to count," Moira said, dismissing long-standing custom with a wave of her hand. "And as I recall, ye always wore your hair covered, even as a wee bairn."

"My mother insisted."

Her mother had been perpetually frightened for her only daughter. *Ye mustn't draw attention to yourself. Cover your hair. Speak softly. Keep your gaze down.*

Until she was eleven, Ilysa sometimes rebelled against her mother's restrictions. She stopped the day Duncan was caught with Moira. After Duncan was sent away, their mother, who had never been a strong woman, was so fragile that Ilysa complied with her mother's wishes without argument.

While her manner was meek, Ilysa never felt meek. Someone had to make the decisions, and her mother was not capable. She began surreptitiously assuming her mother's duties at the castle. Over time, working in the background became so deeply ingrained that Ilysa no longer knew if it was her true nature.

"Now that we know what happened to your mother when she was young," Sìleas said, referring to her mother's rape, "'tis easier to understand why she was so careful with ye."

"But she's gone now, and you're a grown woman," Moira said, taking her hand and squeezing it. "Ye don't have to hide your beauty any longer."

"Hide my beauty?" Ilysa gave a dry laugh.

"Let us show ye," Moira said with a wink at Sìleas.

Sìleas retrieved a comb from the side table while Moira played maid and finished unfastening Ilysa's gown. When her gown fell to the floor, leaving Ilysa in her shift, she crossed her arms over her chest—not that there was much to cover.

"Just as I suspected," Moira said, standing back and crossing her arms under her own voluptuous breasts. "You've a shape under there after all."

"I'm built like a scrawny lad," Ilysa said.

"No, you're not." Sìleas gave her a warm smile. "You're as slender and dainty as a pixie."

"What color gown, Sìl?" Moira asked, narrowing her eyes at Ilysa as if she were deciding how best to skin a rabbit. "Blue or green?"

"She'll need more than one," Sìleas said. "Her coloring is close to mine, and we haven't much time, so I brought a few of my gowns that we can alter."

"Haven't much time for what?" Ilysa asked. "Why are ye doing this?"

The two women drew her over to the bench beneath the window and sat her down between them.

"I know ye have feelings for my brother," Moira said, taking her hand again. "But ye simply cannot devote yourself to Connor any longer. Surely ye know that now."

Ilysa knew it in her head, but her heart had not accepted it yet.

"What a lass needs to forget one man," Moira said, "is another."

"Most of the chieftains will be at the gathering at Mingary Castle," Sìleas said. "And they'll each have a contingent of warriors with them."

"That means Mingary Castle will be filled to bursting with fine Highland warriors!" Moira said, her eyes sparkling. "Duncan is to meet Connor there with a galley of our men, and you and I are going with them. With all those handsome men in one place, you'll have a grand time."

"Men don't notice me," Ilysa said. "I'll only embarrass myself."

"Is this the same lass who braved a pack of pirates to spy for us when Hugh held Dunscaith?" Sìleas said, raising her eyebrows.

"That wasn't so brave," Ilysa said. She'd had it all under control.

"I'll make certain ye don't hide in a corner where the men can't see ye," Moira said. "You'll have your pick of them for a husband."

"But I don't want a husband," Ilysa said.

"Ye could stay here with Duncan, me, and the children forever, if that would make ye happy," Moira said, touching her cheek. "But I don't believe it will."

Different as they were, Ilysa had grown very fond of Moira. If she stayed, Moira would do her best to make Ilysa feel useful, but she was not needed here. Dunscaith had a mistress.

"Don't tell me ye plan to live with old Teàrlag and

waste your life away in her wee cottage," Moira said, "or I'll have to slap sense into ye."

"Moira doesn't mean that," Sìleas said, patting Ilysa's arm. "Much as we all love Teàrlag, she is an old woman who's not long for this world. Ye need someone you can make a life with."

"I know Connor is the one ye want, but ye can't have him," Moira said.

"I've always known that," Ilysa said in a quiet voice.

"Ye need a husband who can give ye children," Sìleas said, her eyes lighting with a soft smile. "I've seen how good ye are with mine, and I know ye want your own."

A tear slipped down Ilysa's cheek. Sìleas had found a vulnerable spot. She did long for children.

"Ye need a man in your bed," Moira said.

*Hmmph.* That had not done Ilysa any good before.

"And there's no one who enjoys making a home more than you," Moira added. "*Is uaigneach an níochán nach mbíonn léine ann.*" It's a lonely washing that has no man's shirt in it.

"Think of it," Sìleas said as she smoothed Ilysa's hair behind her ear. "You can have a family, a home of your own, and a man who will make ye happy."

\* \* \*

"I was sick as a damned dog last night," the MacNeil chieftain said as he joined Connor and Alex, who were sitting with their legs stretched out before the hearth in the hall. "If I didn't know ye better, Connor, I'd say ye tried to poison me."

Connor rubbed his forehead. He did not doubt that the food had made Alex's father-in-law ill. Cook had taken to his bed, and the entire household was in disarray.

"This would never happen if Ilysa were here," Alex said. "*Cha bhi fios aire math an tobair gus an tràigh e.*" The value of the well is not known until it goes dry.

"Thank you for pointing that out," Connor said.

Until everything went amok, Connor had not realized that Ilysa was the reason his household ran smoothly. In truth, he was never even aware that it ran smoothly.

"Another chieftain would believe it was poison," the MacNeil said. "You'd best get your household in order before spoiled meat kills off a guest and leads to a clan war."

"This morning one of the serving maids told me—me, the chieftain—that we are *low on ale*," Connor confessed. "For God's sake, with the MacLeods and Hugh threatening us, I don't have time to concern myself with what goes on in the kitchens."

"What ye need is a wife," the MacNeil said. "This is no way for a man to live."

"I intend to acquire one at the gathering," Connor said.

Alastair MacLeod would be there, which meant Connor could risk leaving Skye without worrying that his enemy would launch an attack in his absence. Neither of them would break the peace until after the gathering because that would upset the Crown and risk interference.

"I'll be looking for a wife at the gathering myself," the MacNeil said, reminding Connor that Alex's father-in-law had recently lost his second wife in childbirth. When he stood, he seemed to have lost his usual proud bearing. "Now I'm returning to my bed to recover from that slop ye fed me."

"Poor man," Alex said after his father-in-law left.

"He's left with a newborn babe, another young son, and Glynis's three sisters."

Alex shuddered when he mentioned the girls, who were pretty but silly and prone to giggling. They were young, but their father and Alex held out little hope the girls would outgrow it.

The MacNeil chieftain's galley would be sailing with Connor's to the gathering, while Alex remained at Trotternish Castle to serve as keeper in Connor's absence. Alex was well established on North Uist and, unlike Connor, had a good man there he could leave in charge.

"Our battle with the MacLeods could come soon after the gathering," Connor said. "I intend to return from it with the matter of the marriage alliance settled."

"Well, I know one chieftain's daughter ye can strike off your list," Alex said. "Alexander of Dunivaig won't be invited to his father-in-law's."

Connor did not tell his cousin that Deirdre was already off his list of prospective wives. If he told Alex why, he would never hear the end of it.

"Has he not come to terms with the Crown yet?" Connor asked.

"Ye could say that," Alex said with a smirk. "I heard he joined our other MacDonald relation, Donald Gallda, in attacking Mingary Castle again."

*Murt!* Connor's near marriage to Deirdre would have been even more disastrous than he thought. With her father still active in the rebellion—attacking his father-in-law's castle, no less—Connor could have been dragged into that lost cause, or accused of it by the Crown.

"Will the gathering still be held at Mingary Castle?" Connor asked.

"Aye, but don't be surprised if ye still smell smoke," Alex said. "Now, there's a cautionary tale about the value of a marriage alliance."

"Ye look well," Connor said to change the subject. "Perhaps it wasn't the food at my table that made your father-in-law ill after all."

"Fortunately, my thoughtful wife packed enough provisions to sink my boat, so I didn't need to risk eating that gray meat," Alex said, making a face.

"I ate it, and it didn't make me ill," Connor said, though it had tasted foul.

"That's because you're drinking enough whiskey to fend off any illness."

Connor had been drinking more of late. Who could blame him?

"At least they can't ruin the whiskey," he said and poured a large measure into each of their cups.

"*Cha deoch-slàint, i gun a tràghadh*!" 'Tis no health if the glass is not emptied! They chanted in unison and threw it back.

Connor choked, and Alex spewed whiskey across the floor.

"What in God's name have they done to it?" Alex asked.

"Ach, they've watered it down," Connor said, shaking his head.

"This is serious." Alex pointed his finger at Connor. "Ye must remedy this situation."

Alex spoke half in jest, but something must be done and soon. Unfortunately, negotiations for a marriage between two chieftains' families generally took considerable time—unless kidnapping was employed to obtain the bride. As often as not, kidnapping led to war, so Connor could not risk it.

He would have to swallow his pride and ask Ilysa to return and restore order to his household until his wife, whoever the hell she was, arrived. While Connor would never forget being imprisoned in his own dungeon, Ilysa had saved him from marrying Deirdre, which did help him forgive her.

Odd, but he missed having her about. He had barely noticed her in all the time they were at Dunscaith. But here at Trotternish, she was one of the few people he could trust absolutely, and he had grown accustomed to sharing his thoughts with her. Without realizing it, he had come to expect her brisk step, her soft smile, and the calm that surrounded her. Connor rarely felt at ease these days, but he could be at ease with Ilysa.

That was not entirely true. When her hands were on his bare skin, every part of him was alive with awareness. While she innocently tended to his injuries, he imagined her kneading, stroking, encircling him until he was awash with guilt and throbbing with need. Thank God his wounds were nearly healed so he would not have to endure that pleasurable torture again. He would put the memory of it firmly out of his mind.

As for his dreams, well, a man was allowed those.

# CHAPTER 17

Ach, you're as adorable as a puppy," Moira said, stepping back to take a look at her handiwork.

Adorable? Ilysa stifled a sigh of disappointment. First a doe, now a puppy. After all Moira had done to her, she had hoped, if not for pretty, then at least for attractive or appealing.

They were in a chamber in the West Tower of Mingary Castle that had been set aside for the few highborn women who had come to the gathering with their men. For what seemed like hours, Moira wove tiny flowers into a loose braid down her back. Then she fixed a headdress to the crown of Ilysa's head that was so delicate, it was more ornamentation than head covering. Finally, Moira laced her into this immodest gown that made Ilysa fear that if she breathed too deeply, her breasts would pop out.

"Ready?" Moira asked, and opened the door without waiting for an answer. As they went down the stairs,

Moira took her arm. "Now ye will enjoy yourself, or you'll answer to me."

Duncan and Niall were waiting in the courtyard just outside the tower door.

"Ach, ye look lovely," Niall said, sounding breathless, after gaping at Ilysa openmouthed for a long moment.

The look her brother gave her, a mix of alarm and disapproval, was even more reassuring. All the same, Ilysa's stomach tightened as she took Niall's arm and they started across the courtyard to the keep.

"Has Connor arrived?" she asked him in a low voice.

"I haven't seen him yet."

As they passed through the arched entrance that led into the Great Hall of Mingary Castle, the noise of a hundred conversations filled Ilysa's ears. There were so many people! In her low-cut gown and with her hair hanging down her back, she felt exposed, as if she had walked into this huge room full of strangers in her nightshift.

She instinctively touched her mother's jeweled brooch, which hung on a silver chain at her throat. Ilysa had no idea how her mother came to own such an extravagant piece of jewelry, but she was glad to have something of her mother's to wear.

"Is this young warrior the lucky man who is your husband?"

Ilysa turned to find a handsome man with graying temples standing next to her.

"Who, Niall?" she asked and laughed. "Poor Niall has been forced to serve as my protector at this gathering, but he's been spared the task of being my husband."

"A task any man with an eye for beauty would gladly take," the man said.

Good heavens. If she was not mistaken, he was flirting with her. To Ilysa's surprise, she found it pleasing.

"I am Alan, cousin to the Campbell chieftain," he said, then took her hand and kissed it just the way she had heard courtiers did.

As Ilysa introduced herself, she glanced sideways at Niall and found him glaring at Alan as if he would prefer to see him at the end of his sword.

"It takes a brave man to approach Duncan MacDonald's sister, which can be the only explanation for why such a gem is yet unclaimed." Alan Campbell's eyes twinkled as he added, "I am a brave man."

Niall coughed. When she glanced at him again, he gave his head a slight shake. Clearly, this Campbell man did not have Niall's approval.

"Excuse us," Niall said and steered her into the crowd.

"Why did ye do that?" she asked. "I was enjoying myself."

"Ye know what they say, *As long as there are trees in the woods, there will be treachery in the Campbells*," Niall said. "And that particular Campbell is no looking for a wife."

"He seemed interested in me," she said.

"He is interested," Niall hissed in her ear, "in getting ye under the blankets."

"Truly?" Ilysa said, pressing her hand to her chest. Other lasses were always talking about men attempting to do this, but they never tried with her. "That's exciting. Do ye suppose other men here will try as well?"

"Ilysa!" Niall looked so shocked that she burst out laughing.

"Will ye share the jest with me, lass?" This time, the

man who spoke was tall, fair-haired, and wore the most elegant tunic Ilysa had ever seen.

Judging by Niall's frown, he did not think well of this one, either. Ilysa, however, found the man's crooked smile quite charming.

\* \* \*

Mingary Castle came into view not long after Connor's galley rounded the tip of the Ardnamurchan Peninsula, the westernmost point of the mainland. The castle was large, consisting of several buildings surrounded by an irregular, six-sided wall, and strategically located to guard the sea routes into the Sound of Mull and Loch Sunart. As they sailed closer, Connor noted the burned tree stumps, remnants of the rebels' latest attack.

Large as the castle was, it could not accommodate so many guests, and camps had been set up along the shore on either side of the castle. Connor smiled to himself when he saw that Duncan, who detested such gatherings, had chosen the spot farthest from the castle and closest to home. After leaving his galley and men with their clansmen, Connor went up to the castle.

A short time later, he stood inside the Great Hall, scanning the crowd. Before the gathering ended, he would have an agreement to marry the daughter or sister of one of the Highland chieftains in this room. The only question was which one.

"Ah, the elusive Connor MacDonald has finally made an appearance."

Connor turned to see an extremely attractive, fair-haired woman wearing a high, elaborate headdress and an equally low bodice.

"Lady Philippa?" he said.

"You remembered," she said, giving him a dazzling smile.

Connor doubted many men forgot Philippa. When his cousin Ian was young and foolish, he was so enthralled with her that he planned to ask for her hand. Fortunately, Ian had been forced to wed Sìleas instead. Philippa had her good qualities, but fidelity was not one of them.

"Why do ye say I'm elusive?" he asked.

"Because you've deftly avoided the chieftains with marriageable daughters up until now," she said, with an amused expression. "With your appearance today, you may as well sound the trumpets and shout, *The handsome chieftain of the MacDonalds of Sleat is prepared to take a wife!*"

Connor chuckled despite himself.

"So who is the lucky lass?" Philippa asked taking his arm and leaning close. "I want to be the first to know."

"I haven't picked her out yet," he said. "Who would ye suggest?"

Philippa was a court creature and would know who was out of favor with the Crown and who was on the rise. She would not waste his time pretending that he could choose a bride based on her beauty and charm.

"The regent is exceedingly grateful to Shaggy Maclean and Alastair MacLeod for capturing the brothers of Donald Gallda," she said, referring to the rebel leader.

"Hmmph."

"Well then, a connection with the Campbells is always worth considering. Or," Philippa said, turning her gaze meaningfully to a well-dressed, dark-haired man with a pointed beard, "if you are willing to take a risk, marriage to a Douglas could pay off very nicely."

Connor eyed the handsome and overly ambitious Douglas chieftain, the Earl of Angus, who had wed the queen soon after the king's death. Everyone, except the queen, realized he had married her in the hope of ruling Scotland in her young son's name. Their marriage, however, had given the council the excuse they needed to take the regency—and the royal children—from the queen, whose brother was Scotland's greatest enemy, Henry VIII of England.

When the council called John Stewart, the Duke of Albany, home from France to be the new regent, there were rumors that the queen planned to abscond with the Scottish heir to England. If that was her intent, she did not act quickly enough. Albany arrived and persuaded her to hand over the royal children by laying siege to Stirling Castle.

"I'm surprised to see the Douglas here," Connor said. "Last I heard, the queen had fled to England, and her husband was lying low at his estates, hoping to avoid a charge of treason."

"The Douglas has made peace with Albany." Philippa gave Connor a mischievous look over her fan. "I fear he will find it far more difficult to reconcile with his wife, though I would never count the Douglas out."

"Why?" Connor asked.

"He's taken up with a former lover and is living openly with the woman *on the queen's money*." Philippa leaned closer, giving Connor a waft of delicate perfume and what he guessed was an intentional look down the front of her bodice. "I've heard a whisper that Albany will return to

France soon and that the queen intends to cross into Scotland the moment he sets foot on the ship. Life at court should be interesting."

With a young child on the throne, the factional fighting was unending. The queen had made a bad situation worse, however, by allowing herself to be blinded by passion and marrying foolishly.

"The rest of us can't change spouses whenever we wish, as you Highlanders do," Philippa said with a smile. "Whether the queen likes it or not, the Douglas remains her husband, and he may rule in his stepson's name yet—which is why I suggest you consider wedding a Douglas."

Connor could not make himself consider a match with either the Douglases or the Campbells. They always had their eyes on other clans' lands and viewed marriage alliances as one more means to acquire them, even if they had to wait a generation.

Which other treacherous chieftains should he consider? As if in answer to his question, he saw his host, the MacIain, coming toward him through the crowd.

"I hear John MacIain has a granddaughter of an age to wed," Philippa whispered, touching his arm again. "I'll leave you to your business."

\* \* \*

"Ye should have a wife by now," John MacIain said after they had exchanged the usual greetings and traded opinions on how much longer the rebellion would last.

When the MacIain put a hand on Connor's shoulder, Connor forced himself not to remove it by thinking of MacIain's hundreds of well-trained warriors.

Connor needed those warriors.

"At eight and twenty," MacIain continued, "I had two strong sons and three daughters."

"You were fortunate in your choice of wife," Connor said, more because MacIain's wife was a Campbell than because of the number of children she gave him.

An additional benefit of wedding MacIain's granddaughter was that it would give Connor a connection to the Campbells without actually having to marry one.

Moira cut their conversation short when she appeared through the crowd, leaving every man she passed staring after her.

"How is my favorite sister?" Connor said and kissed her cheek.

"Is that smoke I smell?" Moira gave a delicate sniff.

Connor closed his eyes at her reference to the recent burning of MacIain's castle.

"I'll leave ye to your *charming* sister," MacIain said. "We'll speak again later."

"Moira!" Connor chastised her after MacIain stalked off. Though Connor was chieftain, he did not fool himself that he could control his sister. He wished Duncan good luck with that.

"I had to do something to get rid of him," Moira said, giving MacIain's back a sour look. "What were ye discussing with that devil before I rescued you?"

"Clan business," he said. "Where's Duncan?"

"Ye know how he hates crowds," she said. "He's gone back to the camp."

"Tell me the news from Dunscaith." Connor hoped she would mention Ilysa without his having to ask. When she failed to, he had a sneaking suspicion it was intentional. Finally, he gave up. "How is Ilysa?"

"Why, do ye have an apology to make?" Moira asked, narrowing her violet eyes at him.

"Did Ilysa say something to make ye believe I do?" Connor asked.

"I couldn't pry it out of her—Ilysa is far too loyal to say a word against ye," Moira said. "But ye must have done something truly dreadful for her to leave."

"I've done nothing to apologize for." In fact, he had punished Ilysa far less than she deserved. Now he was prepared to forgive all and allow her to return. "How is Ilysa?"

"Have ye not seen her yet?" Moira asked.

"Ilysa is *here*?" Connor asked, turning to look for her in the crowded hall. *Why in the hell would she be here?* Regardless, it should not be difficult to spot her drab gown in this room full of lasses dressed like brightly colored birds.

"I'm fortunate to have a sister-in-law I'm so fond of," Moira said as she gazed across the room with a soft smile. "I see I'm not the only one to appreciate what a delight she is."

Connor followed his sister's gaze, but instead of finding Ilysa, he saw a lass surrounded by a group of men. Her back was to him so all he could see of her was a slim outline and lovely reddish-blond hair that fell in a thick braid to her waist and was ornamented with tiny blue flowers.

"I don't see Ilysa," Connor said, though in truth he had stopped looking for her.

He could not seem to drag his gaze away from the lass with hair the color of summer sunlight. When she spoke to the man next to her, he caught a bit of her profile. Then she tilted her head back and laughed, exposing the graceful line of her throat, and his pulse skipped.

"Ilysa is right in front of your eyes," his sister said with a smile in her voice. "Perhaps you're having trouble because of all the men blocking your view."

Men blocking his view? They were talking about *Ilysa*.

# CHAPTER 18

The lass with the red-gold braid turned around. As their gazes met, Connor had the oddest sensation that he was seeing her through a swirling fog. The hall and all the sounds and people in it faded into the mist, and he saw only her.

The lass's eyes widened and her lips parted as if she recognized him before she turned away. Connor's heart lurched, and a terrible longing filled him, just as it had that night in the faery glen. An instant later, disappointment hit him like a fist to his chest because he knew this could not be his faery lass. He had long since realized that the loss of blood from his wounds that night had caused him to imagine her.

How strange that someone in the midst of this noisy, crowded hall had made him think of the faery glen and the ethereal lass who danced with such abandon in his imagination. He was never given to flights of fancy or romantic notions. Yet the fragility of her slender frame engendered an unexpected and powerful urge to protect her.

"Who is she?" he asked.

"Come, let's find out," Moira said and tucked her hand in the crook of his arm.

As they approached, the men surrounding the lass made room for Connor next to her. There were some advantages to being a chieftain.

"Take a stroll with me tomorrow and show me where ye found those wee blue flowers in your hair," one of the men said, which caused her cheeks to blush a pretty pink. "Say ye will, Ilysa."

"*Ilysa?*" Connor did not realize he had spoken the question aloud until the lass spun toward him.

Connor's mouth fell open. This close, he could see that this was indeed Ilysa, but she was so changed—wonderfully so—that his mind was slow to grasp it.

How had he failed to notice how truly lovely her brown eyes were? A man could get lost in them. His gaze dropped to her gown, and his throat tightened. All this time, she had hidden a lithe body beneath oversize gowns.

"I don't recall seeing your hair before," he said and reached out to touch a shining, red-gold strand that had come loose.

She stepped back from him. "Good evening to ye, Connor."

Connor started at the sound of her familiar, calm voice and dropped his hand. What was he thinking, touching her hair in front of a room full of people, as if he were a lover who could not keep his hands off her. How could Ilysa sound so serene when his pulse was pounding at his temples?

"What happened to ye?" he blurted out.

"Your sister and Sìleas have been dressing me." She plucked the skirt of her gown between delicate fingers. "Do ye think the gown suits me? I'm not accustomed to it."

She should not have drawn his attention to it again. The gown was of the French style worn at court, with a tight-fitting, square-cut bodice that revealed the tops of her high, creamy breasts. From there, it fit snugly to her tiny waist, which he could span with his hands, and then flowed gracefully over her hips and down to the floor.

"No, it doesn't look right at all," he murmured to himself. This was not how Ilysa was supposed to look. The sight of her should make him feel comfortable and easy, like a pair of old boots, not send his pulse racing and muddle his thoughts.

Connor was vaguely aware that he had stared at her beguiling shape for far too long and dragged his attention upward, helplessly pausing at each appealing curve. Her shining braid had fallen forward over her breast. He followed it upward over flawless skin until he reached her face, which somehow was both familiar and unexpected.

Her lips looked soft. Her slightly upturned nose was fetching. But her best feature was her dark and luminous eyes, which were set off by her red-gold hair and matching threads of her headdress.

"Ye look exquisite," he said on an exhale, but she was already gone.

* * *

Ilysa ran down the steps and along the side of the keep. When she reached the corner, she ducked into a narrow gap between the buildings. She did not stop until she reached the castle wall at the very end, where she was certain she would be out of sight.

With her chest heaving, she leaned against the wall and closed her eyes. The cold from the stone seeped through her back, but it did nothing to cool her burning cheeks.

She was mortified. At first, when Connor stared at her, she thought he was admiring how she looked, as the other men had. How wrong she was.

*What happened to ye? No, it doesn't look right at all.*

Taking slow, deep breaths, she attempted to calm herself. She had survived worse humiliation with her husband, and she would survive this as well. The disappointment was harder to bear. Ilysa squeezed her eyes shut tighter to force back the tears that threatened.

She had deceived herself. Only now could she admit why she had let Moira and Sìleas persuade her to change her appearance and come to the gathering. She had not done it to gain a marriage offer from a stranger. No, in her secret heart of hearts, she had hoped to make Connor look at her and for once see a desirable woman. Was that too much to ask?

Her pleasure in the attention from the other men evaporated like the mist on a hot day. They had only flocked around her because there were so few women here. Besides, what did it matter if they all thought she was pretty, when the one man she cared about did not find her so?

Ilysa felt someone's presence and snapped her eyes open. *O shluagh!* None other than Alastair MacLeod stood not two feet away, staring down at her. He was huge.

Though she had never seen the famed chieftain of her

enemy clan before, she had heard stories about him all her life. She recognized him by his maimed shoulder, which was caused by a MacDonald axe and figured in the tales as often as the slaughters of her clan.

Sweat broke out on her palms. The MacLeod chieftain towered over her, and she could not get by him in the narrow gap between buildings. She was trapped.

"I am Alastair MacLeod," he said in a voice so deep she could feel it through her feet. "No matter what you've heard, I don't eat captured MacDonald children for breakfast."

Ilysa was caught off guard by his jest and assumed, or at least hoped, it meant he did not intend to harm her. Despite his age and disfigured shoulder, he was unexpectedly handsome. None of the stories had mentioned that.

"I'm honored to meet ye," she said to be courteous, though she could not quite believe she was conversing with the MacLeod chieftain. "How do ye know I'm a MacDonald?"

"I saw ye come into the hall with your clansmen," he said. "What's your name, lass?"

"Ilysa," she said, her voice unnaturally high.

"A lovely name," he said. "It suits ye."

She did not know what to say to that. She was still reeling from his admission that he had watched her enter the hall.

"Did you follow me out?" she asked.

"No," he said. "I was out here enjoying the quiet when I saw ye burst out of the keep like a lamb chased by a wolf."

Ilysa wondered if he was speaking the truth. Remarkably, she was no longer afraid of him. At least not much.

"'Tis growing dark, and there are a great many men here," he continued. "Ye should know better than to wander outside the hall without one of your clansmen to protect you."

"My brother would not be pleased if he knew," she said and gave a humorless laugh. It did not bear thinking about what Duncan would do if he learned she was alone in a secluded corner of the castle with the man her clan called the Scourge of Skye. And that was the nicest name they called him.

"That's an unusual brooch you're wearing," he said.

"It was my mother's," Ilysa said, looking down at it. The brooch was distinctive with its unusual pattern of interlocking leaves surrounding a deep red stone.

"I'm sorry, has your mother passed?" he asked in a surprisingly soft voice.

Ilysa felt a sting at the back of her eyes and nodded. Ridiculous as it seemed, Ilysa felt as though the MacLeod chieftain understood her sadness.

"She died three years ago, when I was sixteen." Ilysa ran her fingertip over the slippery surface of the brooch's red stone. "She dressed plainly and always wore it under her gown where no one could see it."

"Were ye named for her?" he asked.

"No. Her name was Anna."

After a moment, he said, "I hope ye still have your father to look after ye."

"Ach, I never had him, whoever he was." When she looked up, Alastair MacLeod's eyes had that hollow look of someone for whom pain is a constant companion, and her heart went out to him. "Does your shoulder pain ye a great deal?"

"What?" he said, his tone sharp as a blade. His earlier kindness had made her forget who he was, but he was all chieftain now, huge and intimidating.

"I meant no offense," she said quickly. "I'm a healer, and it troubles me to see that ye suffer because your injury was not looked after properly at the time."

"We were a long way from home," he said, glaring down at her, "and no one was concerned about how the shoulder was set because they didn't expect me to live."

"That's a poor excuse," Ilysa said. "Unfortunately, there's nothing I can do to repair it now, but I can make ye a salve that will soothe it."

"I don't mind the pain," he said. "It serves to remind me who my enemies are."

* * *

After working his way around the hall, Connor was once again attempting to have a conversation with the MacIain about his granddaughter when Ilysa caught his eye. The arched entrance was just behind her, framing her like a painting. It was a mystery to him how she could look like herself and yet so achingly lovely at the same time.

His muscles tensed when he noticed that Alastair MacLeod was next to her. It was a testament to how shocked he was by Ilysa's transformation that he did not see the MacLeod chieftain first. He could not bear for her to be so close to their enemy. When he took a step toward them, MacIain stopped him with a hand on his arm.

"I'll have no trouble between you and the MacLeod here," his host warned.

Connor relaxed as the MacLeod moved away from Ilysa and into the crowded hall. Suddenly, the man turned and met his gaze, as if he had been aware of Connor watching him all along. The animosity that burned between them could have set the hall on fire.

# CHAPTER 19

Feels like we've been here a month," Duncan said when Connor found him at their camp near evening on the second day. "When can we leave?"

"As soon as I get this business of a wife settled."

All day, Connor had had careful conversations with other chieftains about their marriageable daughters and sisters without committing himself, which had tested his skills and made him sweat. Now it was time to enter into serious negotiations with one of them.

His near mistake with Deirdre made Connor realize that, if the circumstances allowed, he ought to consider the nature of the lass as well as the strength of her clan. Unfortunately, his own judgment had proved fallible when it came to prospective brides. It was a shame Alex was not here, because Alex *knew* women. Duncan was useless on the subject, and Moira let her emotions rule her judgment.

"Who's that with Ilysa?" Connor asked when he saw

her strolling along the shore with a man. "I'm surprised ye let her walk alone with him this far from the castle."

"That's the MacNeil," Duncan said, which explained why he was not concerned. Alex's father-in-law could be trusted to keep Ilysa safe.

"That's good," Connor said. "With all the men I've seen following her, she needs watching over."

He suddenly realized he had failed to tell her he wanted her to return to Trotternish and decided to do it now.

\* \* \*

Ilysa was grateful to the MacNeil chieftain for taking her outside the crowded castle to enjoy the spring air. Despite his gruff manner, he was easy to talk to.

"Connor isn't the only man who came to the gathering looking for a wife," he said after a while. "As ye know, mine died giving birth a short time ago."

The poor man. "I am sorry," she said and ventured to touch his arm.

"I have both the new babe and a second young son," he said. "Of course, I have a nursemaid for the boys, but they need a mother."

"Mmm," Ilysa murmured to show she was listening. She wondered why he was sharing this with her, but thought perhaps he wanted her advice.

"And I have three foolish daughters," he said, "who are badly in need of a sensible woman like you to guide them."

"Like me?" Ilysa came to an abrupt halt and turned to face him. Could he mean what she thought he did?

"Glynis's mother is the only woman who had my

heart," he said. "Still, I did my best to be a good husband to my second wife, as I will do with my next one."

Was this the best she could hope for? Could no man love her? She told herself not to be foolish. MacNeil was a good man and a far better match than she had reason to expect.

"I..." Ilysa faltered, unable to make herself say the words.

"No need to make a hasty decision," the MacNeil said, putting his hand up. "I can see ye need to think on it."

Before Ilysa could get her bearings, she saw Connor striding toward them. He walked with the unconscious grace of a warrior who trained hard every day. And he was so handsome with his steel-blue eyes and his black hair brushing his shoulders that when he fixed his gaze on her face, Ilysa found it difficult to draw air into her lungs.

"Young men don't know what to look for in a wife," the MacNeil said, but she barely heard him. "I know a prize when I see one."

With the wind blowing Connor's hair and the sunset ablaze behind him, he looked like an ancient Celtic god.

"Connor," the MacNeil greeted him, reminding her of his presence. "Ilysa, I'll leave ye with your chieftain."

"Come," Connor said and took her arm as soon as the MacNeil turned around to head back to the castle. "I must speak with ye."

Ilysa's heart beat too fast as he led her down the empty beach. The heat of his muscles beneath her fingers traveled up her arm and through her body to unexpected places. Connor helped her over a rocky stretch of the beach and continued down the shore until they reached a quiet spot shielded by low trees.

The clouds still held the pink and purples of sunset, but the light was fading rapidly. Ilysa had no idea why Connor had brought her here but suspected it had something to do with her locking him in the dungeon. After all the times he had looked through her and not seen her, now that she had his full attention, she could not force words from her mouth.

"The wind has come up. Ye must be cold." He unfastened the brooch at his shoulder and, in one fluid movement, swung his plaid from his shoulders and around hers. A sigh escaped her as she was enfolded in the warmth and smell of him.

For a long moment, Connor held the plaid together under her chin and stared into her eyes. She was afraid to breathe. Anticipation sang through her. Finally he released the plaid, but he still did not step back.

"When I said your gown didn't look right, I only meant I was not accustomed to it." Connor ran his hand down her arm, sending another wave of warmth through her body, then quickly pulled his hand back. "Ye do look lovely, Ilysa. Very lovely."

She had gotten her wish. For once, Connor had looked at her and found her attractive. Yet no sooner was her wish granted than she realized it was not enough. She wanted more than a flash of desire in his eyes, more than a longing gaze.

She wanted *him*.

It made no difference that it was hopeless. He was the only one she wanted.

"I'd like ye to come back to Trotternish Castle," he said.

Ilysa closed her eyes for a brief moment and told herself not to cry. *Connor wants me back.*

"Does this mean you're not angry with me anymore?" she asked.

"I am not as angry as I was," he said, "but we must have a firm understanding that ye will not interfere in my decisions. Ye must respect me as chieftain."

"I do."

He narrowed his eyes at her. "If ye disobey me again, I will punish ye severely."

Ilysa kept quiet, rather than tell him she would disobey him only if she truly must.

"In truth, I haven't given you the respect ye deserved," Connor said. "I had no idea all that ye do to keep my household in order. Nothing is as it should be without you."

That warmed her heart. She smiled and said, "I'll be happy to return."

"The saints be praised," he said under his breath, and he took her hand. "I promise I won't impose on ye for long. It will only be until my bride arrives."

Disappointment crashed down on her like a great weight, and she had to swallow twice before she could get the words out. "Your bride?"

"I don't have it arranged quite yet," he said. "But I will wed soon."

\* \* \*

Connor needed to get his marriage arranged quickly, and not just because he needed the alliance. He had been so long without a woman that he was losing his mind. Had he really been about to kiss Ilysa?

Aye, definitely.

What was his excuse for bringing her this far away

from the castle? He had wanted to speak with her privately, but it had not been necessary to be quite this alone with her. He reminded himself that this was Ilysa, whom he had known as a babe and a wee girl. He should not have these urges toward her.

But urges he had. With darkness falling around them, he was finding it easier by the moment to imagine laying her down on the sand and having his wicked way with her—over and over. Ach, this was wrong.

"Let's head back," he said and started walking.

"Who have ye decided upon for a bride?" Ilysa asked.

"I'm considering John MacIain's granddaughter," he said. "She is the child of his eldest son, who died in battle while her mother was pregnant with her."

"Mmm," Ilysa murmured, and he noticed a slight tightening around her mouth.

"Why do ye disapprove?" Connor found that Ilysa's opinion of his future wife did matter to him. And she had seen through Deirdre.

"Let's hope the apple has fallen far from the tree," she said.

"Ye shouldn't judge her nature by her grandfather's," he said.

"And ye know her nature?"

"I haven't met her yet," he said.

"Hmmm." She was silent a moment, then she asked, "What are ye looking for in a wife, besides a clan alliance?"

"A quiet, respectful lass, who is loyal and doesn't interfere with my work," he said. "She should make my guests welcome and be a good mother." He wouldn't complain if she were pretty as well.

"Do you not hope for love?" Ilysa asked in a soft voice.

"Hell, no." Connor frowned. It was not like Ilysa to speak nonsense, which was one of the things he liked about her. She was a sensible, practical lass who could be counted on to do her duties and take pride in doing them well.

"Who are the others you're considering?" Ilysa asked.

They discussed each of them in turn, and Ilysa found some fault with every possible alliance.

"I can't help but think...," Ilysa said and turned her head to look off toward the dark sea.

"What?"

"Ye told me never to question your judgment as chieftain," she said, still looking away from him.

"I asked for your opinion," he said. "That's different."

She turned and met his gaze. "Should ye risk tying yourself to either a wife or a clan ye can't be sure ye can trust?"

"I can't trust any of them," Connor said and gave a dry laugh. "I'll never get a wife if I listen to you."

"You're asking them to fight for Trotternish, but what will they want in return?" she asked. "Ye don't know the cost."

"That's true, but I have no choice," he said. "We must fight the MacLeods, and they are too strong for us to do it alone." What concerned Connor more was the risk that his bride's clan would find an excuse not to come to his aid when it was time to fight the MacLeods. Alliances were slippery.

"Perhaps ye should look for a clan that needs us as much as we need them," Ilysa said. After a long pause, she asked, "What about Torquil MacLeod of Lewis?"

If Torquil were not his half brother, Ilysa's suggestion would have been an astute one. They each needed help in ousting another clan from their lands. In a prior rebellion, the Crown had granted the traditional lands of Torquil's clan on the isle of Lewis to a rival, and then Torquil's father had lost possession of the island as well.

"Our mother left his father for mine," Connor said. "I have as much chance of making an alliance with Torquil as I do with his distant relation Alastair MacLeod."

"Ye don't know that," Ilysa said.

But Connor did know. Shortly before he left for the gathering, Sorely returned with the message that Torquil had refused his offer of friendship. As was so often the case with Connor's family, their blood tie, which was born of their mother's passion and disloyalty, separated rather than bound them.

* * *

Lachlan kept his eyes sharp and his hand on his dirk as he and his father approached the house in which Hugh had set up camp.

"I don't like coming back here, Father," Lachlan said in a low voice. "We shouldn't be putting our trust in a viper like Hugh."

"He's useful," his father said and repeated the old adage, "My enemy's enemy is my friend."

The filthy, foul-smelling men who sat on rocks and logs in front of the house continued their games of dice and bones as Lachlan and his father walked past. It made Lachlan feel unclean to be known by such men.

"We must avenge the wrong committed against our

family," his father said under his breath, "for the sake of our honor."

"Honor?" Lachlan hissed. "What honor is there in consorting with the likes of these?"

"Never forget that you have a sacred duty to avenge your mother," his father said, his face hard. "Nothing but blood will satisfy it."

Sometimes Lachlan resented that his father had passed this duty to him because he had not succeeded in taking vengeance himself. When the former chieftain took Lachlan's mother into his bed, he banned Lachlan's father from the castle as a precaution. His father could never get near him. In those days, the MacDonalds were strong and the chieftain always well protected.

"We'll wait outside," Lachlan said when the man guarding the door stepped aside to let them in. "Tell Hugh we're here."

It went against Lachlan's instincts to be in an enclosed space with an unpredictable man he did not trust. Outside, they had a better chance of escape if things took an unexpected turn.

"Haven't seen ye for a long while," Hugh said in a surly voice when he appeared a few moments later.

"We're here now," Lachlan's father said.

"I hear Connor has gone to the gathering at Mingary Castle," Hugh said.

Lachlan grunted in the affirmative since Hugh already knew it. He had not given Hugh any information since he had made his oath to Connor. Although he had been careful to word it as a pledge of loyalty to the clan, and not to Connor personally, the difference between the two seemed a finer line all the time.

"'Twas no thanks to you that I learned my nephew went to Mingary," Hugh said, glaring at Lachlan. "You've brought me nothing."

Lachlan ignored him. Although Connor's departure would be common knowledge by now, Hugh always seemed to be aware of Connor's movements. Hugh must have someone else in the castle who fed him information, and Lachlan wondered who.

"My son is a warrior, not a gossip or a lad who runs errands for ye," his father said. "I trained him from the time he could swing a wooden sword, and now he's the best warrior in all of Trotternish. That is the reason ye want him."

"If your son is so damned good," Hugh said, "why hasn't he killed Connor yet?"

Lachlan was tempted to show Hugh just how good he was with a sword.

"It doesn't have to be Lachlan who kills him—I just want him dead," his father said. "Whether it's you or Lachlan, it must be done in such a way that no one discovers my son's role in it. I don't want him killed for taking the chieftain's life."

*If it can be helped*, Lachlan added in his head. He was not certain his father valued his life above vengeance. But that was the way in the Highlands.

"So tell us," his father said, "do ye have a new plan to kill Connor MacDonald or not?"

# CHAPTER 20

"Why are ye taking Ilysa back to Trotternish?" Moira asked, her eyes blazing.

"Because my household is in chaos without her," Connor said.

"How can ye be so inconsiderate?" Moira asked.

"Calm down," Connor said. "I've no idea why you're upset."

"Men!" Moira said, raising her hands and looking to the heavens. "I finally persuade Ilysa to get out of those ugly gowns and headdresses, and she has men following her around—half a dozen of them serious about wedding her, I might add—and my brother the chieftain decides to bury her at Trotternish Castle and ruin her chances."

"Ruin her chances for what?" Connor asked.

"For happiness!" Moira said. "That lass is so devoted to ye that she'll sacrifice everything for ye—anyone can see that."

Connor always knew Ilysa was devoted to the clan. But devoted to him?

"Ilysa enjoys keeping my household," he said. "And it will only be until I conclude negotiations for my marriage and my wife arrives."

"Don't ask this of her," Moira said, leaning forward with her hands on her hips.

Ach, MacDonald women were the most stubborn, willful women in all of the Highlands. And as for his sister, well, they had not called her Princess Moira as children for nothing.

"Does Ilysa want to marry any of these men?" he asked after taking a deep breath.

"Not yet, but she will," Moira said. "Ilysa loves children. She deserves a husband and family of her own."

*Ilysa, married?* It was hard to think of it.

"Ye seem to have forgotten that it's your duty to help a widow find a new husband," Moira said.

Moira was right about that. As chieftain, his duty to safeguard his clan was all-encompassing and included protecting them from attack, feeding them in famine, and, unfortunately, finding husbands for widows. Connor would rather fight a hundred MacLeods than matchmake. And finding the right man for Ilysa would not be easy. He would have to be a strong warrior who could protect her, but also a kind man.

"If ye let her be, Ilysa will have no trouble finding a husband on her own," Moira said, folding her arms.

"As ye just reminded me, it is my duty to make certain she weds a *good* man," he said, "*if* she wishes to marry at all."

"Ilysa deserves happiness," Moira said. "Give her a chance to find it."

* * *

Ilysa watched for Alastair MacLeod. When he did not appear in the hall for the midday meal, she decided to find him. Duncan had assigned Niall to escort her if she left the keep, but he was speaking with Lady Philippa so evading him would be easy. In fact, she worried that Niall was the one who needed guarding.

Ilysa guessed that a chieftain of the MacLeod's stature would be given a chamber inside the castle and asked a serving maid.

"The MacLeod is in the West Tower," the maid told her.

Ilysa found two enormous MacLeod warriors guarding a door on the second floor of the tower.

"I'm a healer, and I've brought a salve for your chieftain," she said and held out the jar.

The guards exchanged glances. Instead of taking the jar from her, one of them went inside. A few moments later, he returned and demanded her name.

"Ilysa."

The guard opened the door and jerked his head to the side to indicate she should enter.

"I don't need to see your chieftain," she said. "I only brought the salve."

"Go in." The guard gave her a look that said she could walk in or he could carry her.

Ilysa felt uneasy about entering the MacLeod chieftain's chamber. As soon as she crossed the threshold and saw him, however, her uneasiness vanished. His face was drawn with pain. She sat on the stool next to his chair.

"I brought that salve I promised ye."

"It won't help," he said.

"This is always a good salve." She held it up for his inspection. "But this particular batch has special healing powers."

"Lilies?" he asked after sniffing it, just as Connor had. "What makes it special?"

Ilysa hesitated to tell him, but she knew the salve would ease his pain and she wanted to persuade him to use it. "I collected the water lilies from a faery glen on a night of the full moon."

She had seen the lilies in a pond amid the odd, conical hills as she left the glen that night and had stopped long enough to cut a few and put them into her bag.

"The faery glen on Trotternish?" Alastair MacLeod asked. When she nodded, he said, "You're a brave lass. Ye weren't afraid to go there?"

"If I'd seen a faery—or a MacLeod—I might have been," she said with a smile. "'Tis a wondrous, magical place."

\* \* \*

Connor's conversation with Moira put him in a foul mood, and the prospect of the discussion he was about to have with the MacIain chieftain made it worse.

"Your chieftain is expecting me," Connor told the men guarding the door to his host's private chamber and waited while one of them went inside to announce him.

"Just the man I want to see!" The MacIain greeted Connor and slapped him on the back. The man made

Connor's skin crawl, but personal feelings had no place in this.

Connor had thought it through very carefully and concluded that an alliance with MacIain would be advantageous to his clan in every regard. In addition to MacIain's warriors, fleet of galleys, and marriage tie to the Campbells, MacIain's close relationship with the Crown would be useful. Connor hoped that, once he took possession of Trotternish, MacIain could persuade the Crown to grant him the royal charter as well.

"I thought I was to meet your granddaughter," Connor said, glancing about the room, which was devoid of females.

"And you shall." The MacIain signaled for Connor to sit at the table. "I wanted to discuss all the important matters first."

Connor had hoped to meet the lass before this went much further. Although his personal feelings did not count for much, he would be seeing this woman at his table morning, noon, and night for the rest of his life. It felt like a death sentence.

"My granddaughter doesn't take after me in looks, if that's your concern," MacIain said with a gruff laugh.

*God, I hope not.* MacIain had pockmarked skin, bulging fish eyes, and bow legs.

"She's looking forward to meeting you as well," MacIain said as he poured whiskey into the two cups on the table. "When I asked her which of our guests I should choose for her husband, she pointed at you, and said, 'I want that handsome, black-haired MacDonald chieftain.'"

Teàrlag's words rang in Connor's ears. *The lass will choose you.* Surely, this was a sign.

"Fond as I am of my granddaughter, I'd never let her decide such an important matter, of course," MacIain said. "However, her choice coincides with mine. She was born three months after my son's death and has spent far too many years in the Lowlands with her mother's clan for my liking. I want to see her wed to a strong Highlander."

Connor sipped his whiskey. The lass's Lowlander upbringing made him uneasy. "It's a hard life for a lass unaccustomed to it."

"Ach, she has the heart of a MacIain," he said, which Connor did not find reassuring.

"What do you hope to gain from this alliance," Connor asked, "other than a man who will be good to your granddaughter?" No matter MacIain's affection for his granddaughter, or pretense of it, they both knew that was secondary.

"I'll expect ye to respond to my call to arms, should I need ye at some future time," MacIain said.

Connor's pledge would require him to honor the call, no matter what the cause might be. As he had told Ilysa, this was the unavoidable cost of recovering his clan's lands and protecting his people. He hoped to hell that when MacIain called on him it was for a fight that did not turn his stomach.

He and the MacIain went back and forth on the bride's *tochar*, or dowry, and other terms until they reached agreement.

"Can I have the pleasure of meeting your granddaughter now?" Connor asked. He had made it clear earlier that he would not sign a marriage contract until he met the bride. Now that the terms were settled, however, it would be awkward to extricate himself.

"Sadly, she fell ill last night," the MacIain said. "She's a hardy lass, but I fear she'll be unable to leave her bed for a few days."

The timing of her illness was suspicious, to say the least. Connor could not remain here much longer, and MacIain damned well knew it. Was there something wrong with the lass that MacIain did not want Connor to see? Or did MacIain have some other reason for delay?

"The battle for Trotternish will come soon," Connor said, reiterating his key demand. "I must know that you will support me with your warriors and galleys."

"That is the tricky part, isn't it?" the MacIain said, folding his hands.

"What are ye saying?" Connor kept his voice even, but he was so furious he felt as if his head would explode.

"Now that the MacLeod has left the rebellion, ye won't find another chieftain here who is willing to take on the MacLeods with ye."

"Several expressed an interest in a marriage alliance." Even as he said it, Connor recalled how the other chieftains' enthusiasm seemed to wane each time he brought up the coming battle for Trotternish. Several had even suggested he should be content with the lands he had.

"Everyone can see that if ye survive your present troubles, you'll be a powerful force in the isles, the kind of chieftain anyone would want for an ally," MacIain said, spreading out his hands. "But right now, they're no willing to help ye fight the MacLeods."

And Connor was supposed to feel flattered by this?

"I am, however, in a stronger position than most to take the risk," the MacIain continued. "I'll need some time to grease the pig, so to speak, and discuss it with the Campbell chieftain, who may be upset by my attacking one of the Crown's new supporters."

Time was running out. While MacIain professed to be *greasing the pig*, Connor could not enter into serious negotiations for a marriage with another clan. He certainly could not do it while in MacIain's home. And yet, without a signed marriage contract—or a bride—there was nothing certain about his arrangement with the MacIain.

"Three weeks is all I can wait." Connor stood. "Bring your warriors and your granddaughter to Trotternish Castle before Beltane or there will be no marriage alliance between us."

# CHAPTER 21

Alastair MacLeod insisted on escorting Ilysa back to the keep himself. At the entrance to the hall, he fixed his piercing eyes on her for a long moment, then gave her a stiff nod and left her. No sooner had he gone than Ilysa felt another set of eyes burning into her. She turned to see Connor striding toward her from across the room. He looked ready to do battle.

"I didn't expect to find Alastair MacLeod among your admirers," Connor said in his hard, chieftain's voice. "Why were ye talking to our enemy?"

"He doesn't seem like such a bad man to me," Ilysa said. "Alliances change all the time. Perhaps the two of ye could settle your differences."

"The only way the MacLeods and the MacDonalds will resolve our differences is by sword and blood."

"I liked him," she said, which made Connor's eyes flare.

"He's dangerous," Connor hissed. "Stay away from him."

Ilysa refrained from saying she had no plans to visit Dunvegan Castle, the famed MacLeod stronghold, since Connor did not appear to be in the mood for a jest.

"As your chieftain, 'tis my duty to give ye another warning," he said. "Ye must be careful of some of the men you're meeting here."

"None of the clans will raise trouble at the gathering," Ilysa said.

"That's no what I mean." Connor leaned closer. "Ye don't have experience with these sorts of men."

"And what sort is that?" Ilysa asked, though she thought she knew.

"Men of power and wealth."

"Ye mean chieftains?" Ilysa kept her voice pleasant, but she was not accustomed to being lectured about her behavior, which had always been so far above reproach as to be lamentably dull. She especially did not appreciate being lectured on this particular point by Connor.

"I'll speak plainly," he said. "If ye want a man and a home to yourself, don't look to any of these chieftains or their sons."

As if she did not know this. Connor's very being reminded her of it every day.

"Your brother could rise to be keeper of a castle through his skills as a warrior," he continued, apparently assuming her silence showed a feeble lack of comprehension. "You are highborn, but for a lass to be a chieftain's wife, she must bring power and property to the marriage."

"I appreciate your explaining my unworthiness so clearly." It was on the tip of her tongue to tell him about her marriage offer, but it was wiser to keep that to herself until she decided what she wanted to do.

"I did not say ye were unworthy." Connor spoke in a measured tone, as if she were slow-witted. "But ye must be on your guard with such men, for it's not marriage they seek."

"I have been watching out for myself since I was eleven," Ilysa said, biting out the words. "You were all gone, so I did it without your help or my brother's or anyone else's."

"I can see that it's fortunate we are leaving tomorrow," Connor said.

Ilysa never got angry when she argued. She had always found it far more effective to face opposition with perfect calm, but she was failing at that now. Luckily, they were interrupted before she resorted to raising her voice.

"Pardon me," a tall, curly-haired man said as he took her arm, "but this sweet lass made a promise to sit with me at supper."

Ilysa was inordinately pleased that he was not just the son of any clan chieftain, but the son of the Earl of Huntley.

"Thank ye kindly for your advice, Connor," she said over her shoulder.

\* \* \*

"The MacLeod galleys are gone," Connor said when he met Duncan at their camp.

"Yours is loaded, and the men ready to set sail," Duncan said, anticipating that Connor would want to return to Trotternish at once.

"Unless I send word that the MacLeods have attacked earlier, come to Trotternish Castle on Beltane and be prepared to fight," Connor said.

"Hmmph," Duncan grunted in acknowledgment. Instead of looking at Connor, he folded his arms and stared out at the water.

"Bring all the warriors ye can spare and tell Ian to do the same," Connor continued. "I'll send word to Alex."

"Hmmph," Duncan grunted again.

Connor had failed to make a marriage alliance. His sister was barely speaking to him. He had made Ilysa angry, a monumental feat. And now, for the first time in his life, he felt discord between himself and Duncan, his best friend from the cradle.

"What's troubling ye?" he asked. "Come, Duncan, tell me."

"I don't like my sister living at Trotternish with ye," Duncan said, still staring out at the water.

"Why not?" Connor asked.

"People will talk."

"Talk?" Connor asked.

"They'll say she's warming your bed as well as keeping your household."

*Ilysa warming my bed.* Connor could not let himself think about that.

"Ilysa has kept my household since I became chieftain, and you've never mentioned this before," Connor said. "Besides, no one would think that Ilysa and I are..." It seemed too dangerous to say the words, but they blazed across his mind: *lovers, bedmates.*

"The men look at her differently now," Duncan said. "And they will think it."

"They wouldn't dare," Connor said. "Ilysa is your sister."

"Aye, she is." Duncan turned and met his gaze. "She

thinks the world of ye, and you're her chieftain. It would be easy for ye to take advantage of her."

"By the saints, Duncan, I've been as celibate as a monk," Connor said. "It hasn't been easy, but ye know I've held out this long because I won't risk having a babe with any woman but my wife."

"Sometimes things happen between a man and woman, despite their intentions," Duncan said, his gaze still locked on Connor's. "See that they don't with my sister."

# CHAPTER 22

Connor forgot what he was saying when Ilysa passed through the hall balancing a basket on her hip. He knew she must have passed through his hall several times a day over the past two and a half years. And yet, he had never been aware of her movements until their return from the gathering.

The problem was her new manner of dressing. Although she did not wear anything remotely inappropriate, her new gowns did not hide the feminine lines of her body. As she re-crossed the hall, Connor's gaze followed the graceful curve of her neck and the swell of her breasts. Before he could stop himself, he imagined the slender, shapely legs beneath her skirts.

When he finally tore his gaze away, he realized the men were waiting for him to continue whatever in the hell he'd been talking about. He began again but found himself straining to hear her soft voice as she spoke to one of the women.

This could not continue. He was chieftain, and the future of his clan was in his hands.

"We'll speak more of this later," he told the men. "Sorely, lead the practice, and I'll join ye shortly. Our foes do not rest, and neither must we."

Leaving them with that trite admonishment, he strode across the hall to where Ilysa appeared to be in a struggle to the death with a torch that had been rammed too forcefully into a sconce in the wall.

"I'll do it," he said, reaching for it.

When their hands touched, it was as if a lightning bolt went through him. Angry at his reaction to her, he jerked the torch out of the wall and tossed it into the hearth.

Ilysa raised her eyebrows, and he knew he'd offended her careful husbandry of the castle resources. But they belonged to him, damn it, and if he wanted to toss a torch into the fire, so be it. He had a far bigger problem to deal with here than one wasted torch.

"I must speak with ye," he said.

"I was just about—"

"Now." Connor turned, then marched across the hall and through the doorway to the other building and his private chamber. He wanted no risk of this conversation being overheard. But when he shut the door behind her, he was suddenly acutely aware that this was also his bedchamber, and that he and Ilysa were alone in it.

"What is it?" Ilysa asked with a pleasant smile and folded her hands in front of her.

With all his blood leaving his head and filling his cock, he was having trouble recalling his purpose in bringing her here. Something deep inside him made him want to break through her composure, to see if there was fire beneath all that brisk efficiency and calm control.

What was wrong with him? He reminded himself that Ilysa was a lass of undeniable virtue who trusted him blindly. If that wasn't enough—and it should be—she was his best friend's sister. Connor took a deep breath and approached her. Ach, it was a mistake to stand so close to her. The light scent of lilies filled his nose, making him long to smell it on her bare skin.

She glanced at the bed, drawing his attention to it, which was most unfortunate. *It would be so easy to get her there*. His breathing grew shallow as he imagined her naked above him, a tangle of red-gold hair falling over her breasts while he gripped her slim hips. When Ilysa shifted her gaze back to him, she looked a trifle nervous. As well she should.

"I want ye to go back to wearing your old gowns," he said, wanting to get this over with.

Ilysa stared at him wide-eyed. Finally, she said, "I don't have them anymore."

*Damn it.* "Why not?"

"Your sister and Sìleas threw them all away," she said. "Besides, everyone else likes my new gowns."

"You're lovely—I mean, the gowns are lovely," he fumbled. "But you're distracting the men dressed like that."

"Distracting the men?" Ilysa said. "I'm sorry, Connor, but that's ridiculous."

"I don't want ye coming in the hall while I'm speaking with them."

"I try to be quiet." She looked at him with huge brown eyes as innocent as fawn's. "Did I disturb ye?"

She disturbed his peace of mind.

"I can't have ye coming in and out of the hall while I'm meeting with the men until ye have something that is less...less..."—he paused to swallow—"provocative to wear."

When she drew in a deep breath in a huff, he could see the swell of her breasts pressing against the soft fabric of her bodice.

"My clothes are not provocative," she said in a prim tone.

He was being unreasonable. The problem was not her clothes but that he could not stop imagining her without them.

"I don't mean to insult ye," he said and took her hands without thinking.

They were so small in his and her fingers wondrously delicate. Her hands were like the woman herself. Their fragile appearance disguised competence and strength. He turned them over and examined her palms.

"'Tis hard to believe ye cut an arrowhead out of my chest with these," he said.

"They've done more than that to ye," she said and then inexplicably turned a violent shade of red. She tried to pull away, but he refused to let go.

"What have these hands done to me that I wouldn't know about?" he asked with a grin. Teasing her made him feel on safe ground again.

"Ye don't remember?"

Ilysa turned yet another shade of red, as only the very fair could. Now he was intrigued.

"What did ye do, ruffle my hair when ye were a bairn?" he asked.

"No."

"Ye were a perfectly behaved child, as I recall," he said, a smile tugging at the corners of his mouth. "It must have been a strain being so good all the time."

When she dropped her gaze, he realized he had hit the mark squarely and felt badly for it. He ran his thumb over her palm instinctively to soothe her, but when she drew in a sharp breath, it set his blood boiling again. He should let her go. And yet, he did not.

"You're not leaving here until ye tell me what ye meant," he said, attempting a light tone.

Ilysa glanced sideways again, and her gaze appeared to become stuck on the bed. *O shluagh!* He should quit playing these games with her and send her out quickly. He was about to do just that until her next words sent sparks shooting through his veins.

"I bathed ye."

"What?" Surely he had misheard her, yet his whole body was alive with the misunderstanding. "Ah, ye mean ye bathed my wounds."

"Not just your wounds." She spoke so softly that he had to lean forward to hear her. "I washed all of ye. Several times."

Why would she say that? Was she trying to stop his heart and kill him? "I think I would have recalled that," he said.

"After the MacKinnons left ye for dead and Ian brought ye to Teàrlag's, I tended your wounds." She paused and then added in a choked voice, "We feared we'd lose ye."

Ach, tears were suddenly spilling down her cheeks. Connor put his arms around her. He, Duncan, and Alex had been ambushed by two dozen MacKinnons and a few

MacLeods. They had killed a good many of their attackers, but all three of them had been badly injured. It was Connor they were after, and they thought they had killed him.

"Ian cut your bloody clothes off in pieces and tossed them into the hearth fire," she said. "Every inch of ye was bruised and battered. I washed and bound your wounds, then for three days I fed ye broth and sponged your body to fight the fever that wanted to take ye to the other side."

"Shh. It's all right now," Connor said into her hair as he held her.

"Sometimes ye seemed to wake," she said, "so I thought ye might remember some of it."

"I was out of my head and thought I saw an angel watching over me," Connor said. "You must be my angel."

Ilysa laughed against his chest. "Hardly that."

Heat and tension flared between them, and Connor was suddenly aware of how very dangerous it was to hold her like this. He told himself to let go of her, but his arms would not obey.

"Why do ye want me to stay out of the hall, truly?" Ilysa leaned back and looked up at him with brown eyes that could melt the heart of a sea serpent. "I've always done it, and ye never minded my coming and going before."

"I don't know why I didn't notice," he said and touched the back of his fingers to her cheek. It felt so soft that he did it again. "But every time ye enter a room now, I can see nothing else."

Tension coiled in his belly and spiraled down his limbs. It was wrong to hold her like this, wrong to even think of kissing her. He knew it, and yet he wanted to feel her lips. This once, he wanted to be reckless. To do something that was just for him. And how could he help himself when he could feel her body drawing to his?

*What harm could there be in one simple kiss?*

"Ilysa." He breathed her name as he lowered his head.

One innocent kiss, and then he would put this behind him and do his duty, as he always did. But the moment her lips, soft and trembling, touched his, fire burned in his belly.

And yet, he might have had the strength to pull away if she had not curled her fingers into his shirt and pulled him closer. Hot jolts of lust shot through him from every point her body touched his. He thrust his tongue into her mouth and was vaguely aware that he had startled her, but she did not pull away.

When she made a high-pitched sigh against his mouth, he knew it was a lost cause. He pulled her hard against him and gave her deep, hungry kisses that should have frightened her. Instead, she returned them with an urgency that matched his own.

He could never trust a woman to want him, the man, rather than the chieftain. But he trusted Ilysa utterly and completely. She knew him, with all his flaws and shortcomings. She would not be in his arms for any reason except that she wanted him.

And, by the saints, he wanted her. Without lifting his mouth from hers, he backed her up to his bed. He refused to think, refused to let his conscience catch up with him. For once, he was giving in to blind passion.

Part of him wanted her to say no, to be the sensible lass she usually was and push him away. Instead, Ilysa melted into his arms. He pressed her against the side of the bed with his body and devoured her mouth for long minutes. He only tore his mouth away from hers to run his lips and tongue along the divine curve of her throat, which he had been longing to kiss without knowing it.

But as he reached to pull back the bed curtain, guilt reared its ugly head. *This is Ilysa. Duncan's sister.* If ever there was a lass who deserved honorable treatment and his protection, it was she.

Connor unclasped her hands from around his neck. Her breathing was uneven, and her eyes held a dark passion that spoke to the erotic dreams he harbored. And yet, he forced himself to pull away. It was his duty to protect her, even from his own desire—and hers.

Confusion clouded her eyes. If Connor looked into them another moment, he would lift her onto the bed, and they would not leave it for a long, long time.

"This is wrong," he said and turned his back on her. "Forgive me."

"I don't understand," she said, and her light touch on his shoulder pulled him like an undertow.

"'Tis my fault," he said. "I beg ye, Ilysa. Go quickly."

\* \* \*

Ilysa shut her door and leaned against it.

*Connor kissed me!* Not a brotherly peck on the cheek, either. Nor a light brush on her lips. No, this was a real kiss. He wasn't pretending he wanted to do it, as her husband Mìchael had. This was a thrillingly passionate kiss.

And not just one kiss. Ilysa wanted to count them all and remember each one, but they had blended together, one into the next. Her head was still swimming. She had been surprised when Connor used his tongue. Though she was aware people did that sometimes, she had not expected to like it so very much.

She touched her fingertips to her lips. She had dreamed of this, but it had been more wonderful than she ever imagined. Truly, she could have kissed Connor all night and wanted more. When he pulled her against him, his arms felt so strong around her. She hugged herself, remembering how magical it had been. While Connor held her, she had felt as if anything was possible. Anything at all.

Still, Ilysa was no fool. She understood Connor could never be hers, not truly and not for long. That did not keep her from wanting however much of him he would give her.

Connor had not wanted to stop any more than she had. His kisses did not lie. Nor did the desire in his eyes. His sense of honor stood in her way. He had only turned away from her out of some misplaced sense of duty.

Ilysa may not have Connor for long, but she did mean to have him. Then, for the rest of her life, she would have that to remember.

* * *

As soon as Lachlan passed through the gate, he knew that Connor had returned from the gathering. The guards on the wall were more alert, and men in the courtyard were practicing with greater intensity, wanting to earn his praise. Lachlan's awareness of the men's respect for their chieftain was inescapable.

He saw Connor observing the lads who were fourteen to seventeen practicing and crossed the courtyard to stand beside him.

"I see you're back," Connor said, and he did not sound friendly.

"I've been scouting the MacLeod camps," Lachlan said. "They've brought in more warriors."

"I expected as much," Connor said and kept his gaze fixed on the young warriors. "We'll discuss it later."

Sorely, who was a decent swordsman but a poor teacher, was leading the practice.

"They're no better than when I left," Connor muttered under his breath.

"Not like that, ye fooking idiot!" Sorely shouted at an awkward lad named Robbie. Belatedly, he felt their presence and turned around.

"Lachlan and I will work with this group today," Connor said.

Sorely did not enjoy training the younger men. All the same, he resented the dismissal, judging by his sour look before he covered it. If Connor noticed, he did not show it. But then, Connor wouldn't.

"Bless ye for taking this burden from me!" Sorely said and gave a laugh that rang false.

Sorely was an arse.

"Gather 'round," Connor called out. "If I hear any more grumbling, you'll all spend the night in the dungeon with the rats."

The young men went silent.

"The MacLeods will shred ye to bits if ye don't learn to fight better than this—and soon," Connor continued. "Your lives are my responsibility, and I don't intend to see that happen. Now, ye will give me your best, or go home to your mothers."

None of them wanted that humiliation. They shuffled

their feet as Connor's steel-gray gaze moved from face to face.

"Are ye prepared to become warriors worthy of Clan MacDonald?" When they remained silent, Connor raised his claymore into the air and shouted, "Are ye?"

"Aye! Aye!" the lads shouted back.

Connor directed them to form two lines, one in front of Lachlan and the other in front of him. During the long period in which the castle was in the hands of the MacLeods, Lachlan had led practices with small groups in fields, with someone keeping watch. He had discovered he was good at training others in the skills of war, and it gave him satisfaction.

As he worked through his line, practicing with each would-be warrior in turn, he kept one eye on Connor. Again, he begrudgingly approved. Unlike Sorely, Connor never ridiculed the lads' mistakes. He was patient, but persistent. He corrected, praised, and pushed each young man to improve his skills, which could make the difference between life and death for them one day soon.

After a couple of hours, Connor raised his hand to call for a rest. Lachlan started to sheath his blade, but Connor stopped him.

"Let's give them another kind of lesson," Connor said, with a glint in his eye. "I've been dying to fight ye since the day ye arrived and knocked Sorely on his arse."

Unease settled in Lachlan's belly. Though Connor was smiling now, Lachlan was fairly confident that the chieftain would not like being knocked on his own arse in front of the men.

"Pay attention, lads!" Connor shouted and faced Lachlan in a crouch with his sword in his hands.

Sweat broke out on Lachlan's forehead as it occurred to him that if he was going to kill Connor, he should do it now. He could slide his blade between the chieftain's ribs and be done with it. He heard his father's voice in his head, saying the words he'd said to Lachlan from the time he was a bairn with a wooden sword in his hands.

*One day, you will avenge your mother and restore our honor. You must kill him. Kill him! Kill him!*

As they circled each other, Lachlan was aware of the shouts and cheers of the men gathered about them. But once Connor sprang at him with a series of powerful blows, he no longer heard the other men—or his father's voice. He had grown accustomed to being better than every man he fought, but he soon realized Connor MacDonald was his match. The practice with the others had not shown Connor's skills to their fullest. He was good. Very good.

The chieftain should be tired after hours of training, but he showed no sign of it as he slammed his sword against Lachlan's time and again. And he was enjoying himself! Lachlan had not had an opponent who truly tested his skills in a long while, and to his surprise, he began to take pleasure in the fight as well. When Connor leaped over Lachlan's blade after Lachlan was dead certain he had him, Lachlan smiled in appreciation of his opponent's quickness.

They spun and pounded each other back and forth across the courtyard. Finally, Lachlan got lucky and landed a blow with the flat of his sword against Connor's thigh. He hit him hard enough that the blow should have knocked Connor off his feet—but it didn't. Before Lachlan could recover from the force of his swing, Connor spun in a circle.

The next thing Lachlan knew he was lying on his back with Connor's foot on his chest.

"That was good," Connor said, grinning down at him. He was breathing hard and beads of sweat were rolling down his face, despite the cold, misty weather.

It was not until Connor held out his hand to help him up that Lachlan saw the blood soaking through the chieftain's shirt.

Someone shouted, "The chieftain's been hurt!"

Lachlan froze. In a practice, a man was supposed to fight hard, but never strike to kill. Had Lachlan forgotten himself in the heat of their battle? Had he given in to his father's admonition ringing in his head?

Anguish twisted in his gut as he saw that Connor was bleeding both from his chest and his upper thigh.

"I did not mean to do it," Lachlan said, barely speaking the words aloud.

"What?" Connor looked down at himself with a frown. "Ach, ye didn't do this."

Several men jerked Lachlan to his feet and held him by his arms.

"For God's sake, let him go!" Connor thundered. "This blood is from old wounds. They must have broken open in the fight."

Lachlan staggered when the men released him.

"See, there's no cut in my shirt," Connor said, holding it out, then he pulled it off and showed the men the bleeding wound in his chest.

The jagged, circular wound clearly was not made by the blade of a sword, but by an arrow, and Lachlan knew Connor had a matching wound on his thigh.

"I'm sorry," he said.

"I told ye," Connor said, gripping his shoulder and looking straight into his eyes. "Ye didn't do this."

But Lachlan had done it. And not in a fair fight, man-to-man, as Connor deserved.

# CHAPTER 23

Someone fetched Ilysa after the fight, and now Connor had to endure the torture of her hands on his bare skin.

"Why are these arrow wounds taking so damned long to heal?" Connor asked.

He gritted his teeth as Ilysa's fingers drifted down his chest in feather-light touches. This was far worse than the times she had dressed his wounds after they first arrived at Trotternish. Back then, he could convince himself that the nearness of a woman—any woman—would have stirred him. Now there was no escaping that his desire was for Ilysa alone.

He had kissed her, and that had changed everything.

"The arrows went deep, and ye keep re-opening the wounds." Ilysa clicked her tongue in disapproval. "You're not careful at all."

She leaned over him, and her red-gold braid fell over her shoulder like an invitation. Though her bodice exposed nothing, his memory of the tops of her breasts in a low-cut gown was vivid.

"I heard you and Lachlan gave quite a display." She brushed the top of his thigh with her fingertips, taking his breath away. "I hope impressing the men was worth splitting open this wound on your leg."

"Lachlan got in a good hit there with the side of his sword," Connor said in a strained voice. In an attempt to divert himself, he added, "I'm thinking of making him my captain."

Ilysa withdrew her hands, and he felt their absence like a missing tooth.

"What, ye don't agree with my choice?" Connor asked. "Lachlan is the best warrior I have, and the men respect him."

"I'm sure you're right," she said, but her tone was uncertain. "But something troubles Lachlan, and I wish I knew what it was."

Connor forgot Lachlan—and everything else—when she rested one hand on his hip while she used the other to spread her lily-scented salve over the wound high on his thigh. He held his folded shirt over his throbbing erection. When Ilysa tied the bandage, her hand was so close to his cock that sweat broke out on his forehead. He closed his eyes before she caught him looking at her like a starving animal. But as soon as he closed them, his imagination took him in dark, erotic directions.

Connor snapped his eyes open, and there she was, her lovely face just inches from his. He remembered the softness of her lips, and he hungered to taste them again. It would be so easy to encircle her tiny waist, lift her onto his lap, and ravish her mouth.

"Almost finished," she said, sounding a bit breathless.

*Is she thinking of those kisses, too?* He envied the man who would be her next husband. Ilysa had a kind heart, a soothing presence—though Connor was not finding it soothing at the moment—and a calm, competent manner.

His gaze traveled over her as she turned to retrieve another rolled strip of linen from her basket, and he wondered what she was like in bed. When Ilysa took off her clothes and gave up control, was she the kind of lover who drove a man wild?

Connor swallowed. Aye, he suspected she was.

When Ilysa leaned across him to wrap the linen around his chest, her breast grazed his arm. Though it was barely a touch, they both drew in a sharp breath. Their eyes locked, and heat flared between them hot enough to set the room ablaze.

Ilysa's lips parted, and Connor could not see or think of anything else. He gave in to the inexorable pull drawing him closer. Cupping her face, he felt her breath on his lips before he kissed her softly. Ilysa dropped the cloth she was holding and gave a sigh. That was all the encouragement he needed.

He pulled her onto his lap and kissed her with a wild, passionate abandon. Somewhere in the back of his head, the sensible, dutiful part of him was telling him this was a huge mistake. But it felt so right. Ilysa felt right. She was perfect. Extraordinary.

She spread her fingers into his hair at the back of his neck and pressed herself against him. From her sighs and moans as she returned his fevered kisses, she wanted him, too. Though she looked young, she had been married. She must know what she was doing to him and where this was leading. Still, a twinge of guilt made him hesitate and start to pull back. Ilysa sensed it and wrapped her arms more tightly around his neck.

"Please, Connor." Her voice was breathless. "Just this once."

When she pressed her lips against his neck, he shivered with the force of his desire. *Aye. Just this once.* He could not turn away, not when she was kissing him like this.

He stood, lifting her up with him. She was as light as a child, but she was all woman when she wrapped her legs around his waist. He felt the damp heat of her desire against his throbbing cock as he gripped her buttocks, and he was certain he would die if he could not have her.

"I want ye so much," he said between frantic kisses as he carried her to the bed. "I've never wanted anyone like this."

He set her on the edge of his bed and groaned when he finally cupped her breasts. They were small and high and perfect in his hands, just as he knew they would be. As he kissed her neck, she leaned back on her arms and let her head fall back. With her skirts pushed up and her legs wrapped around his waist, the thin layer of his trews was all that was between him and heaven.

His heart raced as he ran his hands under her skirts, along her silky thighs. Aye, he would have her. Right now, right here, like this. The words pounded in his head: *Now, now, now.*

And still, he made himself stop to ask her the question.

"Are ye certain ye want this?" His heart beat wildly, and his breathing was ragged as he waited for her answer.

"I do." As she slid her arms around his neck and leaned forward to kiss him, she said, "More than anything."

# CHAPTER 24

Connor tugged desperately at Ilysa's clothes, trying to touch more of her skin. He had no idea how they had gotten on the bed and didn't care. As he covered her with hot, passionate kisses, his heart beat so hard he thought it might burst from his chest.

He suspected Ilysa's young husband had been the sort who fumbled in the dark with little notion of how to please a woman. For having been married, Ilysa seemed inexperienced. Inexplicably, this was just one more thing about her that drove him wild.

Her every surprised squeak of pleasure and low moan from the back of her throat sent him reeling. She had a natural passion that left him breathless. He felt the self-control that always seemed such a part of her crack, and he could not wait for it to shatter beneath his hands. He wanted to hear her moans and watch her face when she came in his arms.

Her skin was soft as silk. He wanted to taste every inch

of it and to make love to her slowly in a dozen ways. But not now. Not this first time, when he needed her so badly. He would take her fast and hard, pounding into her until she screamed her pleasure and he exploded.

When he touched her center, her body jerked, but she was hot and wet for him. She tossed her head and writhed against him, exciting him so much that he feared he would come against her side like an overexcited fifteen-year-old.

He rolled on top of her, and she felt glorious beneath him. Though he kept his weight on his elbows, she was so slight that he feared he would crush her with the violence of his desire.

"'Tis been such a long time since I had a woman," he said, looking into her eyes. "I can't wait much longer."

"I've waited forever for you," she whispered.

Connor didn't know what she meant by those words, but she was pulling on his hips. His body understood that and was screaming for release.

His shaft found her opening with an unerring sense of direction. He squeezed his eyes shut as he forced himself to slide just the tip in. *O shluagh*, she was so tight. He tried to go slowly, but she felt so good that she was going to kill him. Then she lifted her hips again and destroyed his last shred of control. His ears rang from the surge of pleasure as he thrust deep inside her.

"Ouch!"

That was the last thing he expected to hear. Through the pulsing need that shook him to his core, the realization broke through that he had felt something give way inside her. A tear.

*Oh, Jesu, no, she's a virgin!* The words blazed through

his head, but it was too late. He was already deep inside her.

He tried to make himself pull out, but Ilysa held on to him as if he were saving her from drowning. Need thrummed through him, straining his control like a rope taut to breaking. Her legs tightened around him, urging him on. Then all he knew was the sensation of her tight, wet heat around him and her soft gasps in his ear as he pumped into her again and again. He exploded in a violent burst of unbearable rapture that left him stunned.

As soon as he could gather himself, he rolled off her and covered his eyes with his arm.

"Dear God. What have I done?"

Guilt crashed down on him. He had violated every rule he had made for himself. The one about not risking having a child outside of his marriage was the least of them. Even before he was chieftain, he never took innocent virgins to bed.

And worse, this virgin was his best friend's sister. Duncan's last words to him burned in his ears: *See that it doesn't happen with my sister.* Loyalty mattered more to him than anything, and he had violated his friend's trust. He had violated Ilysa's trust, too. She was his responsibility.

As chieftain, he had blatant offers all the time from women who wanted the status of being the chieftain's lover, or better yet, of having his child. For two and a half *long* years, he had resisted every attempt to seduce him, only to fall to the subtle charms of an innocent lass.

A coldness gripped his heart as he realized he had not pulled out before spilling his seed. It had not even crossed his mind. But then, his mind had played no part in this at all.

"Why did ye not tell me ye were a virgin?" he asked. "I would not have done this if I'd known."

"That's why I didn't tell ye," Ilysa said in a soft voice.

He should be furious with her. Instead, he was just confused. And beneath the confusion, he was foolishly pleased that she had chosen him to be her first lover. What an idiot he was.

Why had she wanted him to take her virginity? Did she hope to bear a chieftain's child? Was she simply curious? Was it because she trusted him, as he trusted her? Or did she fancy herself in love with him? He groaned. God help him, that would make what he'd done even worse.

"You were married," he said. "How could ye be untouched?"

Ach, no, he'd made her cry. Could he do nothing right? He pulled her into his arms and kissed her hair.

"I didn't think ye would regret it so soon," Ilysa said in an unnaturally high voice.

"I should regret it."

Ilysa leaned her head back to look at him with her big, brown eyes. "Why?"

"Because I cannot wed you," he said, brushing back a strand of hair that had come loose from her braid. "You're the last woman in the clan I should have bedded."

"I know ye can't marry me," she said.

Connor sat up straight, suddenly remembering the guards outside his door. How long had he and Ilysa been in here?

"We must get ye out of here before anyone suspects," he said as he leaped from the bed.

It was too late to save her virginity, but he could protect her from having everyone in the castle talking behind their hands about her sleeping with the chieftain. Duncan was right. Though she had been alone with him in his chamber many times before, men looked at her differently now. Connor should not even have closed the door.

After throwing on his clothes, he put his arm around Ilysa's shoulders to help her from the bed. Another wave of guilt swamped him when he saw the swath of blood marring the perfect whiteness of her thigh.

"Wait here," he said and brought her a wet cloth.

After she wiped off the blood, he lifted her to the floor and helped her straighten her gown. Again, Connor wondered how much time had passed and if the guards had heard anything that would make them suspect what had happened.

*What had happened here?* He wished he knew. She had not answered his question about how she could still be a virgin or why she had deliberately not told him, but now was not the time to press her.

When he put his arm around her and started toward the door, Ilysa's legs wobbled. Connor swallowed, remembering how hard he had thrust into her.

"I'm so sorry, Ilysa," he said.

She stared straight ahead, her expression fixed, and he knew she was trying not to weep.

Her first time should have been gentle and loving. God help him, in his rush to have her, he hadn't even taken off her clothes. Of all that he had done wrong, taking her like that was his biggest regret.

* * *

As soon as Ilysa barred her door, she leaned against it and sank to the floor. If only Connor had not ruined it all by regretting it as soon as it was over. She covered her face. For a short time, Connor had wanted her with a fevered passion that was far beyond anything she had imagined or hoped for.

And she had imagined it countless times and hoped for it every single day since he returned from France.

Yet she had never guessed how amazing it would be. When he pulled her into his arms, she felt overwhelmed at first—by the sheer size of him, the press of his hard-muscled chest, and the force of his desire. But when he lost himself, kissing her as if he would die if he could not have her, it was the most wonderful thing that had ever happened to her. Everywhere he touched her, he set off magical sparks. Her skin still tingled, and she ached inside with her need for him.

She had known he might be disappointed, or even angry, afterward, but she hadn't cared. It hurt when he took her virginity, but she hadn't care about that, either.

Their joining engendered such an intense feeling of oneness that she could have wept for joy. When he tried to break away at once, she simply could not bear it. She locked her legs around him and dug her fingers into his arms, refusing to let him go. She had been right to fear that once she released him, she might never hold him again.

When Connor began moving inside her again, she felt sore. At the same time, unexpected sensations spread through her like rings from a rock thrown in a pond. In those precious moments while they were joined, Connor was utterly and completely hers. His burdens were forgotten, the needs of the clan set aside, and there was nothing but the two of them. Her heart soared as he cried out and they were one in a glorious passion.

And then Connor rolled off her. *Dear God, what have I done?*

How could he say that after the extraordinary thing that had just occurred between them? Perhaps it was only extraordinary to her. Or was making love always like that for him? The question flitted across her mind, but she could not let herself think of Connor with anyone else.

Ilysa did not know how she could bear to face him tomorrow and see the regret in his eyes. Who knew where he got his sense of honor? Not from his parents. Regardless, it ran deep, and he had gone against it.

As for Ilysa, she loved Connor—with every breath and every heartbeat. Nothing could ever persuade her that what she had done was wrong.

* * *

Lachlan had left the castle immediately after the practice with Connor and was at his sister's before nightfall. Flora's busy household was overflowing with children, and he was surrounded as soon as he crossed the threshold. After pulling pigtails and tossing his nephews and nieces into the air, Lachlan waded through the chaos to his sister.

"Sorry I haven't been to visit in so long," he said as he kissed her cheek.

"So long as you've been fighting MacLeods, I'll forgive ye," she said with a smile and went back to stirring the pot that hung over the hearth. "Truly, I'm proud of ye."

That was both the reason he had avoided seeing her for weeks and the reason he had needed to come tonight.

"How's my favorite lass?" he said as picked up wee Brigid, the youngest of the large brood.

"Alive, thanks to our chieftain," his sister said. "Ach, that man's a saint."

"The chieftain?" Lachlan asked. "Why do ye say that?"

Flora waved him into a chair at the table, and he sat with Brigid on his lap.

"He came to a meeting here at the house," Flora said. "The MacLeods somehow found out he was here, and we all had to flee for our lives."

Lachlan's chest felt tight at the thought of his sister and her children in such danger. Flora proceeded to tell him how Connor had rescued Brigid, carried her to safety, and then diverted MacLeod warriors from where the family hid on the hillside. So this was where the attack had been the night before he first met Connor. In his mind's eye, he saw the chieftain limping across the field to the castle.

Lachlan leaned his elbow on the table and covered his eyes. Christ above. The man he had tried to kill had saved them.

"The chieftain should have run with the others rather than risk being caught for our sakes," Flora said. "He killed five MacLeod warriors who surely would have found us."

"Have ye told Father this?" Lachlan asked, though he doubted even saving Flora and the children would absolve the chieftain's family in his father's accounting. At least their father had not burdened Flora with their blood debt of honor, if only because she was born female.

"No, I haven't seen Father," Flora said and tossed some herbs into the pot she was stirring. "Malcom doesn't like me to go far from the house these days with the MacLeods and pirates about."

"Malcom is right," Lachlan said. "It would be better still if you and the children moved into the castle."

"I won't leave my home to the thieving MacLeods," Flora said, putting her free hand on her ample hip. Ever the vigilant mother, she shifted her gaze from Lachlan and called out, "Leave your brother alone, or I'll smack ye."

Lachlan sighed, knowing there was no use in trying to persuade her to leave. It was this very MacDonald stubbornness that would drive the MacLeods off their lands in the end.

"I hope Father isn't the reason you've put off marrying," his sister said, demonstrating once again that she could yell at her children and cook without losing her train of thought.

Lachlan loved her to death, but he was grateful that his older sister had so many children to order about. When they were growing up, she'd only had him.

"Just look at ye with my wee Brigid," Flora said, her eyes going all soft. "Ye need to find a lass who will be good to you and give ye bairns of your own."

"With the MacLeods breathing down our necks, this is no time to think of taking a wife and starting a family," Lachlan said, and wondered if the day would ever come when he could.

"Our new chieftain gives me great hope for our clan," Flora said. "May God watch over him."

How could Lachlan satisfy his father's right to vengeance and also protect his clan? When he started this, he believed that one chieftain would serve as well as another. But since then, he had taken both Hugh's and Connor's measure. He had suggested his sister go to Trotternish Castle, knowing Connor would fight to the death to defend the castle and everyone in it. If Hugh Dubh held the castle, Lachlan would not want his sister anywhere near it.

He looked down at his curly-headed niece who had fallen asleep in his lap with her thumb in her mouth. Hugh would never risk his life for wee Brigid.

In the end, that made all the difference to Lachlan. He would give up his father's battle over the past. From this moment forward, he would fight only for his clan's future, and he would do it at Connor's side.

# CHAPTER 25

Connor waited for Ilysa to come to supper, letting the food grow cold before he took up his eating knife to signal the start of the meal. Though his appetite had left him, he forced himself to eat. Nor did he permit himself to glance at her empty chair again, though he was aware of it every moment.

He maintained a pretense of calm and spoke with his men throughout the meal and afterward as well. When he could leave the hall without his departure seeming abrupt, he went up to his chamber.

"Unless we have guests, I will no longer require guards outside my door," he told the two warriors waiting there. "Tell the others."

Having guards outside his chamber was a symbol of chieftainship that now seemed far less important than his privacy. His sword and the bar on his door was all the protection he needed.

He sat in his chair, drumming his fingers and staring at the glowing logs of peat on the brazier. As he waited for the night to come, he tried to plan his strategy for the battle with the MacLeods, but his mind kept returning to Ilysa.

Again and again, he went over what happened in this chamber a few hours earlier. The signs of her innocence had been there, but he had wanted her so badly that he had seen what he wanted to see. She had been willing, but willing to do what? She had done little more than kiss him back, and he had reacted by tossing her skirts up and ravishing her.

Lust had made him deaf, dumb, and blind. For the first time, he understood how his father could disregard the consequences and let himself be ruled by lust. But his father believed he had a right to indulge in his desire, no matter how selfish, and he never felt guilty for it.

Connor was awash in guilt.

Time and again, he saw the swath of blood against the whiteness of Ilysa's slender thigh. Then he recalled how her legs wobbled as he rushed her out the door. Though he had been trying to protect her, that was no way to leave her. He could not make things right. Still, he needed to talk to her and see how she fared.

Finally, the household was asleep, and he could go to her chamber without the entire castle knowing it. A short time later, he rapped his knuckles lightly on her door.

"Who is it?" Ilysa's voice came through the door.

"Connor." He wondered if his name would gain him entry. After a pause, he heard the bar slide back.

He stepped inside quickly—and his breath caught when he saw her behind the door. Her skin and hair glowed in the golden light of the flickering candle in her hand. Though there was nothing revealing about her long white nightshift, it had the power of the forbidden to turn his thoughts in untoward directions. His breathing grew shallow as his gaze traveled down its length to her beguiling bare toes poking out from the bottom.

Connor finally remembered to shut the door. "We must talk."

She gestured toward the lone bench and, after setting her candlestick on the small table next to it, sat down on one end. Ilysa looked so small and fragile that he felt huge sitting next to her. While he usually admired her capacity for silence, he wished she would say something now.

"I was concerned when ye did not come to the hall all day," he said. "Are ye all right?"

She nodded without meeting his gaze. Clearly, she was not all right.

"I am sorry I..." There were so many things to be sorry for that Connor did not know where to start, and so he said the last thing he should have said aloud. "I'm sorry I couldn't hold ye after."

It turned out, however, to be the right thing.

Ilysa raised her gaze and gave him a faint smile. "That would have been nice."

When he gingerly put his arm around her, she leaned her head against his shoulder and gave a shuddering sigh. He held her gently, and neither of them spoke for a long time.

"I've never bedded a virgin before," he said at last. "Did I hurt ye badly?"

"No."

He didn't believe her. "I would have been gentler if I'd known," he said, though he would not have done it at all. "You were married. I don't understand how ye could be untouched."

"Michael was killed at the Battle of Flodden a short time after we wed."

"Precisely how long were ye wed?" Connor asked, leaning back so he could see her face.

Ilysa paused and licked her lips. "Three months."

"Three months?" Connor lifted her chin. "How could a man be wed to ye for even a day and not bed ye?"

Ilysa's bottom lip trembled.

"What happened?" Connor brushed a loose red-gold strand back from her pixie face and resisted kissing her forehead.

"My husband didn't want me in that way," Ilysa said, blinking hard.

"Ye can't be serious."

"It wasn't his fault," she said. "I'm not pretty like Moira and Sìleas."

"Ach, you're as lovely as a woodland sprite."

"Ye don't have to tell me lies," Ilysa said, attempting a smile, "though I confess I like it."

"I don't know how your husband could resist ye once he had ye na—" Connor clamped his mouth shut, but it was too late to stop him from imagining her naked. Desire hit him hard. *Damn*, why had he not paused to take her clothes off today?

He reminded himself that he was here to comfort her— and to get some answers—but it was difficult to concentrate when he could feel the warmth of her skin through the nightshift. He was far too aware that she wore nothing beneath it.

"Mìchael did try sometimes," Ilysa said in a small voice. "But he couldn't, and that was worse."

"Did he like men?" Connor asked, as that seemed the only possible explanation. When her eyes went wide, he asked, "Ye do know that some men are like that?"

She shook her head.

Connor was not surprised. He had met men among the nobility in France who did not hide their interest in other men, but a Highland warrior with any sense of self-preservation would keep it secret. After Connor explained his suspicions about her husband, Ilysa was thoughtful for a long moment.

"Mìchael did have a friend, another warrior, that he was especially close to," she said. "But then, you're close to my brother and your cousins."

"Not like that!" Connor took a deep breath. Ilysa should have had a husband who could share her passion—a passion Connor must stop dwelling on. "I suspect he wanted a wife so no one would guess his secret. You were the perfect choice because you'd never gossip with the other women about what happened—or didn't—in bed."

"That much is true," she said, her face going pink. "As a healer, I'm often told women's complaints about their husbands, but I never told a soul."

"I can see why he wed you, but why did you wed him?" he asked.

"My mother was dying, and she wished it," Ilysa said. "She told me Mìchael would be a good husband because he would not be demanding."

Ach, Anna must have known.

"Duncan was gone, and I had no one else." She shrugged her slender shoulder. "I suppose I was feeling a bit lost, and Michael was a fine man."

Anna had been a kindhearted but excessively fearful woman. The "undemanding" husband, oversize clothes, and severe headdresses must have been her way, misguided though it was, of protecting her daughter. She had succeeded in hiding her daughter in plain sight.

"I don't know how I missed seeing how pretty ye are, even covered up as ye were," he said.

Without thinking, he brushed the back of his fingers against Ilysa's cheek. He was unprepared for the jagged bolt of lust that tore through him, making him want her so badly that his hand shook. In his mind, he was already carrying her to the bed and stripping off her nightgown. This time, he would savor every inch of her and make it last. He would rein in this tumultuous need until she was gasping his name and...

"It will never happen again," he said and got abruptly to his feet. Cool air hit his chest where she had been leaning against him. His arms felt empty. "I just needed to know that ye were all right."

When Ilysa looked up at him, he saw a dangerous longing in her eyes and knew she would let him stay. Temptation dug its talons into him. One word, one touch, and she could be his.

"Ye mean a great deal to me," he said. "I don't want to hurt ye."

He made himself go to the door. As he closed it behind him, Connor was certain he was doing the right thing for her. And yet, it did not feel right—and he had never regretted anything more.

* * *

It had been two nights since Connor had come to her chamber. Though Ilysa knew he would not come again, she lay awake listening for his knock. She finally gave up on sleep, wrapped a plaid around her shoulders, and went to her window to stare out into the night.

Her attention was caught by a movement in the courtyard. It was probably just one of the men assigned night guard duty, but the way the man skirted the edge of the courtyard as if he did not want to be seen, looked suspicious. When the moonlight caught his fair hair, she knew who it was.

Where was Lachlan going this time of night? He was always disappearing. This time, she intended to find out why.

She ran down the stairs and crossed the hall on quiet feet amid the snoring men. After slipping through the outer door, she stood at the top of the steps of the keep searching the dark for him. He was skulking next to the wall, halfway to the gate. Holding her nightshift up with one hand and her plaid around her shoulders with the other, she raced across the courtyard.

Just as she caught up to him, he spun around.

"By the saints, Ilysa!" Lachlan said in a harsh whisper and put his dirk away. "Ye don't sneak up on a warrior in the dark. What in the hell are ye doing out here?"

"You're the one sneaking about," Ilysa whispered back. "Where are ye going?"

"Nowhere," he said, leaning close and keeping his voice low. "I just came in, not that it's any of your business."

"Then where have ye been?" she asked. "If ye won't tell me, perhaps you'll be willing to tell the chieftain."

She could feel Lachlan's eyes boring holes into her through the darkness as the silence stretched between them.

"If ye can keep a secret," he said at last, "I have a confession to make."

"So long as it doesn't endanger anyone else, I'll keep your secret," she promised. "I've been waiting for ye to tell me what it is from the first day."

Lachlan glanced about, she assumed to make sure that none of the guards on the wall was close enough to overhear.

"You were right about Connor," Lachlan said. "He is a man worth serving."

Ilysa's shoulders relaxed. All along she had felt that Lachlan was good at his core and hoped his attitude toward Connor would change. But since he had not said anything yet that could be deemed a confession, she waited for the rest.

"You were right about me, too," he said. "I was a threat to him."

She touched his arm. "What have ye done, Lachlan?"

"'Tis best ye don't know," he said. "But ye can trust me to mind Connor's back from now on."

She believed him. "I'm glad."

"There is someone in the castle ye can't trust, someone who is spying for Hugh Dubh," he said. "I'm trying to find out who it is."

\* \* \*

Connor awoke in a sweat with a throbbing erection. Ilysa haunted his dreams, robbing him of his sleep and peace of mind. Despite his efforts to overcome his desire for her, he wanted to touch every inch of her bare skin, to see her naked above him, and to feel the friction of her breasts against his chest. Most of all, he longed to be inside her and hear her soft moans of pleasure in his ear.

He gave up on sleep and went to his window. From habit, he looked for the outline of the guards on the wall to be sure none were asleep. They weren't. Before turning away, he glanced around the courtyard. He started when he saw Ilysa in the far corner with a man. What was she doing outside in the middle of the night?

*And who in the hell is she with?*

In the moonlight, he could not be absolutely certain who the man was. He was tall, broad-shouldered, and fair-haired. The only man who came to mind was Lachlan of Lealt.

Jealousy, like an ugly green sea monster from the deep, sank its teeth into him and pulled him under. *What is she doing with Lachlan?* The question blazed in his head. No woman had ever aroused jealousy in him before, but the feeling was as unmistakable as it was unfamiliar.

Connor had no right to object if Ilysa turned her attentions to another man. Bedding her once had been a mistake that could never happen again. She was not his *and could not be*. More, it was his duty to find a man to look after her. Lachlan would make a good husband, if a lass did not require much conversation. He had both the courage and the fighting skills to protect a wife and family. In truth, Connor could think of no better choice for Ilysa than Lachlan of Lealt.

And yet, the thought of Lachlan touching her sent murder roiling through his veins.

# CHAPTER 26

Connor was standing by the hearth after breakfast when the doors to the hall swung open. Silence fell over the room as a gray-haired man in shabby clothing entered carrying a young woman in his arms. As Connor watched her long hair and limp limbs sway with the man's steps, the memory of his mother being carried up the beach at Dunscaith slammed into his chest.

He knew at once that the lass was dead.

The people who had been milling about a moment before moved aside to let the gray-haired man pass as he crossed the room with his burden to stand before Connor. Rage rolled through Connor as he took in the cuts and bruises on the dead lass's face and arms and the ugly finger marks around her neck. She was young, sixteen at most.

"My daughter," the man said in a ragged voice. "She was to be wed in a week."

Warriors died in battle. Connor felt sorrow for every

man he lost, but it was an honorable death in the service of the clan, and he accepted it. He could not, however, accept this travesty as part of warfare, though it often was. The violation and murder of an innocent, young lass was unforgivable and merited the strongest possible retribution. He wanted to take his claymore and kill every last MacLeod warrior himself.

"My wife lives, but they raped her as well," the man said, his eyes deep wells of sorrow. "They tied me and made me watch what they did."

Connor's ears rang with the white-hot fury pulsing through him.

"I promise you," he said, clenching his fists. "The MacLeods will pay for this."

The silence in the room echoed like an accusation in Connor's head. Protecting his clan was his duty, and he had failed this man and his family. All he could give them now was revenge. But he would give them that.

"The devils who did this to her," the man said, fighting for control as he looked at his daughter draped in his arms, "were not MacLeods."

"Not MacLeods?" Connor said, stunned. What other clan would have committed this egregious offense against his people. "Who then?"

"They were Hugh Dubh's men."

\* \* \*

Lachlan watched Connor as the old man told him how Hugh's men had gone on a rampage along the east coast of Trotternish, raiding and killing MacDonald farmers who, up until now, had withstood the pressure from the MacLeods to abandon their homes and fields. Connor's face was an expressionless mask, but his rage showed in his clenched jaw and the fire in his eyes.

"Do ye know where Hugh Dubh's men are now?" Connor asked the dead lass's father in a surprisingly gentle voice. "They must have a camp somewhere."

Lachlan was disappointed when the father shook his head. That meant he would have to tell Connor about Hugh's camp himself, which could raise questions he did not wish to answer.

Ilysa appeared at the father's side like the angel she was. With quiet murmurs, she persuaded him to lay his daughter's body on one of the long tables that were still set up from breakfast.

"Warriors, be ready," Connor's voice boomed out in the hall. "We leave within the hour to track down Hugh and his men."

Lachlan followed Connor into the adjoining building and caught up with him on the stairs to his chamber.

"Can I have a word?" Lachlan asked, grabbing his arm.

When Connor turned around, he had battle rage in his eyes. If Hugh could see him now, he would think twice about challenging him. Connor did not answer, but neither did he object when Lachlan followed him into his chamber and closed the door.

"This is a trick meant to trap you," Lachlan said. "Can't ye see it? Hugh's men made certain this poor father knew who they were, and then they let him go. They did that for a purpose."

Connor was glaring at him, but he was listening.

"Hugh can't touch ye while you're inside the castle. He's done this to lure ye out into the open, to a place of his choosing," Lachlan said. "Hugh knows this will make ye come, and he'll be lying in wait for ye."

"Hugh will continue killing and raping until I stop him," Connor said, as he shoved a dirk into the side of his boot. "I cannot sit in this castle while he does this to our people."

A surge of anger swelled in Lachlan's chest at Hugh. How could he have let himself be used by that filth of a man, who attacked his own people?

"Leave Hugh for another day and fight the MacLeods," Lachlan said, though he wanted to punish Hugh as much as Connor did. "More of them are crossing the Snizort River each day."

"We don't have the forces to fight the MacLeods yet. We must hold off that battle until Beltane, when my cousins and Duncan arrive with the rest of our warriors." Connor paused, his face grim. "Pray we have a new ally to come to our aid as well, because we'll need one."

"I don't suppose you're willing to wait for the others to arrive before going after Hugh," Lachlan said, though he knew that after seeing the old man and his dead daughter Connor would not delay. The problem was that Hugh also knew it.

"Unlike with the MacLeods, all I must do to disperse Hugh's pirates is find my slippery uncle and kill him," Connor said. "That's more a matter of luck than strength."

They both knew it would require more than luck. Hugh's men were foul, but they were good fighters.

"This business between you and Hugh is personal," Lachlan said, trying a different tack. "Don't give him what he wants. Send some of us to fight him, while you stay here and hold the castle."

"It is personal," Connor said, pausing in his preparations to fix his steely gaze on Lachlan. "That's exactly why I must be the one to go after him."

If Lachlan had been able to persuade Connor to let him lead the attack, he could have pretended to stumble upon Hugh's lair by chance. Now he had to tell Connor where it was without giving away how he came by the information.

"When I was out among our people this time, I heard that Hugh had taken over the old house next to the creek at the south end of Staffin Bay," Lachlan said, feeling uneasy about giving him a half-truth. "That's a short distance from where the attack occurred, so I suspect he's still camped there."

"We'll look for the house, but if you've heard of it, most likely Hugh has already left it," Connor said. "My uncle is famous for slipping away into the mist."

"I'll see that the men and galleys are ready," Lachlan said, intending to make certain he was in Connor's boat. "How many of us do ye want to take with ye?"

"One galley, twenty men," Connor said as he strapped on his claymore. "Both you and Sorely are staying here."

"But—"

"I can't leave the castle vulnerable to an attack by the MacLeods," Connor said, cutting him off. "I need ye here."

"Take care then," Lachlan said as they gripped forearms in a warrior's farewell. "Watch for an ambush."

"Always," Connor said breaking into an unexpected grin. "Haven't ye heard? I'm a hard man to kill."

* * *

Connor stood at the bow, peering through the dense night fog that lay over the water. They were nearing Staffin Bay. If Lachlan was right, Hugh had his camp here, and he would have men watching. Though Connor could not see it, the long, low offshore island that sheltered the bay lay just ahead. The narrow inside passage was a perfect place to trap a passing boat, and Hugh knew Connor was coming. If he were Hugh, he would post a lookout on the island.

The fog was too thick for the men to see a hand signal and maintaining absolute silence was essential now, so Connor crossed the length of the galley, moving between the men working the oars, to speak to the man at the rudder.

"Steer us to the outer side of the small island," he said close to the man's ear. "Bring the boat to shore there."

Connor's cousin Alex had a sixth sense on the water and could navigate blind, but the man steering tonight was familiar with this part of Trotternish and did well enough. Soon Connor heard the lap of waves hitting the beach, and the shoreline emerged to his right. As they glided into the shallows, Connor moved between the men again and tapped the shoulders of the two he wanted to go ashore with him.

The small island was barren of trees, which meant sound would travel over it almost as well as across the water. Before they left the boat, he whispered instructions to the two going with him. They would not speak again.

The cold, damp air felt heavy in his lungs as they ran the short distance across the width of the island, keeping close enough to see each other. When the ground sloped downward toward the opposite shore, they slowed their steps. Connor strained his ears for the sound of voices or the crackle of a campfire.

Nothing. Damn.

When they reached the shore, he stood still for a long moment, listening hard. He thought he heard a voice across the bay, but none closer. Stopping on the island had been a waste of time. Hugh must have moved his camp or set a different trap for him.

*But wait. What was that?* Connor heard something— probably just a deer—move up the shoreline to his right. Signaling to his partners to follow, he veered inland until he was behind whatever had made the noise. The fog was so thick that he almost fell over Hugh's lookouts before one of them spoke.

"Hugh's nephew won't come tonight in this fog, will he?" the voice said.

Connor made out three men sitting in the beach grass just above the shore, facing the bay.

"Hugh was certain nothing would stop his nephew from coming once that old farmer told him what we did," another of the lookouts said. "The farm is just south of here. If that's where Connor's going, he'll pass through here."

Connor narrowed his eyes, trying to see better. One of the men had his hand on a taut rope that was tied to a rock beside him. The other end of the rope stretched out to sea, a clever method, which he suspected Hugh had devised, for extending their vision on a foggy night. By running a rope from the offshore island to a boat midway across the bay, and probably a second rope from the boat to lookouts on the shore of the bay, Hugh's men would be alerted to a passing galley that would otherwise be hidden in the fog.

Connor considered taking one of the lookouts prisoner to question him, but it was better to keep this simple. The risk of someone calling out was too great.

"Weren't you the lucky one, getting the daughter first," one of the men said, keeping his voice low. "The lass was hardly worth the trouble by the time I had my turn."

"But the mother still had some life in her," the third said, and they all laughed quietly.

On his signal, Connor and his partners slit the lookouts' throats soundlessly. He regretted he had neither the time nor patience to give them a slower, more painful death.

Now that he had discovered Hugh's trap, he could avoid it. After returning to the galley, they continued along the outer shore of the island, rounded its southern tip, and entered the bay from the south, the opposite end from which they were expected. The creek Lachlan described was nearby, and they came upon it quickly.

The fortuitous timing of Lachlan's discovery of the location of Hugh's lair raised questions in Connor's mind, though his information appeared to be correct. He was not completely certain of Lachlan's loyalty to him. And yet he did trust the big, fair-haired warrior to protect his fellow clansmen in the castle—and Ilysa, in particular—in Connor's absence. It had not been easy to leave Lachlan with her. Her safety, however, was far more important than his own petty jealousy.

The fog thinned as Connor and his men followed the creek up the hill, but the night was still dark. When he reached the top of the rise, he saw windows lit by the glow of a lamp or hearth fire. Gradually, he made out the dark shape of a long, one-story building.

His heart beat fast. At long last, he had found his uncle. Hugh had not yet abandoned the house. Connor had been this close before, however, only to have Hugh escape. He was a slippery devil who could be counted on to save his own skin first. This time, Connor was determined to catch him before he slithered away into the black night.

Connor stationed men at every window and positioned himself with the rest at the door. Two men held a log, waiting for Connor's signal to break it down. Connor's muscles were taut with tension. Every sound in the night seemed unnaturally loud to his heightened senses.

That was what finally alerted him that something was wrong. The house was far too quiet.

"Run!" he shouted. "It's a trap!"

An instant later, Hugh's men poured out of the woods behind the house.

* * *

Ilysa was in the kitchen talking with Cook late at night when she felt a coldness pass over her.

"Ye look like someone walked over your grave," Cook said and rested his hand on her shoulder.

"Connor is in danger," she said.

"Of course he is." Cook shoved a cup of wine in front of her. "Our brave chieftain is in danger every time he sets foot out of the castle—and I expect he's in danger here as well, if your suspicion about a traitor inside the castle is true."

Knowing there was a general risk of danger to Connor was different from this certainty in her gut that someone was trying to kill him right now. Ilysa gulped down the wine.

She had said prayers and protective chants for Connor and the other men under her breath all day as she went about her work. If there was a full moon tonight, she would have braved going to the faery glen.

"Tell me who ye think our traitor is," Cook said, "and I'll poison his bowl of stew."

"I'd only be guessing," she said.

"An ounce of prevention is worth a pound of cure," Cook said.

"No poisoning," Ilysa scolded, though she did not believe he was serious—at least, she did not think he was. She kissed his cheek. "'Tis late. I'm going to bed."

Before going to her own bedchamber, Ilysa decided to visit Connor's. She felt his presence most there, and, perhaps it was silly, but it reassured her to touch his things. She slipped through the doorway from the hall into the adjoining building. When she reached Connor's door, she nearly collided with someone coming out.

"Sorely, what are you doing here?" she asked.

"I might ask you the same," Sorely said, and she did not like the way he looked her up and down.

He was a crude man, but then, most of the former chieftain's guards were. She suddenly remembered the servants in the kitchen talking about how the tough old warrior was afraid of the nursemaid's ghost.

"Ye came up here to see the ghost, didn't ye?" she asked.

"Some of the men dared me," he said with a swagger.

If he'd come on a dare, the other men would be watching, not snoring in the hall. So why had he come up here? Perhaps he was aware that he'd been the subject of ridicule and wanted to overcome his fear in private.

"I didn't see anything," he said. After a hesitation, he asked, "Have you seen her?"

"I saw the ghosts of two women here." Ilysa said it to throw him off balance and hurry him along, though it was true.

Sorely's eyes went wide, and he turned to look over his shoulder into the room.

"I don't expect they'll come after ye." She paused. "Unless they have good cause."

"Ye hide a nasty sense of humor behind that innocent face," Sorely snarled, but he left her quickly, which had been her aim.

Ilysa had come hoping to find solace in Connor's chamber. The moment she crossed the threshold, however, she felt engulfed in sadness. Had she inadvertently summoned the despair of the two women, or did it have to do with Connor?

The Sight was fickle and told her nothing.

* * *

Dawn broke over the sea and shone on the haggard faces of the rowers. By a miracle, Connor had only lost two of his warriors in the fight against Hugh's pirates, and all the survivors had made it to the boat. Another six were injured, though none badly enough to force him to return to the castle.

Connor gave the order to continue south. Before long, burned-out cottages dotted the coastline. They stopped at each one, looking for survivors and offering what help they could. By the time they reached the end of Hugh's path of destruction and turned around, Connor was so weary and heartsick he could hardly hold his head up.

He had seen too many burned cottages, heard too many tales of murder and rape.

# CHAPTER 27

Ilysa's heart lifted when she saw Connor at the head of the line of men climbing the steps hewn into the side of the cliff from the beach.

"Praise God, he is alive and well!" she said and turned to smile at Lachlan, who had come with her to the gate to meet the returning warriors.

"Two of the men are missing," Lachlan said, "but that's better than I feared."

Connor walked through the gate, his gaze straight ahead, as if in a daze. He ignored all the people who ran up to him asking questions.

"See to the injured," he said, the only sign that he saw Ilysa as he passed her.

Her stomach tightened. Whatever had happened must have been bad indeed.

Lachlan helped her herd the injured into the hall. As she checked wounds and applied fresh bandages, she

heard snatches of conversation about the confrontation
with Hugh's men.

*We were surrounded…The chieftain must have killed
half a dozen himself…No, it was eight, I'm sure…I was
injured and wouldn't have made it to the boat, but he carried me across his shoulders…He came back for me as
well.*

Ilysa's heart swelled at hearing the men speak with
such pride about their chieftain. Although Connor had not
succeeded in capturing Hugh, he had won the undying
loyalty of these men. Yet a skirmish with Hugh's men did
not explain the look on Connor's face as he walked past
her. He was a hardened warrior.

"What else happened?" she asked.

The men went silent, and none would meet her eyes.
Whatever it was, they did not wish to speak of it, at least
not with her.

That evening, Cook worked his magic to make a feast
from their meager stores to welcome the returning warriors. When Connor came down for supper, he acted more
himself, but Ilysa sensed the anguish behind his mask. He
glanced down the table to where she sat next to Lachlan
once and did not look again. After the meal, he stood with
the men while they again recounted tales of his bravery,
but she could tell he was not listening to a word.

\* \* \*

Connor took another long drink of his whiskey, then
rested his head in his hands. The evening had been interminable. Finally, he was alone in his chamber where
he did not have to pretend that the chieftain had the situation well in hand and that the clan would overcome this

last round of trouble and triumph over their enemies.

He cringed when he heard the knock on the door. He could not face one more person congratulating him on his exploits after he had failed so utterly and miserably to protect his people.

The knocking persisted. Finally, he dragged himself to his feet and went to the door. When he opened it, he leaned against the door frame to block his visitor from entering. If that was not sufficient discouragement, he'd repel whoever it was down the stairs.

The one person he could be happy to see stood in his doorway like a gift.

"Ilysa."

"Let me come in," she said.

Without waiting for an answer, she ducked under his outstretched arm. She sat at the table and folded her hands in her lap, looking prim and determined. There was no use attempting to kick her out, and he did not want to anyway.

When he sat in his chair beside her, she pinched her brows together and swept her gaze over him, the jug of whiskey, and the empty cup. That served to remind him that he wanted another, so he poured it and drank it down.

"Tell me about it," she said, and when he glanced sideways at her, she was looking at him with her big, doe eyes.

"No." He could not burden her with this.

Ilysa ignored the rebuff and touched his face, a gesture of kindness all the more compelling after the vileness of the last two days.

"I'm worried." She pushed her chair back and stood next to him. Before he knew what she meant to do, she pulled his head against her chest and wrapped her arms around him. Ilysa had seen his despair. It touched his wounded soul.

He could not trust himself with her. He needed her arms around him too badly.

"You should go now," he said and firmly pushed her away.

She kept a hand on his shoulder and gave him a soft smile that pierced his heart. When she brushed his hair back with her fingers, his eyes closed. He felt her breath and then her soft lips on his forehead.

"I want to comfort you," she said.

"I want a hell of a lot more than comfort from ye." He gave her the truth in a hard voice to frighten her off.

He wanted to lose himself in her arms, to make love to her until he stopped seeing the horrors of the last days in his mind's eye—the dead girl draped in her father's arms, the smell of burned cottages, the vacant stares of the children he had been powerless to protect.

"I know," she said. "That's why I'm here."

He wanted her so much it hurt. Nay, he needed her tonight. There were a dozen reasons not to take her to bed, but he didn't give a damn about any of them. Ilysa wanted him, and that was all the reason he needed.

\* \* \*

Ilysa swallowed at the naked hunger in Connor's eyes. She had started this, and she was not going to lose her courage now. When she reached back to untie her brèid, the cloth tied over her hair, he stopped her.

"Let me."

When he stood, he towered over her. She fixed her

gaze on the vee of his shirt as he untied the knot at the back of her neck, lifted the brèid off her head, and drew her braid over her shoulder.

"Ye look so pretty," he said as he cupped her face between his hands. "This time, we'll go slowly—and we will most definitely be naked."

*Naked?* Ilysa's breathing grew shallow as he kissed her cheeks, her nose, the point of her chin, and the sensitive spot beneath her ear.

Connor released her and said, "I'll bar the door."

He pulled his shirt over his head and tossed it into a chair as he walked across the room, at ease in his body and unconscious of his beauty. And Connor MacDonald was beautiful. Ilysa's head felt light as her gaze traveled the lines of his broad, muscular back and down to his narrow waist. The muscles of his buttocks and long legs flexed beneath his trews as he moved with the sure grace of a warrior.

When he came back toward her, Ilysa's body prickled with awareness and her chest felt too tight. Without taking his gaze from her face, Connor stripped off his trews—and Ilysa stopped breathing altogether. Her brief look at him naked when she had barged in on him that first day after his bath had been wholly inadequate.

When she dropped her gaze lower, her mouth fell open. His staff was standing straight up, and it was far bigger than she expected. She had not seen it the first time. Though she had not ever gotten much of a look at her husband's, either, she was certain it had never been like this.

After realizing she was gaping, she dragged her gaze to his face. *O shluagh!* The heat in his eyes singed her skin and made her pulse leap wildly. Everything about the intimidating warrior before her was overpowering—his nakedness, his wolf-hungry eyes, his erect shaft. She had to remind herself that this was Connor, and she could trust him.

She did trust him. More than that, she loved him.

When he pulled into her arms and kissed her, she soon forgot her nervousness. For such a hard-muscled man, his lips were soft and pliable. While he deepened the kiss, he ran his hand from her hip up to the side of her breast. Her head spun as their tongues entwined. All the while, she was excruciatingly aware of his shaft pressing against her stomach through the layers of her skirts.

She felt the tension of his taut muscles beneath her fingers as his kisses grew more urgent. Connor groaned into her mouth as his hand covered her breast. When he rubbed his thumb across her nipple through her gown, sharp sparks of pleasure shot through her, and she had to break the kiss to gasp for air.

Connor moved to her neck, giving her a sucking kiss that pulled sensations all the way from her toes. Then he grew gentle again, and she sighed as he ran his tongue along the skin above her bodice.

When he pulled back, his black hair fell over his eyes, making him look dangerously handsome. "Let's take your gown off and get into bed."

A squeak of assent was all she could manage.

Connor's hand shook as he slowly pulled at the loose end of the bow at the top of her bodice. She watched the rise and fall of his chest as he unfastened the laces that held the front of her gown together, revealing her chemise beneath it. Then he pulled her against him and kissed her until she could not think at all. One hand supported her back, while the other was inside her bodice kneading her breast. When he found her nipple again, he sent shivers of pleasure spiraling through her body until she was breathless. And far too warm.

Once he took his hand from her breast, he was remarkably quick at removing her gown. Ilysa was uneasy, but at least she still had her chemise on. She crawled into the bed and pulled the bedclothes up to her chin. When Connor got in, the mattress sank under his weight. She had to brace herself to keep from rolling into him as he stretched out beside her.

The tension between them jangled her nerves as they lay face-to-face across the pillow. Connor's eyes, which sometimes looked gray, were steely-blue now, and his jaw was dark with the day's beard. He lay still as a wildcat watching its prey.

"What's wrong?" she asked when he made no move to touch her.

"I'm waiting for ye to stop being afraid of me."

"I'm a bit nervous is all." It was ridiculous since they had done this before. But as he said, this time was different.

"Have ye changed your mind?"

"No!" she said quickly, and his white teeth gleamed in a sudden smile.

"I can understand if you're frightened after last time," he said. "I hadn't had a woman in a very long time, and I didn't know that... Well, I regret I was too rough and rushed."

"No, ye weren't." She shook her head against the pillow, wanting to reassure him. "It was... quite exciting."

"Ahh, Ilysa," he said on an exhale, and his eyes held that darkness again that robbed her of air.

She dropped her gaze to his chest, taking in the well-defined muscles, the dark curly hair, the arrow wound that had finally healed, and the white lines of old injuries. Of its own accord, her hand went to the long gash that ran across his ribs on his left side.

"You have so many scars," she said as she traced it with her finger. "I remember this one from the MacKinnon attack."

"I don't notice them." He enfolded her hand and brought it to his mouth. His breath was warm on her fingers. "Do they bother ye?"

"It pains me to know how many times people have tried to kill ye." She withdrew her hand from his to brush her fingers through the hair at his temple. "But each scar reminds me of how very precious your life is."

"The last two days have reminded me how quickly life can be cut short," he said, and his eyes clouded.

Ilysa feared she was losing him to the darkness that had engulfed him earlier and rested her hand against his cheek to draw his attention. The scratch of his whiskers felt good against her palm.

"Save your worries for tomorrow. Tonight, it's just you and me." She leaned across the pillow. "Forget everything else and kiss me."

Connor gathered her into his arms and gave her a long, melting kiss that made her toes curl. His hands roamed her body, slowly and deliberately, sending waves of heat everywhere he touched. She wanted to touch him, too, but she did not know where or how she ought to do it. Last time, she was caught in a maelstrom before she had time to fret about being so ignorant. But now, she did not know what she was supposed to do.

As his kisses grew more fervent, she forgot her worries and let her hands go where they would. She ran them through his hair, letting the dark strands slide through her fingers, then traced the muscles of his shoulders and back.

Connor's breathing grew harsher, and he rolled her onto her back. He was all heat and passion, and she lost herself in the feel of his body pressed against hers. How had she lived without his touch? He kissed her throat, and then she felt his breath through her chemise as he moved down her breastbone.

It startled her when she felt the moist heat of his mouth on her breast through the cloth. Needles of pleasure shot to her womb as he suckled her breast. Unexpected little moans came from her mouth, and she had a fleeting concern that he would wonder what was wrong with her.

"I love the sounds ye make," he said, looking up at her with such heat in his eyes that she knew he was not just saying it.

After a time, she felt cold air on her thigh. She was in such a daze that it took her a moment to realize Connor was pulling her chemise up.

"What are ye doing?" She tried to sit up, but he was in her way.

"I'm desperate to feel your skin against mine," he said. "I sorely regret leaving your clothes on ye last time."

Ilysa swallowed. She had never been completely naked in front of a man before. Was this necessary? From the determined way Connor was tugging at her chemise, it appeared he thought it was.

"Lift up for me," he said.

"I fear you'll be disappointed," she said.

"I won't."

He said it so firmly that she gave in to the inevitable and lifted her hips. Leaving her chemise gathered around her middle, he pulled her up to a sitting position and kissed her long and hard until she forgot her awkwardness. As he kissed the side of her neck, his hand moved up her back under her chemise. The scratch of the calluses and the strength of his hand felt good.

She was beginning to understand why he wanted to be skin-to-skin with nothing between them. When he broke the kiss to lift her chemise over her head, she raised her arms for him. He immediately enfolded her in an embrace again, and she squeezed her eyes shut against the rush of desire that radiated through her as his chest pressed against her sensitive breasts.

She kept her eyes closed as he laid her down. When she finally opened them, it was to find him staring down at her. She instinctively brought her hands up to cover her breasts, but he caught her wrists and pressed them against the mattress.

"Don't. I want to see you."

She held her breath as his gaze burned over her.

"You're more beautiful than I imagined," he said, then lifted his gaze to her face. "And I've spent a good deal of time imagining having ye naked in my bed."

She did not know which surprised her more—that he had imagined her naked or that he had called her beautiful. After yearning to have Connor want her like this for so long, it was hard to believe it was truly happening.

"I imagined this, too," she confessed, which earned her a long, heated kiss. She did not tell him that when she imagined it, she had her chemise on. She had a strong suspicion that was only one of many surprises in store for her tonight. Not that the first time hadn't been surprising. That had been like being swept into a sudden thunder and lightning storm.

She swallowed as Connor moved down her body. When he reached her breast, bare to his touch this time, she was aware of nothing else but his tongue as he slowly circled her nipple. Then he flicked it, setting off jolts of desire, before drawing her breast into his mouth. She clenched her fingers in his hair to anchor her against the wild tumult cascading through her.

When he moved up to take her mouth again, she was acutely aware of his shaft pressing against her hip. Would it fit? It had before, but barely. His hand slid up the inside of her thigh, and her unease gradually melted away. She followed the course of his fingers as they moved in languid loops ever higher up her thigh. Her body was taut with anticipation long before his fingers reached their destination. When he finally did touch the sensitive place between her legs, she nearly rose off the bed.

Then his tongue was exploring her ear, and she felt as if she were floating. She never would have expected that to feel good. Another surprise.

"Ye feel like heaven," he said, his breath warm against her ear.

She thought she should say something back, but for long moments, she could not form words, even in her head. His fingers circled round and round, creating an unbearable tension until she thought she might snap in two. Yet she did not want him to stop.

"You have magic in your fingers," she finally managed to say.

When he leaned over her to kiss her, his chest rubbed against her nipples and she drew in a sharp breath. She wrapped her arms around his neck and held him close as their tongues entwined in deep, mindless kisses. All the while, his fingers drove her to near madness.

"Closer," she said, digging her fingers into his shoulder. Though his body was touching the full length of hers, it wasn't enough. She wanted to meld into him.

"I want ye so much," he said in a ragged voice. "Tell me ye want me, too."

"I do." *Always.*

Bracing his weight on his arms, he moved to lie between her legs. She bit her lip when the tip of his shaft touched her center. Connor paused above her, his black hair hanging down, framing his perfect face. Their gazes locked, and she saw the tumult raging inside her reflected in the storm in his eyes.

The air pushed out of her lungs in an "ooh" as he slowly slid inside her. Every part of her body was alert with awareness of his shaft inside her, stretching and filling her.

"I don't know how long a lass might be sore from her first time," he said, his breathing hard. "Am I hurting ye?"

"No."

"Ye must tell me the truth," he said, his eyes searching hers. "I couldn't bear to hurt ye again."

"Ye feel wonderful inside me," she said and ran her hands up his chest.

Connor sucked in his breath when she lifted her hips, drawing him deeper. Then, with slow, deliberate movements, he pulled out nearly all the way and thrust deep inside her, again and again. Ilysa's skin felt too sensitive, her body too tight. Connor continued moving inside her, slowly and relentlessly, until she vibrated with need. She felt on the verge of something, but she did not know what.

"Faster, harder," she pleaded.

Connor made a growling sound deep in his throat. She wrapped her legs around him like a vise and held on as he drove inside her. Through the blood pounding in her ears, she heard him call her name. He was hers. Waves of pleasure swelled and crested, washing over her in a storm of wonder.

# CHAPTER 28

Connor awoke to sunlight streaming through his windows and Ilysa in his arms again. Instinctively, he pulled her closer and kissed her hair. They had slept together every night for a fortnight.

He prided himself on always making decisions logically. He weighed his options carefully, taking into account all the ramifications before making his move, as in a game of chess. He was, in fact, an extraordinarily good chess player. When the situation called for it, he was quick and decisive. But even then, he made his decisions based on logic and the information available to him at the time.

There was nothing logical, however, about his falling into bed with Ilysa. He had not meant for it to happen the first time—or the second. In fact, he had decided it would *not* happen.

And now, he could not imagine awaking without her smell in his nose, her silky skin under his fingers, and her warmth against his side. In so short a time, she had seeped into his very bones until he did not know where he ended and she began.

With Ilysa, he was able to forget his responsibilities and burdens as chieftain for a while. He could just be a man lost in his woman's arms. What she did for him went far beyond their physical passion, as remarkable as that was. She filled the empty places inside him that he had not known were there. She made him feel whole.

All his life, he had strived to be better than he was—a better son, a better man, a better chieftain. He supposed his mother's abandonment and his father's disapproval had something to do with that. But Ilysa thought he was enough, just as himself. Her faith in him made him all the more determined to become the man and chieftain she thought he was.

Connor's growling stomach finally drove him from the bed. As he dressed, he watched Ilysa's peaceful form. Sometime in the night, he had shaken her hair loose from its braid, and it spilled out around her on the bed like a red-gold sunrise.

She left him breathless. He was tempted to wake her and make love to her again, but he should let her sleep after keeping her awake half the night. Once again, he told himself that he must cut this off. There was no future in it, and Ilysa deserved a future.

Ilysa rolled onto her side and opened her eyes. When she gave him her soft smile, Connor felt his resolve draining from him like sand through an hourglass. Soon enough, he must take a bride for the alliance, and Ilysa would take a husband.

She sat up, holding the bedclothes over her breasts.

Her modesty amused him after all they had done in bed.

"Slaying dragons again today, Connor MacDonald?" she asked with a smile in her eyes.

And the wonder of it was that Ilysa believed he could.

\* \* \*

Ilysa wrapped a blanket around her shoulders and got out of bed to join Connor. She slid her arms around his waist and sighed with contentment as she rested her head against his chest. Her days and nights were a blur of happiness.

"I must go," Connor said, but he held her closer. "The men need training."

"I'll get ready and come downstairs with ye," she said, though she knew what he would say.

"'Tis best if we aren't seen coming into the hall together," he said.

This pretense that he insisted upon was the only mar to her happiness. "Are ye ashamed of me?" she asked.

"Ashamed?" Connor took her by the shoulders and leaned back to look into her face. "Why would ye ask that?"

"What else am I to think when ye don't want anyone to know I sleep here?"

"I do it to protect you," he said. "I'm ashamed that I've taken advantage of ye, but I could never be ashamed of you."

"Protect me from what?" she asked. "You're not the first chieftain to keep a woman without making her a wife, and 'tis usually considered an honor for the lass."

"An honor? Hmmph." The happiness seemed to drain from him. With gentle fingers, he brushed a loose strand back from her face. "I don't want them talking about ye."

"I love ye," she said as she flung her arms around him and held him fiercely. "I don't care who knows it."

"I wish ye could be my wife," he said, regret dragging at his voice.

That he wished it was more than Ilysa had ever hoped for.

She told herself it was enough.

\* \* \*

How Connor dreaded his marriage. He held Ilysa's lithe body against his and closed his eyes as he breathed in the scent of her hair, wanting this moment to last forever. He should not have told her he wished he could marry her. What value was there in a wish he was not free to follow?

He should have heard from the MacIain by now if he was coming with his warriors—*and his granddaughter*. It was traitorous for Connor to hope that the MacIains would not come, and foolish as well, for his reprieve would be temporary. Connor would just have to make a different marriage alliance.

Without help, the chances of the MacDonalds prevailing against the larger forces of the MacLeods were slim to none. Alastair MacLeod was a formidable chieftain who had led his warriors for nearly forty years. He was unlikely to make mistakes.

Connor cupped the side of Ilysa's face and ran his thumb across her bottom lip. No matter how little time the reprieve bought him, he wanted it.

"Come back to bed with me," he said. "I need ye."

# CHAPTER 29

Ilysa was passing through the hall on her way to the kitchens to speak to Cook about supplies when she saw Lachlan. He stood alone, leaning against the wall next to the door that led outside. The other men respected Lachlan, but he mostly kept to himself.

When she met his gaze, Lachlan jerked his head to the side, then went out the door without a backward glance. Exasperated, she followed him outside and caught up with him between the buildings by the well.

"If ye wish to speak to me, Lachlan of Lealt," she said, putting her hand on her hip, "ask me politely."

He gave her his bored look with his eyelids half closed, but the corner of his mouth quirked up, giving away his amusement. "Ye came, didn't ye?"

Ilysa rolled her eyes, but she smiled, despite herself. "Now that you've dragged me away from my tasks, what is it ye want?"

"I've had no luck discovering who in the castle is spying for Hugh," he said. "Have you?"

"I thought I had it figured out—until ye told me it wasn't you," she said.

"I'll be leaving in the morning for a few days," Lachlan said, ignoring her remark. "The chieftain wants me to see if I can find out where Hugh's new camp is. I may hear something about this spy as well."

"I'll keep my eye out for clues here," she said.

"That's why I'm talking to ye," Lachlan said. "Don't try to uncover the spy on your own."

"I can't help looking," she said and gave him a pleasant smile.

"Don't," Lachlan said. "You're a bright lass, and ye might guess right. If the spy realizes it, you'll be in danger."

"I appreciate your concern," Ilysa said, which was what she always said when men felt compelled to give her orders she did not intend to follow. She rose up on her tiptoes and gave him a peck on the cheek. "You be careful out there, Lachlan."

A short time later, Ilysa was enjoying a chat with Cook amid the clatter of pans and the savory smells of the midday meal preparation. She took the opportunity to ask him something that had been on her mind.

"What do ye know about the ghosts in the castle?" she asked.

"Hmmph. There's more than one now?" Cook paused in his chopping to turn to her and raise a skeptical eyebrow. "I've only heard about the nursemaid in the tower."

"Then tell me about her," Ilysa said.

"She dropped our last chieftain's baby son out the

tower window," Cook said. "Ach, she was a sweet, cheerful lass, but she didn't have the sense of a turnip."

"Ye knew her?" Ilysa had assumed the tale was an old one, as ghost stories usually were.

"It only happened about twenty years ago." Cook shook his head. "God knows what that silly lass was doing hanging half out the window with the babe when he slipped from her arms."

"I thought the chieftain had no sons after Connor."

"Not by his wife, he didn't." Cook turned to the kitchen maids who were scrubbing pots behind them. "We need more meat for the stew. Go fetch that hen that's stopped laying eggs and kill it outside. I don't want that squawking in here."

"What happened to the nursemaid?" Ilysa asked.

"The chieftain ordered her cast adrift at sea in a boat," Cook said as he reached for another leek to chop. "Neither the lass nor the boat was ever seen again."

Ilysa bit her lip. It was a harsh punishment, though not unexpected for such a grave offense. The loss of a chieftain's son was a loss to the entire clan.

"Ye haven't heard about the other ghost?" Ilysa asked in a low voice, though no one else was in the kitchen now.

"The nursemaid is the only one I know of," Cook said, slanting her another skeptical glance.

"I've seen a second woman with the nursemaid and the babe." Since sleeping in Connor's bedchamber, she had awakened several times to see them. The image always faded quickly, and she was never sure if it was a vision or a dream.

Cook did not respond for a long while. When he finally did, his question surprised her.

"Have ye told Lachlan?" he asked.

"Why would I?"

"I believe your second ghost must be his mother," Cook said. "The poor soul. It was her babe who died."

"Her babe?" Ilysa asked. "Lachlan's mother had a child by our last chieftain?"

"Aye. Becoming the chieftain's mistress brought her nothing but sadness in the end." Cook set down his knife and turned to face Ilysa. "See that the same doesn't happen to you, lass."

"I didn't realize ye knew about me and Connor," Ilysa said, her cheeks going hot.

"Half the castle knows you're sharing his bed," Cook said. "The rest suspect it."

"Ye needn't fret about me," she said when he continued looking at her like a mournful dog. "I've never been so happy. Truly."

"Lachlan's mother was as joyful in the beginning as you are," he said. "Now she's a ghost who cannot rest."

\* \* \*

Winter made a return with freezing rain that blew in gusts and hit Connor's face like pellets. He should have taken it as a sign.

They were practicing in the field outside the castle in mud up to their ankles, but no one complained. A Highland warrior had best be prepared for fighting in the rain.

"You're favoring your right side—ye may as well point to where I should strike ye," he shouted over the wind at Robbie, his practicing partner. "Aye, that's better."

Robbie was small for his age at sixteen and lacked natural talent, but the lad was determined, and the extra time

Connor spent with him was paying off. In fact, all the younger men were improving.

"Connor!" someone shouted. "Isn't that your small galley headed this way?"

He glanced out to sea and, sure enough, the galley they had stolen from Shaggy Maclean was entering the bay. Before leaving the practice, Connor took one last swing and knocked Robbie backward into the mud. Next time, the young man would know to block it.

He took the steps cut into the side of the cliff two at a time and arrived on the beach just as the galley neared shore. Niall, his chestnut hair dark with rain, was alone in the boat, so Connor waded out to help haul it in.

"Am I welcome?" Niall asked with a sheepish grin.

"Get out of the damned boat and help me," Connor said.

Niall vaulted over the side, and together they carried it above the tide line.

"'Tis good to see ye," Connor said, slapping Niall on the back. "But next time ask permission before ye take my boat."

"I was under the impression that it was my boat now," Niall said as he reached inside it for his claymore and a leather bag. "Admit it, ye were planning to use her for kindling before I repaired her."

"For kindling? This beauty?" Connor said, though the galley had been nearly destroyed in a storm and looked unsalvageable before Niall got hold of it. "Never."

Connor looked forward to a long discussion over whiskey regarding who had the better right to the stolen boat. Since the MacDonalds acquired the sleek vessel from Shaggy, it had changed hands at least once on a wager.

As soon as they burst into the hall, dripping rain, mud, and seawater, Connor's eyes found Ilysa across the room, and she smiled at him. Each time he entered the castle now, he felt as if he were coming home to her. It was a good feeling. After a long moment, Ilysa's gaze shifted, and she noticed who was standing beside him.

"Niall!" She picked up her skirts and ran across the hall to throw her arms around him.

Niall blushed and grinned while he hugged her longer than Connor thought necessary. "Let her be," he said. "You're getting her all wet."

After finally setting Ilysa on her feet, Niall swept his gaze over her. "I haven't grown accustomed to ye looking so fetching."

Ach, it appeared Niall had acquired his older brother's charm. Time to hide the women.

"Change out of those wet clothes before ye catch your death," Ilysa told Niall.

"Can I eat first? I'm starving," Niall said, sounding young again. While Ilysa sent servants scurrying, Niall thrust a sealed parchment into Connor's hands and, pitching his voice low, said, "Ian sent me with this as soon as it arrived."

With a sinking heart, Connor recognized the MacIain chieftain's seal. He stuck the missive inside his shirt to read in private. Would it say MacIain was coming or no? Either way, it could be nothing but bad news.

# CHAPTER 30

Connor and Ilysa had formed the habit of talking over the day's events and business of the castle when they met at night. Usually, they made love first, but the matter Connor had to discuss with her tonight should not wait. When she came to his chamber, he pulled her onto his lap and sat with her before the brazier.

"I saw ye speaking with Lachlan outside today." This was not what he needed to discuss with her, but the words came out of his mouth.

"Aye." Ilysa's face lit with a smile that was like a needle in his heart. "Have ye thought any more about making him captain of your guard?"

"For now, I need him to travel around the peninsula gathering information," Connor said.

"He said he's going off to look for Hugh's new camp."

"That's what I told him to do," Connor said. "Who knows if that's what he'll actually be doing."

"I'm certain he is." Ilysa drew her brows together and searched his face.

"I thought ye didn't like the idea of me making him captain," Connor said, keeping his own gaze on the burning peat logs. "Ye didn't trust him."

"I don't recall saying that," she said.

"What ye said was that something troubled Lachlan, and ye wish ye knew what it was." Connor turned and fixed his gaze on her face. "I take it ye found out."

Ilysa fussed with her sleeve and did not respond.

"I see that ye don't want to tell me," he said.

"I do," she said. "But it's no my secret."

Connor did not like the idea of Ilysa and closemouthed Lachlan sharing secrets. "Why would he tell you?"

"He didn't, precisely. He just gave me a general idea of the sort of secret it was," Ilysa said, looking decidedly uncomfortable. "He thinks Hugh has a spy in the castle."

If Lachlan was the spy, that is exactly what he would say to divert suspicion.

"So now that ye know—*in a general sort of way*—what troubles Lachlan," Connor said, "what is your opinion of the man?"

"I believe ye can trust him," she said, meeting his gaze dead-on now, "and that he's the best choice to be your captain."

"What about Sorely?" Connor asked, just because he was feeling sour.

"Ye said yourself that Sorely is no good at training the younger men." She paused. "And I don't like him."

"Perhaps if he told ye his troubles like Lachlan does, you'd feel differently about him."

The hurt on Ilysa's face made Connor regret the words

as soon as they were out of his mouth. She removed his arm from around her waist and slid off his lap. Then she stood before him, hands folded in front of her, looking at him with her doe eyes and making him feel like dirt.

"Why are ye speaking to me this way?" she asked.

"Ach, I'm sorry." Connor went to the window and stared out at the black sea and sky. "I see ye with Lachlan and know he could give ye all the things I wish I could, and I'm so jealous I can't think straight."

He heard Ilysa's soft steps as she crossed the room to him. He felt the venom go out of him as she put her arms around his waist from behind and leaned against his back. Her kindness was a gift he did not deserve.

"Don't talk like that," she said. "What could anyone give me that I'd want more than being with you?"

*I can't even give her that for much longer.* Though it was true that he had suffered a bout of jealousy when he saw her with Lachlan in a quiet corner of the castle yard, it was the message from MacIain that made his jealousy so sharp that he lashed out at her.

Connor turned around to face her. There was no avoiding it any longer. He had to tell her. What would she do?

She would leave him.

"Come to bed," Ilysa said and took his hand—and he put off telling her a little longer.

They prepared for bed like he imagined a young married couple would. After helping her off with her gown, he watched her cross the room in her chemise to drape it neatly over a chair. He dropped his own clothes by the bed. He left the candles burning because he liked to see her and crawled in beside her.

As he held her to him, he closed his eyes, but he could

not prevent the words of the message from blazing across his mind. It would be wrong not to tell her before they made love in case it changed her mind about wanting to be in his bed. But he was tempted.

"*Mo chroí.*" He brushed the hair back from her face and kissed her forehead. "I have news I must tell you."

He felt her body tense in his arms, and she said, "I don't want to hear it."

"Niall brought a message from the MacIain chieftain," Connor said. "He writes that the Crown will look favorably upon a marriage between me and his granddaughter."

Ilysa seemed to fold in on herself. Though he understood why she was withdrawing from him, he hated it.

"What do ye intend to do?" she asked in a small voice.

"I sought this match," Connor made himself say. "Our clan needs the alliance."

He had racked his brain since reading the message, trying to think of a way to avoid the marriage. No matter how he looked at it, his clan could not defeat the MacLeods without the help of an ally, and his warriors' lives would be sacrificed for naught. As chieftain, Connor did not have the right to put his own happiness, or even Ilysa's, above the lives of his warriors or the recapture of their rightful lands.

"Does that mean it is settled?" Ilysa asked, and the slight catch in her voice plucked at his heart.

"MacIain is on his way now," he said. "He'll be here in a few days—with his granddaughter."

As the silence stretched out, Connor wished just this once that Ilysa was the sort of lass who yelled and threw things. Anything would be better than this terrible stillness that made him feel as if she were slipping away from him moment by moment.

"I have no choice," he said, "I must enter into this marriage for the good of the clan."

*But you're the one I want.* Connor did not say the words aloud. He had caused enough harm without begging her to stay and be his lover.

In her methodical way, Ilysa folded the bedclothes back in neat turns and sat up, leaving his arms empty of her warmth. The candlelight picked up gold and red in her hair as she sat on the edge of the bed with her back to him.

"If ye want to leave, I'll send ye home to Dunscaith tomorrow," Connor said, though he prayed she would not go.

He loved her so much.

* * *

Was her happiness to end this quickly? Connor called Dunscaith her home, but it could never be that without him. She had no home.

"What do you want me to do, Connor?" Ilysa managed to keep her voice calm, though she felt as if her life hung in the balance. It was easier with her back to him.

"I'm trying to do the right thing, if belatedly, by you and by...my future wife," he said. "I swore I would have but one woman as chieftain. If you remain here, I won't be able to keep that pledge."

"I didn't ask what ye thought was right or what ye feel your duty is," she said, speaking carefully. "I asked what ye want me to do."

"I want ye to stay here more than anything I've ever

wanted," he said, his voice rough. "I need ye at my side every day and in my bed each night—but I can't ask that of ye."

Ilysa swallowed against the surge of emotion that closed her throat. Connor still wanted her.

"You don't have a wife yet," she said. "I'll stay until ye do."

*And after that?* She could feel his unspoken question, but she was not ready to answer it.

Connor moved to sit behind her, sliding his long legs on either side of hers and wrapping his arms around her in a protective cocoon.

"I'll cherish every hour we have together," he said and kissed the side of her neck.

"I have one condition," Ilysa said, remembering Teàrlag's warning. *Our chieftain can only find happiness if he weds the lass who chooses him on Beltane night.*

"What is it?" he asked, his breath warm on her skin.

"Promise ye won't wed before Beltane."

"Is that all?" he asked. "I doubt there would be time to wed before then, even if I wanted to."

"Promise," she insisted.

"I promise."

Why had Teàrlag not said Connor must wait to find his bride until the summer solstice—or better yet, Lamas, when August arrived warm and golden?

Beltane was only a week away.

* * *

Connor awoke abruptly and sat up. It was dark, but he sensed morning was not far off. He held very still, listening for the sound again.

"What is it?" Ilysa asked in a sleepy voice.

"Did ye hear that?"

"Hear what?" she asked.

He could not say what precisely had roused him from a deep sleep, but his warrior instincts had been alerted by a sound that should not have been there. He threw back the bedclothes and walked naked to the windows. He peered out into the darkness, looking for movement, first on the sea side and then from the windows overlooking the courtyard.

"I can't see well enough from here," he said. "I'm going to the tower."

He opened the small door at the end of his chamber and ran up the three steps to the tiny tower room. In addition to the ghost who supposedly dwelled here, the tower had a single large window. Connor opened it and leaned out. He heard nothing but the wind and the crash of the waves against the cliff.

Then he saw them, a line of dark figures coming up the steps.

# CHAPTER 31

Connor took the three steps from the tower in one stride, tossed his clothes on, and grabbed his claymore as he ran out the door.

"What is it?" Ilysa called after him.

"We're being attacked!" He repeated the cry to awaken the men when he reached the hall. "Everyone outside!"

Connor burst out of the keep and ran hard for the gate. Ensuring it was secure was the first task in defending the castle. The sky was already a shade lighter with dawn nearing.

*O shluagh!* Connor's heart flipped over in his chest as he made out two figures slumped on the ground inside the gate. When he was a few yards from the downed guards, he could see in the growing light that the gate was unbarred. He heard running feet on the other side and ran faster. Leaping over the bodies, he flung himself against the gate.

*Thump, thump.* The gate bounced against his shoulder

as men banged on the other side, trying to force the gate open. Connor braced his legs against the weight pounding against it. A gap inched open, and the shouts of the attackers rang in his ears. He rammed the heavy bar across, but he could not bring it home.

"No!" All would be lost if the enemy came through the gate. Gritting his teeth, Connor gave a final push and slammed the bar across.

No sooner had he secured the gate than he was surrounded by a dozen warriors who had followed him from the hall. He had only been alone at the gate for a few short moments, but battles and wars were won or lost in such moments.

"Drop the portcullis!" he shouted.

Someone followed his order, for he heard the rapid *clank clank clank* of the chain as the heavy iron grate fell free, quickly followed by the anguished cries of the men caught under its sharp points.

"To the walls!" Connor shouted, and waved for the men to go up to repel the attackers.

While he gave orders, a part of his mind grappled with what he had seen. The two dead guards. The unbarred gate. It could have been a disaster, the battle for the castle over almost before it began. That was the plan. While the MacDonald warriors slept, someone had killed the two guards and opened the gate.

There was a viper inside the castle.

\* \* \*

After Ilysa had seen to all of the wounded who had been carried into the hall, she left Cook in charge and went outside to look for more injured. From the steps of the keep, she surveyed the chaos of the attack in the slanting streaks of dawn light. Arrows sailed into the courtyard. Several men were busy propping logs at an angle against the gate, which shook with a rhythmic pounding. Above her, warriors were fighting hand-to-hand with attackers who had scaled the walls.

She watched in horror as one of the MacDonald warriors fell backward off the wall. He landed with a *thud* and lay twitching with his legs splayed at awkward angles. Ilysa ran across the courtyard and dropped to her knees beside the fallen man. There was a dirk in his chest. His body was still now, and his eyes open and unseeing. There was nothing she could do for him.

Overcome, she covered her face and keened over him. But this was no time for weakness, so she forced herself to stop. There were others who needed her attention.

As she struggled to her feet, she saw Connor watching her from across the courtyard. When their eyes met, the sounds and sights of the battle faded, and there was only the two of them. It could not have lasted more than an instant, but she felt as if time itself stopped.

Then he waved his arm and shouted, "Get inside!"

She ran back to the keep. From the protection of the doorway, she turned and saw him climbing a ladder up the wall with a dirk between his teeth.

Lachlan followed him, carrying a bow and arrows. Once they were on the wall, Connor fed arrows to Lachlan, who shot them, one after another in quick succession. Between shots, Connor pointed, apparently choosing targets. She guessed he was picking out the leaders or the most formidable-looking warriors.

Connor left Lachlan on his own while he knocked one

enemy and then another off the wall. Ach, he was a wonder with a sword. Ilysa had her own part to play. When she saw a man limping toward the keep, dragging his bleeding leg, she hurried to help him. This one, she could save.

* * *

Connor was not surprised to find that the attackers were Hugh's men, rather than MacLeods. A traitor in the castle was far more likely to have a connection to Connor's rival within the clan than to their enemy clan.

The one bright light in this miserable day was discovering Lachlan's deadly skill with a bow and arrow. Hugh's men shot their arrows blindly into the castle, occasionally making a lucky hit. But there was no luck involved with Lachlan's bow—except bad luck for anyone in his aim. Unfortunately, Hugh did not show himself. Connor suspected he was watching from the safety of his damned boat. Hugh could wield a sword with the best of them, but he was judicious about risking his neck when he could be.

"Bring buckets of water!" Connor shouted when he saw that the thatched roof of one of the storerooms along the wall was in flames.

Before the words were out of his mouth, he saw Ilysa leading three women across the courtyard, all of them carrying sloshing buckets. An arrow whizzed by Ilysa's head, and his heart stopped. If the woman did not stay inside, he was going to tie her to a goddamned chair.

When he caught up with her, he handed her bucket to the nearest man, picked her up, and shouted at the other women to leave their pails and get the hell inside.

"Stay in the keep where ye can't be hurt," he ordered Ilysa after he set her down on the steps.

"I'll try," she said.

By the saints, she was stubborn. But what a woman—she was as courageous as any of his warriors. Connor gripped her shoulders and kissed her full on the lips.

"I have a battle to fight," he told her. "I can't be worrying about ye, so you'll do as I say."

This time, she nodded, and he kissed her again for that.

*  *  *

Though he was tired from the battle, Connor could not sleep. He kept thinking about the two men at the gate, murdered by someone they thought was a friend. At least his men would be less vulnerable now that they knew to be on guard against an enemy within. Trust was essential, however, for them to fight well together. Connor must find the culprit and soon.

His thoughts bounced back and forth between that scene at the gate and the arrow whizzing by Ilysa's head. Dear God, if something had happened to her, he would never forgive himself.

The attack on the castle served to reinforce how important it was to control the surrounding countryside and, hence, to secure MacIain's help. Soon, his bride would arrive, and he would lose Ilysa. What would he do without her?

In truth, he was not even trying to sleep. The little time he had left with her was too precious to waste in oblivious slumber. Each night was both a valued gift and a torture, knowing it could be his last.

"Are ye awake?" Ilysa asked in a soft voice.

"Aye." He kissed her hair and held her closer.

"I've made up my mind," she said.

"About what, *mo chroí*?" He steeled himself to hear her ask him to have a boat ready in the morning to take her back to Dunscaith. His heart was in her hands.

"If ye want me to, I'll stay after she comes"—her voice caught as she added—"and after you're wed."

He closed his eyes. This was both what he wanted and what he hoped she would never say.

"I fear it will make ye unhappy to share the household with another woman." Connor did not add, *and share me*, but it hung in the air between them.

"It may," she said, "but I would be more unhappy without ye."

Connor felt overwhelmed with relief and guilt.

"I will feel badly for her," Ilysa said, turning her face away from him.

That was so like Ilysa. "Most chieftains have more than one woman. Her grandfathers are chieftains, so she will expect it," he said, stroking her back. "Having no woman but my wife was my rule, made in the arrogance of ignorance."

"'Tis the church's rule as well," Ilysa said without much conviction.

The church had many rules that were not strictly followed in the Highlands. Here, priests were so few that marriages were generally blessed, if at all, at the same time the couple's first child was christened. Under Celtic tradition, illegitimate children were claimed with no shame. Both men and women could set aside a marriage for a variety of grounds, including the woman's failure to bear a child and the man's failure to perform his husbandly duty in bed.

"I expect my wife will be content so long as I treat her with respect and"—he made himself say it—"give her children."

Ilysa was so still Connor wanted to take it back and tell her he wanted only her, which he did. But he needed to be honest about how it would be—how it *had* to be—if she stayed.

"I have a duty to her. This is not her fault, and I will give her what is her due," he said. "Can ye accept that?"

Ilysa nodded against his chest, and he hated himself.

"She will understand that our marriage is an alliance between clans, nothing more," he said.

"She's a woman," Ilysa said. "No matter what she understands, she'll hope for love."

"That she can never have," Connor said. "No matter if ye stay or go, my heart is yours."

He made love to her slowly, needing to show her with each touch, each kiss, each stroke, how much she meant to him. Until now, he had held back some essential part of himself that he had never trusted to a woman—at least not since he was a boy of seven and his mother left without a second thought for him.

He was a cautious man who laid aside all caution. He bared his soul to Ilysa and let her own his heart.

# CHAPTER 32

Connor was in his chamber when Lachlan stormed in and banged the door open with such force that it bounced against the wall.

"Next time, you'll knock and await permission before ye enter my chamber." Connor folded his arms and raised an eyebrow at Lachlan, who was seething over something, judging by his clenched hands and heaving chest. "I take it ye lost Hugh?"

At the end of the battle yesterday, Connor had sent Lachlan with a galley of men to follow Hugh's departing boats in the hope of discovering his new lair. After seeing how Lachlan fought against Hugh's men, he had decided Lachlan could not be his uncle's man. That did not mean Connor trusted him completely.

"Aye, I lost him," Lachlan bit out.

"Well, you're not the first. Hugh has a well-earned reputation for disappearing into the mists." When Lachlan did not relax his stance or offer an explanation, Connor asked, "Is there something else?"

"I thought ye were different from your father—better than him," Lachlan said. "But now that I see how you're taking advantage of that sweet, innocent lass, I know you're just the same."

Lachlan must have seen him kiss Ilysa in the midst of the battle. It was unlike Connor to forget himself like that, but his attempts to hide their relationship were probably futile anyway. In the close quarters of a castle household, that sort of secret was nearly impossible to keep.

"It wasn't enough that she takes care of your household, heals your wounds, and sees to your guests," Lachlan said, spreading his arms. "By God, that lass cares for ye—she threatened to kill me to protect ye. How could ye mistreat her?"

Connor did not defend himself, though he could have argued that he was not mistreating her. Chieftains took wives to make alliances, and they had mistresses and second "wives" to please themselves or to make other alliances. It was expected. Yet he knew in his heart that it was wrong to do this to Ilysa. She was meant to be a man's one and only.

"You're right. I should give her up." Connor sank into his chair and rested his head in his hands. "But I'm a weak man. I love her too much to let her go. At least not yet."

"Do ye mean that?" Lachlan asked. "That ye love her?"

Connor didn't bother lifting his head to answer.

"Then why don't ye make her your wife?" Lachlan said. "If a lass like Ilysa loved me, I'd do the right thing before she changed her mind."

The thought of Ilysa falling out of love with him hit him like a blow to the chest.

"I am chieftain," Connor said. "I must choose for the clan and not for myself."

"For such a clever man, Connor MacDonald," Lachlan said, "you're a damned idiot."

\* \* \*

"Chieftain, we have visitors!"

They were practicing in the muddy field again, and Connor crossed it to take a look. From the top of the cliff, he watched as a single war galley drew into the bay. He narrowed his eyes, wondering whose it was. It was not one of the MacDonald's, and MacIain would be coming with half a dozen galleys.

The bad feeling in his gut turned sour when he saw two women, whose brightly colored gowns showed from beneath their capes as they were lifted out of the boat. For a moment, he thought perhaps MacNeil had come with a couple of his daughters, but Alex's father-in-law would not bring them here just days before the battle for Trotternish was to begin.

This was a poor time to entertain guests, but there was no exception to Highland hospitality. Connor took a deep breath and started down the steps. As he approached the group gathered on the beach, the two women clutched each other and stared at him as if in fear for their lives. What was wrong with them? He stood alone, while they had two dozen warriors to protect them, and no Highland chieftain would attack his guests.

The blade of Connor's claymore made the familiar *whoosh* as he swung it over his shoulder and slid it into the scabbard on his back. Unaccountably, the younger woman emitted a loud gasp and buried her face in the older woman's bosom.

"A thousand welcomes," Connor greeted the group. "I am Connor, son of Donald Gallach, and chieftain of the MacDonalds of Sleat."

This set off a flurry of excited whispers between the women. Connor felt sorry for the men who traveled with them. After a day at sea in the confines of a galley with them, Connor would be ready to drop over the side and drown himself.

An old warrior separated himself from the others and stepped forward. "I bring ye greetings from my chieftain, John MacIain of Ardnamurchan."

No, it could not be that MacIain had sent only one galley.

"Where is your chieftain and the rest of his warriors?" Connor demanded.

"They've been diverted for a short time."

"Diverted?" Connor asked, holding his temper with an effort.

"Aye, more trouble with the rebels," the man said, shrugging as if it were nothing. "My chieftain expects to be here within a couple of days with his fleet of galleys."

Connor's shoulders relaxed a fraction. He could not fight with promises, but if MacIain arrived with his warriors in two days, that should be soon enough. Alex, Ian, and Duncan would be here by then as well, and it would begin. Connor's thoughts went to the attack he planned to launch on Beltane night.

"While my chieftain is detained..." The old MacIain

warrior cleared his throat, dragging Connor's attention back from his battle plans.

"Aye?" Connor asked when he tired of waiting for the man to continue.

"He gave me the great honor of delivering his grand-daughter to ye."

* * *

Ilysa watched for an opportunity to speak with Lachlan while Connor was busy elsewhere. She did not want to raise Connor's suspicions unnecessarily. After Lachlan left the keep, she waited a bit and then followed him outside with her basket over her arm. She caught a glimpse of him as he went into the armory. Perfect.

Rather than go directly, she took the long way around the courtyard. She went into one of the storerooms, pretending she needed something there, before circling around to the armory. When she tugged open the heavy, wooden door, she found Lachlan sitting on the long bench that ran the length of the room while sharpening his dirks with a whetstone.

"Ilysa in the armory?" he said, in lieu of a greeting. "Looking for a new axe?"

Despite the dry humor, his eyes were wary. This time, Lachlan's perpetual mistrust was well founded.

"No," she said. "I'm looking for a lighter weapon."

"Ye shouldn't be going into places like this alone," he said. "Our spy has killed two men. If I were him, you'd be dead now."

Connor had given her a similar lecture. "I am careful," she said, though her reason for following Lachlan into the armory belied that.

"Hmmph."

When Lachlan went back to sharpening his blade, Ilysa snatched an arrow from the quiver that lay beside him on the bench. As she stared at the distinctive, jagged tip, she felt as if the ground were tilting under her feet. It was a perfect match for the arrows she had cut out of Connor's chest and thigh.

Truly, she had not expected this. After watching Lachlan shoot with such skill during the battle, the idea that he could be the archer who'd tried to murder Connor had come into her head. She had only wanted to assure herself that it could not be true.

Ilysa's eyes blurred with tears at the memory of Connor's head slumped forward while Alex and Ian half carried him into Dunscaith. Then tears, this time of bitter disappointment, slid down her face because it was Lachlan, her friend, who had done it.

Her hands shook as she held the arrow out to him, her gesture an accusation. The tension between them was like a taut rope. Lachlan did not pretend he did not understand; nor did he try to rip the evidence from her hands.

"How could ye do it, Lachlan?"

\* \* \*

Connor was furious.

He had been absolutely clear that his willingness to enter the marriage was wholly dependent upon MacIain's joining the fight against the MacLeods for Trotternish. Given that understanding, MacIain should not have sent his granddaughter ahead of his war galleys.

In the event that MacIain failed to arrive in time to participate in the battle, Connor would be in the awkward position of returning a bride. On the other hand, Connor would probably lose the battle and be dead, so any awkwardness would be short-lived.

It was a complex situation, and he would have liked to have Ilysa's advice. Of course, she was the last person he could discuss this with. How would Ilysa react when she learned that MacIain's granddaughter was here?

By the saints, how was *he* going to live with two women? He suspected that removing the MacLeods from Trotternish would be the easier task.

Connor hid his growing despair as he approached the two women. He assumed they were mother and daughter, for they were twenty years apart and looked very much alike. They were tall, dark-haired, pretty women with heart-shaped faces and meat on their bones. Their fashionable headdresses and delicate slippers had not fared well on the sea journey in an open boat.

"This is Lady Eleanor, widow of our chieftain's first son, and her daughter, Jane," the old warrior said.

"Welcome, ladies," Connor said and gestured toward the steps. "I'm sure ye would like to get out of the wind and rain."

The two women continued staring at him without budging.

"I hope ye speak Scots or English," the old warrior said. "Neither of them have the Gaelic."

MacIain's granddaughter did not speak the Highland language? Connor was beginning to understand why MacIain had not allowed him to meet the lass sooner. Still, he told himself she could learn Gaelic. But one thing was certain—this lass sure as hell had not chosen him.

MacIain had lied about his granddaughter wanting him for her husband.

"Mind the steps." Connor spoke in Scots because it was slightly less distasteful to him than English. "They can be slippery when they're wet—and they're always wet."

The old warrior laughed, but neither woman showed any sign that she appreciated his jest. Connor stifled a sigh and held out his arm to the older woman, but she took the old warrior's arm and indicated he should help her daughter.

Connor's bride-to-be leaned her head back to look up the cliff. "I can't go up those steps! What if I fall?"

"Take care that ye don't," Connor said, struggling for patience. "I live on top of the cliff. There's no other way to get there from here."

When he offered his hand, she looked at it as if it were a poisonous snake. In the end, he had to heft the lass up the steps on his back. He found it hard to believe that such a helpless creature had any Highland blood in her at all. Between her cloying perfume and her arms clenched around his neck, she choked him all the way up the steps.

# CHAPTER 33

Connor was in hell.

He glanced down the head table at Ilysa, but she would not meet his eyes. When would this interminable meal be over so he could talk with her? He'd had no opportunity to forewarn her of his bride's arrival. He did not like how pale Ilysa looked, and it did not appear that she had touched her food.

"Must we come to this place often after we're wed?" Jane asked, her Scots harsh in his ear.

"Trotternish Castle is my home." Connor took another long swallow of whiskey. "This is where I stay."

"But we will spend a good deal of time at court," she persisted. "My grandfather promised me."

"I only go to court when commanded to appear," Connor said, then added, "and not always then."

"Not go to court?" Jane said and made that irritating gasp that had him reaching for his whiskey again.

Good God, the lass was going to turn him into a drunkard. He rubbed his forehead and reminded himself how badly he needed MacIain's warriors. Marriage for a chieftain was a political arrangement, and he had no cause to complain. He glanced sideways at her. Jane looked strong and healthy, and she was pretty—just not his kind of pretty.

How many times would he have to bed her to fulfill his duty to get her with child? The thought of bedding her made him feel dirty when his heart was elsewhere. Men did it all the time. Certainly his father had without it ever troubling him.

Connor's gaze returned to Ilysa. Niall appeared to be telling her quite a tale, judging from his wild gestures. Perhaps she would retell it to him later, when they were in bed...

"Is that your mistress?"

The question startled Connor out of his reverie. When he turned to Jane, she was looking down the table at Ilysa with narrowed eyes. Had she really asked him that, in the midst of supper? He hoped no one sitting near them understood Scots.

"I must say, she doesn't look the sort," Jane added.

*The sort?* That was such a Lowlander way of thinking. Since there was nothing polite Connor could possibly say in response, he poured himself more whiskey.

"My mother says Highland men are...demanding, and that I should be glad if you keep another woman," Jane said, making Connor choke on his drink.

"Keep your voice down, lass." After taking a deep breath, he decided he may as well ask, as long as she raised the subject. "And what do you say about it?"

Jane shrugged. "Why should I care?"

Though Connor had felt guilty at the prospect of hurting his wife's feelings, the idea of her being wholly indifferent to his bedding another woman did not sit well with him, either.

"So long as she knows her place," Jane added.

*Knows her place?* "So, you're looking forward to managing a large household?" he asked, deciding to take her statement in the least offensive way possible.

"Oh yes," Jane said, her eyes lighting up with the first spark of interest since her arrival. "To start with, there is so much I'd want to change in this hall."

"What, in particular, would ye wish to change in my hall?" Connor asked, speaking slowly. Someone who knew him better would take heed from the dead-calm of his tone, but not Jane.

"I'd buy all new tapestries and replace the paneling as well," she said, turning her head from side to side as she glared at his walls. "And I'd love to have one of those elaborate ceilings with rows of carved paterae, like I've heard the English king has in his palaces."

By the saints, Connor had to nip this in the bud. There was so much he objected to that he hardly knew where to begin.

"We Highlanders do not emulate the *filthy* English," he explained in a calm, reasonable voice, and he even managed to call the English filthy rather than what Highlanders usually called them, "most especially their king, who is responsible for the deaths of a great many Scottish warriors."

"I could be content with the French style—" Jane began.

"My clansmen have suffered great hardship," Connor

said, cutting her off. "As chieftain, it is my duty to provide for those who cannot provide for themselves before spending coin redecorating my perfectly good hall."

Tears filled Jane's eyes, and she abruptly fled the room in a rustle of fine silks. He was so relieved to have her gone that he could not even feel guilty for driving her from the table. Perhaps she would take her next meal upstairs with her mother, who had refused to come down at all.

And he had thought he had no romantic notions about marriage just because he did not expect love. Ha. His hope of a quiet, companionable partnership—a friendship even—in which they fulfilled their respective duties to the clan with consideration and respect for each other now seemed like a foolish dream.

He had a thousand memories of Ilysa quietly and efficiently bringing order to his household—decorating the hall with wildflowers, cajoling the servants with an encouraging word here and a firm suggestion there, and winning over the obstreperous cook. Without flinching, she bandaged wounds, helped babes into the world, and prepared the dead for burial.

Connor could not imagine his bride-to-be doing any of that. Jane was utterly useless. He was even more grateful, if that was possible, that Ilysa had decided to stay. Perhaps she could keep him from murdering his wife.

* * *

Ilysa made herself as small as possible and lay as close to the edge of the bed as she could without falling out. Jane and her mother breathed too loudly and flopped around like beached fish. While it had been a luxury to have a bedchamber to herself as the only highborn female in the castle, Ilysa was accustomed to it.

Or to sleeping with Connor in his bed.

Unfortunately, the other chambers in the keep either lacked beds or were in need of repair, due to the MacLeod occupancy and the castle changing hands twice through violence. Regardless, Ilysa intended to have her things moved to one of the smaller chambers first thing in the morning.

A lass could only take so much, and sharing a bed with Connor's bride—and the bride's mother—was more than Ilysa could bear.

The moment she saw Jane enter the hall on Connor's arm, she felt as if she had been struck in the heart with one of Lachlan's arrows. All day, the wound festered, spreading poison through every vein. She went about her duties, seeing that a fine meal was prepared for their guests, all the while enduring looks of sympathy from everyone. If she had any doubts before, it was clear that every man, woman, and child in the castle knew about her and Connor—and pitied her now.

Ilysa had hoped Connor's bride would be a duplicitous creature like her grandfather so she could hate her and not feel guilty about what she and Connor did. Instead, Jane was a guileless lass.

What was she going to do? Ilysa already knew. The decision had taken hold in the back of her mind, but she could not yet face it.

"Ilysa," Jane whispered, ruining Ilysa's hope that she was asleep. "Is the chieftain always so frightening?"

"Frightening?" Ilysa asked.

"When he came down the cliff to meet us, he was

streaked with mud like a barbarian, and he was carrying that enormous sword." Ilysa heard a *thump* as Jane slapped her hand to her bosom. "Truly, I feared for my life."

"Connor would never harm a woman or a child," Ilysa assured her.

"Hmm." Jane did not sound convinced.

"I imagine this is a harsh place compared with what you're accustomed to," Ilysa said. "Here, you'll be glad to have a husband who can protect ye so well."

"Without the mud, he is no doubt handsome, though he's a bit large," Jane said. "I just wish Highlanders were not such barbarians."

Ilysa refrained from pointing out that, despite her diminutive size, she was a Highlander. Eventually, Jane's breathing grew even, and Ilysa believed she was finally asleep.

She heard a soft knock on the door. As a healer, she was often awakened in the night to tend to someone. She quickly slipped out of bed, wrapped a plaid around her shoulders, and went to see who it was.

When she cracked the door, she saw Connor in the torchlight from the stairs. He did not speak a word until she slipped out and closed the door behind her. Then he enfolded her in his arms like a dying man clinging to life and said her name into her hair. He held her for a long, long time before he spoke another word.

"I couldn't wait any longer for ye to come to me," he said. "I need ye so much."

How could she resist him? When he lifted her in his arms to carry her to his chamber, she buried her face in his neck. He smelled of sea air and peat smoke—and Connor.

After he closed the door to his chamber, he pressed her against it. His kisses were demanding, urgent, desperate.

"I know what you're thinking," he said, his mouth against her ear. "But ye can't leave me. Ye can't."

When he hiked up her nightshift, the roughness of his shirt against her breasts sent tingles of awareness through her. She felt the familiar soft scratch of the calluses on his palms as he ran his hand up her side and over her back.

Tomorrow, she would think it all through, but right now she just wanted to be with him. Tonight, he was still hers. She wanted to touch him, to feel his warm skin and strong muscles under her hands, to be surrounded by his heat and passion.

He drew in a sharp breath when she reached between them and ran her hand up his shaft through his clothes. While their tongues entwined in a slow, sensual kiss, he unfastened his trews. When she wrapped her hand around his freed shaft, he deepened their kiss and sucked on her tongue.

"I'm going to show ye that you're mine," he said in a ragged voice against her ear.

He dropped to his knees and covered her breasts with his hands. His breath was hot and moist on her skin as he kissed and ran his tongue along her breastbone. All the while, he rubbed her nipples between his fingers and thumbs, sending jolts of desire sparking through her and causing a throbbing ache between her legs.

She clenched her fingers in his long hair as he sank lower and encircled her thighs with his hands. Tension curled inside her like a spring as he teased her with his tongue and mouth, planting moist kisses across her abdomen and down her hip.

"Aye," she gasped when he finally dipped his tongue between her legs. Her breasts ached, and her breathing grew shallow as she watched him pleasure her. But then she dropped her head back against the door. She gave herself over to the sensations coursing through her body as he worked his magic, licking and circling and sucking, until her knees grew weak.

He gripped her buttocks, holding her up and pulling her harder against his mouth. When he slid a finger inside her, her vision went black behind her eyelids. She heard herself cry out as if from a distance as bursts of bright light sparked and shimmered through her in waves.

Connor rose to his feet and lifted her off hers. Her nipples were so sensitive that she gasped when they brushed against his chest.

"I need to be inside ye," he said between frantic kisses. "Now."

"Aye," burst from her throat as he thrust deep inside her in one stroke, and her body clenched around him in another spasm of pleasure. Before she could catch her breath, he thrust into her faster and harder. Her back was banging against the door, but she didn't care. She could never get enough of him, never. She held on to him more tightly as he moved against her, sending hot shards of pleasure darting through her that were almost painful. He shuddered, and she cried out again as he called her name and exploded inside her.

He rested his forehead on the door and held her up, which was good because she could not have stood on her own. They were both panting and sweaty. After a long while, he leaned back just far enough to look into her face with his silvery blue eyes.

"I love ye with all my heart," he said, rubbing his thumb across her cheek. "You're part of me, and I am part of you. We are two halves of one whole."

* * *

Connor turned to Ilysa again and again in the night, trying to persuade her with his body to stay, to show her how much he loved and needed her. As he watched the room in the eerie light of dawn, lack of sleep made him feel as if he were floating. And yet, he did not want to close his eyes for fear she would slip away from him while he slept.

She stirred, restless in her sleep. When she opened her eyes, he saw farewell in them.

*No, I cannot let her go.* He caught her tear with his finger, and then her arms came around his neck. He breathed in the familiar scent of lilies and held her.

"Make love to me as if it were the last time," she said.

He did as she asked.

He pressed his lips to her palm, then he laid her on her back and kissed every inch of her, starting with her toes. Though he already had her body embedded in his memory, he memorized it again as he traced the arch of her foot, her slender ankle, the softness on the back of her knee.

He let the gold and red strands of her hair slide through his fingers.

He knew her, knew how to make her sigh, knew what the slight hitch in her breath meant. He used it all against her, trying to convince the stubborn woman he loved that what was between them was all that mattered. That it was enough.

She was quivering with need before they finally joined.

"Ye belong to me," he told her. She did not argue, but with Ilysa that never meant agreement.

They made love with a desperate passion.

\* \* \*

Ilysa held Connor to her a final time, then she forced herself to pry her arms loose and slide out of bed—and out of his reach. She slipped on her nightshift before she changed her mind.

"I thought I could do this," she said, swallowing back her tears. "But I've met her now, and I can't."

"Ilysa, please," Connor said but stopped when she held up her hand.

"I wish I could say it is only because I don't want to take your attention from her," she said. "But the truth is that she's far too pretty, too lively, too sweet."

"Sweet? She cares nothing about the welfare of my clan. She frets about silly things."

"Jane is just young," Ilysa said.

"She is the same age as you are."

"She hasn't had responsibilities and doesn't know any better, but she will learn," Ilysa said. "Ye will love her in time."

That was what had finally convinced her she must go. She could neither bear to be the reason Connor did not fall in love with his wife, nor watch him fall in love with her.

"I've told ye that no one else will ever have my heart," he said.

"I can't share ye. *I just can't do it.*" Ilysa briskly re-braided her hair out of habit and to calm herself. "I want something of my own. A home, a family, a husband."

Connor got out of bed and clasped his hands around hers.

"We can have children," he said. "Your sons will have chieftain's blood, and the same chance to be chosen chieftain as my other sons."

"Isn't that precisely what ye feared?" She looked away from him so he would not see the tears that threatened to spill from her eyes.

"That doesn't matter to me now, and it's too late anyway," he said. "Ye could be carrying my child already."

"I'm not." At least, there was no sign of it yet. "I'm a healer. I would know."

"But I *want* to have children with you," Connor said.

She closed her eyes against the answering surge of longing in her heart. How she would love to have Connor's children, to have a son with his fine looks and stalwart heart. But that was not to be.

"While we were at the gathering, I had an offer of marriage," Ilysa said. "I plan to take it."

Connor straightened and stared at her. She tried not to be insulted or hurt that he was so shocked, but she was.

* * *

Connor felt as if he had been kicked in the stomach.

"Ye didn't mention it before," he said through his teeth. "Who is he?"

"I know ye thought no chieftain would want to wed me because I'm not important enough," she began.

"I never said ye were not important—you're everything to me," Connor said, wondering if she were deliberately misunderstanding him. "I only meant that ye don't bring a clan's power and warriors to a marriage."

"Regardless of all I lack," Ilysa said, "the MacNeil chieftain said he wants to wed me."

"Glynis's father?" Connor said. "Ye can't want to marry him. Why, he's an old man."

"He's not old," she said. "He's a fine man, and I like him."

"He has all those children, that's why he asked ye," Connor said, raising his arms. "He wants a wife to mother his children."

Ilysa turned and fixed her direct gaze on him. "Is that the only reason ye believe a man would want me for his wife?"

"Of course not, but he doesn't love ye as I do." He tried pulling her into his arms, but she pushed him away.

"Mothering his children appeals to me," she said. "I like children. Perhaps we'll be blessed with more. I know that would please him as well as me."

The thought of Ilysa having any man's child but his made Connor feel physically ill.

"I want a family. I want to be mistress of my own home. I want a man I can call husband, who will take a vow to be faithful and keep it," she said, relentlessly ticking off the things he could not give her. "I believe marriage to Gilleonan MacNeil will provide me with all that."

"But will ye love him?" Connor asked, hating the desperation in his voice.

"I will feel useful and valued." She wrapped her plaid around her shoulders and tied the corners together with a snap. "I will be content."

"It sounds as though you've given this a great deal of thought." Just how long had she been planning to leave him?

"I have," she said.

"Who else did ye consider in all this thinking ye did? Lachlan of Lealt perhaps?" Connor asked. "Ye seem to have developed a true fondness for him."

"Lachlan?" Her face showed surprise, and he wondered if she was feigning it. "I'd never wed a MacDonald now, especially one who would keep me here on Trotternish. I'm going where I won't ever see ye again."

Never see him again? Could she mean it? His anger drained out of him, leaving only emptiness in its place.

"I'll tell the MacNeil when he comes here to join the battle against the MacLeods." She busied herself adjusting the plaid over her nightshift and avoided looking at him as she spoke.

"If you'll be happy with him, then I shall be content as well." Connor made himself say it, though it was a lie. "But there's no need for ye to make a hasty decision."

"If the MacNeil still wants me, I'll leave with him as soon as the battle's done."

That gave Connor almost no time to persuade her to change her mind.

"Remember, ye promised not to wed before Beltane," Ilysa said. "Ye owe me that."

"Does it matter now?" he asked.

She finally looked at him, and in her eyes he saw the deep sorrow that she had tried to hide behind her brusque manner.

"Aye," she said softly, "it still matters."

# CHAPTER 34

No one leaves the castle without my permission," Connor reminded everyone before they settled down to their meal.

He had first issued the order the moment Jane set foot in the castle. If word of her grandfather's imminent arrival with three hundred warriors reached the MacLeods, they would attack at once while the odds were still in their favor.

Jane sat next to him, and his appetite steadily dwindled as she prattled on about the latest court fashions. His thoughts grew blacker as he scanned the faces of his men while they ate, wondering which of them had murdered the two guards and left the gate open for Hugh. He had no better idea of who the culprit was now than the night it happened.

He was relieved when Lachlan entered the hall and strode to the head table, interrupting the meal.

"You and Sorely, come with me," Connor said, rising from his chair.

Whatever Lachlan had discovered on his latest excursion around the peninsula, Connor did not want him to speak of it in front of everyone in the hall. And he was glad for the excuse to leave.

As he turned to go, he caught the question in Ilysa's eyes and gave a slight nod. Before he left, he saw her pick up a flask of wine from the table as a pretext for coming into his chamber while he met with the two men. He had become accustomed to having her listen in on his private meetings and sharing her insights with him afterward. Apparently she had decided not to abandon him entirely yet, though she had avoided him all day up until now.

"What news do ye bring?" Connor asked Lachlan once the three of them were settled at the table in his chamber.

Sorely kept glancing over his shoulder, as if he expected the nursemaid's ghost to sneak up behind him and strangle him. Connor withstood the temptation to knock some sense into him.

"The MacLeods have gathered more men at the Snizort River," Lachlan reported. "They're harassing the few MacDonald farmers who still live near the river."

"Our warriors from Sleat and North Uist will be here soon, as well as MacIain's," Connor said. "We cannot let ourselves be drawn into battle before they arrive."

"While we're waiting," Lachlan said, "can we rattle some MacLeod cages a bit to divert them from the farmers?"

Connor had precisely the same idea. "I'll send you two and the other men I can spare to the Snizort River."

"Both of us?" Lachlan asked in a flat voice.

"Aye." Connor did not think either of them was Hugh's man, but it always paid to be cautious. The two disliked each other, and they could not both be spies, so he could count on them to watch each other. "All I want ye to do is create some havoc. Just enough to make the MacLeods cautious about straying too far from their camp."

"Who's in charge?" Lachlan asked.

He was right to ask, for one man had to lead. Sorely was paying close attention now and had a smug expression, anticipating Connor's answer.

"Sorely," Connor said and stood, dismissing them both.

Lachlan was the better man, but Connor was less certain he could trust him. He told himself it was a logical decision and had nothing to do with Lachlan's friendliness with Ilysa.

"Leave before daybreak and return as soon as ye can," he told them.

As the two men left, Connor watched Ilysa meet Lachlan's eyes and some message pass between them. Connor's claim on her was weakening by the hour. He could not bear that she might choose to be with Lachlan—or any man but him. She had said it would be MacNeil, but there was something between her and Lachlan.

"I'm surprised ye picked Sorely," Ilysa said as soon as the door was shut behind them.

"I thought we agreed ye wouldn't question my judgment again," Connor snapped, jealousy making him angry.

"And I thought ye wanted me in the room because ye valued my opinion," Ilysa said, crossing her arms. "I can see I was nothing but a bedmate to ye—and a temporary one at that."

When Connor put his arms around her, her body was stiff and unyielding.

"I'm sorry. The prospect of losing ye is making me behave like an ass." Sadness filled him as he breathed in the familiar scent of lilies in her hair. "You're everything to me."

"Would you be willing," she said in a quiet voice as she pushed him away, "to share me with another lover?"

The thought of her with anyone else made him murderous. If the circumstances were the other way around, he could never leave her—but her husband would be found with Connor's dirk in his chest.

"You're right," he said. "I am asking too much."

She touched his cheek with the tips of her fingers, filling him with longing. But it was only a gesture of farewell.

"We must both try to be happy," she said.

It was not his fate to be happy. It was his fate to save his clan, no matter what it cost him.

\* \* \*

The moon was full.

Ilysa pulled her hood over her head, carefully closed her door without a sound, and slipped down the stairs. Outside the hall, she paused to listen. When she was certain she heard nothing but snoring men, she tiptoed into the hall. The hearth fire cast a dim, eerie light over the slumbering bodies on the floor and benches. Ilysa skirted the edge of the room, staying in the shadows.

Connor would never agree to let her go if he knew, and

she did not want an escort. She must do this alone. With a glance over her shoulder to reassure herself that she had awakened no one, she eased the heavy door open just far enough to slide through and closed it softly behind her.

"There is an ill child who needs me," she told the guard at the gate, and he gave her no trouble, despite Connor's order. Men simply did not see a threat when they looked at her. Besides that, everyone knew she had Connor's trust.

Before she left to marry MacNeil, she would do everything she could to safeguard Connor. Tonight, she was making her second and last trip to the faery hills to cast her protective spells for him.

* * *

Connor looked up to see Sorely in the doorway to his chamber. Judging from the dwindling candlelight on his table, it was near midnight.

"You're not going to like this," Sorely said.

There was nothing Sorely could tell him that would be worse than the news that Ilysa was leaving. But it must be serious for Sorely to brave the ghost. He nodded for Sorely to come in.

"I've found our spy," Sorely said.

"No matter who our traitor is, 'tis better to know." He hoped it wasn't Lachlan. Despite his jealousy, he liked the man, and Lachlan was his best warrior. And odd as it seemed, he felt a connection between them because of the shared brother they had lost. "Who is it?"

Instead of answering, Sorely shuffled his feet and looked distinctly uncomfortable. If he had proof that Lachlan was Hugh's man, Connor would have expected him to be gleeful. Perhaps he had not given Sorely sufficient respect.

"Damn it, tell me," he said, but still Sorely did not answer. Connor had lost all patience with him when he finally spoke.

"Ilysa."

# CHAPTER 35

Ilysa?" Connor felt the blood drain from his head. "What about Ilysa?"

"I saw her sneak out of the castle a short time ago," Sorely said.

"She's a healer," Connor said. "I'm sure she's helping one of the farmer's wives deliver a babe or some such."

"When she does that, someone always comes asking for her first," Sorely said. "No one came. She stole out like a thief in the night."

Connor knew Ilysa was no spy for Hugh. The suggestion was ridiculous. But where was she going in the middle of the night if no one had come seeking a healer?

*Can Ilysa be meeting a man?* The thought struck him like a blade to his heart. No, she would not do that, not so soon after they had been together.

He hated himself for thinking it. But now that the idea

took hold, he could not shake it. A lass like Ilysa needed a lover. After Connor had uncovered her passionate nature buried beneath her layers of calm control, he hated the idea of her sharing it with another man.

"You're certain it was her?" he asked.

"Aye," Sorely said, looking mournful. "I've seen her go before."

Had she found another man while they were still lovers? Could that be the reason she was able to turn her back on him so utterly?

"Ye gave a clear command that no one was to leave without your permission," Sorely said, lifting one shoulder.

"I'm sure there's an innocent reason." He hoped to God there was. "She probably woke up worrying about some child she saw days ago with a fever."

Ilysa would not want to hurt his pride. If she were meeting a man for a liaison, she would not do it here in the castle where he was certain to find out. She was nothing if not *considerate*.

"Perhaps we should follow her?" Sorely suggested. "That would answer it."

Sorely was a fool to suspect Ilysa was their traitor. If she was meeting a man tonight, Connor did not want anyone to discover it but him.

"No, this is a trivial matter. I'll send a couple of the young men who need to practice their tracking skills," Connor said. "You and Lachlan will be leaving early, so get your rest."

"I came as soon as I saw her leave," Sorely said, "but whoever you're sending will need to be quick to catch her before she's crossed the field and is out of sight."

* * *

Ilysa's breathing was loud in her ears as she ran, then walked, then ran again along the dark path. It was a long distance to the faery hills, and she had to hurry to make it there and back before dawn. As she hastened her steps, she was grateful for the moonlight that shone intermittently between the windblown night clouds and kept her from losing her way.

After a couple of hours, the outline of the odd, conical hills emerged against the blacker night. White dots of sheep lay scattered across them, like stars in the sky. Ilysa set down her bag and caught her breath as she unpacked her things. Before starting the fire, she changed into her robe. Though no one was here to see her, she felt too exposed to remove her clothes in the firelight.

Once she had the blaze going, she found a stick the right length. She needed to calm herself and focus her thoughts for the spell to work. She stood facing the fire and drew in deep breaths until her heartbeat slowed.

Gradually, she pushed back the fear that had dogged her steps while traveling alone at night, as well as the tiredness from running and lack of sleep. Finally, and hardest of all, she set aside the hurt, the anger, and the desolation that had engulfed her since the arrival of Connor's bride.

She released all the emotions that crowded her heart and thoughts. All she kept of them was the longing, for that helped her to focus not on herself, but on the man. On Connor, for whom she was casting her spell.

She tossed a handful of the herbs she had brought onto the fire, and a burst of sparks shot above her head. The fire glowed in hues of blue, green, and orange. As she stared into the flames, she conjured an image of Connor, and she felt his presence so strongly that she was hopeful her spell would succeed.

Slowly, she began to circle the fire, left to right, in the direction for good fortune. As she walked, she dragged her stick behind her. It made no mark on the grass-covered ground, but the strength of the circle of protection she was making around Connor had nothing to do with what the eyes could see.

"Connor, son of Donald Gallach, grandson of Hugh, and great-grandson of the Lord of the Isles," she chanted as she circled, keeping his image in her mind, "may you be the chieftain who brings security and peace to our clan.

"May your feats be so great that the bards write poems and sing songs about them for many generations," she chanted as she circled a second time.

"May ye live to be an old man," she said, and in her mind's eye, she aged his beloved face, giving him deep lines and snowy white hair. "May your children be bonded to each other by great affection, and may ye have grandchildren who bring ye joy."

When she had circled three times, she flung her head back and raised her arms to the night sky. "May this circle protect and keep you until all these things have come to pass."

Now that she had completed the simple protective charm of the circle, she was ready to begin the more powerful fire dance. With every movement of the dance, she must please the faeries and thereby win their favor. In exchange, they would employ their magic for Connor's protection. Highlanders were good Christians, of course, and so the chant also called on God's help.

> Blades may cut you,
>     Yet none shall kill you.
> False friends may deceive you,
>     Yet none shall kill you.
> Allies may desert you,
>     Yet none shall kill you.
> Enemies may trap you,
>     Yet none shall kill you.
>
> *Seun Dhè umad!*
> *Làmh Dhè airson do dhìona!*
> Spell of God about you!
> The hand of God protect you!

* * *

Connor knelt on one knee in the grass, mesmerized. So he had not imagined the dancing faery the night he stumbled into the faery glen injured and bleeding. Somehow, it made sense that his dancing faery was Ilysa. As her hair caught the light of the fire and her body swayed back and forth, he thought of her above him and the magic of their lovemaking.

When he left the castle, he had been lucky to spot her at the far edge of the field in the moonlight. He had kept close enough to protect her should trouble find her, yet far enough behind her that she would not sense him following. The distance she traveled had surprised him. The longer she walked, the lower Connor's opinion sank of the man who had asked her to come so far alone to meet him. But when he recognized the odd, conical hills of the faery glen, he realized he had been wrong.

Instead of a romantic liaison, she had come all this way to reach the faery glen and recite some sort of spell. Connor set less store by the power of the Old Ways than most Highlanders—and clearly less than Ilysa did. With too little thought, he had dismissed the rumors that she was learning more from Teàrlag than headache cures.

He could not make out the words of her chant, for he kept his distance, not wanting to interrupt her until she finished her enchantment. Or curse. When he was injured and thought she was a faery, he had not seen her circle the fire with a stick as she was doing now. But he had fallen asleep that night and could easily have missed it.

As she circled the fire, long-ago memories of his mother cursing his father flashed through his head. What Ilysa was doing looked the same, and yet was markedly different. His memory of his mother was black as night, from the hate in her eyes, to her harsh words, to her hair writhing like snakes, while everything about Ilysa radiated light—her hair, her face, her robe.

When Ilysa began to dance around the fire, Connor forgot to breathe. Her movements were so erotic that desire swept through him like a storm. He imagined making love to her in the firelight and watching her dance above him with her golden hair falling all around him.

\* \* \*

Ilysa dropped her arms and closed her eyes, drained by her effort. When she recalled the image of an aged Connor, she smiled to herself. Ach, he would be a handsome old warrior. Her smile faded as she remembered that she would not be there to see him grow old.

When she opened her eyes, a jolt of fear coursed through her. Across the fire, she saw the outline of a huge warrior coming toward her out of the darkness. Her heart raced. In this magical place, he could be the faery king or a warrior from the dead. She quickly made the sign of the cross.

"Ilysa." The phantom said her name in a voice so deep she could feel it in her toes. "I was hoping to find ye here."

Her mind had been so focused first on Connor and then on her fear that it was a long moment before she took in his disfigured shoulder and realized who he was.

What was Alastair Crotach, chieftain of the MacLeods, doing here in the Faery Glen?

And why was he looking for her?

# CHAPTER 36

Greetings and God's blessing upon you," Ilysa formally addressed the MacLeod chieftain. Now that she knew who he was, she was far more curious than fearful. "What brings ye to the faery glen this night?" *Or any night.*

"I remembered that ye collected healing herbs in the glen when the moon was full." He lifted his hand toward the moon that shone through the night clouds. "I took a chance that ye would be here."

"But why?" Ilysa asked. "Our clans are on the verge of spilling each other's blood. 'Tis dangerous for ye to come to Trotternish alone."

"I have fifty warriors within calling distance," he said. "I needed to speak with ye."

"Me?" Ilysa could think of nothing that would bring the great MacLeod chieftain into a faery glen just to see her.

"I believe I know who your father was," he said.

"*My father?*" This was the last thing she expected to

hear. As exhausted as she was, it was one surprise too many. The MacLeod chieftain took her arm to steady her as tiny sparks crossed her vision.

"Come sit with me," he said. "I'll tell ye a story."

Ilysa had given up expecting to find out who her father was years ago, yet Alastair MacLeod did not seem the sort of man to make a joke of this. Blindly, she let him lead her to a log, then she sat with a *thump* as her legs gave way. He sat beside her and put a hand on her shoulder, an unexpectedly kind gesture.

"Do ye know about your mother being stolen away by one of my warriors?" he asked. "This would have been a long time before ye were born."

"Aye, though I only learned about it a short time ago," Ilysa said. "She returned to our clan with my brother when he was a babe."

"I was at our fortress on the isle of Harris and knew nothing of what happened at the time," he said. "In my absence, your mother's MacCrimmon relations complained to my son Ruari. He commanded her release and escorted her to the MacCrimmons himself."

"I thought your children were all younger than that," she said.

"I married late, but I had a natural son many years before my marriage," he said, staring off into the darkness. "Ruari was sixteen at the time, same as your mother."

"I am grateful to your son for coming to her aid."

"Ruari was kindhearted and gentle like his mother, not at all like the warrior he should have been." The MacLeod's silver hair shone in the moonlight as he shook his head. "From the time he was a bairn, he cared for three-legged dogs and birds with broken wings."

"Was he a disappointment to ye?" Ilysa asked, her thoughts on Connor. Although Connor was a gifted warrior, his father had never been able to see his other strengths because the two were so different.

"I tried my best to make a warrior out of him, but he was never more than passable with a sword." The MacLeod chieftain gave a deep sigh. "I could not name such a son my *tànaiste*, successor, but I did love him. I grieve for him still."

The sorrow in his voice made Ilysa's eyes sting, but she kept silent. Pity would only offend such a proud man.

"I recognized the brooch ye wore at the gathering," he said. "I had given it to Ruari's mother upon his birth, and it became his when she died."

Though she was not wearing it now, Ilysa's hand went to her throat where the brooch had rested. How did her mother come to possess a brooch belonging to the MacLeod chieftain's family?

"After seeing ye wear the brooch, I returned to Dunvegan and spoke with those who knew my son best. Eventually, I pieced it all together." He paused. "I believe Ruari was your father."

Ilysa sat up straight and blinked at him. She had been so caught up in the tale that she had forgotten where it was leading.

"'Tis easy to imagine how it happened. Your mother was a fragile creature who had been hurt—my son was bound to think himself in love with her. As for your mother, my son would not have frightened her as other men did. Ruari was the one who rescued her, and he had a gentle nature."

"He could not be my father," Ilysa said after she had gathered her thoughts. "What ye speak of happened near the time of my brother's birth, which was many years before mine."

"Nothing happened then, but they met again nine years later when your mother accompanied your chieftain's family to a large gathering of the clans," he said. "When they both disappeared soon after, no one guessed it was with each other."

"How do ye know it was?" she asked.

"My son confided in his best friend, who I recently persuaded to tell me all about it," he said. "Ruari knew, of course, that I could not approve a marriage to your mother, as she was not close kin to a chieftain."

"Of course," Ilysa said, unable to keep a touch of bitterness from her voice.

"They became lovers, and he begged her to come live with him at Dunvegan and bring her son," he continued. "But she refused. She told him she had made a promise to care for your chieftain's children, and she would not break it."

"I can't imagine my brother Duncan raised as a MacLeod," she said. "His first chance, he would have run away." Then it struck her that if her mother had gone, she would have grown up as a MacLeod herself. As much as the prospect of being parted from Connor grieved her, the thought of never knowing him was worse.

"When your mother chose to return to her own clan, it broke my son's heart. Ruari died in a battle not long after." He paused. "I don't believe he knew she carried his child."

"I'm sorry ye lost your son." Ilysa could not yet think

of the young man in the story as her father. "Do ye want his brooch back? Is that why ye came to tell me this?"

"I didn't come for the brooch." The MacLeod chieftain's gaze was intent on her face. "I came for my dead son's only child. I came for my granddaughter."

# CHAPTER 37

Connor was the worst kind of fool.

He had caught Ilysa red-handed. And yet, as he followed her slight figure through the darkness back to the castle, doubts assailed him. That's how much he loved her. Passion for a woman could rob a man of rational thought if he let it. Ilysa had sneaked out of the castle for a secret meeting in the middle of the night with the chieftain of their enemy clan. There could be no innocent explanation. And yet, his heart could not accept that Ilysa would commit this treachery.

Even if she hated him for taking a wife, he could not imagine Ilysa doing anything that would put the clan in danger. It made no sense. Yet he had seen her with his own eyes, sitting and talking with the MacLeod chieftain as if they were old friends.

Or more than friends.

Connor wanted to shout at her and shake her—and

most of all, to hold her in his arms and beg her to say she had not betrayed him. But his emotions were too raw, the pain too fresh. Until he could think this all through with a clear head in the cold light of day, it would be unwise to confront her. In his current state, he would believe anything she said, grasp at any straw.

Connor kept his gaze on Ilysa, slipping in and out of the moonlight ahead of him like a sprite, while he tortured himself going over and over again what he had seen in the faery glen. When the MacLeod first appeared like a wraith from the darkness, Connor had reached for his sword. He was on the verge of sprinting toward Ilysa to save her when instinct born of years of fighting froze him in place.

First, he sensed the presence of other men in the darkness. When he paused to listen, he heard the telltale sounds of a large group of warriors trying to be silent: a nervous hand sliding a dirk in and out of its sheath, the shuffling of feet, a muffled cough. The hidden warriors would not have stopped him from rescuing her, but only led him to be cautious and cunning in devising a plan to do it.

What truly halted him was Ilysa's reaction to the MacLeod's sudden appearance. She did not attempt to run, or even take a step backward, when he approached her. Instead the pair appeared to exchange greetings. While Connor watched from his hiding place, she allowed their clan's greatest enemy to take her arm and sit beside her. Ilysa showed no resistance even when the MacLeod chieftain rested his goddamned hand on her shoulder.

Connor had been too far away to hear their conversation. With so many MacLeod warriors hidden in the darkness, he dared not draw closer. Yet their ease with each other was obvious, as was the MacLeod chieftain's reluctance to part with her at the end. The MacLeod held Ilysa's hands, as if trying to persuade her not to leave him.

When did Ilysa have the opportunity to become acquainted with the MacLeod? Connor had been away in France for five years. It could have happened then, somehow.

Each instance Connor had seen the two of them together at the MacIain gathering came back to him with sharp clarity. The first time, he thought it an unfortunate coincidence that Ilysa was standing next to Alastair MacLeod at the hall entrance. But now, in his mind's eye, he saw the pink of her cheeks from the cold outside and Alastair striding away from the doorway as if he had just entered.

The second time, Ilysa had not denied speaking with the MacLeod. *He doesn't seem like such a bad man to me. I liked him.*

How long had she been meeting him in the faery glen? The MacLeod was far from young, but the MacNeil's age had not troubled her. Connor did not believe they were lovers—at least not yet. The pair had neither kissed nor embraced. Again, he cursed himself as a fool for wanting so badly to believe she was innocent—as if a clandestine rendezvous with the MacLeod chieftain when the two clans were on the verge of war could mean anything except that she was disloyal.

Connor recalled how he had repeatedly given her all the reasons he could not wed her. Consorting with his enemy would be the perfect revenge, rivaling his mother's vengeful curse on his father's other sons.

*Ilysa came to me a virgin. She chose me first.*

Whatever Ilysa had done was his fault. She had come to him innocent, not just in body, but in heart and spirit. And he had brought her to this.

# CHAPTER 38

"Our warriors did what?" Connor thundered at Lachlan.

His head pounded from lack of sleep, and his temper was frayed. The first rays of dawn were slanting through his windows when he finally fell into his cold, empty bed. After a few hours of tossing and turning, he had finally fallen into a restless sleep. He was dreaming of Ilysa dancing around the MacLeod chieftain with sparks flying from her fingertips when Lachlan and Sorely banged on his door to report on their excursion.

The moment he saw them, he knew something had gone terribly wrong. The animosity between the two men veered to the edge of violence.

Connor shifted his gaze to Sorely, who had given a glowing report of their success, then back to Lachlan, who had spoken last.

"Our warriors chopped off the heads of the dead MacLeods," Lachlan repeated, "and sent them floating down the river."

After his night at the faery glen, Connor had mistakenly thought things could not get worse. He was so angry his vision went blood-red around the edges.

"We have every right to fight for the return of our lands," Connor said through his teeth. "But this sort of barbarism turns it into a blood feud. Our grandchildren will still be fighting because of what you've done."

"I knew ye would be angry," Lachlan said.

"Then why in the hell did ye not stop it?" Connor said, clenching his fists.

"I wasn't the one in charge," Lachlan spat out.

"Did the two of ye just stand by and let this happen?" Connor demanded, shifting his gaze from one to the other.

"I had my hands full keeping Sorely and the others from murdering a MacLeod farmer's wife and daughter, after they raped them," Lachlan said, his nostrils flaring. "I thought that was more important than saving the heads of those already dead."

"You participated in this travesty?" Connor said, turning on Sorely. When he saw the smirk on Sorely's face, he knew. "Christ, ye ordered it, didn't ye?"

"Ye said to rattle their cages," Sorely said with an insolent shrug. "That's what I did."

"Trotternish is not MacLeod homeland, so they would not have fought to the death for it as we will," Connor said. "Now that you've made it a matter of honor for them, they'll bring the full force of their fury upon us, and it will cost us many more lives."

"I fought under your father and your brother Ragnall for years," Sorely said. "This is exactly what they would have done."

"Not my brother, not Ragnall." Connor's anger was cold and hard, like ice in his chest at the accusation, though he could not say for certain that his father would not do such a thing.

"Ragnall was a fearsome warrior," Sorely hissed, "*just* like your father."

Sorely appeared to have no idea how close he was to being skewered with Connor's sword.

"Well, I am *not* like my father," Connor said, and for the first time he saw himself as a better leader than his father was. "I should have made my expectations clear. We do not rape women or defile the dead!"

"'Tis a mistake to show an enemy mercy," Sorely said, his face going an angry red. "Your father and brother understood that."

Connor picked Sorely up by the front of his shirt and slammed him against the wall. "Get out of my sight before I order ye cast adrift at sea as my father did to the nursemaid you're so frightened of," he said between his teeth. "Unlike that lass, you'd deserve it."

"You'd best mind your back with Sorely after this," Lachlan said in a low voice after Connor tossed Sorely out the door. "Better yet, lock him in the dungeon."

He was tempted instead to hand Sorely over to Alastair MacLeod, who would give him a far worse death than casting him adrift at sea.

"Sorely is too loyal to my father's memory to go to Hugh, who was the brother my father hated most," Connor said. "I will deal with Sorely later. For now, I need every warrior."

"What do ye think the MacLeod will do now?" Lachlan asked.

Connor went to the window and imagined a mass of MacLeod warriors charging across the field toward the castle.

"Taking the castle by force would cost him too many men," Connor said. "He'll want to consolidate his control of the countryside first so that he can keep food and our clansmen from reaching the castle."

"Up until now, he's held Trotternish with relatively few warriors," Lachlan said. "His control is thin."

Connor had come to the same conclusion from his night forays.

"After what Sorely and the others did, Alastair MacLeod will be angry, but not foolish," Connor said. "My guess is he'll sweep across the Snizort River with a large force, burning MacDonald homes in retribution and strengthening his hold on the countryside. We must stop him from crossing the river with all those men, and he knows it. He'll hope for a sound defeat to show us the futility of our cause. After that, he'll lay siege to the castle and bide his time while he starves us out."

"Sounds about right to me," Lachlan said. "How long will it take him to gather his forces?"

"Even if he moves quickly, it will take him a couple of days," Connor said. "If we're lucky, he'll want to wait until after the purification of the fields and herds by the fires of Beltane, which gives us three days."

He hoped to hell the other MacDonald warriors and MacIain's arrived before the MacLeod attack began. It would be a disaster if the enemy crossed the river en masse.

"I'm making ye captain of my guard," Connor said. "Come, I'll speak to the men now. We must prepare for battle."

\* \* \*

The sun was high when Ilysa awoke. Though she still felt groggy from her long night, she told herself she must go downstairs to see that everything was going as it should. She sat up. But then she remembered that the responsibility for managing the household was not hers— or at least it would not be for much longer—and flopped back down.

She stared at the ceiling and contemplated the events of the last two days. Between the arrival of Connor's bride and the discovery that her father was the son of the MacLeod chieftain, she felt shaken to her foundations.

*Alastair MacLeod is my grandfather.*

No matter that by Highland tradition she belonged to her father's clan, she would always be a MacDonald. She had told Alastair as much. She could no more go live with him among the MacLeods than she could live among the hated English. And yet, it made her feel less alone in the world to know that she had a grandfather who wanted her.

Alastair was gruff, much like her brother, and he seemed an honorable man. Despite the briefness of their acquaintance, she found she liked him a great deal. She felt certain that under different circumstances he and Connor would get along well. It pained her that her newfound grandfather and the man she loved would soon be waging war against each other, as MacLeods and MacDonalds seemed destined to do with regularity. If Ilysa needed it, that was one more reason to wed the MacNeil chieftain and leave Skye.

When she finally dressed and went downstairs to the

hall, she found the men preparing for war. She stopped one of them, who told her that the chieftain expected the battle against the MacLeods to come soon, perhaps even before their other warriors arrived.

Connor was busy giving orders to the men, who all seemed to be in motion. When he saw her, he stopped in place. For an instant, his eyes burned into her. But then, he broke their gaze and abruptly left the hall.

Seeing him filled her with such a painful longing that she told herself it was just as well Connor could not bear to be in the same room with her. All day, Jane and her mother were constantly underfoot, adding to her misery. The two expected to be waited on and entertained, while all the other women oiled plaids to keep the warriors dry and prepared food for them to carry.

Just before sunset, a cheer went up in the castle when Alex arrived with fifty warriors from their stronghold on the isle of North Uist. Connor looked as if a weight had been lifted off his shoulders as he greeted his cousin.

"Am I glad to see ye," Connor said as they gripped forearms.

"I didn't want to risk missing any of the fun, so I came early," Alex said.

The sail from North Uist was shorter than the journey Ian and Duncan would make from the far end of Skye, but it was across open water, which meant Alex had a greater risk of being held up by bad weather—not that he would ever admit a mere storm could delay him.

"There's my favorite lass in all of Trotternish," Alex called out when he saw Ilysa.

He strode over to her and lifted her off her feet. As he spun her around, his laughter rang in her ears, and the oppression that had closed in on her all day lifted for a brief moment.

"Alex!" Connor's voice cut through the hall, his tone so sharp that it was like a blade to her heart. "We must speak without delay."

Connor turned on his heel and marched through the doorway to the adjoining building without a backward glance. When Alex raised his eyebrows at Ilysa, she shook her head.

"Ye can't keep anything from me—I'll get if from ye later," he said with a wink before he left to follow Connor.

"Ilysa!" Jane called.

Ilysa was too weary and profoundly unhappy to humor Jane. Instead, she pretended not to hear, which was so unlike her, and went straight to her new bedchamber at the top of the keep. She began packing her things at once, determined to move forward with her plans—and to not give in and go to Connor's bedchamber. Somehow, she must learn to live without him.

Despite his coldness toward her today, Ilysa felt her resolve weakening by the moment. All that saved her from going to him was the knowledge that Alex was in his chamber. The two would likely be up until all hours talking.

But how she wanted him. She fell across the bed and pounded her fists. *Why, why, why can't I have him? Why can't I be the one he weds?* She felt both confused and overwhelmed by loneliness. Perhaps things would look better in the morning when she was not so tired and did not miss him so much. But tonight, she let the tears come.

Tomorrow she would be brave again.

\* \* \*

"Praise God you're here," Connor said when he and Alex were alone in his chamber with the door closed. "I need someone I know I can trust."

"'Tis like that, is it?" Alex raised an eyebrow. "I thought ye would have weeded out Hugh's spies by now."

"They are like weeds," Connor said as he poured them both cups of whiskey from the jug on the table. "Pull one and two more appear in its place."

Connor told him about Hugh's attack on the farms on the east side of Trotternish, the murder of the two guards, and the skirmish with the MacLeods that ended with heads in the river.

"Ach, that is bad," Alex said, making a face.

Though it did not solve anything, Connor felt better after discussing all the disasters with Alex—all of them, that is, except Ilysa.

"I have news as well," Alex said.

"I can't take more bad news, so this better be good," Connor said and tossed back another whiskey.

"I wouldn't call it bad news, but your uncle Archibald is dead."

"Dead?" Connor straightened. "I saw him not long ago. What happened?"

"He let Hugh Dubh into his home is what happened." Alex paused to take a drink. "Hugh murdered Archibald *while he was a guest in his brother's home.*"

Hugh was not only guilty of a cowardly act and murdering his last brother, but he had violated the ancient and sacrosanct Highland code of hospitality between host and guest, which was almost worse.

"The story is that, after enjoying a fine meal at Archibald's table, Hugh called his brother to the window to look at his new galley—then stuck his dirk in Archibald's back."

After a long silence, Connor said, "I was invited to join them."

"Ye were wise not to go," Alex said and lifted his cup to Connor.

"I would have gone," Connor said, feeling the weight of his errors and misjudgments like a boulder on his back, "except that Ilysa locked me in my own dungeon to prevent me."

Alex threw his head back and laughed. There was nothing for it then but to tell him the full tale, which caused his cousin to laugh so hard that tears rolled down his face.

"I always knew that lass had more spark than she let on," Alex said, slapping the table. "I can't wait to tell Ian and Duncan."

Connor would never hear the end of it from the three of them, though he could count on them never to undermine his authority by speaking of it to anyone else.

"Ilysa is as stubborn as her brother. She just hides it behind a sweet manner," Alex said. "That must have been why ye sent her packing to Dunscaith, aye? I'd say ye owe her an apology."

Connor's stomach dropped. Alex had no idea how wrong he was.

"A large gift is in order, for she saved your sorry arse," Alex said. "What would ye say your life is worth? A fine horse? A bag of gold?"

Ilysa had saved him. Did this mean he was wrong

about the rest? But he had seen her meeting with the MacLeod. There was no mistaking that. He could think of no reason for their meeting except treachery, but he should have heard her out. He owed her that.

He was anxious to go talk to her. Yet he had such a weakness for Ilysa that he decided to tell Alex about her meeting with the MacLeod and hear his thoughts first. Connor took a gulp of his whiskey. He dreaded telling him what Ilysa had done, knowing how fond Alex was of her.

"Alex, there is something I must tell ye." He paused. "'Tis about Ilysa."

"For God's sake, Connor," Alex said, springing to his feet. "You're fooking Duncan's baby sister, aren't ye? I knew it!"

This was not what he had intended to disclose to Alex, but his cousin was exceptionally perceptive about such things.

"Ye can stop worrying about Hugh and the MacLeods," Alex said, gesturing with his hands as he paced the room. "Duncan will kill ye first."

* * *

Ilysa must have fallen asleep, for she was dreaming of Connor when a knock on the door awoke her. Her first thought was that it was him, and she scrambled out of bed and opened the door without bothering to wrap a plaid about her.

In the glow of the torchlight from the stairwell, she saw that it was Lachlan. Disappointment weighed down on her chest. It was a long moment before she realized Lachlan was staring holes into her and still longer before she remembered she was in just her nightshift. When she swung the door closed, Lachlan stuck his foot in it. He looked past her, taking in the open chest and the clothes laid out.

"What do ye want?" she asked, leaning out from behind the door.

"My sister's youngest is gravely ill," he said. "She sent my nephew to fetch you. He's waiting in the boat. Will ye come?"

"Of course," she said. "I'll just be a moment."

She did not even know Lachlan had a sister, yet there was no mistaking the worry in his voice. After closing the door, she quickly donned her gown and heavy cloak, then gathered the herbs she thought she might need into her basket.

# CHAPTER 39

Let me do the talking," Lachlan told Ilysa as they approached the gate. Fortunately, the guards were Trotternish men who knew him well and were accustomed to his comings and goings in the night.

"The chieftain said no one is to leave," one of them said without much conviction.

"I'm the new captain of the guard," Lachlan reminded them—and wondered if he still would be when he returned tomorrow. "The chieftain gave me permission to take Ilysa to visit an ill child."

Some truth was better than none, and it satisfied the guards. Lachlan had not bothered seeking Connor's permission once he discovered how adamant Connor was that Ilysa, in particular, not leave the castle. He assumed the pair were having a dispute over the arrival of Connor's bride. Love may make the chieftain behave foolishly, but Lachlan was not about to let his niece die because of it.

"This is Ewan," Lachlan told Ilysa, nodding toward the

shadowy figure of his nephew in the small boat when they reached the shore. In quick succession, he lifted her into the boat, pushed off, and leaped over the side.

"You're coming with us?" Ilysa asked, sounding surprised.

"Ewan is a good lad, but I can't send ye off in the night with only an eleven-year-old to protect ye." Lachlan spoke in a low voice as he took up the oars and began to row. "Besides, if wee Brigid should... well, I'd want to be there."

Lachlan was grateful that Ilysa was not one of those lasses who had to talk. Since Connor had a habit of staring out to sea from his windows and the sail on his nephew's little boat was white, Lachlan rowed until they were well away from the castle.

"Why did ye wait to raise the sail until now?" Ilysa asked, astute as always.

"Why did Connor have guards stationed at your door?" he countered. Lachlan had told that set of guards he would take the night duty for them, and they'd been happy to let him.

"I suppose he did it because of those two men being murdered," Ilysa said. "But he needn't worry. I have a bar on my door."

Did she really not know?

"The guards were not there to protect ye," Lachlan said, "but to keep ye in."

\* \* \*

"What?" Ilysa felt as if she had been kicked in the stomach. "Why would Connor do that?"

"You tell me," Lachlan said. "On our way to harass the

MacLeods, Sorely was bragging that he'd caught ye leaving the castle against orders and ran to tell the chieftain. Then I heard from the men on duty last night that Connor left the castle shortly after you did. So I'm guessing he followed ye and didn't like what he saw."

Of all the ill luck. The one night Connor followed her was the night she went to the faery glen and spoke with Alastair MacLeod.

*Good heavens, does Connor believe I'm a traitor?*

She could think of no other reason why he would imprison her. Of course, she understood how suspicious it must have looked, but Connor had known her all of her life. More, they had shared every intimacy, and he said he loved her. He could not truly love her and believe she was capable of turning on him and her clan.

She understood now why Connor could not bear to be in the same room with her today. But why did he not simply ask her what happened? True, he had been busy preparing for the coming battle, but if he had time to order men to guard her door, he had time to put the question to her.

The blood drained from her head as she realized Connor must have followed her all the way back from the faery glen without once attempting to speak to her. He had already condemned her. How could he think so little of her?

She must finally accept in her heart that there was no hope for them.

While the small boat glided through the darkness, the terrible thoughts swirled round and round in her head. She was glad Lachlan could not see her silent tears. She did not know how she would live through this, but she would. When she was only eleven, her brother was sent away and her mother fell apart, leaving Ilysa to take over her mother's duties and be responsible for them both. She told herself that if she could survive that, she could survive anything.

As soon as they entered his sister's cottage, Ilysa forgot her own troubles. Lachlan's sister was weeping with the sick child in her arms while five or six other children looked on with big eyes.

"*Beannachd air an taigh*," a blessing on this house, Ilysa said in a low voice.

"This is Ilysa," Lachlan said when they stood next to his sister. "She is a good healer, Flora. If anyone can save Brigid, she can."

The child's lethargy and the sound of her labored breathing rattling in her chest worried Ilysa deeply.

"I can see you've been doing just right, washing her with cool cloths," Ilysa said, attempting to reassure the mother. "Your other children are frightened. I'll take good care of wee Brigid while ye see to them."

She exchanged a glance with Lachlan, and he nodded.

"Where is Malcom?" he asked as he helped ease the ill child from his sister's arms and into Ilysa's.

"I don't know," Flora said while Lachlan led her to where the other children were huddled together. "I've been worried sick about him, too."

"When ye have a moment, Lachlan, I need a pan of hot water," Ilysa said, keeping her voice calm.

Brigid's hacking cough was sapping her strength. Ilysa hummed to soothe her as she rubbed a salve over the little girl's chest to ease her breathing.

"Feels good," the child whispered.

Ilysa brushed the damp curls back from her face and kissed her forehead. Her fever was high. She was a pretty, curly-headed thing, but so ill that Ilysa anticipated it would be a long night—and the outcome was uncertain.

* * *

"I do love Ilysa, for what little that's worth," Connor said after letting Alex rant at him for a while. "Now you'd best sit down, for I have worse to tell ye."

Connor proceeded to tell him about Ilysa's secret meeting with the MacLeod chieftain. "There's no getting around it. Ilysa has betrayed us."

"By the saints, how could ye believe Ilysa would do anything against you, let alone the clan?" Alex said. "She's been in love with ye from the day we returned from France."

"She has?"

"Ach, you're a fool." Alex gave him a crooked smile. "But then, most of us are when it comes to love."

"I don't know what to do about her," Connor said, sagging lower in his chair.

"Groveling would be a good start."

"I meant about her treachery," Connor said. "How can ye believe she is innocent?"

"I'll admit that meeting the MacLeod in the faery glen is strange," Alex said. "But there must be an explanation. What did she say when ye asked her?"

"I didn't."

"Tell me I misheard that," Alex said.

"I was afraid I'd believe anything she told me," Connor said, holding his head in his hands, "despite the facts."

"Ye should believe her because Ilysa is incapable of

doing anything vile," Alex said. "When it comes to judging people, sometimes ye have to go with your heart, not your head."

"That's what Teàrlag told me," Connor said, rubbing his forehead.

"Ilsya is too brave for good sense. Don't forget, she stayed at Dunscaith to spy for us while Hugh held it," Alex said. "Hell, she probably thought she could talk the MacLeod out of fighting for Trotternish or some such foolishness."

Connor wanted to believe it. "I'll go talk to her now."

Hope, like a wildflower sprouting from a rock, sprang up in his chest as he raced to her bedchamber. When he reached Ilysa's door, the guards were gone. His heart felt as if it were being torn in two as he pushed the door open and stepped into the empty room.

She was gone.

\* \* \*

Near dawn, Brigid's breathing finally eased. Ilysa put the child in her mother's waiting arms and went outside. Lachlan followed her out, and they leaned against the cottage wall watching the sun rise over the water.

"I must return to the castle this morning," Lachlan said after a time. "Whether I'm still captain of the guard or no, I want to fight the MacLeods with my clan."

Ilysa had made her own decision during the long hours of caring for the ill child.

"I'm not returning to the castle," she told him. "Ever."

"My sister will welcome ye here as long as ye wish to stay."

"The MacNeil chieftain asked me to be his wife," Ilysa

said, and her voice wavered only a little. "When he arrives at the castle, I want ye to get word to him that he can fetch me here."

"No need to decide that yet," Lachlan said. "Do ye want me to tell Connor where ye are?"

"No."

* * *

Lachlan's heart was full as he sat next to the cot watching Ilysa's sleeping face in the morning light. He was so grateful to her for saving his niece. He pushed a strand of red-gold hair away from her cheek. Asleep, she looked deceptively frail.

"She's a tough one," Lachlan said to his sister who had come to stand behind him. "For such a tiny lass, she has a lot of courage."

Flora squeezed his shoulder. "Don't let this one get away, Lachlan."

"Her heart is elsewhere," he said.

"Hearts change," his sister said.

Not Ilysa's. That was just one of the things he admired about her.

"Once ye put your mind to it, what lass could resist ye?"

He put his hand over his sister's. "I'd best be off."

The door to the cottage swung open, and Malcom entered. His face was haggard, and he looked as though he had traveled hard. When Flora embraced him, he eased her aside and looked at Lachlan.

"The MacLeods are coming."

# CHAPTER 40

Connor was torn between fear and jealousy, not knowing if Lachlan had kidnapped Ilysa or if she had she gone willingly.

After he found the two men he had assigned to guard Ilysa sound asleep in the hall and hauled them outside to question them, he had grilled the guards at the gate. They all told him the same story. Lachlan and Ilysa were both held in such regard that they were allowed to walk out of the castle with nary a question, despite Connor's explicit command.

"I don't know where she is," Connor said for the hundredth time as he wore out the floor pacing. Alex had chosen to believe the obviously fabricated story about an ill child and was annoyingly unconcerned.

"Let's work on a problem we can solve." Alex stretched out his long legs and yawned. "I believe I can tell ye who your spy is."

"Do ye claim ye have The Sight now?" Connor asked.

"Ach, 'tis a simple matter once I have the right information," Alex said with an amused glint in his eye.

"I'm in no mood for games," Connor said.

"We're looking for a man, or a woman, who has a grudge against ye or something important to gain by helping Hugh," Alex continued, undeterred. "Our culprit also must be ruthless enough to murder two innocent men of his clan to serve his purpose."

Alex was right. There was always a reason people did what they did; it was just a matter of discovering what it was.

A knock on his door interrupted his contemplation of suspects. When Connor opened it, one of the men he had upbraided earlier for letting Lachlan and Ilysa leave was there.

"Thought you'd want to know that Lachlan's returned."

\* \* \*

Lachlan was hauled up the stairs and into the chieftain's private chamber. While Connor clenched his fists and looked ready to murder him, a long, lean, warrior sat with his feet propped up on Connor's table. The visitor had the look of an ancient Viking except for the amusement in his sea-green eyes.

"What have you and Ilysa done? Betrayed us to the MacLeods or to Hugh?" Connor shouted at him, looking every inch the warrior chieftain. "How could you, a man who has been hailed as a hero of our clan, commit this egregious act? After I trusted ye enough to make ye my captain, this betrayal cuts deep."

Lachlan felt himself sinking fast in a sea of disaster.

Somehow, Connor had discovered his crime. But why did he mention Ilysa, as if she had been an accomplice in the attempted assassination?

"Tell me what I'm accused of," Lachlan said, instinctively defending himself, though he was guilty as hell. "As for Ilysa, your imagination far exceeds mine if ye can conceive of her betraying the clan."

"I saw the two of ye talking alone time and again," Connor said, his eyes flashing. "And now, ye sneak her out of the castle against my orders. You've betrayed me."

Oh, Jesu, was that all? Being caught violating Connor's order to keep Ilysa in the castle was a slight offense compared with Lachlan's near-successful attempt to murder the MacDonald chieftain.

"My sister's child was ill," Lachlan said. "She would not have lasted the night without Ilysa's care."

"An easy claim to make," Connor said, folding his arms. "Why should I believe ye?"

"I think we can rule him out as Hugh's spy," the warrior lounging in the chair put in. "Evidently, he has no need to stab your guards to get them to leave their posts or open the gate for him."

*O shluagh*, Connor suspected him of that? "Ye can ask my sister—ye know both her and the child," Lachlan said. "Ye were at her and Malcom's home the night the MacLeod warriors attacked. My sister told me ye saved wee Brigid."

"That's your sister's family?" Connor asked. "Is the child all right?"

"Aye, thanks to Ilysa's healing skills," Lachlan said.

"Ye brought Ilysa back with ye?" Connor asked and started heading for the door.

"No," Lachlan said, bringing Connor to an abrupt halt. "She didn't want ye to know where she is, and she claims she's never coming back."

"What else did she say?" Connor asked.

Lachlan hesitated. "She may have mentioned something about marrying another chieftain..."

Connor made a growling sound and started pacing the room.

"See, Ilysa's safe, and ye can sort this out later," the tall blond warrior said and stretched his arms as if he hadn't a care in the world. "'Tis time for fighting, aye?"

Lachlan was more than ready to change the subject. "Malcom crossed the inlet to the other peninsula and saw scores of MacLeod warriors moving south, toward the river," he told Connor. "Ye were right—if they were attacking the castle, they'd come by sea."

At the sound of shouts from the courtyard, he and Connor rushed to the windows. Even the visiting warrior was stirred to drop his feet from the table and join them.

"A fleet of war galleys is coming!" one of the men shouted up to Connor. "Our men from Sleat are here!"

Connor strode out of the room. When Lachlan started to follow him, the other warrior stopped him with a steel grip on his arm.

"I'm the chieftain's cousin Alex," he said. "Is Ilysa all right?"

"Aye," Lachlan said.

"Good," Alex said with a smile that did not reach his cold, green eyes. "Because I'll skin ye alive if you've harmed her."

* * *

With a mix of relief and anguish, Connor watched the MacIain galleys—all six of them—sail toward the bay behind Ian and Duncan's boats. MacIain had arrived in time for the battle and met Connor's condition for the marriage alliance.

"Shame I asked my father-in-law to use his warriors to guard North Uist for me so I could bring more of our own men to this fight," Alex said as they waited on the shore for the galleys to come in. "If I'd known Ilysa wanted to marry him, I would have brought him along instead."

Connor ignored the taunt. He understood why Alex was angry—hell, he was angry with himself.

"Hope you're ready to fight," he greeted Duncan and Ian after their galleys were pulled onto the shore.

"How is my sister?" Duncan asked.

"She's away from the castle caring for a sick child," Connor said. This was not the time to tell Duncan that his sister did not intend to return to the castle—and it would never be a good time to tell him why. *Duncan, I took your sister to bed, then condemned her for a traitor and attempted to hold her prisoner. She's a wee bit upset with me.* If Alex was right and Ilysa was innocent, he had committed another great wrong against her.

"Have ye found Ilysa a husband yet?" Alex asked.

"Not yet," Connor said keeping his voice even. He wanted to strangle Alex for goading him in front of Duncan.

"Ach, you're slacking in your duty to her," Alex said. "But I suppose ye have been *busy*."

Ian raised an eyebrow and shot a look between him and Alex—and just like that, Connor could tell that Ian had guessed that something had happened between him and Ilysa. It was one thing to know each other so well that they could read each other's minds on the battlefield; this was quite another. Praise God Duncan had a blind spot when it came to his sister.

"Ach, no, why did MacIain bring a Campbell with him?" Connor asked when he caught sight of the boar-head crest of the Campbell clan on the sail of one of the galleys. *Damn it*. He had hoped to have the battle with the MacLeods concluded before the Crown's lieutenant learned of it.

"That's John Campbell in that galley," Ian said, refer-ring to the Campbell chieftain's brother, who was also the Thane of Cawdor. "The other galleys are his as well."

"MacIain is no coming?" Connor asked.

"No," Ian said. "He's dead."

# CHAPTER 41

Connor gripped his cup so tightly his knuckles were white as he listened to John Campbell tell how Alexander of Dunivaig had attacked and killed MacIain and MacIain's two oldest sons, who were his own wife's father and brothers. Twenty-some years of marriage and six children of shared blood had only masked, not erased, Alexander's drive for vengeance against his wife's clan. MacIain had finally been held to account for his treachery that resulted in the execution of three generations of Alexander's family—his grandfather, father, and brothers.

How could Alexander face his wife after killing her father and brothers? Connor recalled sitting at their table and observing what he thought was genuine affection between Alexander and his wife. Connor felt sorry for the poor woman. His own efforts to create a reliable alliance through marriage seemed futile. While such marriages sometimes succeeded in forging strong allegiances, just as often they ended in blood feuds.

"Can I call upon the friendship between our clans and ask ye to join our battle?" Connor asked John Campbell, though he knew it was pointless.

"That friendship is what will keep us from fighting on the side of the MacLeods," John said, raising his cup to Connor. "I do hope you're not too aggrieved that I came to retrieve MacIain's granddaughter."

The Campbells had moved with their usual stunning speed to take control of the MacIain's lands. Before the dead chieftain's body was in the grave, the Campbells claimed guardianship over his only surviving son, a boy of nine, whose mother was a Campbell. Connor doubted the son would ever gain control over MacIain lands. Similarly, John Campbell had been dispatched to collect Jane, whose marriage would be arranged to better suit Campbell interests.

"I regret giving up my bride, of course," Connor lied, as there was an advantage to letting the Campbells believe they owed him a favor. "But Jane and I part on good terms."

That much was true. Jane, who was upstairs joyfully packing, was almost as relieved as he was to avoid a marriage destined to make them both miserable. But Connor could not help thinking that if she had never arrived, Ilysa would still be spending her nights in his bed.

* * *

Lachlan decided he was still captain since Connor had not said he wasn't. While the chieftain drank whiskey with his guest, Lachlan made sure the men had their weapons and supplies ready. He marveled at Connor's patience. With a battle to be fought, he had to sit inside the keep playing host to the Thane of Cawdor, who looked to be an arrogant son of bitch if there ever was one.

"Lachlan!"

He turned to find Robbie, one of the young men he and Connor had trained, running toward him with a bloody dirk in his hand.

"What's happened?" Lachlan asked.

"I think I killed Sorely."

"Take me to him," Lachlan said. "Ye can tell me why ye did it on the way."

His own calm seemed to settle Robbie, which was good. Lachlan didn't want a garbled explanation.

"I was guarding the gate, like ye told me," Robbie said as they crossed the courtyard. "I let everyone in and no one out."

The gist of the story was that when it was most chaotic with all the newly arrived guests and warriors coming in, Sorely tried to leave. When Robbie stopped him, Sorely started to argue and then suggested they go inside the gatehouse to discuss it.

"As soon as I went through the door, he tried to dirk me," Robbie said, his eyes wide. "Without thinking, I did exactly as ye taught me. Next thing I know, Sorely's on the floor bleeding. I think he's dead."

"Sometimes a man isn't as dead as he looks." Lachlan walked faster and hoped Sorely was still there.

When he entered the gatehouse, Sorely had dragged himself a few feet across the floor.

"Ye don't look as if you're going to last," Lachlan said, kneeling beside him. "That will save us the trouble of executing ye since I assume you're the one who murdered the two guards."

"To hell with ye, Lachlan," Sorely said and spit out blood.

"Ye want to tell me why you're a miserable traitor to your clan?" In Lachlan's experience, men wanted to talk at the end, and he suspected Sorely would want to justify himself.

"Ye think ye know so much," Sorely said in a rasping voice. "But I'd wager ye don't know your mother was murdered."

"Mind the door," Lachlan said to Robbie, wanting him out of earshot.

Lachlan was not going to give Sorely the satisfaction of asking. Sorely wanted to tell him, so he waited, hoping the man wouldn't die before he got the words out.

"Hugh pushed her! Aye, that's right. Your da has been helping the man who killed her. Isn't that a laugh?" Blood seeped through Sorely's teeth in a grisly grin. "I told Hugh that your mother was carrying another child of the chieftain's, so he got rid of her."

Lachlan was tempted to put his hand around Sorely's throat and speed his journey to hell. Instead, he asked, "How would ye know she was with child?"

"Jenny told me," Sorely said, and tears suddenly filled his eyes. "No one knew, but we were sweethearts."

Who in the hell was Jenny? Then it struck him. "Jenny was the nursemaid. That's why ye see her ghost."

"She was waving to me when she dropped the babe," Sorely said. "The chieftain didn't have to cast her adrift at sea. She never meant to harm the child."

He was blubbering so that Lachlan could almost feel sorry for him—until something else occurred to him. "Ye didn't try to save Jenny, did ye? Ye didn't speak to the chieftain on her behalf or go out in a boat to rescue her."

"I couldn't!" Sorely choked out. "The chieftain would have banished me, and I would have lost my place in his guard."

"I guess that explains why she haunted ye." Lachlan was disgusted with him. "I suppose ye held what the chieftain did to her against Connor." That's what his own father had done.

"I was willing to forgive all…when I thought Connor…would make me captain," Sorely said, his voice growing weaker with each breath. "But he kept delaying…and delaying…"

His voice faded, and his head fell to the side.

"What a sorry excuse for a MacDonald." Lachlan got up and went to the door. "Ye did well, Robbie. It would have been a damned shame to lose a good man like you to his blade. I'll report this to the chieftain."

Lachlan would tell Connor everything except what Sorely said about his mother and father. That was no one's business but his own.

\* \* \*

"The MacLeods are coming," Connor called out, raising his arms. "'Tis time to raise the clan."

Every man, woman, and child in the castle was gathered around the blazing bonfire that had been built in the center of the castle yard for the ceremony of the *crann tara*.

Duncan, Ian, and Alex, the three men Connor trusted above all others, stood to his right, each holding a wooden cross. He thought of their wives and children and prayed the men would survive the battle ahead. To his left stood three of the young Trotternish warriors he and Lachlan had trained.

Duncan's eyes were fierce as he gave Connor the first wooden cross. "We fight to the death!" he shouted, and all the men cheered.

Connor held the cross in the bonfire until the dry wood caught flame, then he held it high for all to see it blaze against the afternoon sky. It hissed as he doused the flames in the waiting tub of sheep's blood. He raised the charred cross over his head again and shouted the MacDonald battle cry, "*Fraoch Eilean!*"

The castle yard reverberated with the deep voices of the men as they shouted it back. Finally, he motioned to Robbie, the first young warrior to his left, who had earned the honor by catching Hugh's spy.

"Let our men know the MacDonalds are gathering at the standing stone to fight!" Connor shouted, and Robbie took the charred cross from him and ran out the open gate.

Connor repeated the ceremony two more times, taking the crosses from Alex and Ian, and sending each of the young warriors to raise the men in a different part of the peninsula.

The *crann tara* was a call to every man, whether he be warrior, farmer, or shepherd, to gather at the designated rallying point, prepared to fight for the clan. Most of the clan's trained warriors came from Sleat and North Uist and were already at the castle. The *crann tara* would be a test of the confidence Connor's Trotternish clansmen had in him as chieftain, and he wondered how many of them would come.

When the ceremony was complete, the men shouted

and raised their claymores. Connor saw the battle lust in their eyes, and he was glad to see they were ready to fight. The responsibility for the lives of these brave men fell on his shoulders.

He knew he would have found the burden easier to carry if Ilysa were here to send him off to war.

# CHAPTER 42

In the glow of sunset, Connor and Ian lay flat on their bellies and watched the MacLeod warriors across the river. There were so many of them converging on the camp that they looked like a swarm of bees returning to the hive.

"Doesn't look good," Ian whispered. "Damn MacIain for getting himself killed."

"I fear I am leading our warriors to a slaughter," Connor said.

"Ye have no choice," Ian said. "If we let a force this size cross the river, we'll have no hope of getting them out."

"'Tis good we arrived before Beltane," Connor said. "I think Alastair will strike tomorrow, rather than wait another day."

When he and Ian returned to the standing stone, Connor's heart lifted at the sight of so many of his clansmen gathered on the far side of the hill. And all through the night, more men joined them.

When the day broke, bleak and damp, Connor stood in front of the assembled men. His gaze moved from the hardened warriors who had fought with his father, to the young men he and Lachlan had trained, to the farmers who carried scythes and axes as weapons. More men had come than he had hoped, and yet there were not nearly enough.

"These lands were granted to my grandfather, the first chieftain of the MacDonalds of Sleat, by his father, the Lord of the Isles. It falls to us to secure them for our children's children. Today, we will take our stand. The MacLeods will learn that they must pay in blood for each foot of our land they hope to claim."

The men raised their weapons in silent response so that the MacLeods would not hear the echo of their shouts in the river valley below.

"We must hold them at the river," Connor said, raising his claymore. "They shall not cross it!"

\* \* \*

Lachlan fought until sweat rolled into his eyes and the blood of his enemies drenched his sleeves. The odds were terrible, but he was accustomed to worse. After two and a half years of leading clandestine raids against the MacLeods, he was glad to finally let loose his rage in open battle against the occupiers of his homeland.

So far, the MacDonalds had held the line and kept the huge MacLeod force from gaining a foothold on the Trotternish side of the river. But the MacLeods kept coming.

Lachlan understood now why the four warriors who returned from France had become legend in such a short time. Connor, his cousins, and Duncan were at the center

of the MacDonald line, and no matter how many Mac-
Leod warriors converged on them, none got through.
Though Lachlan could spare no more than a glance now
and then, he saw how, in the midst of the chaos of battle,
they coordinated their movements and fought as one
deadly force.

Some might say it was foolish of the chieftain to risk
his life, but their situation was desperate, and his example
inspired the others to fight harder.

On a slight rise behind the MacLeod warriors, Lachlan
saw a massive warrior with white hair, regal bearing, and
the telltale hunched shoulder, watching the slaughter at
the river. After a half day of bloodletting, he raised his
arm, and his warriors withdrew to regroup.

\* \* \*

Connor dunked his head in the river to wash off the sweat
and blood. When he looked up, he met the hard gaze of
the MacLeod chieftain who stood fifty yards away.

*Give up, old man. This land belongs to the MacDon-
alds.*

He found Ian, Alex, and Duncan with the other men a
few yards back from the river.

"How's that leg?" he asked Ian, who was tying a strip
of cloth around a wound to stanch the bleeding.

"Good," Ian said.

Alex had also been wounded. Connor scanned the
dead bodies along the riverbank. There were far more
MacLeods than MacDonalds, but he had fewer to lose.

"I fear they'll break through next time," Connor said
in a low voice to the three, and none of them argued. His
only hope was that the MacLeod was losing more men

than the lands were worth to him. Connor looked again for some sign that the men across the river were dispersing, but he saw none.

"What order will ye give if the line breaks?" Ian, always the pragmatist of the group, asked. "Everyone makes for the castle?"

Connor did not have a chance to answer.

"Grab your weapons!" Duncan shouted and was on his feet pointing behind them with his claymore.

Two hundred warriors were streaming down the slope behind them.

# CHAPTER 43

Is that my brother Niall?" Ian asked, looking up at the descending horde. "I thought he was with Ilysa."

"Put down your weapons!" Connor shouted, breaking into a grin. "These are friends."

Torquil MacLeod of Lewis had come, and they had Ilysa to thank for it. When she told him she did not trust Sorely, Connor had dismissed her concern at first. But Torquil's lack of response to the message he had sent with Sorely troubled him. On the chance Ilysa was right, he had sent Niall with a second message.

"A thousand welcomes to ye, brother. I'm glad to meet ye at last," Connor greeted Torquil, a rough-looking warrior of about thirty years, who had the same jet-black hair as Connor and Ian. "These are your MacDonald cousins, Alex and Ian, and our friend Duncan."

"I accept your offer," Torquil said. "My warriors will fight with yours today in exchange for you doing the same for me when the time comes."

Torquil was a chieftain without lands. After his father had supported the last rebellion, the Crown had punished him by taking away his clan's traditional lands on the isle of Lewis.

"I gladly give ye my pledge," Connor said, grasping forearms with his brother.

"Good," Torquil said with a broad smile. "My men are ready for a fight."

* * *

All day, Ilysa and Flora had kept busy while they waited for news. Malcom had left a couple of hours before dawn. The cottage was fairly close to the mouth of the Snizort River, so they had been among the last to receive the *crann tara*.

After hours of sewing, Ilysa had worked her way through the pile of children's clothing that needed mending. She stuck her needle in a scrap and carefully set it in her medicine basket. As she did, her fingers touched the rock she had found at the faery glen, which she had put in the basket along with her brooch for safekeeping. She took the rock out and turned it over in her palm, watching it sparkle in the firelight from the hearth.

Flora came over with Brigid on her hip and looked over Ilysa's shoulder. "I do believe that's my rock," she said.

"How can ye be so sure?" Ilysa said with a laugh. She was not about to tell Flora that she had found it in the faery glen.

"I carried it in my pocket for years as a gift to appease the faeries should one cross my path," Flora said. "I gave it to our chieftain the night he was here in case he needed it. Did he give it to ye?"

"I believe he thought I was a faery," Ilysa said in a soft voice as she rubbed her thumb over it.

Flora's laugh was cut short when Lachlan burst through the door. He was carrying Malcom, who was bleeding from the head. While Flora and Ewan rushed to help him, Ilysa fetched a blanket and spread it on the floor in front of the hearth where the light was best.

"There were hundreds of MacLeod warriors," Malcom said after they lay him down. "I thought they'd never stop coming."

"The wound is worse than it looks," Ilysa said as she stanched the blood, then she looked to Lachlan. "What other news can ye give us?"

"The MacLeod force is three times the size of ours, and it was looking grim at midday," Lachlan said. "But then the MacLeod of Lewis arrived with his warriors."

"Flora, ye would have been proud of Lachlan," Malcom said. "Ye should see him fight."

"Hush now," Flora said. "Ye must save your strength."

"I just wanted to bring Malcom home," Lachlan said. "I must get back. The battle will continue tomorrow."

Ilysa followed him to the door and asked in a low voice, "How bad does it look, truly?"

"I fear there's no end in sight," Lachlan said. "That old goat MacLeod shows no sign of giving in."

\* \* \*

Celebrating Beltane made for a strange end to the toughest day of fighting Connor could remember, but the ritual, which brought purification and luck, was important to the clan. Connor was the first to pass between the two giant bonfires, followed by all the warriors and a few families who lived nearby. Finally, some cattle were driven between the fires.

Now that the herds and crops were protected for the coming year, Connor hoped it would not be for the benefit of the MacLeods. He looked across the river to where the MacLeod bonfires blazed against the night sky while he listened to the soft voices of his own men talking. After their cries for blood earlier, they were subdued.

He had lost too many men today. If this fight continued much longer, there would be no winner. Thanks to Torquil's arrival, they had succeeded in holding the MacLeods at the river. But Torquil had only half the men Connor had expected from MacIain, and it was not enough for a decisive victory.

He could not blame Alastair MacLeod for taking Trotternish when the MacDonalds were weak and it had been easy. That was the way of it in the Highlands—the strong survived. That was also why Connor had to take back Trotternish. Either you defended your lands or you risked being attacked on all sides.

But if Sorely and that handful of fools had not defiled the MacLeod dead and raped their women, the MacLeod would likely have decided by now that losing so many warriors was not worth taking land that did not belong to him. Connor hoped Sorely was burning in hell.

"I'm grateful to ye for coming," Connor said to Torquil as they sat with their backs against a log watching the bonfires.

"We have a blood tie," Torquil said, as if that explained it.

"Frankly, I'm more accustomed to that leading to murder," Connor said with a dry laugh. After a long while, he said, "I am sorry for how our mother left ye."

"Ach, I had a pack of older half sisters who spoiled me," Torquil said. "I don't remember our mother, and I surely didn't miss her."

"When I was a bairn, she was the moon and stars to me," Connor admitted. "The older men still talk about her beauty."

"As our fathers learned, she was more trouble than she was worth," Torquil said. "I count myself lucky to have the love of a kindhearted woman who has stayed with me through my present hard times."

"If I live through this, I'm going to marry a lass who is like that—if she'll still have me," Connor said.

He stared into the dwindling bonfire thinking about Ilysa. Looking back now, he recalled the many ways, big and small, that Ilysa acted to protect the clan—and him. Since she left, he had received still more proof of her loyalty. Now he knew that she had saved his life when she locked him in the dungeon. And it was only because she had cautioned him about Sorely that Torquil was here today to help beat back the MacLeod attack. Connor was ashamed of his doubts, but trusting in a woman's love and loyalty came hard to him.

Teàrlag had told him the right lass would choose him, but he had not been wise enough to know it. He had sacrificed their happiness to make a marriage alliance, which now seemed like a slender reed on which to rest his clan's future. Belatedly, he realized that Ilysa was the best wife he could choose not only for himself, but for his clan. No other woman would be as devoted to the clan's welfare or as wise and steadfast a helpmate to him. And only with her at his side could he become the chieftain his clan needed him to be.

He still could think of no good explanation for why Ilysa would meet with their clan's worst enemy, that devil Alastair MacLeod. But if God gave him another chance, he would put his faith in the woman who had always had faith in him.

His thoughts were interrupted by Lachlan, who appeared out of the darkness, his hair bright in the firelight.

"Ye fought well today," Connor told him, and he refrained from mentioning that he also noticed that Lachlan disappeared afterward.

"I brought ye a message." Lachlan slanted a look at Torquil. "It's private."

Connor was bone-weary, and his shoulders ached from swinging his claymore all day, but he hauled himself to his feet. The air was chilly when he stepped away from the fire.

"What is it?" he asked.

"Ilysa wants ye to meet her," Lachlan said. "She says it's important."

Connor's weariness fell away. Ilysa wanted to see him.

"You're to come alone to the abandoned church on Saint Columba's Island after midnight," Lachlan said. "If she's not there by an hour before dawn, you're to leave because she's not coming."

Saint Columba, a small island in the Snizort River, was the site of the church of the Bishops of the Isles for five hundred years before it was abandoned near the time the Lord of the Isles submitted to the Scottish Crown. Its burial ground was crowded with the graves of ancient chieftains and warriors, including some who had fought in the Crusades.

"That's a strange place and time to meet," Connor said. "Why can't I meet her at your sister's?"

"I had the impression Ilysa meant to leave the cottage as soon as I was out the door," Lachlan said.

"How do I know this message is from Ilysa and not a trap you're setting at Hugh's behest?" Connor asked. "Ye expect me to leave my men in the midst of battle and go alone to this isolated place in the black of night on trust?"

If Connor died, the clan would be forced to choose a chieftain between the only other males with chieftain's blood, Moira's young son and Hugh. The chance they would put the clan in Hugh's hands was too great for Connor to risk his life lightly.

"Ilysa said to give ye this."

Connor stared at the stone that Lachlan dropped into his palm. Even this far from the fire, it picked up the light. He recognized it at once as the glittering stone he had left for his dancing faery. For Ilysa.

The question was no longer whether he trusted Lachlan with his life and his clan's future, but whether he trusted them to Ilysa. Connor had not expected the test of his faith in her to come quite so soon or to be so stark.

# CHAPTER 44

Ilysa shivered against the cold as Ewan rowed his little boat from the inlet to the mouth of the river. It would be too difficult for him to row upstream against the current, and the distance was not too far to walk. She directed him to land the boat on the MacLeod side of the river.

"Thank you," she whispered to Ewan as she got out. "Be careful and go right home."

Though an eleven-year-old could hardly protect her, Ilysa felt very alone as his boat disappeared into the darkness. She brushed off her fear and walked briskly along the riverbank until she saw the glow of campfires through the mist. They were farther away than they looked. By the time she reached the edge of the enemy camp, her gown and cape were soaked up to her knees from the tall, wet grass.

Despite the cold, damp night air, her palms were sweaty as she approached it. All her life she had heard stories of the terrible things MacLeod warriors did to captured women. Her own mother had never recovered from what they had done to her. She saw a tent at the center and guessed that was where the chieftain slept. Was it possible she could simply walk through the sleeping camp to his tent?

She screamed as rough hands grabbed her from behind. Before she knew what was happening, she was jerked off her feet and her back slammed against a solid frame. She kicked and tried to bite the hand that clamped over her mouth.

"Damn it!" the man cursed when she rammed her heel into his shin.

They were making such a ruckus that several men awoke and surrounded them.

"We all want turns," one of them said, sending a wave of panic through her.

"Wait," another said. "We should find out who she is first."

Ilysa praised the saints for that one, for her captor finally removed his hand from her mouth.

"Get your hands off me," she said. "I'm a MacLeod, and I have a message for the chieftain."

"Ha, I'm sure ye do," one of the men said.

"I promise he'll be very angry if he doesn't get it," she said.

"And I'll be angry if I don't get something from you, lass," one of them said.

"I've been spying on the MacDonalds for the chieftain, and he will punish ye most severely if ye harm me." Ilysa was proud of herself for thinking of such a good lie.

"Ye know the chieftain doesn't approve of abusing

women," one of the men said, which gave her hope until he added, "We'd best take her into the wood."

"I have proof!" she said quickly.

That seemed to give them pause.

"Take this to him," she said, holding out the brooch. She hoped they would not steal it, but she had no choice now but to take the risk. "You'll find that he does wish to see me."

* * *

Connor left his guard fifty yards up the river from where it split around the island. The stream was wider on the far side of the island, but the gap on the Trotternish side was narrow enough for him to leap over it. Between the darkness and the heavy mist that lay over the island, he could not see the lumpy ground beneath his feet. He suspected he was walking over ancient graves and prayed their souls were a long way away.

Though his claymore was useless against spirits, he carried it in his hand, ready to meet a more solid opponent hiding in the night mist. He had decided for once to trust in his heart, not his head, and proceed on blind faith. Still, he would be cautious. This was the perfect place to capture him, and Ilysa the perfect bait.

Questions rolled around in his head as he stole over the uneven ground. Why had Ilysa chosen this eerie place of the dead to meet? Where in the hell had she gone that she was not certain she would return before dawn? It was near midnight now, and he wondered how long he would have to wait.

The outline of the small church appeared out of the mist. The old, weathered door creaked as he pushed it open, and he heard a gasp from inside. It was a distinctly feminine sound.

"Ilysa?"

"Connor! Praise God it's you."

It was even darker inside the church, but he heard the swish of her gown as she stepped toward him. The next instant, they found each other, and she was in his arms. He clasped her tightly to him, unable to speak at first. He had feared he would never hold her again.

"I've missed ye so much," he said. It seemed impossible that she had only been gone a couple of days.

"I missed ye, too," she whispered.

"Don't leave me," he said. "I don't want us to ever be apart again."

She shook her head against his chest.

"This time, I'm asking ye to be my wife," he said. "I can't go on without ye."

Ilysa was crying. Could she not forgive him? He had to persuade her.

"I love ye so much, and I'm sorry I failed to trust ye," he said. "If you'll marry me, I'll strive to be the man ye believe I can be."

"You already are that man," she said, which was no answer.

"Ilysa, *mo rùin*, will ye have me?"

"I choose you for my husband, Connor MacDonald," she said with a smile in her voice as she echoed Teàrlag's prediction. "In truth, I've been yours for the asking since the day ye returned from France."

The world fell away as he kissed her. Connor forgot the battles of today and tomorrow, the dangers facing his clan, and even the tombs of the dead surrounding them.

At this moment, the lass who had danced away with his heart was in his arms. Ilysa had agreed to become his wife, and all things seemed possible.

"Your clothes are damp. Ye must be frozen, *mo rùin*," he said when they finally broke apart. "Why did ye want to meet in this abandoned church, among the dead?"

"'Tis close to the battle," she said, "and I thought we should do this in a neutral place where we could be certain of secrecy."

"Secrecy? A neutral place?" he asked. "Why?"

The door creaked, and Connor whirled around, brandishing his claymore. In the doorway, he saw the outline of a giant warrior with a distinctive hunched shoulder.

"Connor," Ilysa said from behind him and rested her hand on his shoulder. "Meet my grandfather, Alastair MacLeod."

\* \* \*

Ilysa grew weary as the two chieftains went around and around in negotiations that seemed to go nowhere. At first, it appeared they would come to a quick agreement after Connor informed her grandfather about their upcoming marriage and apologized for Sorely's atrocities. But generations of bloody history could not be overcome so easily. The two men did not trust each other, and the discussions soon stalled.

Dawn was nearing, and the only point the two could agree upon was that Ilysa's parentage should be kept secret. Alastair was adamant that a future chieftain of the MacDonalds not have a claim to the chieftainship of his clan, and Connor feared the taint of MacLeod blood could be used against his sons when his successor was chosen.

"The child I carry," she said, interrupting them, "has the blood of both of ye."

This was not how she had planned to tell Connor, but this had gone on long enough. Her announcement was met with startled silence, then Connor pulled her into his arms and kissed her soundly.

"Would ye kill the man who is my grandfather and our child's great-grandfather?" she asked him, and then she turned to Alastair. "And would you have my babe be fatherless?" For good measure, she added, "I'm tired, and I need my rest."

After that, matters were settled swiftly. As Connor accompanied her back to Flora's cottage, Ilysa was so filled with joy she could hardly contain herself. The agreement the two chieftains had reached to resolve their current conflict was an enormous victory. It had been too much to expect that the two rival clans would form a close alliance, but she had hope now that they could live in peace. And she would soon be Connor's wife.

"Shh, don't wake them," she cautioned Connor outside the cottage door.

"I'll come back for ye as soon as I can," he said and embraced her once more. "You've made me the happiest of men."

She watched his back until she could no longer see him in the dark. Hugging herself, she quietly opened the door so as not to wake the family, though she felt like shouting her news.

*Connor and I shall marry! The battle for Trotternish is over!*

She eased the door closed behind her. As she started to tiptoe across the room, a muffled sound made the hairs on the back of her neck stand up. Before she could scream, for the second time that night, a hand covered her mouth.

"Hello, Ilysa," a familiar, deep voice rumbled in her ear. "I always knew a lass would be my nephew's downfall, but I never guessed it would turn out to be you."

# CHAPTER 45

Connor was relieved when everything went as he and Alastair MacLeod had agreed. Though he had learned to trust Ilysa, he doubted he would ever fully trust her grandfather.

They made a pretense of negotiating the truce in the presence of their respective guards. As promised, Alastair agreed to withdraw his warriors from Trotternish, and Connor pledged a payment to compensate for Sorely's acts. Though he had no idea how he would raise such a vast sum, he would do it. His clan's lands were finally restored. And, without the constant threat from the MacLeods, he could turn his full attention to Hugh, who had been suspiciously quiet.

Connor sent the Trotternish men to their homes to share the good news and sent the rest of his warriors ahead to the castle so he could speak freely with Duncan, Ian, and Alex.

"Ilysa and I plan to marry," he told them, which seemed to surprise only Duncan.

Duncan was too stunned to speak at first, and before he could get any words out, Lachlan came running toward them from up the path.

"They're gone!" Lachlan shouted.

Connor's stomach tightened into a knot. "Who's gone?"

"Malcom is dead. My sister and the children are gone." Lachlan's chest heaved as he spoke between gasps for air. "Ilysa is missing as well."

The blood drained from Connor's head. *God, no!*

He ran until he reached the cottage. Just outside the open door, he saw a child's rag doll. Inside, Malcom lay sprawled across the floor, a thick line of blood across his throat. The table was on its side and broken crockery littered the floor.

"It has to be Hugh who took them," Connor said.

"He must have found out Ilysa was here," Lachlan said, behind him. "He wouldn't have done this just to take Flora and the children."

Duncan knelt beside Malcom's body. "He's been dead a couple of hours, at least."

"So many of our men passed this way since then," Alex said, "that we won't be able to find Hugh's tracks."

"Where would Hugh take them?" Connor ran his hands through his hair, trying desperately to think.

"We must go to my father's," Lachlan said. "He can lead us to Hugh."

\* \* \*

"The children can't walk this fast," Ilysa called to Hugh, who was at the front of the motley group of men herding them east across the peninsula. "We must slow down."

"Any who can't keep up will join their father," Hugh said, which made the children cry harder.

"Damn ye, Hugh." Ilysa was furious. "You're making it worse."

Hugh walked back to the girl who had fallen farthest behind, lifted her off the ground by her thin arm, and pulled his dirk.

"No!" Ilysa dropped Brigid and threw herself over the girl. As they crashed to the ground, she felt a sharp pain where Hugh's dirk caught her shoulder. She looked up into his hard eyes and said, "I'll carry her, too."

"Just remember, I only need one of these bairns to make sure ye do as you're told," he said. "I'll not risk having those four find us before I'm ready."

"If ye harm these children, you'll have the entire clan after ye," she said.

"Once Connor is dead, I'll be chieftain," Hugh said with a smirk. "And people have a way of forgiving a chieftain."

* * *

"Why would your father know where to find Hugh?" Duncan demanded, his eyes as cold as a winter's pond.

Sweat broke out on Lachlan's forehead at the thought of his nieces and nephews in the hands of Hugh's men, and the fate of the two women was sure to be worse. Nothing else would have made him confess what he'd done to the four warriors glowering at him.

"My father is a traitor, and for a time, I was as well." He paused. "I'm the man who shot the arrows at ye when ye were hunting near Dunscaith."

Duncan roared and had his hands around Lachlan's throat before the others pulled him off.

"Let him speak," Connor commanded.

"I can explain on the way," Lachlan said. "I've seen these foul men, and we must hurry."

"Let's go," Connor ordered.

Lachlan led them on the path across the peninsula that he had taken a thousand times between his sister's and his father's cottages. It was a distance of several miles and, on the way, he told them everything about his parents and how his father raised him to seek vengeance for the family.

"Ach, let's kill him now," Duncan said after Lachlan finished. "There's no excuse for what he did."

"Ilysa trusts him," Connor said. "I want to know why."

"Some say she has The Sight, and I believe it," Lachlan said. "She was the only one who saw that I harbored a dark secret that threatened you and was destroying me. She set out to persuade me that ye merited my loyalty."

"Ilysa never told me she suspected ye were a traitor," Connor said, turning eyes like blue ice on him.

"She had no proof. My guess is she didn't think you'd believe her," Lachlan said and saw a flash of pain cross Connor's face. "She did threaten to kill me if I caused ye harm."

"She would have done it, too," Alex said with a laugh.

"Eventually I saw for myself that she was right. I've done nothing against ye since."

When they reached his father's, Lachlan went inside alone. He had not been here since he had told his father he would never act against Connor again.

"How dare ye step into this house after turning your back on your duty," his father greeted him.

"Hugh has murdered Malcom and taken Flora and the children hostage. Ye must tell me where to find him."

Lachlan's heart sank when his father's stony expression remained unchanged. "What kind of man are ye?"

"One who will have my vengeance," his father said.

"You're a fool. All these years, ye blamed the wrong man," Lachlan said. "Your friend Hugh murdered her."

"You're lying!"

"I heard it from a dying man's lips that Hugh pushed her off that bluff," Lachlan said. "But I think it was you who put her there. She couldn't stand to live with ye, could she?"

His father crumpled into a chair and covered his face.

When Lachlan picked him up by the front of his shirt, he was surprised by how light he was—the man he had looked up to all through his boyhood was a pathetic bag of bones.

"Now you're going to tell me where to find Hugh," Lachlan said. "And then you're going to be a man and save Connor the trouble of dealing with ye."

# CHAPTER 46

Hugh's camp is on Creag-na-Feile, the high cliff just up the coast," Lachlan said, looking pale and grim after emerging from his father's house. "He has fifty men there."

"Ten for each of us, not bad odds," Alex quipped, though Connor knew he was as worried as the rest of them.

They took the path up to the soaring basalt rock cliffs at a dead run. Connor looked down the sheer two-hundred-foot drop, and a shiver went through him as he thought of the battered body of Lachlan's mother at the base of the cliff.

When he saw the smoke from a fire rising from a small stand of trees, he raised his hand to signal that the camp was just ahead. They crouched in a circle to make their plan.

"Hugh has too many men. A simple attack would put the women and children at risk," Alex said. "We must come up with some other plan."

"Leaving them with those men puts them at risk as well," Duncan said. "We can't wait."

"You're both right," Connor said. "It's me Hugh wants. I'll offer myself in exchange for the hostages."

"No," Ian said, "the clan cannot afford to lose ye."

"I've made my decision," Connor said, rising.

"Wait, there is another way."

The four of them turned as one to look at Lachlan. The circle of trust among Connor, his cousins, and Duncan stretched back to boyhood, and they were unaccustomed to relying on anyone else in matters as grave as this.

"I shot my first arrow at Ian that day because I mistook him for Connor," Lachlan said. "From any distance, 'tis impossible to tell the two of ye apart."

"I see," Ian said at once. "I can go in for Connor."

"No," Connor said. "You're not dying for me."

"I don't intend to," Ian said, a slow smile spreading across his face. "I think Lachlan is suggesting I serve as bait to lure Hugh out."

\* \* \*

The few trees around the camp afforded little protection from the wind and rain. As Ilysa huddled with Flora and the children near the smoky fire, she kept a wary eye on the men who encircled them like wolves. The throbbing cut on her shoulder was nothing to what these foul men had in mind for her and Flora. While she was certain Connor and the others would find them, it might not be soon enough.

"I fear we've no chance of escaping before dark," Flora breathed in Ilysa's ear.

"Aye, I must act now," Ilysa said and whispered her plan.

She reached into the leather pouch tied to her belt for her dried herbs. In the weeks that Hugh had held Dunscaith, she had protected herself by spreading the rumor that she had learned dark magic from Teàrlag. Only a few of these men had been with Hugh then, but that was a start.

"I am a daughter of the Sea Witch!" she cried out in a loud voice as she stood and raised her arms. "I will curse any man who harms us!"

She tossed some of the herbs onto the fire and sparks flew high into the sky. The men who had started to laugh stopped abruptly.

"I was born at midnight on a night of the full moon," she said as she walked slowly around the fire, meeting the eyes of each man. Every Highlander knew these were signs of someone born with The Sight. "I can see your future. Every one of ye who remains here shall be dead by morning."

* * *

As Connor crept through the grass toward the camp, he was astonished to hear Ilysa's voice carried on the wind—and no others. He moved closer and saw her circling the fire.

"I see your blood!" she called out, and sparks flew from her fingers as they had at the faery glen. Then she swept her arm around the circle, pointing as she spoke in an ominous voice. "*Mìle marbhphàisg ort!*" A thousand death shrouds on you. "*A' phlàigh ort!*" A plague on you!

With their attention riveted on Ilysa, none of Hugh's men noticed Alex and Duncan, who were creeping around the other side of the camp to get closer to Flora and the children. Their task was to separate Flora and the children from their captors as quickly as possible and protect them. When Duncan and Alex were in position, Connor signaled to Ian and Lachlan.

"Hugh!" Lachlan called from the opposite side of the camp and twenty yards out. He held Ian in front of him, with his arm locked around Ian's throat and his dirk pricking his side.

Hugh dumped Rhona off his lap and strode to the edge of the camp.

"I've captured Connor," Lachlan shouted, "and I'm willing to make a trade."

Ian's black hair fell over his face as he lolled his head forward. Blood ran down his temple—a nice touch—and the chieftain's brooch was visible on his shoulder.

Connor waited, every muscle taut. Hugh hesitated, then finally signaled to his men to follow him. As soon as they moved away, Alex and Duncan put themselves between Hugh's men and Flora and the children. Fear choked Connor when he saw that Ilysa was on the opposite side of the fire and unprotected.

"Here I am, Uncle," he said, rising to his feet. "Come and get me."

Hugh looked back and forth between him and Ian, confusion on his face. By now, Lachlan and Ian had also pulled their swords, and the three of them converged on Hugh. If they could kill him, there was a good chance the others would flee.

Hugh was quick and fell back among his men. The fight began in earnest then. Connor swung his claymore side to side, slashing pirates and dodging blades, trying to get to Hugh, but there were always more men in his way.

After a while, the odds did not seem quite as bad. He saw a few of the pirates and Rhona fleeing across the field. A moment later, he saw sparks and knew why.

"Every one of ye shall die!" Ilysa was shouting from beside the fire. "I see your blood! I see your death shrouds!"

Ilysa's efforts were helping considerably, but he wished to hell she would not call attention to herself. He looked to Alex and Duncan, who were closer to her, but they had their hands full battling men near the children. Leaving Hugh to Ian and Lachlan, Connor worked his way toward Ilysa.

Then, through the melee, he saw Hugh moving toward her, too. Connor fought like a madman, killing one, two, three men who stood in his way. By then, Hugh was dragging Ilysa away from the camp.

Connor finally broke free and followed Ilysa's screams at a dead run. Hugh had her over his shoulder and was headed for the path along the cliff. Connor was younger and faster, and he was sure he could catch Hugh before he got very far. But when Hugh reached the edge of the cliff, he did not turn and follow the path.

Fear struck Connor like a bolt of lightning, and he slowed his steps. Hugh held Ilysa off her feet against his side as he stood with his back to the cliff. Connor couldn't breathe when he saw how close Hugh's heels were to the edge. The ground could easily crumble beneath his feet and send them both plunging backward.

"It's finished, Hugh," he called over the wind. "There's no escape."

"Then I'm taking her with me!"

Hugh glanced over his shoulder, and Ilysa shrieked as

he teetered backward. Connor's heart stopped beating until the man regained his balance.

"For God's sake, Hugh, get away from the edge," Connor said and started toward them.

"Stay back, or I'll toss her over right now," Hugh said.

"Let her go," Connor said. "Ye have no grudge against her."

"No, but I'll take my revenge against you the same way I did your father."

"I know what ye did to Lachlan's mother." Connor caught Ilysa's eye and inched forward. Somehow he would get to her in time. "But ye can't do that this time and save yourself."

"I admit," Hugh said with a laugh, "I'll enjoy this less than sending your father's lover over the cliff alone."

"My father had lots of women," Connor said. "Ye were a fool to think ye could hurt him that way."

"Oh, I did have my revenge," Hugh said. "He had a mindless passion for your mother, and he never recovered from her death."

"What do ye know about that?" Connor said, trying to divert Hugh as he moved forward a bit more.

"It was me she ran off with," Hugh said.

Connor maintained his focus, though he was shocked by the revelation. A few more steps, and he would be close enough to lunge for Ilysa.

"Ye didn't know that, did ye?" Hugh said. "I was eighteen, half my brother's age, with the good looks he used to have, when she chose me."

"My mother didn't give a damn about ye," Connor said.

"We loved each other!" Hugh shouted.

"She only used ye to punish my father," Connor said, easing forward. "Ye were nothing next to him."

"No, she wanted me," Hugh said, his eyes wild.

"She couldn't love a coward like you," Connor spat out. "Why didn't ye die in that storm, Hugh?"

"I—I—"

"You were too afraid of my father to meet her yourself," Connor said, cutting him off. "Ye sent someone else to fetch her."

Sweat trickled down his back. He was almost close enough now. He could not risk shifting his gaze from Hugh to signal Ilysa.

"I did love her," Hugh said. "I just wasn't willing to die for her."

"Then ye don't know what love is."

"I understand it well enough to know how much this is going to make you suffer," Hugh said, his eyes gleaming.

Connor's dirk was already flying through the air when Hugh stepped backward off the cliff, clutching Ilysa. *Thunk!* The blade struck Hugh through the eye. His arms jerked out, releasing Ilysa, as the two toppled backward.

Connor lunged for her and caught her wrist. With a sudden jerk, he fell flat and was pulled forward until his head and shoulders went over the edge, but he held on.

Ilysa screamed as she dangled from his hand while Hugh fell spread-eagle down the two-hundred-foot cliff.

"Don't look down," he shouted. "I've got ye."

Ilysa fixed her gaze on him and nodded.

Connor's hand was slippery with sweat. He died a thousand deaths as she started sliding from his grasp. *Nay, I will not lose her.* He dug his toes into the dirt and stretched still farther over the cliff until he caught her forearm with his other hand. He swallowed as he watched her body sway with nothing but the distant sea below her. Then, with all his strength, he hoisted her over the edge to safety. They fell backward tangled together with her lying on top of him.

"That was far too close." He brushed her windblown hair out of her eyes with a shaking hand. His heart was beating so hard he feared he might never recover. "Dear God, I almost lost ye."

"No, ye didn't." Ilysa looked down at him with her sweet smile. "I knew ye would never let me fall."

# CHAPTER 47

*Two Weeks Later*

Hold still!" Connor commanded as he spread the lily-scented salve over the cut on her shoulder. "Don't make me tie ye to this chair, *mo rùin*."

"'Tis a wee scratch," Ilysa complained.

A wee scratch? He shuddered as he remembered feeling the damp stickiness on her back while he held her on the cliff. When he looked at his hand and saw blood, fear struck his heart like a shard of ice.

"'Twas lucky Lachlan was there to show us where Hugh had taken ye," he said.

"Luck had no part in it," she said, tilting her head back to smile at him. "Lachlan was there because you're a leader who engenders loyalty. That's why ye prevailed over Hugh and why you'll be one of the great chieftains of our clan."

She merited a kiss on her forehead for that. Fortunately, he had been able to bring her home quickly after the skirmish. Lachlan had also learned from his father where Hugh's boat was hidden a short distance up the coast. Despite Ilysa's foolish objections, Connor had carried her there on his back, and they had sailed home in their new galley.

They had found some of Hugh's plunder hidden on his boat, which meant Connor could make good on his pledge to Alastair MacLeod. He would give the remainder to the families whose homes had been raided or burned.

"Are ye finished yet?" Ilysa asked.

"A healer makes a poor patient." As he made the final knot in the bandage, his gaze drifted to where her pink nipples showed beneath her chemise.

"Ye do take good care of me," she said, and from the heated look in her eyes, she didn't mean just the bandage.

"Ye know me—I take my duty seriously," he said as he ran his finger along the curve of her cheek.

She moved his hand to her breast and pulled him down for a long kiss. After one turned into several, she asked in a breathless voice, "Do we have time?"

"I'm chieftain, aren't I?"

Just as their lips touched again, the door banged opened. Connor sighed as women and small children burst into the chamber like a spring flood.

"You'll have plenty of time for that after the wedding," his sister Moira said. "Out with ye now. We've come to help the bride dress."

Before he could greet Alex's wife, Glynis, who had arrived with their newborn son, one of Silèas's twins climbed on the table and the other escaped up the stairs to the tower. If those wee red-haired lasses were half the trouble at sixteen that they were at two, Ian would grow old long before his time.

"I'm glad I had the masons narrow the tower window." Connor exchanged glances with Ilysa, who had thought the measure he had taken to protect their future children a tad excessive. If he could have, he would have removed the nursemaid's ghost as well, though Ilysa assured him she was harmless.

"Your brother Lachlan is a fine-looking man," Moira said to Flora from where the two of them stood at the window overlooking the courtyard. "We must find a wife for him."

There was a general murmur of assent from the women, as if that were an obvious conclusion.

"Will ye find a wife for Niall, too?" Connor asked out of curiosity, which made the women laugh.

"Niall's not ready," Silèas said. "And when he is, he won't need our help."

Joking aside, Flora would be needing a new husband to help her with all those children, after her grief over Malcom eased. Connor intended to hand over that particular chieftain's duty to his wife, although Ilysa had expressed the strange notion that Cook was just the man for Flora.

"Go," Moira said, with a hand on Connor's back. "Everyone's waiting."

"I'll see ye in the hall," he said to Ilysa and leaned down to give her a last lingering kiss.

When Moira cleared her throat, they broke the kiss and smiled into each other's eyes.

The sound of pipes and the buzz of voices filled the stairwell as he descended. As soon as he entered the hall, the crowd began chanting his name and stomping their feet. The clan was in the mood for a celebration. Connor raised his fist in acknowledgment, and the crowd roared.

By good fortune, Father Brian had arrived for his annual visit, which ensured the festivities would go on for days. Today was devoted to the chieftain's wedding, but the priest would later bless all the babes that had been born and the marriages that had taken place since his last visit.

With all the greetings and wishes of good fortune, it took Connor some time to reach the far end of the hall where his cousins and Duncan waited, dressed as he was in their best saffron shirts and plaids. At Duncan's signal, the boisterous crowd parted down the middle and went quiet, save for the occasional voice of a child.

Connor stood with Ian and Alex on one side of him, and Duncan on the other, as he waited for his bride. It was right that these men, who were his close companions since childhood and who had each played an essential part in restoring their clan, be at his side on this special day. The four of them had accomplished what they set out to do when they returned from France to find their clan in near ruin. Their lands and people were secure once more. And with Hugh's death, the hatreds and sorrows caused by the previous generation were finally laid to rest.

He smiled to himself thinking how it was not a fierce, sword-wielding MacDonald warrior who had wrested Trotternish from the MacLeods, but a deceptively frail-looking lass. That was Ilysa's wedding gift to the clan.

At last, his bride came through the doorway—and

stole his breath away. Sweet Ilysa had surprised him once again by coming to their wedding as his faery dancer. She was a vision in gold in the luminous gown, which was so light it floated as she walked. He was relieved to see that she wore a chemise beneath it so he did not have to order all the men to turn their backs. Her glorious red-gold hair fell in loose tendrils to her waist, and there were tiny blue flowers in it like the ones she had worn at Mingary Castle.

His heart swelled as she joined him. They clasped their hands, palm-to-palm, and he wrapped the strip of linen Duncan handed him around their wrists three times. After they exchanged the traditional pledges, she started to turn for the next part of the ceremony, but he held her in place. She widened her eyes and tilted her head to the side to remind him what came next.

"I'm no finished," he whispered. A simple vow wouldn't due for such a lass. "I pledge my sword, my body, and my heart...," he began and then continued, pausing between each line:

> ... to the angel who watches over me
> the healer who mends me
> the efficient lass who keeps my household
> the seer who warns me of danger
> the helpmate who makes my burdens lighter
> the mother of my future children
> the faery lass who weaves magic in my nights
> and
> the woman who makes me whole,
> You are everything I ever longed for and every
> woman I will ever need.

Connor turned then to present his bride to his clan, and the hall erupted into wild cheers of approval. This chieftain's wife was beloved by her clan. With Ilysa at his side, he would be the man and chieftain she believed he could be.

# EPILOGUE

## 1525

"Children, stay here with your father," Ilysa said. After kissing Connor, she left them to throw stones in the pond while she carried her new babe to meet the man waiting beyond the next hill.

When she reached her grandfather, she embraced him warmly and put her new babe in his arms.

"This one looks like you," he said, after they sat down on the log. "What's her name?"

"Teàrlag," she said. "We named her for the old seer who died the night she was born."

The seer had foretold that the child's gift of The Sight would rival her own, and the babe was born at midnight on a full moon. Ilysa sighed. She missed the old seer.

"The other children have grown," he said, watching them from between the hills. "The lads are tall—they take after the MacLeod side."

Ilysa refrained from mentioning that the boys had

Connor's fine looks as well as his height. After they had talked at length about the children, she had business to discuss with him.

"My husband received another summons to appear before the regent to settle the dispute between the two of ye over Trotternish."

"I received one as well," the MacLeod said, "same as last year and the year before."

"Connor would prefer to ignore it, if you're willing to do the same."

"Ach, 'tis always perilous to go to court," the MacLeod said. "I intend to stay home."

"He'll be grateful, as am I." She kissed his weathered cheek.

They had kept this secret pact for years now. Except for the time the MacDonalds had helped Torquil reclaim Lewis, her clan had lived in peace since her marriage.

Ilysa handed her grandfather the pot of salve she had made for him and took her babe from his arms. "I'll see ye next year."

It was hard to see him so rarely. She embraced him one more time before returning to where her family waited.

Connor had already built the fire. Before they left, she made the protective circle for her family and her clan, as she did each year.

"...May ye live to be an old man."

When she came to this part of the chant, she conjured her beloved as a handsome old man with deep lines and snowy white hair. Unlike the first time, she saw herself as an old, happy woman beside him.

"May your children be bonded to each other by great affection," she said as she circled the fire the third time, "and may ye have grandchildren who bring ye joy."

When she finished, Connor wrapped his arms around her.

"Come, *mo rùin*," he said in her ear, "let's go home and make another kind of magic."

# HISTORICAL NOTE

Most of the scenes in this book are set in actual places on the Isle of Skye that I visited on a trip I took with my daughter. (Readers can find photos on my website.) I envisioned the cliff scene as taking place on Skye's famed Kilt Rock, but I changed the name because—I really hate to tell you this—Highlanders did not yet wear kilts in the early 1500s. For simplicity, I also changed the name of Duntulm Castle to Trotternish. The castle is in ruins, but the site is gorgeous. One of the ghost stories associated with this castle is about a nursemaid who was cast out to sea after accidentally dropping the chieftain's baby out the window to its death.

My daughter and I were lucky to discover, despite the lack of signs and our terrible sense of direction, the faery glen near Uig and the ancient graveyard on Saint Columba's Island in the Snizort River. The faery glen truly does feel magical with its odd, conical hills. Though the sheep looked bored, I found it delightfully eerie. Saint

Columba is an incredibly lovely and peaceful spot. All the same, it was unnerving to walk over the uneven ground knowing that we were probably stepping on ancient graves. Despite their beauty, I would not want to be in either place after dark—which of course is what led me to put my characters there at night.

As usual, I incorporated several real historical characters into this book and filled in their personalities based on the facts I could find and the needs of my story. The historical figures include Alexander MacDonald of Dunivaig and the Glens, John MacIain, Margaret Tudor, Archibald Douglas, and the wonderful Alastair Crotach ("Hunchback") MacLeod. I did, however, invent some of the chieftain's children, including Alastair's "natural" son.

Connor MacDonald is a fictional character, but most of his family members were real people. Hugh, the first MacDonald of Sleat, had six sons all by different highborn women. I changed details, but the conflict among these six half brothers led to two generations of murder within the family. To create Connor, I borrowed bits from the lives of Hugh's son Donald Gallach, and his grandson, Donald Graumach, both of whom served as chieftains. Donald Graumach drove the MacLeods of Dunvegan and Harris from Trotternish with the help of his half brother, the MacLeod of Lewis. Years later, Donald returned the favor by helping his half brother take possession of his lands on the isle of Lewis.

The MacDonalds of Sleat and the MacLeods of Dunvegan and Harris were bitter rivals. Since they appeared to commit atrocities against each other with regularity, I was intrigued when I came across an unexplained break in the bloodletting, which occurred after the MacDonalds re-took the Trotternish Peninsula from the MacLeods. During these years of relative peace, the two chieftains ignored royal summons to appear at court to resolve their dispute over Trotternish, which added to the mystery. I saw this as an opportunity for a story and made up a wholly fictional explanation.

I moved their fight for Trotternish several years forward and changed many details to suit my story. The key battle did take place near the Snizort River, and the victorious MacDonalds supposedly floated MacLeod heads (it's unclear to me whether they were attached to their bodies) down the river, where they collected in a pool called Cauldron of the Heads.

As I've noted before, researching clan histories of five hundred years ago is challenging, and I apologize for any inadvertent mistakes I may have made.

Discover how it all began—
in the first book of this sizzling series
featuring fearless Highlanders!

Please turn this page
for a preview of

*THE GUARDIAN.*

# CHAPTER 2

THE DUNGEON IN DUART CASTLE
ISLE OF MULL
OCTOBER 1513

Damnable vermin! The straw is alive with the wee crit-ters." Ian got to his feet and scratched his arms. "I hate to say it, but the Maclean hospitality is sadly lacking."

"'Tis the Maclean vermin on two legs that concern me," Duncan said. "Ye know they are upstairs debating what to do with us—and I've no faith they'll chose mercy."

Connor rubbed his temples. "After five years of fight-ing in France, to be taken by the Macleans the day we set foot in Scotland…"

Ian felt the humiliation as keenly as his cousin. And they were needed at home. They had left France as soon as the news reached them of the disastrous loss to the English at Flodden.

"'Tis time we made our escape," Ian told the others. "I expect even the Macleans will show us the courtesy of feeding us dinner before they kill us. We must take our chance then."

"Aye." Connor came to stand beside him and peered through the iron grate into the darkness beyond. "As soon as the guard opens this door, we'll—"

"Ach, there's no need for violence, cousin," Alex said, speaking for the first time. He lay with his long legs stretched out on the filthy straw, untroubled by what crawled there.

"And why is that?" Ian asked, giving Alex a kick with his boot.

"I'm no saying it is a bad plan," Alex said, "just that we won't be needing it."

Ian crossed his arms, amused in spite of himself. "Will ye be calling on the faeries to open the door for us?"

Alex was a master storyteller and let the silence grow to be sure he had their full attention before he spoke. "When they took me up for my turn at being questioned, they got a bit rough. The chieftain's wife happened to come in, and she insisted on seeing to my wounds."

Connor groaned. "Alex, tell me ye didn't..."

"Well, she stripped me bare and applied a sweet-smelling salve to every scratch from head to toe. The lady was impressed with my battle scars—and ye know how I like that in a woman," Alex said, lifting one hand, palm up. "It was all rather excitin' for both of us. To make a long story short—"

"Ye fooked the wife of the man who's holding us? What is wrong with ye?" Duncan shouted. "We'd best be ready, lads, for I expect the debate on whether to kill us will be a short one."

"Now there is gratitude, after I sacrificed my virtue to set ye free," Alex said. "The lady's no going to tell her husband what we done, and she swore she could get us out."

"So when's she going to do it?" Ian didn't question whether the lady would come; women were always doing unlikely things for Alex.

"Tonight," Alex said. "And it wasn't just my pretty face, lads, that persuaded her to help us. The lady is a Campbell. Shaggy Maclean wed her to make peace between their two clans. She hates him, of course, and does her best to thwart him at every turn."

"Ha!" Ian said, pointing his finger at Connor. "Let that be a lesson to ye, when you go choosing a wife among our enemies."

Connor rubbed his forehead. As their chieftain's son, he would be expected to make a marriage alliance with one of the other clans. With so many men dead after Flodden, a number of clans would be looking to negotiate such a match.

"Interesting that ye should be giving advice on wives," Alex said, raising his eyebrows at Ian. "When it doesn't appear ye know what to do with yours."

"I have no wife," Ian said with a deliberate warning in his voice. "So long as it hasn't been consummated, it's no a marriage."

While in France, Ian had done his best to forget his marriage vows. But now that he was returning home to Skye, he would put an end to his false marriage.

Alex sat up. "Anyone willing to make a wager on it? My money says our lad will no escape this marriage."

Duncan grabbed Ian before he could beat the smile off Alex's face.

"That's enough, Alex," Connor said.

"Ye are a sorry lot," Alex said, getting to his feet and stretching. "Ian, married but doesn't believe it. Duncan, who refused to wed his true love."

*Ah, poor Duncan.* Ian glared at Alex—the tale was too sad for jesting.

"And then there's Connor," Alex continued in his heedless way, "who must try to guess which of a dozen chieftains with unwed daughters would be the most dangerous to offend."

"Ach, my da's brothers will likely kill me first and save me the trouble of choosing," Connor said.

"Not with us watching your back," Duncan said.

Connor's half-uncles would be pleased to have one less obstacle between them and leadership of the clan. Connor's grandfather, the first chieftain of the MacDonalds of Sleat, had six sons by six different women. The sons had all hated each other from birth, and the ones still alive were always at each other's throats.

"I hope when my brother is chieftain he'll save the clan trouble by keeping to one woman," Connor said, shaking his head.

Alex snorted. "Ragnall?"

That was a false hope if there ever was one, though Ian wouldn't say it. Connor's older brother was no different from his father and grandfather when it came to women.

"So who will you wed, Alex?" Duncan asked. "What Highland lass will put up with your philandering without sticking a dirk in your back?"

"None," Alex said, the humor thin in his voice. "I've told ye. I'll never marry."

Alex's parents had been feuding for as long as Ian could remember. Even in the Highlands, where emotions tended to run high, the violence of their animosity was renowned. Of the three sisters who were Ian's, Alex's, and Connor's mothers, only Ian's had found happiness in marriage.

At the sound of footsteps, Ian and the others reached for their belts where their dirks should have been.

"Time to leave this hellhole, lads," Ian said in a low voice. He flattened himself against the wall by the door and nodded to the others. Plan or no, they would take the guards.

"Alexander!" A woman's voice came out of the darkness from the other side of the iron bars, followed by the jangle of keys.

\* \* \*

Ian drew in a deep breath of the salty air. It felt good to be sailing again. They had stolen Shaggy's favorite galley, which went a long way toward restoring their pride. It was sleek and fast, and they were making good time in the brisk October wind. The jug of whiskey they passed kept Ian warm enough. He grew up sailing these waters. Every rock and current was as familiar to him as the mountain peaks in the distance.

Ian fixed his gaze on the darkening outline of the Isle of Skye. Despite all the trouble that awaited him there, the sight of home stirred a deep longing inside him.

And trouble there would be aplenty. They had spoken little during the long hours on the water since the Campbell woman had given them the terrible news that both their chieftain and Connor's brother Ragnall had been killed at Flodden. It was a staggering loss to the clan.

Duncan was playing sweet, mournful tunes on the

small whistle he always carried, his music reflecting both their sadness and yearning. He tucked the whistle away inside his plaid and said to Connor, "Your father was a great chieftain."

Their chieftain had not been loved, but he was respected as a strong leader and ferocious warrior, which counted for more in the Highlands. Ian found it hard to imagine him dead.

He took a long pull from the jug. "I can't believe we lost them both," he said, clasping Connor's shoulder as he passed him the whiskey. "To tell ye the truth, I didn't think there was a man alive who could take your brother Ragnall."

Ian knew that the loss of his brother was the harder blow for Connor. Ragnall had been fierce, hotheaded, and accepted as the successor to the chieftainship. He had also been devoted to his younger brother.

"I suspected something," Duncan said, "for if either of them was alive Shaggy wouldn't have risked a clan war by taking us."

"Even with our chieftain fallen, Shaggy should expect a reprisal from our clan," Ian said after taking another drink. "So I'm wondering why he didn't."

"Ian's right," Alex said, nodding at him. "When Shaggy said he was going to drop our lifeless bodies into the sea, he didn't look like a worried man to me."

"He had no extra guard posted outside the castle," Ian said. "Something's no right there."

"What are ye suggesting?" Connor said.

"Ye know damn well what they're suggesting. One of your da's brothers is behind this," Duncan said. "They knew we'd return as soon as news of Flodden reached us, so one of them asked Shaggy to keep an eye out for us."

"They're all wily, mean bastards," Alex said. "But which of them would ye say wants the chieftainship most?"

"Hugh Dubh," Connor said, using Hugh's nickname, "Black Hugh," given to him for his black heart. "Hugh never thought he got his rightful share when my grandfather died, and he's been burning with resentment ever since. The others have made homes for themselves on the nearby islands, but not Hugh."

"What I want to know," Ian said, "is what Hugh promised Shaggy to make sure ye never showed your face on Skye again."

"You're jumping to conclusions, all of ye," Connor said. "There's no affection between my uncle and me, but I won't believe he would have me murdered."

"Hmmph," Alex snorted. "I wouldn't trust Hugh further than old Teàrlag could toss him."

"I didn't say I trusted him," Connor said. "I wouldn't trust any of my da's brothers."

"I'll wager Hugh has already set himself up as chieftain and is living in Dunscaith Castle," Duncan said.

Ian suspected Duncan was right. By tradition, the clan chose their leader from among the men with chieftain's blood. With Connor's father and brother both dead and Connor in France, that left only Connor's uncles. If half the stories told about them were true, they were a pack of murderers, rapists, and thieves. How a man as honorable as Connor could share blood with them was a mystery. Some would say the faeries had done their mischief switching babies.

They were nearing the shore. Without needing to exchange a word, he and Duncan lowered the sail, then took up the oars with the others. They pulled together in a steady rhythm that came as naturally to Ian as breathing.

"I know you're no ready to discuss it, Connor," Ian said between pulls. "But sooner or later you'll have to fight Hugh for the chieftainship."

"You're right," Connor said. "I'm no ready to discuss it."

"Ach!" Alex said. "Ye can't mean to let that horse's arse be our chieftain."

"What I don't mean to do is to cause strife within the clan," Connor said. "After our losses at Flodden, a fight for the chieftainship would weaken us further and make us vulnerable to our enemies."

"I agree ye need to lay low at first," Ian said. After an absence of five years, Connor couldn't simply walk into Dunscaith Castle and claim the chieftainship—especially if Hugh already had control of the castle. "Let the men know you're home and see they have an alternative to Hugh. Then, when Hugh shows he puts his own interests above the clan's—as he surely will—we'll put ye forward as the better man to lead."

Alex turned to Duncan, who was on the oar opposite his. "You and I are like innocent babes next to my conniving cousins."

"All great chieftains are conniving," Ian said with a grin. "'Tis a required trait."

"Connor will need to be conniving just to stay alive," Duncan said without a trace of humor. "Hugh has been pirating in the Western Isles for years without being caught. That means he's clever and ruthless—and lucky as well."

They were quiet again for a time. Connor may not be

ready to admit it aloud yet, but Ian agreed with Duncan—Connor's life was in danger on Skye.

"If you're going to the castle, I'm going with ye," Ian said. "Ye don't know what awaits ye there."

"Ye don't know what awaits you either," Connor said. "Ye must go home and see how your family fares."

Ian sent up a prayer that his own father had survived the battle. He regretted that their parting had been angry—and regretted still more that he had ignored his father's letters ordering him home. He should have fought alongside his father and clansmen at Flodden. He would carry the guilt of not being there to his grave.

"And ye need to settle matters with the lass," Connor added. "Five years is long enough to keep her waiting."

Ian had managed to forget about the problem of Sìleas while they talked of Connor and the chieftainship—and he didn't want to think about it now. He took another swig from the whiskey jug at his feet while they rested their oars and glided to shore. As soon as the boat scraped bottom, he and the others dropped over the side into the icy water and hauled the boat up onto the shore of Skye.

After five years gone, he was home.

"I'll wait to go to Dunscaith Castle until I know which way the wind blows," Connor said, as they dragged the boat above the tide line. "Duncan and I will take Shaggy's boat to the other side of Sleat and find out the sentiment there."

"I still think I should go with ye," Ian said.

Connor shook his head. "We'll send word or come find ye in two or three days. In the meantime, talk to your father. He'll know what the men are thinking on this part of the island."

"I know ye can't mean to leave your best fighting man out of this," Alex said. "Should I come with ye or go north to hear what the folks there are saying?"

"Stay with Ian," Connor said, the white of his teeth bright in the growing darkness. "He faces the greatest danger."

"Verra funny." At the thought of Sìleas, he took another swig from the jug—and choked when Alex elbowed him hard in the ribs.

"You'd best give Ian a full week," Alex said. "Ye don't want him leaving his poor wife wanting after such a long wait."

The others laughed for the first time since they had heard the news about Connor's father.

Ian, however, was not amused.

"I have no wife," he repeated.

"Sìleas's lands are important to the clan, especially Knock Castle," Connor said, draping an arm across Ian's shoulders. "It protects our lands on the eastern shore. We can't have it falling into the hands of the MacKinnons."

"What are ye saying?" Ian asked between clenched teeth.

"Ye know verra well my father did not force ye to wed Sìleas out of concern for the girl's virtue. He wanted Knock Castle in the hands of his nephew."

"Ye can't be trying to tell me to accept Sìleas as my wife."

Connor squeezed Ian's shoulder. "All I'm asking is that you consider the needs of the clan."

Ian shrugged Connor's hand off him. "I'm telling ye now, I'll no keep this marriage."

"Well, if ye don't," Connor said, "then ye must find a man we can trust to take your place."

"Perhaps ye should wait until you're chieftain before ye start giving orders," Ian snapped.

# CHAPTER 3

The wind whipped at Sìleas's cloak as she stood with their nearest neighbor, Gòrdan Graumach MacDonald, on a rocky outcrop overlooking the sea. The mountains of the mainland were black against the darkening sky. Despite the damp cold that penetrated her bones and the need to get home to help with supper, something held her.

"How much longer will ye give Ian?" Gòrdan asked.

Sìleas watched a boat crossing the strait, its outline barely visible in the fading light, as she considered his question.

When she didn't answer, Gòrdan said, "'Tis past time you gave up on him."

Give up on Ian? Could she do that? It was the question she asked herself every day now.

She had loved Ian for as long as she could remember. Almost from the time she could walk, she had planned to marry him. She smiled to herself, remembering how kind he had been to her, despite the teasing he got from the men and other lads for letting a wee lass half his size follow him like a lost puppy.

"Five years he's kept ye waiting," Gòrdan pressed. "That's more time than any man deserves."

"That's true enough." Sìleas brushed back the hair whipping across her face.

Her wedding was the worst memory of her life—and she was a woman with plenty of bad memories to choose from. There had been no time for the usual traditions that made a wedding a celebration and brought luck to a new marriage. No gifts and well-wishes from the neighbors. No washing of the bride's feet. No ring. No carrying the bride over the threshold.

And certainly no sprinkling of the bed with holy water—not with Ian threatening to toss the priest down the stairs when he attempted to go with them up to the bedchamber.

None of the traditions for luck were kept, save for the one. Ian's mother insisted Sìleas wear a new gown, though Sìleas didn't see how a bit more bad luck on top of what she already had could make a difference. Regardless, Ian's mother wouldn't hear of her wearing the filthy gown she had arrived in. Unfortunately, the only new gown to be had upon an hour's notice was one Ian's mother had made for herself.

Sìleas rushed through her bath, barely washing, so she would be out and dressed before Ian's mother returned to help her. Quickly, she dabbed at the long gashes across her back so she would leave no telltale blood on the borrowed gown.

When she slipped the gown over her head, it floated about her like a sack. She looked down at where the bodice sagged, exaggerating her lack. If that were not bad enough, she wanted to weep at the color. Such a violent shade of red would look lovely on Ian's dark-haired mother, but it made Sìleas's hair look orange and her skin blotchy.

When Ian's mother burst in the room, her startled expression before she smoothed it confirmed Sìleas's worst fears.

"'Tis a shame we can't alter it," his mother said, clucking her tongue. "But ye know that brings a bride bad luck."

Sìleas was sure the gown's color canceled out any good luck its unaltered state was likely to bring her. A bride was supposed to wear blue.

Then came the worst part of all. As she descended the stairs, with his mother's hand at her back pushing her forward, she heard Ian shouting at his father. His words were the last blow that nearly felled her.

*Have ye taken a good look at her, da? I tell ye, I will not have her. I'll no say my vows.*

But with his father, his chieftain, and a dozen armed clansmen surrounding him, Ian did say them.

Sìleas blinked when Gòrdan stepped in front of her and took hold of her shoulders, bringing her sharply back to the present.

"Don't try to kiss me again," she said, turning her head. "Ye know it's not right."

"What I know is that ye deserve a husband who will love and honor ye," Gòrdan said. "I want to be that man."

"You're a good man, and I like ye." Gòrdan was fine looking as well, with rich brown hair and warm hazel eyes. "But I keep thinking that once Ian returns, he'll..."

*He'll what? Fall on his knees and beg my forgiveness? Tell me he regretted every single day he was away?*

Truth be told, she wasn't ready to be married when they wed. She had needed another year or two before becoming a true wife. But five years! Each day Ian didn't return deepened the wound. By now, she should have a babe in her arms and another grabbing at their skirts, like most women her age. She wanted children. And a husband.

Sìleas drew in a deep breath of the sharp, salty air. It was one humiliation after another. Ian could pretend they were not wed, because he was living among a thousand French folk who did not know it. But she lived with his family on this island in the midst of their clan.

*Where every last person knows Ian has left me here waiting.*

"If you cannot ask for an annulment..." Gòrdan let the question hang unfinished.

Though she could ask for an annulment, she could not tell even Gòrdan that—at least, not yet. She had been lectured on that point quite severely by both Ian's father and the chieftain. If her MacKinnon relatives heard that her marriage was never consummated, they would attempt to steal her away, declare the marriage invalid, and force her to wed one of their own.

Yet her marriage to Ian was not a trial marriage, as most were. Through some miracle, the chieftain had found a priest. The chieftain had wanted them bound—and her castle firmly in the hands of the MacDonalds of Sleat.

For the same reason, it would have been useless to ask her chieftain to support a petition to annul her marriage. A bishop wouldn't send a petition to Rome on her request alone. Consequently, she had written a letter to King James seeking his help. For six months, the letter lay hidden away in her chest, awaiting her decision to send it.

But now, both King James and her chieftain were dead.

"If you can't ask for an annulment," Gòrdan said, "then simply divorce Ian and marry me."

"Your mother would no be pleased with that," she said with a dry laugh. "I don't know if she would faint dead away or take a dirk to ye."

Although it was common in the Highlands to wed and divorce without the church's blessing, Gòrdan's mother had notions about the sort of woman her precious only son should wed. A "used" woman was unlikely to satisfy her.

"'Tis no my mother's decision," Gòrdan said. "I love ye, Sìleas, and I'm set on having ye for my wife."

Sìleas sighed. It was a precious gift to have a good man tell her he loved her, even if he was the wrong man. "Ye know I can't think of leaving Ian's family now."

"Then promise ye will give me an answer as soon as ye are able," Gòrdan said. "There are many men who would want ye, but I'll be good to ye. I'm a steadfast man. I'd never leave ye as Ian did."

Though he meant to reassure her, his words pierced her heart.

"'Tis time we returned to the house." She turned and started toward the path. "I've been gone too long."

"Ach, no one will begrudge ye a wee time away after you've been working so hard," Gòrdan said, taking her arm. "And if ye marry me, they'll have to learn to do without ye."

As they walked up the path, Sìleas looked over her shoulder at the dark water. *Where was Ian now?* Even after all this time, she missed the boy who had been her friend and protector. But she didn't think she still wanted the angry young man who had left her—even if he deigned to return to claim her after all this time.

Five years she had waited for Ian. It was long enough. Tomorrow, she would rewrite her letter and send it to the dead king's widow.

\* \* \*

"Perhaps ye should ease up on the whiskey," Alex said.

"Ye can't expect me to face this sober," Ian said.

Ian tipped the jug back one more time to be sure it was empty then tossed it aside. When they rounded the next bend, he saw the smoke from the chimneys of his family home curling against the darkened sky and felt a piercing longing for his family. It would be good to be home...if not for having to face the problem of Sìleas.

"Most women don't appreciate a man who is slobbering drunk, cousin," Alex said. "I hope ye haven't had so much you'll have trouble doing your husbandly duty."

"Will ye no leave it alone?"

"Ach," Alex said, rubbing his arm where Ian had punched him, "I only meant to cheer ye up with a wee bit a teasing."

"'Tis good you're coming home with me," Ian said. "Since Sìleas will be needing another husband in the clan, it may as well be you."

"And I thought ye were fond of the lass," Alex said.

In truth, Ian was fond of Sìleas. He wanted a good husband for her.

He just didn't want it to be him.

For five years, he had this false marriage hanging over him. Not that he'd let it constrain him, but it was always there in the back of his mind like a sore that wouldn't heal. Now that he had come home to Skye, it was time to take his place in his clan. He supposed he would have to take a wife—which meant he had to deal with the problem of Sìleas first. He still got angry every time he thought of how he'd been forced to wed her. And whether she'd done it on purpose or not, it was her fault.

Once he was out from under the marriage, he could forgive her.

A dog barked somewhere in the darkness to herald his homecoming. The smell of cows and horses filled his nose as they passed between the familiar black shapes of the byre and the old cottage where his parents had first lived. Just ahead, lamplight filtered through the shutters of the two-story house his father had built before Ian was born.

Swaying just a wee bit, Ian found the latch and lifted it. The earthy smell of the peat fire enveloped him as he eased inside the door.

Ignoring Alex's nudge from behind, he paused in the dark foyer to survey the people gathered around the hearth. His mother sat on the far side. Her face was still beautiful, but she was too thin, and her thick, black braid had streaks of white.

Across from her, a couple sat on a bench with their backs to the door. Neighbors, most likely. Between them and his mother, a young man with his brother's chestnut hair was sprawled on the floor, as if he lived here. Could this long-limbed fellow, talking in a deep voice, be his "little" brother Niall?

There was no sign of his father or Sìleas, so he would have the easy greetings first.

"Hello Mam!" he called, as he stepped into the hall.

His mother shrieked his name and ran across the room to leap into his arms. He twirled her around before setting her back down.

"Mam, mam, don't weep." Her bones felt sharp under his hands as he patted her back to soothe her. "Ye can see I am well."

"Ye are a wretched son to stay away so long." She slapped his arm, but she was smiling at him through her tears.

"Auntie Beitris, I know ye missed me, too," Alex said, as he held his arms out to Ian's mother.

"And who is this braw man?" Ian said, turning to his brother.

Their mother had lost three babes, all of them girls, before Niall was born, so there was a nine-year gap between Ian and his brother. When Ian left for France, his brother had barely reached his shoulder. Now, at fifteen, Niall stood eye to eye with him.

"Surely, this cannot be my baby brother." Ian locked his arm around Niall's neck and rubbed his head with his knuckles, then passed him to Alex, who did the same.

"Look at ye," Alex said. "I'd wager all the lasses on the island have been after ye, since I wasn't here to divert them."

Niall and Alex exchanged a couple of good-natured punches, then Niall caught Ian's eye and cocked his head. Ian had forgotten all about the couple on the bench, but at his brother's signal, he turned around to greet them.

The room fell away as Ian stared at the young woman who now stood in the glow of the firelight with her eyes fixed on the floor and her hands clenched before her. Her hair was the most beautiful shade of red he had ever seen. It fell in gleaming waves over her shoulders and breasts and framed a face so lovely it squeezed his heart to look at her.

When she lifted her gaze and met his, the air went out of him. Her eyes were a bright emerald, and they seemed to be asking a question as if her very life depended upon it.

Whatever this lass's question was, his answer was aye.

# THE DISH

*Where authors give you the inside scoop!*

♥ ♥ ♥ ♥ ♥ ♥ ♥ ♥ ♥ ♥ ♥ ♥ ♥ ♥ ♥

## From the desk of Kristen Callihan

Dear Reader,

I write books set in the Victorian era. Usually we don't see women with careers in historical romance, but one of the best things about exploring this "other" London in my Darkest London series is that my heroines can lead atypical lives.

In WINTERBLAZE, Poppy Ellis Lane is not only a quiet bookseller and loving wife, she's also part of an organization dedicated to keeping the populace of London in the dark about supernatural beasts that roam the streets—a discovery that comes as quite a shock to her husband, Police Inspector Winston Lane.

Now pregnant, Poppy Lane develops a craving for all things baked, but most especially fresh breads. Being hard-working, however, Poppy has little time or patience for complicated baking—an inclination I share! Popovers are a great compromise, as they are ridiculously easy to make and ridiculously good.

## Poppy's Popovers (yields about 6 popovers)

**You'll need:**

- 1 cup all-purpose flour
- 2 eggs

- 1 cup milk
- 1/2 teaspoon salt

Topping (optional)

- 1/2 cup sugar
- 1 teaspoon ground cinnamon
- a dash of cayenne pepper (to taste)
- 4 tablespoons melted butter

## Directions

1. Preheat oven to 450 degrees F. Spray muffin tin with nonstick spray or butter and sprinkle with flour. (I like the spray for the easy factor.)
2. In a bowl, begin to whisk eggs; add in flour, milk, and salt, and beat until it just turns smooth. Do not overbeat; your popovers will be resentful and tough if you do! Fill up each muffin cup until halfway full–the popovers are going to rise. (Like, a *lot*.)
3. Bake for 20 minutes at 450 degrees F, then lower oven temperature to 350 degrees F and bake 20 minutes more, until golden brown and puffy.
4. Meanwhile, for topping, mix the sugar, cinnamon, and dash of cayenne pepper—this is hot stuff and you only want a hint of it—in a shallow bowl and stir until combined. Melt butter in another bowl and set aside.
5. Remove popovers from the muffin pan, being careful not to puncture them. Then brush with melted butter and roll them in the sugar mix, shaking off the excess. Serve immediately.

Inspector Lane likes to add a dollop of raspberry jam and feed them to his wife in the comfort of their bed.

He claims they make Poppy quite agreeable…*Ahem*. You, however, might like to enjoy them with a cup of tea and a good book!

*R.C. Ryan*

♥ ♥ ♥ ♥ ♥ ♥ ♥ ♥ ♥ ♥ ♥ ♥ ♥ ♥ ♥

## From the desk of R.C. Ryan

Dear Reader,

To me there's nothing sexier than a strong, handsome hunk with a soft spot for kids and animals. That's why, in Book 3 of my Wyoming Sky series, I decided that my hero, Jake Conway, would be a veterinarian, as well as the town heartthrob. Now, who could I choose to play the love interest of a charming cowboy who has all the females from sixteen to sixty sighing? Why not a smart, cool, sophisticated, Washington, D.C. lawyer who looks, as Jake describes her, "as out of place as a prom dress at a rodeo"? Better yet, just to throw Meg Stanford even more off her stride, why not add a surprise half-brother with whom she has absolutely nothing in common?

I had such fun watching these two try every possible way to deny the attraction.

But there's so much more to their story than a hot romance. There's also the fact that someone wants to harm Meg and her little half-brother. And what about the mystery that has haunted the Conway family for twenty-five years? The disappearance of Seraphine, mother of Quinn, Josh, and Jake, chronicled in Books 1 and 2, will finally be resolved in Book 3.

In writing the stories of Quinn, Josh, and Jake, I completely lost my heart to this strong, loving family, and I confess I had mixed emotions as I wrote the final chapter.

I hope all of my readers will enjoy the journey. I guarantee you a bumpy but exhilarating ride.

Happy Reading!

R. C. Ryan

RyanLangan.com
Twitter, @RuthRyanLangan
Facebook.com

## From the desk of Margaret Mallory

Dear Reader,

Ilysa is in love with her older brother's best friend. Sad to say, the lass doesn't have a chance with him.

As her clan chieftain, Connor MacDonald is the sixteenth-century Highland equivalent of a pro quarterback, movie star, Special Forces hero, and CEO all rolled into one. And the handsome, black-haired warrior never even noticed Ilysa *before* his unexpected rise to the chieftainship.

Other women, who are always attempting to lure Connor into bed—and failing, by the way—are drawn to him by his status, handsome face, and warrior's body. While no lass with a pulse could claim to be unaffected by Connor's devastating looks, Ilysa loves him for his noble heart. Connor MacDonald would give his life for the lowliest member of their clan, and Ilysa would give hers for him.

Connor MacDonald is the hope of his clan, a burden that weighs upon every decision he makes. Since becoming chieftain, he has devoted himself to raising his people from the ashes. With the help of his cousins (in *The Guardian* and *The Sinner*) and his best friend (in *The Warrior*), he has survived murder attempts by his own kin, threats from royals and rebels, and attacks by other clans. Now all that remains to secure his clan's future is to take back the lands that were stolen by the powerful MacLeods.

Through the first three books in The Return of the Highlander series, Ilysa has worked quietly and efficiently behind the scenes to support Connor and the clan. None of her efforts has made him look at her twice. Clearly, it's time for me to step in and give Connor a shake.

The poor lass does need help. Her mother thought she was protecting Ilysa in a violent world by covering her in severe kerchiefs and oversized gowns and admonishing her to never draw attention to herself. Ilysa's brief marriage left her feeling even less appealing.

But Ilysa underestimates her worth. After all, who helped our returning heroes in *The Guardian* sneak into the castle the night they took it from Connor's murderous uncle? And who healed Connor's wounds and brought him back from death's door? Even now, while Connor fights to protect the clan, Ilysa is willing to employ a bit of magic to protect him, whether from the threat of an assassin or a deceitful woman with silver-blue eyes.

Unfortunately, Ilysa's chances grow more dismal still when Connor decides he must marry to gain an ally for the clan's coming fight with the MacLeods. As I watched him consider one chieftain's daughter after another, I knew not one of them was the right wife for him or the clan. What our chieftain needs is a woman who can heal the wounds of his heart—and watch his back.

But Connor is no fool. With a little prodding, he finally opened his eyes and saw that Ilysa is the woman he wants. Passion burns! Yay! However, my relief is short lived because the stubborn man is determined to put the needs of the clan before his own desires. Admirable as that may be, I can't let him marry the wrong woman, can I?

Despite *all* my efforts, I fear Connor will lose everything before he realizes that love is the strongest ally.

With Ilysa's life and his clan's future hanging by a thread, will he be too late to save them?

I hope you enjoy the adventurous love story of Connor and Ilysa. I've found it hard to say goodbye to them and this series.

You can find me on Facebook, Twitter, and my website, www.MargaretMallory.com. I love to hear from readers!

*Margaret Mallory*

♥ ♥ ♥ ♥ ♥ ♥ ♥ ♥ ♥ ♥ ♥ ♥ ♥ ♥ ♥

*From the desk of Cynthia Garner*

Dear Reader,

My latest novel, HEART OF THE DEMON, takes two of my favorite preternaturals—demon and fey—and puts them together. Tough guy Finn Evnissyen has met his match in Keira O'Brien!

I come by my fascination with the fey honestly. My family came to America from Donegal, Ireland, in 1795 and settled in the verdant hills of West Virginia. One item on my bucket list is to get to Donegal and see how many relatives still live there.

My fascination with demons, I guess, has its roots in my religious upbringing. Just as I have with vampires and werewolves, I've turned something considered wicked into someone wickedly hawt! I hope after reading HEART OF THE DEMON you'll agree.

To help me along, my Pandora account certainly got its workout with this book. From my Filmscore station that played scores from *Iron Man*, *Sherlock Holmes*, and *Halo 3*; to my metal station that rocked out with Metallica, Ozzy Osbourne, and Rob Zombie; to my Celtic punk station that rolled with the Dropkick Murphys, Mumford & Sons, and Flatfoot 56, I had plenty of inspiration to help me write.

I have a more complete playlist on my website extras page, plus a detailed organizational chart of the Council and their liaisons.

Happy Reading!

*Cynthia Garner*

cynthiagarnerbooks@gmail.com
http://cynthiagarnerbooks.com

# *Find out more about Forever Romance!*

Visit us at
www.hachettebookgroup.com/publishing_forever.aspx

Find us on Facebook
http://www.facebook.com/ForeverRomance

Follow us on Twitter
http://twitter.com/ForeverRomance

## NEW AND UPCOMING TITLES

Each month we feature our new titles
and reader favorites.

## CONTESTS AND GIVEAWAYS

We give away galleys, autographed copies,
and all kinds of exclusive items.

## AUTHOR INFO

You'll find bios, articles, and links to personal websites
for all your favorite authors—and so much more.

## GET SOCIAL

Connect with your favorite authors, editors, and
other Forever fans, and share what's important to you.

## THE BUZZ

Sign up for our monthly romance newsletter,
and be the first to read all about it.

# VISIT US ONLINE AT

WWW.HACHETTEBOOKGROUP.COM

## FEATURES:

**OPENBOOK BROWSE AND
SEARCH EXCERPTS**

•

**AUDIOBOOK EXCERPTS AND PODCASTS**

•

**AUTHOR ARTICLES AND INTERVIEWS**

•

**BESTSELLER AND PUBLISHING
GROUP NEWS**

•

**SIGN UP FOR E-NEWSLETTERS**

•

**AUTHOR APPEARANCES AND TOUR
INFORMATION**

•

**SOCIAL MEDIA FEEDS AND WIDGETS**

•

**DOWNLOAD FREE APPS**

Bookmark Hachette Book Group
@ www.HachetteBookGroup.com